Spirit Bound
The Guardians: Book Two

Tessa McFionn

DEDICATION

To all my great friends and family members who wouldn't let me give up on my dreams. To my husband who makes me laugh and never stops believing in me. To Mom. I hope I do you proud.

PROLOGUE

Plataea, Greece 479 BC

"That was enjoyable. Let us do that again tomorrow."

Strategos Galen Theodoris Alexiou threw back his head, laughter rolling easily. The sun had descended only moments ago, cushioning the outlying coast in a pale red glow. Boats bobbed in the shores of the Gulf of Lepanto, tents littered the sands, each campfire coiling fragrant smoke toward the clear heavens.

The day had been another long and bloody one, but successful nonetheless. Darius the Usurper had paid dearly for his arrogance, legion upon legion of his army now lay scattered and broken on the land Galen called home. Gripping Ioannes, his lieutenant, on the shoulder, Galen smiled easily as they made their way toward the glowing fire-lit silhouette of his large round general's tent. The faint sounds of the men's laughter mingled with the moans of injured. Still, more had died on their enemy's side, so there was cause for celebration.

"We need to find new hobbies for you, little brother. Perhaps one of these days that damned Persian will tire of sending so many of his people to an early grave."

"So what would ya be doin' if that were the case?"

Galen stopped the young lieutenant from drawing his steel with a simple thought as the familiar voice filtered in through the fog. He sighed as the tall, copper-haired figure strode toward them. With a sharp nod to his captain, he stood firm, his arms folded across his chest as the hulking Celt approached.

1

"Eamon. What brings you to this end of the world?" Galen's mind traveled back to their first meeting, three years earlier on a similar field of battle. The man had spoken of strange things, of battles in a faraway future and evil forces. He had easily dismissed his ravings as battle fever. Yet as the days progressed, all he had spoken of had come to pass. Perhaps the man had been sent by the Oracle, and he could spare a moment for prophecy.

Bright sapphire blue eyes sparkled as the rugged face broke into a warm grin. "Why, you do, to be sure. Have ya been givin' any thought to the new army I told ya of?" He stopped in front of Galen, both men meeting each other eye-to-eye at a menacing six and a half feet. Both sported broad shoulders and a physique honed by years of vicious campaigns, their bodies scarred and strong.

Galen arched a dark brow as he held the man's gaze. "You still believe I am some kind of… What did you call it again?"

"A Guardian Warrior. I am certain of it. You're what we call a Marshal, for ya got the skills to fight and control the physical actions of others. Ya just did it right now, did ya not?" He paused, his eyes dancing with some unknown secret before he continued. "He coulda killed me where I stand. How did ya stop him? Did ya reach out and touch him? No. Ya tell him? Aye, ya did, but not with words, did ya? But the how is the real question now, isn't it now?"

Galen quietly pondered the man's odd speech, but the truth of his words began to bleed through. He had always been a strong commander, the men under him following every order, even the most dangerous and deadlier ones without ever batting an eye. Many of his superiors thought him to be enchanted, blessed by the Gods to have risen as far and as fast as he did. Could there be something to this foreigner's tale?

Still deep in contemplation, Eamon stepped in closer and clasped him firmly on the shoulder. Images poured into his mind as Eamon continued to speak. "I am in need of one such as yourself. The enemy I face is one bent on nothing less than the destruction of the peace and harmony both you and your men have fought so hard to ensure. These Rogues plant the seeds sowing disharmony, chaos, and death. And time and again, you have shown yourself to be a true warrior, fighting with courage and honor. Truth be told, I would not be surprised to hear that they have already tried to turn you. If they were to get their hooks into you…" With a shake of his head,

Eamon stepped away as he gave Galen breathing room to let his words sink in.

Galen slowly pulled the tense air into his lungs, his brows furrowed as his mind churned this new information. True, of late there had been some rather strange warriors on the field. Men who fought and whispered of foul deeds had descended upon his men, fighting without honor, resorting to trickery and underhanded methods. These despoilers drove fear into his men, and anger into his heart. He and his men battled these vagabond thieves as well as each other when darkness fell for far too many nights.

Long had he fought, and his enemies ranged from seasoned Spartan generals to headstrong Roman praetors, but something else drove these men, and the only way to describe it was evil. The oily voices that crept into his camp under cover of the night's shadows were twisted by evil and driven by the need to foment dissonance.

"You have a gift, my son. The gods have seen fit to make you a true leader of men. Be sure you follow a path that will do honor to those same gods."

The words of his father drifted in from a half-forgotten memory when he was beginning to learn of his natural abilities to see and even control the way the pieces moved on every battlefield. Battle strategies were in his blood, his mind innately knowing exactly where the enemy would strike and how to rally his men to achieve victory. At the age of only twenty-seven, he was responsible for leading the largest of Greece's armies against the entire might of Persia and he was winning.

If his father were still alive, he would have told him it was now time for him to find a wife and start a family of his own. But no woman had ever caught his eye for longer than one night, and he was damned sure not going to spend the remainder of his days with just any female to ensure his lineage continued.

This was to be his last fight, not the beginning of another campaign, this one lasting for an untold span of time. Was he ready to quit? Had he done all to protect his land and his people? His mind unraveled the myriad of possible paths as his gaze stayed locked with smiling bright blue eyes across from him.

As he pondered the other signs and omens, he caught a wave of concern from the young lieutenant to his left. Ioannes, as well as his other men, gave allegiance to him with unquestioning loyalty and devotion, but he sensed his trepidation at this stranger and his curious words. The concern was a physical force to Galen, a breath of energy that spoke to him and him alone. He knew when his men were scared or angry, hungry or horny, the latter sensation the most rampant as well as the most unsettling.

With a comforting smile, he nodded, his eyes shifting back toward the tents and the men waiting just beyond. Something told him the rest of this conversation would be best in some semblance of privacy. The young man balked for an instant, then his shoulders drooped, his head bobbed in a quick acknowledgement before he backed away from the pair.

"And if I were to believe your claims?" Galen continued. "What then?"

The smile that greeted his words reminded him of felines and small yellow birds. Galen raised his hands quickly, palms open. "Not that I am giving credence to your words. I am only asking about the next steps from here."

"The next steps will take you places you never dreamed of, my friend. Not in your wildest of fantasies." Once again, Eamon clapped a hand on his shoulder, but this time, energy rocketed down through his arm, flooding his being with power.

"Welcome to the Guardians, brother."

ONE

"I am so not drinking that." Calliope Vandeen watched as her blonde-dreadlocked roommate Maggie lowered the steaming mug from under her nose. She wiggled into a pair of jeans as she studied Maggie's bright blue eyes behind coke bottle thick lenses, full of anticipation and eager for approval. Cal dropped her gaze to study the contents of her friend's latest healthy concoction as she shoved her arms into her standard go-to for class, a blue San Francisco College of Arts and Humanities hoodie.

"Aw, Cal. Why not?" Maggie sniffed the bubbly and frothy liquid before thrusting it toward her again. "This has all sorts of stuff to help you sleep."

Cal laughed at her friend's efforts, her straight black bobbed hair bouncing as she shook her head. "Yeah, but I refuse to drink from something while its inhabitants are still paddling." She reached down, snatched her favorite black Pumas, and laced the sleek shoes. The odiferous cup once again appeared in her vision.

She gently pushed the mug away as she stood, her fingers instead grasping her beaten olive green messenger bag off the couch before slinging it over her shoulder. "Don't wait up for me, Maggs. Got a meeting with Professor Archibald after class tonight, and you know how he loves to hear himself talk."

"You need to get some real sleep, Calliope. You can't keep burning the candle at both ends—"

The rest of the reprimand was lost behind the shutting door. Cal

5

sighed, mulling over the parting words of her hippie roommate.

Burning the candle at both ends. What candle? That metaphor had long since lost any deep significance to her. And sleep? Yeah, that would be nice. Scoffing at that minor impossibility, she tightened the strap on her bag before making her way out of her dorm/condo. Her feet plodded along on their memorized course. The early November air smelled faintly of approaching rain as the skies blazed in the golden red sunset. She glanced at her watch, noting the lateness.

Shit.

Her pace quickened and she moved easily, weaving through the late night college crowd. Her mind did some weaving of its own, pondering what Maggie had said. How long had it been since she'd slept through the night? She counted the nights, using her footfalls as rhythm. It was going on five years.

Five years. Wow. Long time to be living on twenty-minute catnaps. Her thoughts drifted back to her senior year in high school as she jogged along the footpath leading toward Stewart Hall, pressing her way through the throng of exiting students, anxious to start their night of freedom. Five years since she noticed that each night she slept less and less. At first, she'd thought it was just stress, nerves about the impending entrance into the real world. Or for her, worry about her college entrance exams.

By the time she started her freshman year of college as a seventeen-year-old, her normal night of sleep lasted around five hours. No biggie. It was only a few minutes of sleep here and there that she no longer needed. Her mind was still sharp, and she kept herself busy working on her degree in Classic Civilization with an emphasis on Medieval Literature. Yet as time went on, her days became longer, sleep more and more elusive.

At first, she used the extra time for more classes and continued her eager search for knowledge of all things ancient and chivalrous. However, little things had begun to slip during her junior year. Sometimes her steps would falter, sometimes voices sounded distant and muddled. Her hands shook and her eyes lost focus if she read for longer than an hour.

The thick wooden doors rose in the distance as she hurried up the stone stairs. Her breath puffed out, foggy signals as she reached the entrance and slipped inside the massive brick hall. She rounded the corner and began the thigh-burning ascent to Professor Laurent's classroom, her thoughts still lost in her past. Now, as she had finally got her wish and began her work as a grad student, she could only sleep for intermittent snoozes. Total amount of sleep per day: one hour. Maggie and her equally New Age-y, but on the darker side, boyfriend, Ajax, were convinced that unless she got some serious sleep soon, her mind would rebel and her body would soon follow.

She would smile at them, pooh-poohing their fears. Too bad, she had learned the truth. After many long hours both online, searching medical sites and in the stacks, perusing psychological texts, she'd reached a frightening and sobering conclusion

Her body, unable to reach a recuperative REM state of sleep, would eventually shut down. Her mind, too, needed this downtime to recharge and file away the events of each day. Without this, her goose was as good as cooked.

She was living on borrowed time. Now it was only a matter of how much she truly had left.

Arriving at Room 416, she spied the note taped to the door.

CLASS CANCELLED. QUIZ RESCHEDULED FOR NEXT SESSION.

She squinted her eyes, allowing her breathing to slow as she stepped closer then further away, making sure she wasn't imagining her own night of freedom. Convinced of its authenticity, she shrugged her shoulders at the unexpected bit of happy news before she turned back toward the stairwell. This might turn out to be a good night after all.

"Calliope Vandeen?"

"Yes?" Cal turned toward the voice before a sharp sting bit her arm and darkness swallowed her.

TWO

Pain exploded against Cal's right temple, awakening her to another round of torment and interrogation. She couldn't get her right eye to stay open and she swore a couple teeth were too loose. The circulation to her hands had long since disappeared, her wrists raw and bloody from the heavy manacles that kept her suspended above the floor.

She knew time had passed since that night in the stairwell, but for the life of her, she had no idea how much. Sometimes it seemed like mere minutes, other times... Other times, she couldn't remember what her life had been like without pain. The questions started as soon as consciousness returned, and so did the torture. To each strange inquiry, for every "I don't know" or stumbled half-answer, violence was her reward. Her kidnappers used words like Mate and Guardian and Marshal, among other words that held no deep meaning to her. Yet neither her adamant denials nor angry rush of tears and curses could convince these apparitions of agony to believe her feeble words.

Open hands were the first weapons used, followed by closed fists. Other, more solid implements came soon after. With each new tool, the same questions remained. Where was her spiritmate? Why hadn't she called for him yet? How many Guardians lived in the city? She distinguished five separate voices, never seeing any faces since she was either blindfolded or simply blinded during all the interrogations. As her thin sweater gradually gave up the ghost, she could feel the heat of lecherous eyes on any revealed bit of flesh. Occasionally, a stray hand would grope at her breasts or trail up her inner thigh, but sharp words from one certain voice and these more terrifying attacks would stop. Those brief moments were the ones that shook her the most, her tears falling silently long after her captors had left.

Blood dribbled down her cheek and added to the half-dried puddle on the ground. Her breath rattled in her chest as one rib poked into her lung while at least one more poked out. If only her legs were longer... But she realized it wouldn't have made a difference, her bent knees were still tantalizing inches away from the tile floor.

Fingers grabbed her jaw, twisting her face upward. Bright light crept through her swollen lid and blinded her one good eye. Tears streamed unbidden down her bruised cheek as her shoulder hunched and she struggled to hide from the next onslaught.

"Why are you protecting him? He obviously doesn't give a fuck about you or he would have come to your rescue by now. Where is he?"

Goddammit, this broken record thing is getting really old. The hazy silhouette before her continued his tirade, leaning in closer with each word. During the first interrogation, she feared he would kiss her, his foul breath a mix of stale cigarettes and rotten eggs. She scoffed, cringing as her sharp wit kicked into overdrive. "Do you even know what a toothbrush is?"

Cal's head swiveled with a snap, pinpoints of light dancing on the edge of her vision. Her tongue swept across her teeth, the quick tally returning with the magic thirty. Finding them all intact, she spit out the blood she could no longer stomach and prayed for another hit to send her once again into the dark.

A sharp yank on her hair jerked her back to the here and now. Trenchmouth got up close and personal this time, flecks of spittle dusting her cheeks as his anger grew. "Listen here, you little bitch. We've been asking nicely so far..."

Nicely? Was he for real? She stifled a laugh, figuring her brain no longer fired on all cylinders. "...keeping things, let's just say superficial."

Don't make me get into the uglier, more personal parts. Because my friends would love to see if you feel as good as they think you do."

Cal's blood turned to ice in her veins and her face paled. She had overhead, numerous times, her jailers discussing who would take her first. She had fought to play possum even as her heart knocked in a terrified rhythm against her aching ribs.

A flash of red caught her eye, followed by the chemical tang of burning metal. Panic took root in her bones as the glowing iron came closer.

"I still say we ask the crazy blonde she hangs out with. I'm sure she'd tell us about him."

Fear gripped her heart, and she struggled weakly. "You leave her alone."

"Then tell us where your lover is and we can end this now."

Tears of exhaustion and rage spilled down off her chin. "How many different ways do I have to say I have no *fucking* idea who or what you're talking about? You're making a mistake."

Fetid breath washed over her and she swallowed hard, staving off the urge to throw up. "We don't make mistakes."

The sizzling sound met her ears as the stench of a forgotten roast filled the air. Quick on its heel was blinding pain, centered on her right shoulder. She squeezed her eyes tight, her jaw locked as the scream echoed through her mind.

The crisp, early autumn night was still, the trees a silent haven to Galen Alexiou. Smiling, he inhaled deeply, filling his lungs with the clean scent of the ancient redwoods as he looked out from his vantage point high in the treetops. Living in the heart of San Francisco for the past four decades, his duties as a Guardian Warrior kept him busy at all hours of the day. Never a dull moment, except for now. He decided to treat himself to an escape since things had been quiet for a couple days. And knowing his adversaries as he did, these stolen moments of peace would end all too soon. Running a hand through his shaggy black hair, he laughed lightly, thinking maybe it was time to update his style as he climbed up higher, pausing a couple stories off the forest floor.

He enjoyed the peace of nature, the soul-deep hush when stillness wrapped up the technological world in a neat package and a man could almost believe he was the only person on the planet. Perhaps it was also time for him to update his home as well. Thoughts of his homeland, of that war-raved beach all those centuries ago and the changes that had transpired, brought a wistful smile to his lips as he replayed the events in his mind.

He gasped, caught off-guard by the sudden surge of the unexplainable, and in the distance, a strong voice spoke above the thundering din.

"You have been chosen to take up the mantle of the Guardian Warriors. You were chosen for your skills and for your valor. You have been called to do battle with your sword, your wits, and your soul. To this arsenal, we give you an extended life in your current form and the ability to move with wind."

Sounds sharpened to a painful intensity as more words bled into his mind.

"You can hear the thoughts of any mortal and can heal with a touch. Many miles will you travel and many lands will you discover. No place will you call home for more than two score and ten years. You will be drawn to your enemy across time and space. Your enemy will hide within the hearts of men and within the realm of the In-Between, the void betwixt the land of the living and the land of the dead. They will influence dreams and move in shadow."

Strains of Denis Leary's less-than-melodic "I'm an Asshole" brought his attention back to the present, his eyes sliding down to his pocket. A grin split his face at the sound of his old friend's set ringtone, and he slipped the phone out with a laugh.

"Eamon. To what do I owe this late night ring- up?" Loud music seeped through the line, informing him of its suspected origination.

"Hey, boyo! Ya hearin' me?"

Galen winced at the sloppy shout that met his ear. He shook his head and sighed. He knew Eamon lived his life like there was no tomorrow, but there were times when he really did rue technology. For Eamon, drunk dialing could be considered an Olympic event, or at least a Guinness Book-worthy endeavor.

A tired laugh escaped from his lips as he crouched onto the branch currently holding his weight. "Yes, I can hear you fine. You have no need to yell. So, how are things in San Diego?"

Tittering laughter rose and fell in the background. "Good as always, my man. Good as always. Ladies, a moment please." Galen rolled his eyes, his mind picturing the model-quality females he was sure flocked around the copper-haired devil. The clattering of stilettos heels clicked into the distance, and giddy giggles followed along in their wake. "Well, Malakai found his spiritmate." Eamon's voice was now clear and all business. "And she's a Conduit."

"Whoa."

"You will vanquish your foes, sending them back into oblivion. You will fight until you find your spiritmate. She will bring you balance and quiet your restless soul. Once you have made her your own, you will choose to find another to take up the battle in your

stead or to bring her into the service of the Guardians."

The news was both good and bad. He was happy that Malakai had finally found true happiness, but would he still stay and fight? So many Guardians chose to find a replacement and live out their lives as humans rather than endanger their spiritmates.

"That's, um...wait, you said she's a Conduit. Can't she be recruited? I mean, would he be willing to let her fight?"

A devilish chuckle met his ears. "Ya sound like I've not been thinkin' the same thing myself, now. But I will talk to them both about it. He's a right bit, um, protective of her now. Heard ya had a bit of excitement in your neck of the woods lately. How'd that turn out?"

He sighed as he relaxed against the rough bark with a smile. "Well, nothing I couldn't handle. But the fact that the snaky shits disappeared without a huge fight has got my ears to the ground. It feels like that damned Roman. You know his M.O., finding a bunch of poor saps to do his dirty work while he sits in the shadows."

"Ya tellin' me you were expectin' a stand-up fight? After all these years, I see you're still such an optimist."

He chuckled lightly, rubbing a hand against the stubble on his cheek. "You know me, I keep hoping to be pleasantly surprised one of these days. I can dream, can't I?" His eyes caught the lazy flight of a brown owl, cruising the dark skies in search of its nightly repast. "But something's up. I just know the other shoe has yet to drop."

"Need any reinforcements?"

"Not yet, at least. But should things begin to turn more sinister, I will give you a call." He opened his mouth but the rising chatter and giggles of the women bled through the phone again. Galen laughed deeply. "Well, since it sounds like your, ah, companions have returned, I will let you go."

A hand muffled the voices for a moment before returning to the line. "Right, boyo. Keep your eyes peeled and watch your ass." The music and dithering voices disappeared, the serene quiet of the night swallowing him back. A crooked grin touched his lips as he slipped the phone back into his pocket.

He did miss a good battle. All the years spent waging minor skirmishes only whet his appetite for the massive campaigns of his early days. He had learned to fight at the feet of his father, fending off marauding invaders as he protected his island home on Naxos while he was still very young. Soon, he found that the other men in the village looked to him and followed his orders even though he had yet to grow a beard. As the months turned to years, his skills continued to blossom and grow, as did the stories of the young man rallying the men of Delos, Nelos, and even the warriors of Cnossos to hold off the other warring city-states.

He turned his eyes to the night sky, the familiar stellar formations of his youth replaced by this new place and time. The constellations had spun around their orbits scores upon scores of times since he'd first stared up.

His reminiscence was cut short as a focused shaft of agony split his mind. His balance fled, branches rushed past him as the ground came up fast. He windmilled his arms and clutched at anything to slow his descent. An unknown voice cried out, definitely feminine, terrified and in terrible pain. His heart stuttered as a gut-wrenching anguish threatened to rip out his very soul. His palms slammed down as he dropped to his knees on the mossy ground, cushioning his fall.

What the hell was going on? Was this truly possible? It couldn't be. But his heart, thundering in his ears, told a much different story. It was her. His body knew it. She was calling to him. His spiritmate; his destined. And she was hurt. His hands threaded through his hair as another wave of pain shot through his brain. Closing his eyes, he anxiously reached out, tracing the faint lingering line.

"Agapi mou, where are you?"

Her response was understandably leery. *Fabu, now I'm hallucinating voices. Well, at least it sounds sexy. And foreign, too. Maybe Greek.*

A smile tugged the corner of his full lips; his eyes flicked behind his lids. Her voice was soft, light and angelic, slick like brushed velvet against the edges of his mind. The kind of voice that whispered the promise of erotic things in the dark. His fingers gripped the bark of the nearest tree as he crawled up to stand. The roughness of the redwood against his back centered him.

"I assure you it's not a trick, agapi. I'm coming for you. Do you know where you are?" Galen knew the longer he could keep contact with her, the sooner he'd be able to find her. She was close, maybe a hundred miles or so. The first spike of connection sparked in his darkened vision. His eyes popped open and he *moved*, distance vanishing in a blink as he sped toward her.

Cal dared not open her eyes. If her capturers believed she was passed out, she might have a moment to pull her thoughts together. And discover why she had the most amazingly sensual voice rattling around her head. Agapi...agapi. Where had she heard that word before? It was so familiar to her. A lecture, some ancient text. Her head swam trying to unravel this new mystery.

And someone was coming for her? Her mind must have finally broken, creating her own imaginary hero. A purely male figure, dark hair, dark eyes, rushing to her side and kissing her senseless. He would be strong, defeating all these fuckers and whisking her to safety. He would swoop in and save...

Dread hit her stomach like a fist. *Aw, crap. Well, if you are real, then you can't come here. Need to stay away.*

The warm voice in her head sounded puzzled. *"Why? Why would you say that?"*

She attempted a deep breath to steady her, but only succeeded in a shallow gasp before her aching ribs stopped her. *Because if I'm right, then this is a trap.* With a resigned sigh, her shoulders dropped slightly, the ceiling cuffs biting deeper into her wrists. *And I'm just the bait.*

An odd wave of heat brushed against her skin, the sudden intensity terrifying. "Do not fear, agapi. I will find you."

She held her breath as the seconds ticked on in silence. With no more answer, she sighed with a renewed sense of hope, her thoughts lost in her fantasy until all-too-familiar voices bled into Cal's consciousness, their words somewhat muddled, but their intentions all too clear.

"We've been waiting too damn long. Are we even sure she's tied to one of them?" She imagined him as short, fat and stubby, sausage fingers and greasy-haired to boot. "All we have is the Stefan's word on it."

"Yeah." This one she pictured as tall and skinny, looking like a deranged jackrabbit, judging by his lisp. "And from what he said, any Guardian worth his salt would have come long before now. I say we take her spoils now and be done with it."

"She's been quiet too long. All right. Wake her up and let's finish this thing." Fucking Trenchmouth. All business and torture, him she envisioned as a wannabe Soldier of Fortune type. Crewcut, too much muscle and rage brought on by 'roids, and not enough brains to make the combination anything but hazardous to those he deemed weaker.

Footfalls headed her way, the telltale squeak of combat boots on the dingy linoleum beneath her. Tubby's unexplored cross trainers and Bugs' worn-out loafers soon joined in the trek. She struggled to still the pounding of her heart, unsure if it was fear for an untimely demise or hope for an impending rescue. Whichever the outcome, she had to keep her wits about her.

"Hey, wake up." One second passed. Then two. A stinging slap did not allow the third to pass in peace. Cal felt the blood drip from a new split on her already battered lips. Lifting her head as best as possible, she cracked open her eye.

Bugs leaned over, eager to sneak a peek down her tattered and blood-soaked shirt. "Looks like you've become an expired commodity, sweetheart." His fingers slithered out, groping at her skin in eager anticipation. "I guess that leaves you here to party with us."

Squirming only pushed her body closer to the others and opened up new gouges along her wrists. Evil laughter rippled through the air at her feeble thrashing.

"I called first dibs." Tubby's tracksuit inched closer, his pudgy fingers dug into her hair. He wrenched her neck and brought her face dangerously close to his crotch. "Been wanting to see that mouth do something useful for long enough. And she's at the perfect height, too." A mocking pair of sinister voices made encouraging remarks as the nylon before her eyes shimmered and slid. Leaning down to whisper in her ear, flecks of spittle splattered against her cheek. "Such a shame your boy didn't care enough about you to save you."

"*I am here!*"

A delicious warmth crept into her body, stealing away her growing fears. Her lips broke into a weak smile, a light laugh giving way to a painful bout of coughs. Cal wondered about the looks on their ugly faces right now, her vision too blurred to make out any real details.

"Be careful what you wish for," she whispered as the room exploded and the dark enveloped her.

THREE

Galen latched onto her mental link, rushing down the path to find an abandoned-looking shack, set apart from the lights of any nearby town. She was inside. He knew it. His eyes narrowed into slits as he surveyed the scene from afar. Three men were there with her. They stood very close to her, and the knowledge fired his blood as his ancient skills bubbled to the forefront.

His anger took tangible form as he blasted through the wall with a thought. Wood splintered and rained down in the tiny cabin, the thin barrier no match for his rage. Debris shimmered as it filtered through the musty air. He made a quick survey of the scene. Three stunned men were scattered around a bloodied and broken figure suspended by thick iron chains from the low-beamed ceiling.

Galen struck as the men tried to stagger to their feet, his fists flying, smashing into anyone stupid enough to stand in his way. Blood sprayed as bone cracked. Reaching into a hidden pocket inside his leather coat, he grasped the short staff. With a flick of his wrist, the innocuous stick transformed into three feet of sharp, polished steel. The blade flashed and crimson filled the air, followed by gurgled screams. A man dressed in army fatigues clutched at his chest and gut, trying to hold the looping entrails inside as they slithered out into the open air. The vicious blade shimmered in the fading light as he thrust backward without a glance. A satisfied smile appeared on his lips before he gave a practiced flick of his wrist as he stepped away.

Galen stalked the two remaining men with murderous intent as a gurgled death rattle sounded behind him. The weaselly business-suited man cringed in terror, but to no avail. A glint of silver creased the air, and his shocked expression slid from his face as his head slid from his shoulders. Galen watched for another heartbeat as the body buckled and crumbled to the floor. Scuffling footfalls behind him drew his gaze from the headless corpse.

"W-w-w-what the fuck are you?" The final man, a gluttonous creature in a food-stained tracksuit, slipped on the blood-slick floor. In his haste to run, he misjudged the recently rearranged furniture and his body jiggled as it bounced off table pieces and rebounded off walls. Galen tracked his prey with ease, maneuvering the paling blob of flesh into an inescapable corner. His icy gaze burned as he closed the remaining distance.

"I am your worst nightmare." One firm thrust and the eyes before him widened, swallowing up the man's sallow features. A stream of scarlet sprang from his gaping mouth and spilled down, adding to the mustard and guacamole splatters. Galen yanked the blade back, wiping the bloodied edge against the filthy fabric and stepping out of the way as the mountainous mass toppled.

He snapped his wrist and the weapon retracted, vanishing once again to its quiet, unassuming form as he tucked it back inside his jacket. A stray rag on a nearby table caught his eye and he snatched it up, eager to wipe the filth off his bloodied fingers. He forced in a calming breath before facing the grizzly scene behind him. He fought to slow his ever-increasing heart rate as he turned his attention toward the broken marionette in the center of the shattered room.

Galen approached the hanging figure with tender caution, his eyes drinking in every cut and bruise. His stomach turned at the lumped and burned pale skin. The tattered remains of what might have been a soft blue shirt hung in ribbons off long lean arms, dark with dirt and dried blood. Shapely legs were wrapped tight with blood-stiffened denim and bent at an uncomfortable angle, knees inches away from the floor below. A mop of short dark hair drooped down. His fingers trembled as they dipped and lightly touched the chin beneath, and with infinite care, he knelt to peer into the face he'd only ever imagined he would find.

Cal woke to an almost forgotten and unfamiliar sensation: kindness. A gentle hand caressed her chin, urging her head away from the solace and silence of the ground. A violent rush of air was the last thing she remembered before the dark swallowed her again. And now... She dare not imagine.

"Theós mou."

The sound took on the shape of words as they slipped out in a hollow sigh and she fought to peel back her lids. The voice, deep and rich, rolled through her like warm chocolate, the fingers along her skin firm, strong and yet tender. The delicious dichotomy had her wishing her eyes would open, yet all she could muster was a shadow silhouetted by other not- so-dark shadows.

"Did we get 'em all?" she asked.

Galen felt the blood drain from his face as he stared into the broken and battered face of a young woman. His woman. His eyes did a quick scan, taking an inventory of her visible wounds, as well as the not- so-visible ones. Her left eye was swollen shut, deep purple and angry red, and the right was not far from the same fate. A fight bite oozed from a yellowing blossom on her left cheek, and her full bottom lip was split in numerous places. Straight black hair fell in clumps, the tangled edges tickling his palm. A blackened furrow marred her right shoulder, the jagged tip dangerously close to her soft curves. He swallowed hard against his growing rage.

Brave words whispered slipped from her broken jaw. We. The sound alone fired his blood.

"Yes, *moraki mou*. Yes, we did." By the gods, how long had she been tortured? A growl slipped from his lips as he glanced around the room. For the first time in his long life, he secretly wished for the skill to raise up the dead so he could kill them over again, this time with more relish and less haste. Grabbing onto the chains, he yanked, easily ripping the anchors from the ceiling. He scooped her into his arms and carried her to the table. The instant her body fell against his, his shaft thickened to the point of pain in his confining black leather pants.

Oh, you have got to be kidding me. His teeth clamped down hard, locking tight to stop him from groaning during the short trip to the kitchen. A weak cry escaped from her as he lowered her with loving care to rest on the cold wood. Her head lolled as her body struggled to adapt to its new setting.

"I have to get you out of here," Galen murmured, brushing at a stray lock of the midnight hair off her brow. The skin beneath his fingers was deathly pale, so much damage and so much blood.

Breath rattled in her chest and a ghost of a smile formed on her lips. "Yes, please."

Air rushed out of Galen's lungs in a heavy sigh. Leaning down, he slid one arm behind her neck only to be stopped by a feather-light touch on his arm. Her delicate fingers rested against his skin, her all-too-ivory against his olive. His mind fired wickedly as he wished to see this beautiful contrast played out on a much larger canvas.

"I...I..."

"Shhh." He brushed the pad of his fingers against her battered lips, careful not to hurt her. "Don't speak. You are badly hurt, agapi." Gods, even in her broken state, his body screamed for her. He knew, once she was whole again, she would be exquisite. Something in her touch drew him closer to her, his ear close to replacing his fingers against her lips.

"Greek, maybe..." she murmured, her voice weak and breathy against his cheek. "Know...n-n-n- name..."

Unsure if he heard her correctly, he followed the path into her thoughts. In her mind, he found her imagination furiously at work, giving form to his voice, using her imaginings as a shield against the ordeal she'd just endured. Tall, dark and deliciously handsome.

Galen's smile broadened at her innocent question, as well as her not-so-innocent thoughts. This only proved the truth of their connection even further. Plus, he was quite impressed by her ability to create a rather accurate visualization. Now, he only hoped she was indeed interested in the truth of him.

"My name is Galen Alexiou, *glykiá mou*."

Galen sensed she was weakening. His heart caught in his throat. She was a fierce one, blessed with a sharp mind. Even now, she struggled to discover the meaning of his native Greek words. Without another thought, he gathered her into his strong arms and moved, speeding over the night-darkened landscape. He held her with infinite tenderness, but her stifled groans of agony whispered softly against his skin.

Trees and mountains disappeared around Galen, the city gaining in size and nearness, his eyes affixed firmly on his destination. Only a few more moments.

Buildings sprung up like dandelions around them and his top-floor penthouse loft loomed in the distance. He disengaged the security perimeter, opened the large door to the rooftop access stairwell, and lit the way to his bedroom before his feet crossed the threshold. Forcing himself to slow his pace, knowing the journey was not pleasant for her, he deftly maneuvered to the farthest room in the house before he carefully set down his precious cargo.

"Could we please not do that again?" Or at least that was what his brain told him she had said, her fractured jaw making clear speech impossible. Her voice was little more than a whisper against his chest.

"Shh. Close your eyes and rest." He brushed his fingertips along her forehead, willing her into sleep. As he added a final push, her soft laughter tinkled in his head with a puzzling statement: *Yeah, like that's gonna happen.*

Sure she was deep under sleep's spell, he dashed into the bathroom to return with towels and a basin of warm water. His healing abilities would fix both her internal and external damage but would not clean off the dried blood.

Not to mention, he wanted to touch every inch of her skin. No, he thought as he stepped back into the room where her battered body sprawled against the white of his thick down comforter. It was something much more, much deeper than a simple want. He needed to touch her, to feel every part of her, to pull her deep into him as he drove himself into her.

His hands shook as he placed the towels in a pile next to the wrought iron bed frame. Shades of red varying from bright crimson to deep brick red and even crusted brown covered nearly every inch of her exposed flesh, as well as the tattered remains of her clothes. He shoved down his fury, locking it away until later.

His movements smoothed as he knelt beside her broken form, willing his body into the focused stillness he would need to heal her. He closed his eyes as he took a deep cleansing breath, hovering his hands above her, barely containing the urge to hold her again. His mind strayed at the remembrance of her slight form against his, his body unable to ignore the press of her full breasts and narrow hips as he pulled her close.

His blood began to rebel, slinking on a downhill route. Shaking his head violently, he willed the life-giving force back under his control. Later, he mentally reprimanded his body, his cock aching and straining against the taut binding. He opened his eyes slowly, knowing they glowed from within as his hand descended.

Inhaling sharply at first contact, he was assaulted by the ferocity of the damage and was sickened by his discovery. He found partially healed wounds. And judging by the degree of scarring and the Technicolor shades of her bruises, she had been in the hands of those men for at least five days. His vision blurred, a red cast on the edges of his sight. *Stay focused. She needs you to stay focused.*

He sobered in an instant and his mind called forth his curative skills. The light stemmed from his spirit, building in strength as he channeled his concentration. Gradually, he poured the healing glow through his hands, directing the flow to seek out each tiny muscular tear and every fractured bone. With his mind's eye, he followed the light, ensuring everything was restored to its original state. The internal bleeding stopped, the punctured lung re-inflated. Her poor ribs, spiraled and fractured or only connected by slender threads, were reassembled, their puzzle pieces locking seamlessly into place.

Sweat trickled down his spine as he progressed. Normally, he would have blasted his energy into his patient and trusted all would be well. But with her... No, he would take all the time in the world, pushing himself close to his own demise to ensure she was fully healed.

Her cheekbones reformed, revealing strong, high lines that spoke of a natural beauty. Next, he stitched together the shattered jaw. His hands shook, violent trembles he struggled to still, knowing these breaks were designed to keep her from crying out. Taking extra time, he anchored her loose teeth and straightened her narrow nose.

And I have yet to truly hear her voice or even to know her name.

He knew he could pull her name from her mind, but we wanted to hear it from her lips. Needed to...

Get my damned head out of my pants and into the game! Another growl and his traitorous body snapped back to the task at hand. Major repairs still need to be completed and now wasn't the time for such thoughts. His guidance sent the light toward her torn wrists and dislocated shoulders. As the tendons and ligaments eased into back into place, he sensed she was fit, her body lean yet supple and strong. Perhaps she was an athlete of some kind. His groin twitched as his mind strayed to images of her slender body, slick with sweat, her head thrown back with her hands pressed against his chest as she straddled him.

His pants shrunk another size as his mind entertained his fantasies.

Once again, he clenched his teeth, working to dismiss his latest sojourn into the erotic when something odd happened. She started to push her way up from unconsciousness, muttering as her head lolled from side to side. He frowned and his knuckles brushed against her forehead as he soothed her back into the depths of sleep.

Shaking his head, confused by her resistance to remain at rest, he returned his focus to the smaller wounds, relieving the deep bruising along her pale skin and smoothing the torn flesh of her soft lips. He paid special attention to the tender area around her eyes as well as her face. The reds and purples faded to greens, the last vestiges of bruising damage disappearing bit by bit.

He gingerly touched the angry burn, taking care to knit together the deep trench in her soft flesh. He had seen wounds like that before. He knew it had been caused by one thing: a heated iron. He made a promise to himself no lasting bruise or scar would mar her, but some of these had already begun to heal on their own, the scars already firmly in place. He wished he could remove the memories of the entire event, but he knew too much time had passed and someone would have inquired about her whereabouts by now.

A possessive spike of jealousy flared in his heart as imagined another man in her life. That thought dragged forward another one, equally as terrifying. His heart raced as he sent his healing energy out again, this time, searching for signs of the most heinous of violations. Rape. His breath stilled as he focused on her delicate feminine flower, exhaling in a sigh of relief when he found no injury. At least she would not have to suffer the long years with that stain on her heart. The simple fact she had endured any of this at all caused him to rage once again.

This would not do.

Another mental shake and his mind made one final pass. The damages had been fixed, but something was still off. There was a sense of unbalance, a view askew. His brow furrowed in deep concentration, seeking to find the source of his unease. The longer he studied his repairs, the more he realized it had nothing to do with her ordeal. Lingering tears and faint shreds in the fiber of her soul seemed to permeate her whole being. And he had no more energy to spare.

She was in no danger. For the moment. But Galen sensed that, in time, he would need to return to solve this mystery. For now, however, she was safe. As he pulled his spirit energy back into himself, he added a push toward sleep, willing her yet again into a deeper slumber.

Exhaustion threatened to spill him across her, undoing some of his hard work. He groaned, his body both tense and weak. He turned his focus toward the restored beauty spread before him. Her skin was a soft and pale alabaster, a hint of rosiness shining from within with only a slight discoloration still visible along her cheek. He reached toward the stack of towels, grabbing a washcloth and pulled the basin of now cold water onto the bed. A focused pulse from his hand and steam billowed along the surface.

Opting to start as innocently as possible, he rinsed her short locks with tender care. Her sleek black hair slipped seductively through his fingers and a groan slipped from his lips. He savored the softness, leaning close to inhale the fragrance that was exclusively hers. His body tightened beyond the point of pleasure, racing at light speed toward excruciating, as he continued his task, gently removing the tattered scraps covering her to begin the process of washing away the only remaining physical evidence of her torture. The emotional scars, however. Those would take more time.

Each pass of the cloth over her skin only increased his raging desires. His hands trembled, fighting the fiery urge to trail his tongue along each new bit of flesh unveiled. His efforts revealed lush, kissable lips set into a heart-shaped face. He dragged his eyes further down, reveling in her ample breasts partially hidden by the fragile remnants of a lacy bra, his mouth watering as the lucky cloth touched the tops of her soft mounds. Pale yellow bruises still peeked along her ribs, stomach and disappeared under the edge of her shredded denims.

His resolve nearly shattered as he peeled her jeans from her long, slender legs. He clamped down on the inside of his cheek to keep from growling, forcing sobering thoughts on an endless loop through his frazzled mind. Images of puppies and kittens bubbled up alongside mundane poems, multiplication tables, even scientific theorems in his feeble attempt to squash his raging hormones as the soft square skirted along the edges of her black briefs. Yet each new topic strayed to the eventual and delicious promise of passion.

Sweat of a different kind dripped down his brow, his jaw clenched tight enough to crack his teeth. One last pass of the cloth and her skin glistened, clean of all brown, rust- and red-stained traces. His shoulders sagged as he released the breath he'd been holding. His vision began to fade in and out, life losing its sharp edges and contrasting colors.

He had pushed himself too far and too hard, using too much of his own energy to heal her, and now he was going to pay the price for his perseverance.

Dammit all. He would have to move fast before the darkness swallowed him. He slipped her into one of his shirts and tugged the blanket up from the end of the bed, further covering her sleeping figure. Tucking the edges around her, he gave into a small temptation, pressing a soft kiss against her brow.

"Kalinýchta sas omorfiá mou." Galen barely managed to strip off his own bloodstained shirt as weariness overtook him and he collapsed face down, his arm draped possessively across his newly acquired reason to live.

FOUR

"No, dammit. I'm not going to say it again." Malakai Vadim pinched the bridge of his nose, sighing and counting to ten. For the umpteenth time in the last two minutes. "You have to lead with your shoulder and let the body follow, flowing through the movement. Your arm is only an extension of the body. That gives more power to your attacks and makes you less of a target if you miss." Easily shoving his pupil off balance, he heaved another sigh, shaking his head, his sweat laced hair dripping into his eyes. "Again."

The shoulders of the masked figure before him drooped slightly, the thick mesh shroud bobbing up and down in understanding. The hulking mass clad in black hakama recovered to a more appropriate fighting stance, drawing the narrow wooden staff up to begin his attack anew. The bamboo sang through the air, snapping sharply down repeatedly against Kai's lazy defenses. Onward he pressed, parrying each attack and responding in kind.

Seizing an opening, his student struck, the staves hitting center, and his opponent dragged both weapons downward. With a dancer's grace, his leg snapped out and caught the back of Kai's leg, driving him to his knees. Kai grunted as he fell, following the momentum to roll forward, spinning low as he crouched, his leg swiping out his partner's wide stance. The heavy man landed hard on his back, a hand slapping flat on the mat to absorb the fall.

"Good. You're improving fast, Adrian." Kai rose smoothly, his hand extending to his soon-to-be replacement. He was still teetering on the idea of continuing to remain as a Guardian now that his spiritmate, his reason for living, Siobhan Wheeler, had come into her abilities as a Conduit. Her safety was now his only priority in life. Only problem was, with her newly acquired skills to peer into the minds of others, even to control their thoughts, she was an enticing target for his enemies.

And that would not do.

Familiar electronic tones filled the quiet. Tucking the staff under his arm, he fished the phone out of his deep pocket. He didn't bother to wait until the party on the other end spoke. "No, Eamon. I still haven't made a final decision yet." He knew that ringtone and since the same question had been asked for the past two months like clockwork, he figured he would spare himself the agony of hearing it again.

The laughter rolling through the connection told him he was right on all counts. "Well now, boyo. Are ya sayin' I'm gettin' predictable or somethin'?"

Kai responded with a chuckle of his own. "Perish the thought." His voice was laced so heavily with sarcasm, he stepped back to make sure it didn't drip onto his bare feet. "So did you call for anything other than your regular inquisition?" He nodded to Adrian, who bowed sharply and took both staves, returning them to the weapons rack and headed toward the showers. He had made a wise choice on his replacement. The young man was eager to learn, his heart and soul pure and honest.

Now, if he could only find the guts to relinquish his powers to Adrian and be done with his lifetime of Guardianship.

"I might be needin' ya to take a little trip up the coast. Ya up for it?" Eamon asked.

Kai frowned and grabbed a towel to wipe his dripping sweat. "Galen has something he can't handle? Didn't think that was even possible."

The mirthless laughter ringing in his ear told him a different story. "What is it with you two? Too alike, the pair of ya, I say. Just might be some trouble brewin', and since Konstantin's not likely to be showin' his face for a while, thought ya might be open to a change of scenery. Consider it a favor to me, boyo."

Kai let out a heavy sigh. "All right. Just give me enough warning so I can prep and let Voni know."

"Would ya be bringin' her along?"

The question was innocent, but it did set his mind working. Did he leave her here, unprotected, in the hands of his apprentice? Should he bring her along, possibly into yet another dangerous situation with the Rogues? "Fuck," he murmured in answer. "Between a rock and a hard place on that one. Not to mention, I'd rather not be away from her, but it wouldn't feel right throwing her back into all that shit again." His feet began their memorized path up the circular stairs to the living room, making one quick stop to grab a bottle of water from the large silver Viking refrigerator in the kitchen.

"Well, guess that choice'll be yours there, boyo. Make it a vacation, if ya'd like."

Growling into the phone, he knew his only choice would not make him happy. Another eloquent string of physically impossible profanities flew from his lips as the knowledge sank in.

"I owe ya one," Eamon continued. "And this is only a possibility, too. Things might not get dicey, but just in case. Well, I'll let ya get back to trainin'. Say, how's that goin', by the way?"

Kai finished half of the bottle in a long pull before answering. "The kid's got the right mindset and some decent skills. But these modern times don't create the same survival skill sets like we had. Guess never having to fight for your dinner makes people soft."

The chuckle on the other end told him his friend agreed. "That's one way to put it. Keep your ears open, *bráthair*. And give your beautiful lady a squeeze from me."

As if on cue, the front door opened, the fleeting day's light silhouetting the tiny figure in the entranceway. He grinned as the petite dancer stepped inside. "Uh huh. Yeah, sure. Later." He barely registered Eamon's laughter before he ended the call, his long strides swallowing the distance between him and his prey with ease.

"*Am fost dor de tine, dragoste meu.*" His lips crushed against hers as he wrapped his arms around her, pulling her close. His hands journeyed north and south, tunneled through her sweat-slicked hair as he pinned his growing erection against her black fleece-shrouded core.

Voni tried to laugh against the ferocity of his passionate greeting, but her own desires quickly rose to meet his. Her eyes shuttered close, her tongue dueling as equally possessive as his. Her hands splayed against his damp chest and a giggle escaped from her lips as she playfully pushed him away.

"Ewwww. You're all slimy." Her wriggling only tightened his vice-like embrace, her hips grinding erotically against his thickening shaft. He leaned over, purring into her ear as his hands roamed over and under her baggy clothing.

"Gods, get this off. I need to have you. Right now." His fingers gripped her thigh as his other hand yanked and tore at the offending materials of her pants. Underneath, her legs were still sheathed in more confining dance gear. His primal growl rolled between their lips, followed by the sounds of shredding cloth.

She cringed, hearing her brand new tights fall prey to her spiritmate's erotic appetite. Complaining would not mend the tattered synthetics, nor would it cool his desires. Since they had completed the Claiming Ritual a few months ago, she learned his desire to touch her, his need to please her, had only increased with each passing moment.

She also found she did not mind. Since leaving the ballet company and coming to the "dark side" as her new company members called it, her self-confidence had also grown stronger. The fusion of jazz, hip-hop, and contemporary styles into her ballet training created a completely new version of herself, one she was comfortable with. Her Conduit skills were sharpening with practice. No longer did they cause her excruciating headaches.

But right now, her "Spidey senses" were tingling. Big time. Pressing her palms against his chest, fighting her own urge to curl her fingers against strong muscles beneath them, she broke the seal of his kiss.

"Huh uh, not so fast, mister. What did Eamon want?" Her voice was breathy, but steady. She was getting better at this. Prying her eyes open, she found his ice green eyes half-lidded and dangerously dark. Her skin flushed under his sinful gaze, but she knew he was trying to avoid the subject. She leaned back in counterpoint to his lunge toward her lips and smiled crookedly.

"Nice try, Kai." She reached up, touching his warm lips with her fingertips. "You usually get overly amorous after you've gotten some news from Eamon you don't want me to know. So, spill it, bub."

His wicked grin formed beneath her fingers lying against his mouth. She was a quick study in learning to read people. "I get overly amorous the moment you walk into a room, *dragoste meu.*" He sucked one of her fingers into his mouth, swirling his tongue over the soft tip. Her flat stare spoke silent volumes as she moved her hand away from his distracting mouth. Rich laughter bubbled from his chest and spilled across the short distance between them as one graceful brow arched along her perfect face.

"Eamon just wanted to give me a heads up on the need for a possible trip up the coast." One hand traveled up the length of her back under her voluminous shirt, pulling her closer still. "Up San Francisco way." His tongue flicked out, laving the shell of her ear as his other hand skimmed beneath the band of her sweatpants. "We could make it vacation." His voice purred along her skin, sending tremors of anticipation in the wake of his words, his rock hard cock tenting the thick cotton trousers.

Voni sighed, her head lolling on her shoulders. "I can tell there's something you're not…aah…not telling me." She pulled a shaky breath, her hands mirroring his trails on her body, except she didn't have as many obstacles as he did. "Please…"

A wicked smile curved along his lips, his teeth nibbling the salty skin on the column of her throat. "I live to please you, baby. Always and in all ways." He ground his raging erection against her hips to drive his point home and was rewarded with a deep moan, her spine bowing against his demanding frame. Not wanting to waste a second of this passionate moment, he devoured her mouth, his tongue coaxing hers out to play.

"Baby, I promise. He had no other news." Gliding smoothly in reverse through the living room as the darkness deepened around them, his lips never released hers as the back of his knees found the couch. *"Gods, I miss you when you're away."*

He braced one arm and lowered her onto the soft leather, breaking their kiss to peer into her passion darkened pools of honey. As she reached up, caressing his stubbled cheek, he nuzzled her soft palm. He answered her directed pull and he leaned down, brushing his lips against hers. His mouth curved into an impish grin as her voice echoed in his head.

"Don't think is getting you off the hook."

FIVE

San Francisco, CA

Time ceased to flow in a forward direction in Cal's mind. Instead, it seemed to spin around her, creating pools and currents, even pulling her sideways in its journey. Faces appeared and disappeared, evil ugly images bobbed up before being pulled beneath the surface. Voices ebbed and flowed as well.

Yet above the cacophonous din, one tender whisper brushed against her soul, soothing her pain and touching her spirit. She had heard it once before, the voice of her savior, while she was soaring through the night sky. Was it all just a dream? When she opened her eyes, where would she be?

Her body was slowing coming back to itself, and she tensed, preparing for inevitable rush of her daily dose of pain. Seconds ticked by and agony did not rear its ugly head. *Could this be real?*

Cal dared a deep breath, feeling the air fill her lungs and still no pain. She inhaled as much as her body would allow and puffed out the air in a happy sigh. Maybe it had all been a really bad, pizza-induced nightmare. A slight stitch in her side broke her celebratory mood. *Well, too bad it didn't last.*

This had to be the dream. And now she had shattered the illusion, so she might as well open her eyes and get back to the daily business of torture and torment. Peeling back her lids, she squinted at the light filtering through the narrow wooden window shades.

Huh?

She pushed herself onto her elbows…

Elbows? What the hell?

Cal's head swiveled as she took in the completely unfamiliar room. She was lying down on a huge soft bed, wrapped in a blanket and wearing a black T-shirt at least three sizes too big for her. She grasped at the blurry images from her last bout of consciousness, their fuzzy pictures dancing just along the edges of her waking mind.

As she hesitantly lengthened and stretched her body, her hand met with another rather interesting surprise. Skin. Warm, solid and a bit on the naked side. Her eyes followed the line of her arm to discover the defined ridges of strong shoulders and the sculpted muscular plains of a well-honed back that tapered into a pair of leather pants. The paleness of her hand appeared ghostlike against his olive skin. Pale scars scattered in all directions across his body and created a crosshatched roadmap, telling of battles and deeds of old.

Fire of a uniquely physical variation rushed through her body, the flames igniting from her fingertips and pooling low in her gut. Her mouth grew arid and her eyes widened, eager to drink in every inch of his amazing anatomy. *Whoa.* She felt like a kid eying the best jungle gym in the world, wondering where she wanted to hang first. He was huge, his body sharp and strong. Thick black hair fell in jumbled waves, begging for her to run her fingers through it. She hungered to know what it felt like. She tried to catch a glimpse of the face attached to this image of male perfection, but his arm denied her that pleasure.

Cal took a moment to admire her personal view before crawling out of her cushiony cocoon. She ached with a strange detachment, as though all the parts of her body had been torn apart then put back together with too much haste. Her fingers traced over her face, her cheeks tender, but she couldn't feel any kind of swelling. A quick glance down at her arms and legs poking out from the huge shirt/dress showed her normal ivory skin, with only scattered patches of the telltale chartreuse of healing bruises. Also, she noted the lightening of the outside sky, telling her the day was many hours old. Did...did she really sleep?

How the hell did you do that? A smile touched her lips as she marveled at the mystery man beside her. Galen. He said his name was Galen. This would definitely require much more study. Escaping from the comforting shroud of soft sheets and firm flesh, she slid her legs out until her toes touched the cool cherrywood surface beneath the massive, black iron bed frame. As she sneaked silently over to the floor-to-ceiling picture window, she peered out to the shadowy skyscape beyond the bright haven surrounding her. Somehow, she was back in the city and not too far from the campus as well. Convenient.

"And exactly what do you think you're doing?"

The voice tickled along her skin, the sound spilling along her arms and wrapping her in velvety chains. Closing her eyes, she sighed against the feel of that voice. She turned around to see…

The figure still unmoving, lost in the sea of white.

Cal arched a brow quizzically. "Excuse me?"

"You should still be in bed."

She took a cautious step back, bumping into the thick glass. "Huh? I mean, how are…what… How come I can hear you in my head and you're not talking?"

"All that can wait until later, agapi. You still need to rest."

Her eyes never left his body, but no part of him moved. His back rose and fell with the ease of sleep, but if he were talking to her, his voice would have been muffled and drowsy. But the sounds echoing in her ears were nothing short of pure masculine power, strong and clear. And unbelievably sexy.

"Rest? Uh, yeah, sure. I'll get right on that. And how did I end up here in the first place? Unless…wait. All that…that. It wasn't just a bad dream, was it?" The comforting warmth created by his husky voice vanished as fear chilled her blood. Tiny tendrils of pain crept around her spine and threatened to travel elsewhere. She hugged the last of the fleeting heat to her chest, a tremor running down her arms.

"I am afraid not. Please, come back to me."

The overwhelming desire to retrace her steps and fall into the pillowy softness was almost too much to fight. Almost. Cal still had too many unanswered questions. She shook her head to restart her brain on a track other than one that included the yummy hunk of male perfection on the bed before her. Timidly she stepped around the room, keeping a healthy distance from the dominating wrought iron frame.

"I…I need to check out a couple things. I have to go." *What? Why the hell would you even think that?* Cal dragged her fingers through her short and rather mussed hair, her inner voices whining about timing and priorities. She could definitely imagine herself crawling across the expansive sea of white and losing herself in an uncharted island of flesh.

"Agapi mou, I need you to stay. I am sure these "things" can wait. And I would not mind if you did some exploring."

A soft sigh escaped from her lips as warm laughter rolled through her mind, her blood racing like lightning through her body. Her lids fluttered down as a strange tingling pooled between her legs. And there was the word again. Had she read it before? Maybe in one of her texts from Professor Carmichel's Modern and Medieval Languages class.

"Who are you?" Her voice was breathy and light, the question loaded like Chicago dice.

"Come back to bed and I will tell you everything."

The promise of those few words was so enticing, she almost caved. Almost.

Sighing heavily, Cal shook her head. "I…I'm sorry. God, I must sound like a horrible person. Here, you save my life and I haven't even said thank you yet. But I'm just… Aw hell, I don't even know any more."

"You are still in need of rest and of time to recover from your ordeal. Your wounds have not fully healed."

Cal wanted nothing more than to hear that voice along her skin, whispered into her hair and brushed against her lips. His words tumbled around her rattled mind. Wounds. Ordeal. And rest? Every part of her knew he was right, but she still needed…

Needed to have my damn head examined. Looking down, she realized she was only wearing a rather baggy shirt. And somehow she didn't think she'd be able to convince a cop it was the latest fashion statement. Yet when she remembered the veiled threats against her roommate when she refused to answer their questions, she just had to be sure she was OK.

"Look, I feel fine. Really. I need to check something out really quick. I can see my apartment from here. I'll only be a couple of minutes. And this whole talking-without-talking thing…yeah."

The sigh that blew through her mind nearly shattered her, the soundless breath brushing against the sensitive parts of her long-forgotten feminine self. Her fingers clenched into tight fists to curb her urge to touch and to caress. She had never felt anything this powerful in her whole life, and it was both terrifying and exhilarating.

"Please, will you at least wait until I can accompany you?"

Cal was touched by his concern. As she looked around the room, trying to find something to use for bottoms without rummaging through her sexy stranger's closet, she spied the remnants of her jeans. Her blood froze as fragments of her encounter seeped into her mind. One voice in particular, the creepiest of them all, had said something about watching her and made reference to a daft blonde. It had to be Maggs.

Had she put her friends in some kind of danger? She shook her head and without another second's hesitation, she crammed her legs into the filthy denims and opted to go barefoot. Heck, this was San Francisco after all, and filled with trendy New Agers and modern day hippies, so she shouldn't stand out too much.

"I'm sorry. I won't be gone long and I'll be back and—"

"Can I at least have the pleasure of your name, since you would deny me the pleasure of your company?"

Her hand stilled a cat's whisker away from the doorknob. She had asked his name when he swooped in to rescue her and she hadn't even returned the gesture. A sheepish blush touched her cheek as she realized she had not even used his name once. Turning to face the sleeping form, she gathered her courage.

"Calliope… Galen. My name is Calliope Vandeen. And I will come back, I promise."

Before her courage failed her, she slipped out.

Calliope.

Galen had sensed the moment she arose. Yet locked within the cage of his all-too-deep slumber, he could do nothing more than listen. She'd moved hesitantly around the room, her mind full of questions. Her movements were graceful and elegant. He imaged the shirt he had hastily thrown over her, the black fabric clinging to the lush curves of her breasts.

Lucky shirt.

The longer she was awake, the more confused and apprehensive she became. He had hoped his soft words and gentle nudging would ease her back to the bed, but her mind was strong and determined. She had survived for the gods-only-knew how many days and hours of brutal torture, and her first thoughts were steered toward those with whom she dwelled.

Raging at his inert body, he scrambled within his own mind, trying to speed along the process. His efforts met with the same results as had every attempt in the past nine hundred years. As one of a handful of Marshal Guardian Warriors, he was able to control the physical body, focusing on attack, defense, or in the case of his beautiful damsel, healing. Yet, when it came to the healing arts, he discovered that while healing himself was rather painless, whenever he performed similar medical procedures on others, the price he paid was a period of immobility, the degree and nature of wounds healed determining the length and intensity of his wet spaghetti impression. The last time he attempted a healing like hers, he had been comatose for more than half the day.

That had been centuries ago.

The sound of her voice was paradise. She had a soft, rich voice, deliciously feminine and driving him insane. Her life energy pulsed in the dark surrounding him, her brightness rivaling the sun. He wished he could see her with his own eyes. Her aura enticed him, glowing, yet still he saw the tremors and imperfections only imagined last night. She needed to stay with him.

Who was he kidding? He needed her to stay with him. He needed to hear her quiet voice, hot against his skin, breathy and urgent. Wanted to feel her long firm legs wrapped around his ass, her nails biting into his shoulders as he tunneled his way between her wet folds, plunging deeper and deeper.

And all he could do was lay here like a piece of luggage as she walked out the door. With their mental link firmly established, he would be able to follow her movements, a biologic GPS tuned to only her. He could find her no matter where she was, awake or asleep. His only fear: if anything were to happen to her before his body finished recharging, she would be on her own. And that simply would not do.

The longest he had ever needed to rest was twelve hours, and judging by the color of the sky beyond the bamboo blinds, he had only an hour tops left to wait.

Calliope. My own personal muse. Please, my beautiful Calliope, stay safe for just a little while longer.

The energy that buoyed Cal's feet out of the high-rise tower in the middle of the city was rapidly seeping through the soles of her bare feet as she padded down the concrete paths leading her home. Yet every step further away from the mirrored steel tugged on her heart. The feeling was not comfortable, the sensation like a string yanking on her insides, and it brought a tinge of sadness with each new step.

Swallowing back an uncharacteristic sob, she shook her head violently. *Come on, Cal. Get a hold of yourself. You're only checking to see that Maggs and Ajax are fine. Then…*

Then what? Would she run back to Mr. I'm-Too-Sexy-for-My-Clothes?

Her steps slowed as the campus apartments appeared around the corner. Her gut was telling her someone she wouldn't like was near. A darkness oozed around her, slicking her skin in the waning afternoon sun. It was strangely familiar, not welcome, but still familiar. With each step, the dread followed her just beyond the edges of her vision.

Self-preservation and battle strategies kicked into high gear, propelling her feet past the front door of her building. She continued on, leading her strange stalker away from her home and toward her second home, the History building. The darkness seemed to follow her, slinking from shadow to shadow, its inky presence raising the hairs along the back of her neck. She fought to remain cool and collected, avoiding the urge to run screaming back to the solace of that ginormous bed.

The mere thought of her recently departed pillow-topped ivory playground spurned her closer to her new destination. If she was indeed being followed, then she was going meet the bastard on her own terms. On her home turf. A crooked smile touched the edge of her lips as she sauntered down the hall, her bare feet whispering against the tiled floor. She spent countless hours as Professor Archibald's grad student, so it had given her some special privileges. Namely the key code to the department's antiquities lab. Her fingers danced over the keypad, quickly tapping out the right sequence. The door clicked open as she walked into the cluttered closest, shimmying between boxes and crates as she avoided protruding stacks of papers and teetering tomes. She underestimated the space between her ass and an overloaded table and she banged her hip on the corner.

"Shit," she muttered as a wayward book caught the hem of her shirt. Readjusting her, or make that *his*, shirt, her eye was caught by a gleam of highly polished copper, the sleeping blade just beyond the leather bound pages. She filed this tidbit away for later and stepped toward the exit. She was brushing the gathering dust off the black fabric when rolling laughter filled the cubicle.

Cal's head snapped in the direction of the room's only door. Standing inside the threshold was a nondescript-looking man wearing a rather forgettable business suit. Everything about him made her want to dismiss him. Then it dawned on her: that was his weapon. He could move about in a crowd, causing God-only-knew what kind of damage and no one would even remember he was there, much less what he looked like.

"You know, we figured it was only a matter of time before he came for you," he said.

Cal honed in on every little detail, from his bland sandy blonde hair cut in a standard men's short style to the nasally tone of his vanilla voice. Damn, he had perfected the art of the unremarkable. Yet something was still familiar to her. She knew that voice. But from where? She focused on cataloguing everything about him. She knew she'd need it later.

"I still have no idea what you were talking about then and I know even less now. I don't know why you thought I was…whatever you thought I was. I'm just a college student, that's all." Keeping her eyes on the approaching man, she held her ground, hoping the more he talked, the more she'd learn. And the closer she could get to the Sumerian dagger next to the binding.

"You think to trick me, sorceress?"

Sorceress? Her brows furrowed in confusion. Her mental balking did not stop his tirade. A light flared in the back of her mind, and her eyes widened in dim recognition. He had been in that room with her. He had called her that before and now he continued to press the issue.

"We've been watching you for some time now. You think you're so secret. Running around all hours of the day and night. The powers of your lover keeping you fit and healthy." He pressed further into the room, inching his way closer to his prey. His arrogance and complete ignorance astonished her, giving her the advantage she needed. *Where the hell did he come up with this crap? I feel like I stepped into a bad episode of the Twilight Zone.*

Cal shuffled backward, knocking her ass into the table and rattling its precariously balanced display items. Her hand shot out to steady the teetering terra cotta urn before it became another lost relic. Scant inches away from her hand rested the smooth wooden handle. She sent a silent prayer to the gods of historical items, hoping the blade wouldn't disintegrate if she needed to use it.

"You are no mystery to us. We will stop him, and once I have his head, my place in the future will be unquestionable. Right now you hope he will hear your pleas and he'll again come to your rescue." He sneered, beady brown eyes behind wire-rimmed glasses dancing with malice. "But you are trapped here. You've already lost and now you'll be mine. I have already foreseen this. Your thoughts are like an open book to me."

His hand snaked out, grasping at her wrist, intent on yanking her away from her barricade.

Cal moved fast and smooth, years of martial arts training kicking in. Her fingers closed around his extended wrist, slamming his palm flat against the table. Without missing a beat, she grabbed the dagger, plunging the blade deep into his hand, pinning him to the wood.

"Really?" She locked furious green eyes with his stunned brown orbs, her voice cold. "Then learn to fucking read."

Seizing a handful of his hair, she smashed his face against the solid table, and his head bounced back from her force. Bone crunched and blood splashed across the wood as his body slumped in a mangled pool at her feet. The explosive rebound took her by surprise and sent her to her knees, agony tearing through her side.

Her hand clutched at her ribs, her fingers meeting with bones not in their expected place.

Aw, crap.

CHAPTER SIX

"CALLIOPE!"

"Calliope? Agapi, what has happened? Answer me, please!"

Cal hissed through the pain as the welcomed warmth of his voice flooded her mind. A hint of a smile touched her lips. No one had ever really been worried about her for years. She'd distanced herself from friends and family once she figured out the limited shelf life on her existence. As a lover of history, she was oddly terrified by the idea of leaving someone behind or something unfinished after she was gone. So she had opted to remain separate, losing herself in her studies and her books.

She closed her eyes, savoring his deep, rich voice. The words he chose, the style of speech, even his devilish accent promised a history lesson not to be slept through. *And there was that "agapi" again. I'm gonna figure it out.*

"I'm all right. Just...damn." The act of pulling air into her lungs to form words made the cracking rib spiral further into her side. Sweat formed on her head as she struggled to her feet. Images swayed before her eyes. She grabbed the table as she swallowed down a wave of nausea. She squeezed her eyes shut, waited a moment while her mind focused on returning all wayward body parts into their expected places.

"Calliope?"

"Cal. Please, call me Cal." Risking a glance, she peeled her lids open and found straight lines and solid walls. *Yay for me.* She regarded the figure in the cheap brown suit, hanging like a hastily discarded sweater, half-on and half-off the table. She knew he'd have one hell of a headache, not to mention a broken nose and maybe a couple teeth as well. Sighing, she cautiously made her way toward the door, hobbling at a snail's pace.

"Cal. Hmmm. I like how that sounds. But I can tell you are hurt. Please stay where you are. Will you not tell me what happened?"

The door clicked shut behind her as she walked down the hall, cringing with every jarring step. "Let's just say I guess I should've stayed in bed," she mumbled. Thank God with today's technology, if you found someone talking to themselves, most people assumed you were on a Bluetooth device. She tried to walk as upright as possible, but the stabbing pain against the left side of her torso was not making this a viable reality.

"But I'm fine. I'm leaving the campus now and I'll be back in a few. It's a short walk and I'm OK."

"I admire your courage, but you are not a very convincing liar, ómorfià."

Cal wove awkwardly between the crowds of college students, avoiding any large clusters if possible. Yet for each group she managed to dance around, one passerby would bump into her or nudge the arm cradling her side, and the pain almost drove her to her knees. Most did not give her a second glance, but an occasional hand would touch her shoulder in way of apology. Biting her lip to stop from crying out and nodding sharply, she stumbled further down the street, working her way toward the steel spires of downtown and closer to the source of the sexy voice in her head.

"Yeah, well. I don't think courage is quite the word that I thought of," she finally replied. A red light stopped her progress, and she leaned against the light post, her strength beginning to seriously wane. Closing her eyes, she imagined how she must look, dressed in a shirt looking more like a dress, blue jeans stiff and rust-stained, bare toes peeking out, and sweat pouring down her face like she'd just run a marathon. Lucky for her, she was surrounded by the famous hills of San Francisco's streets, so her lack of breath could be easily ignored. As she sneaked a peek to check on the light's progress, she also gave a small prayer of thanks for the fact her return path did not include any of those hills.

"Why did you not stay where you were safe?"

Cal felt a rush of heat race through her blood at the imagined feel of fingertips caressing her cheek. "Like I said, I don't think courage is the word you're looking for. More like stubbornness." Opening her eyes, she was disappointed to find herself still alone as the light turned back to red. "Or stupidity," she muttered. Crap. So much for getting back to the body housing that amazing voice any sooner.

"Callie? Is that you?"

That was definitely not the voice she wanted to hear. She only had to look up to find Paul McCormack power walking toward her as gracefully as a giraffe charging down a flight of stairs. The expression on her once-lab partner's square face fluctuated from perturbed to feigned concern. Blue eyes too big for his face squinted at her, making her feel like a bug on display. She rolled her eyes as his rail-thin frame ambled closer, his blonde high and tight crew cut at odds with the fire-engine-red Hawaiian print shirt and Bermuda shorts. Maybe if he stood in the middle of traffic, she could cross the street in peace.

"What is it, Paul? Kinda busy right now." She stood on her own legs, barely, as his steps closed the final distance. *Ok, Mr. Super Sexy. Now would be a good time to swoop in and rescue me.* She bit the inside of her cheek to stifle the smile twitching along the corner of her mouth. Paul would think she was happy to see him.

"Yeah, really? Busy doing what? I've had to take over your duties for the past week with Professor Archibald, cover your classes and even met with… Oh my God, Callie, are you all right?"

Cal leaned back against the pole, exhaling in a hiss as she ducked to avoid the arm about to land across her shoulders.

"Yes, Paul. I'm fine." Her head snapped up, the blood draining from her face. "Wait, did you say a week?"

Galen became aware of his heart, then his lungs. Blood pumped and air flowed, bringing life to his body, seeping down to his hands and feet. His mind spun in deadly circles, finding her trace and flaring the path to a dizzying brightness. He traced the line between them and found a bloodied body with an arm reaching toward something protruding from a table. Oh, that would be a hand. A hand, to be exact, stuck like a butterfly on display, the hilt of some ancient and still quite useful weapon pointing skyward with a slight quiver.

Seconds ticked by until long-awaited energy coursed through his body. With a curse, he lurched off the bed, tugging on the first shirt within arm's reach as he shoved his feet into his motorcycle boots in one swift movement. He moved with a single-minded focus, stalking down the stairs, his hand grabbing the leather duster off the chair back, and out the door he stormed. It was still too early to pop in and grab her, too many people out and about. And most normal people did not respond too well to the sudden appearance of a 6' 5" hulk of pissed-off black leather.

Opting to take the longer route, he entered the building's main stairwell and blinked to the ground floor, emerging onto the street. He shifted his focus, concentrating on her scent, which still lingered in his soul. His groin tightened as he inhaled deeply, the innocent flowery fragrance that was hers and hers alone hit him like a cross-town bus. It was clean and pure, reminding him of bright spring mornings.

And she was in great distress. Something had added to the pain she felt and he was compelled to seek her out and to save her. Grumbling with a tense sigh, he shook his head as his feet followed her lingering path. He had the feeling saving her was going to be a full-time job, one he would be eager to fulfill.

In more ways than one.

Opening his eyes and stalling his newest erotic daydream, he stepped onto the sidewalk, his long strides eating up the distance between him and his lovely quarry. His feet moved with purpose through the milling students as he followed the wake of her earlier passing, his single-minded determination clearing his path. He had traveled several blocks, his pace insistent yet smooth. He could sense she was beginning to weaken, whether from her wounds or from whatever was causing her current tension he did not know. Nor did he truly care. His woman was in need of him, and he was not going to fail in that task.

As he turned the corner, the picture before him slammed into him with the fury of lightning blast. Cal, his beautiful mate, still draped in his clothes, staggered as another man moved to gather her into his arms. *Oh, I think not.* No sooner had the thought crossed his mind then he was standing behind her, glaring down at the skinny young man wrapped in a violently loud flower-print shirt.

Cal's knees started to buckle, and she leaned against the streetlight before landing on her ass. Or worse, in Paul's spindly arms. Her mind fired in a flurry, ideas and images floating through the chaos like scraps of paper in a wind tunnel. She knew her strength would not last her much longer, but she had to get out of this very public place so she could pass out in peace.

"Yes, Callie."

God, she really hated that name. She had given up correcting him about her name back during her sophomore year. He thought she looked more like a "Callie" than a "Cal." She scoffed at the memory, even back then, she didn't care what he thought about her or her name. He creeped her out, still did. There was always something just...off about him.

Shaking her head to bring her back to the here and now, she tried to pick out the important facts of his ongoing soliloquy.

"...you had us all so worried. What happened? Where have you been?"

Think fast, Cal.

"Look, Paul, it's been a really weird few days, and I just want to get home, all right?" Her vision began to waver, edges losing their straight lines and colors paling. *No, please,* her mind screamed. *Not without him here.*

Paul brown eyes widened as she swayed. "Fuck. I mean, oh my God, Callie. Are you OK? I've got—"

"There you are, agapi."

Cal wanted to weep when the voice from her dreams melted into her ears. He was here. He had found her. Forcing her eyes to focus, she stared into the taut black fabric before her, the slickness of more leather flowed like dark water down his strong arms and pooled around this legs, still sporting those second skin, thigh-hugging pants. He was made up of night and shadows, but there was nothing about the mountain of pure male before her that gave her any fear. Just the opposite in fact, and this knowledge spurred her on. Her gaze traveled higher, examining every rise and curve, starting with the defined cut of tight washboard abs and chiseled pecs and finally reaching the destination she craved.

Any air remaining in her lungs escaped in a heavy sigh as she stared into a face from her wildest imaginings. Thick waves of black hair brushed the tops of his shoulders, framing a strong, square jaw dusted with a purely masculine unshaven shadow. Piercing black eyes peered out from long feathery eyelashes, one thick brow arched as a slight smirk graced his lips. Her mouth grew arid as she focused on those full, and very kiss-worthy, lips.

"Oh…hi."

Her blood heated, warming her from tip to toe and settling just south of her navel. Under the intensity of his gaze, she felt self-conscious, yet desired and empowered as well. *I think I could get used to being looked at like that.* She knew if she touched her cheeks, she would singe her fingertips.

If only her other arm wasn't busy trying to stop her body from flying apart.

The angel before Galen turned with timid care, her eyes working their way up. His body locked, his breath caught in his chest as he waited patiently for her to finish her visual journey. When her face finally raised to meet his, Galen sent a silent howl of thanks to the gods of old. She went beyond beautiful and ventured into the realm of the divinely exquisite. His heart knocked hard against his ribs as he stared into her mysterious emerald green eyes. Only once he heard the catch in her breath was he reminded of her current state of peril.

He hastily cleared his throat to restart his vocal cords, hoping to reroute the blood fleeing his brain for the already ramrod stiff shaft in his way-too-confining pants. His gaze dragged from the lovely vision before him to lock eyes with the garish beanpole who thought to touch his woman. He wrapped a possessive arm around her, pulling her into the shelter of his body.

"I believe I can handle this from here, sir." Dismissing the other man, he redirected his eyes to the bundle close to his heart. "I tried to warn you were not recovered enough for a venture outside. You still need time and rest." The driving urge to claim her where they stood shook his foundations. Hoping to assuage the hunger inside him, he reached down, stroking her cheek with the back of his fingers, the temptation to pull her into a kiss undeniable.

"Yeah, well, you know me. I don't listen very well." She attempted a light laugh, but the sounds was cut short by a sharp hiss. She reached out, her fingers digging into his arm keeping her upright as her legs finally gave up the ghost.

Galen swore under his breath as she began to collapse in his arms. "All right, that is enough. I am getting you back home." He moved swiftly, intending to sweep her into his arms only to be stopped by a panicked glare.

"Don't you dare," she whispered hastily, her eyes flashing with embarrassment and pride. "I'll not be carried out like a sack of potatoes."

A nasally and almost forgotten voice piped up over Galen's shoulder. "Um, excuse me? Just who are you and what do you think you're doing with Callie?"

Galen twisted his head to see the frail chest puffed out as much as possible, stick arms folded across the floral nightmare. If not for the fast-fading beauty in his arms, he would have found the entire scene amusing.

"Who I am is of no consequence to you. Know that I am here to protect Calliope and right now, she needs to rest to complete her healing." He growled, one corner of his lip curling up and he fought the urge to bear his teeth to seal the deal. Sighing, he swiveled his attentions away, only to have a rude yank on his shoulder, attempting to spin him around.

"Healing? Listen, pal. I have a right to—" The rest of the statement died on his lips as Galen jerked around and leveled his cold, predatory eyes into the fear-filled mouse brown eyes before him.

"It is YOU who have no right here, little man. And if you wish to continue your existence, you will step back. Right. Now." Adding Insistence to his voice, he watched as the would-be competitor stumbled backward, driven away from the wrath and ire in his command. Galen rolled his tightening shoulders, hoping to ease the growing knot in the center of his back. Sucking in a calming breath, he warred with his conflicting desires; pull her into his embrace and kiss her senseless, scoop her up and pop home, or snap the scrawny neck before him.

Decisions, decisions.

"Paul, stop." Her weak voice further fueled his protective desires and he held her closer. He felt her slight resistance and he released his iron grip on her. She eased her shoulders away from him and faced her colleague. "Look, I just need to rest for a while, all right? You don't have to cover any more of my work. I'll get—"

"Nonsense, Callie," Paul said, and Galen was unable to control the low growl rumbling in his chest. "Don't you worry your head about anything. It's my pleasure to help you. You know that, babe."

Babe?

This Paul was pressing his luck.

"Yeah, OK. Um, thanks, then. A day more and I should be back—"

"Agapi, you will take as much time as is needed before you return to your duties." His patience was beginning to fray, and he had no wish to continue the pointless bantering with Paul. Especially as he could feel her growing weaker with each passing moment. She swiveled her head, looking up over her shoulder, an inquisitive twinkle in her green eyes. Her mind began to spin. *Spell. That guy talked about me being a sorceress.*

"And yes, you are on the right track. I will explain everything to you, but I'd rather do that in private."

"Yeah, yeah." Nodding slowly, she leaned further into him, her thoughts becoming hazy and blurry.

He trembled as he placed an innocent kiss atop her smooth black hair, sneaking a whiff of the fragrance that was all her. The light scent of April flowers and clean rain masked a dark secret, one he would take time soon to unravel. She was slipping slowly into unconsciousness; he sensed her faltering legs and her waning strength. He locked eyes with the man she addressed as Paul, nodded sharply then began to guide her away from his stunned face. He ignored the continued dribble aimed at the back of his jacket, spying the perfect darkened alleyway.

He kept his attention tuned to her hesitant movements, his pace cautious. It was about a mile or so back to his building and he was seriously wondering if she could make the trip vertically. Her arm trembled as she white-knuckled his shirt, fighting to keep her legs underneath her. Her gaze skittered up from the ground, seeking a vehicle to whisk them away. He tightened his hold on her shoulders as her mind began to wander this new tangent. What kind of car would he drive? Would it be something sleek, powerful, and incredibly fast?

Galen smiled as her thoughts busied to keep her awake and in the moment. "It is that and more, *ómorfiá mou*," he whispered against the shell of her ear. "But I have a much better and much quicker method of transport in mind." The dark privacy of the narrow passageway swallowed them.

Paul watched in stunned silence as the hulking mass of black leather walked off with the woman he had painstaking courted for the past two years. He brought her coffee, smiled at her, even rearranged his entire future, changing his major from Business to the boring ass study of all that ancient shit she fawned over to spend time with her.

And she just left with that fucking *300* reject.

She even smiled at the bastard, like he was something special. Who did he think he was?

"Well, now that must have hurt."

A soft voice whispered in his ear, through his mind. His eyes stayed glued on the receding duster as it turned the corner, most likely heading toward some suped-up expensive sports car to drive his girl away from him. And contrary to what she might think, she was his girl. He hadn't thrown his whole life away not to get the sweetest piece of ass on this whole goddamned campus.

"Doesn't she realize the sacrifices you've made for her?"

A light touch on his shoulder drew him back to the present. Turning, he looked into a pair of unearthly lilac eyes locked within a face of cruel yet compelling beauty. Auburns and deep red tones sprang out of the dishwater-blonde locks meticulously slicked back, framing the image and forever burning into his memory.

"No," Paul found his voice, laced with anger and disdain. Words poured into his mind, spilling out of his lips in time with those of his newfound friend. "No, she doesn't. That little bitch. Well, if she thinks this is over, she's got another thing coming. I'm not giving up that easily."

Paul watched as the lips curled into a sardonic grin, the mirth never reaching his cold eyes. "You can't bear to think of what would happen if she were hurt. Or if someone else were to claim the prize rightly yours. You should follow her, make sure she's all right."

"Yeah," the words rang though his head, sounding perfectly logical. *My prize. Fucking A, she's my damn prize. Been making sure no one else tapped that ass before me. And I'm not gonna let this asshole get into her pants first.* Paul hurried after the pair, not more than a few minutes behind. He figured he could at least grab the license plate number on his car. He knew people who knew people, and information was easy to obtain when you knew where the bodies were buried.

As he turned the corner, he found himself alone in the very empty alley. *Fuck.* They must have gone out the other way. His brown eyes danced as he thought about the way she practically fell into his arms. Yeah, until that fucking leather wearing pansy showed up. She was so close, he could almost taste her, all but smell her sex.

Scowling at the victory torn from his grasp, he followed the alley back toward the campus and contemplated his next move. He had always been fascinated by Callie, even created his own pet name for her. But now? Now, there was another dog in the fight, and he was gonna show how much fight was in this dog. Grinning, he decided to start by keeping a closer eye on her flaky roommate.

Back at the signpost, a figure receded into the growing shadows, leaving only a trail of dark laughter.

CHAPTER SEVEN

Galen slipped easily from the shadows of the alley and stepped into the shadowed alcove in his entryway.

"Hey, that's a neat trick," she whispered, and he lead to the rumpled ivory comforter, her heart beat escalating as they crossed the bedroom floor.

He begrudgingly honored her earlier request, his arms itching at the need to gather her close and lay her on the tousled bedding. His groin jumped in agreement, shoving against his zipper with single-minded and sharply painful determination. Clenching his teeth to tamp down the growl in his throat, he acted the perfect gentleman, letting her set the pace to the bed. He had faced legions of enemies; he could be patient and do this.

But the hiss against his chest finally spurred him in action. He swept her gently into his arms and set her down on the bed. With quick and deft movements, his fingers traced along the arm cradling her ribs.

"I've got you, my sweet. Now relax and let me see what went wrong."

She winced when he moved her arm. A half-mumbled apology in his native tongue slipped between his lips as a tear slipped down her cheek. Swearing at himself for his fumbling, he hovered above the bed and placed a gentle hand against her side, the other resting on her feverish and sweat-slicked brow. He forced himself to set aside his rage and concentrated on re-mending her fractured rib.

The repairs were simple and completed in a blink. Yet never before had a healing simply not taken. It was as if her body refused to let itself be fixed and was determined to be in pain. He sent a second charge into the misbehaving marrow, hoping the extra boost would encourage the errant break to stay mended. He stroked her cheek, the soft skin beneath his fingers too warm for the chill in the room. Opening his eyes, he peered down into her angelic face. The skin beneath his hand was a delicious and tempting shade of pink. His body lurched at her naive blush, his groin tightening to an excruciating level. Clenching his jaw hard enough to crack, he swallowed his hungry growl, curbing his need to lower his lips and claim his rightful prize. He gave his head an angry shake. He must give her the choice to accept him; the terms must be hers and hers alone. If she denied him, he would be lost for all time. He sent a silent prayer to the old gods as he willed her to open her eyes.

Cal listened to the melodic voice washing over her. She recognized his accent as Greek. And she had heard enough spoken to be able to pick out words sounds, but not enough to know their meanings. But, she was pretty sure he was not happy right now. *Fabu, you've managed to piss off the sexiest man on the planet. So much for some action on this amazing bed.* Another mental shake, this one much more forceful and accompanied by a noticeable blush. His voice was soothing and she felt the welcome flow of air returning to her starved lungs.

The gentle voice whispered in her mind, drawing her eyes open. Her lids fluttered and, close enough for her to touch, was a set of eyes so dark that she felt as if part of the night had been trapped midway between his wavy black hair and strong, full lips. She sat mesmerized as those lips curved into a wicked smile that sent heat pooling between her legs. What had she done to warrant such a gorgeous dark hero? Oh yeah, got herself kidnapped and tortured for a week.

That stray thought slammed the brakes on her raging hormones. The weight of her ordeal crashed over her with the force of a hurricane. He heart began to beat out a frantic and ever-increasing staccato rhythm; her breath came in short gulps. She knew all too soon, she would be a quivering, bawling mass of Jell-O. Opting for some privacy for her impending breakdown, she feebly rolled onto her side, her knees curling into her chest as her hands climbed to hide her face from his heated gaze.

Her resolve was truly tested when he embraced her, his words in a seductively exotic language brushed against her skin and she was undone. At first, the tears trickled down her cheeks. Yet, as the hypnotic voice spoke soft encouragements, they rained down with more gusto, her shoulders knocking against his chest, her face buried in her hands.

His hands rubbed lazy and comforting circles along her back as her sobs rocked her body. Emotions ranging from anger to confusion raced through her mind, chased by exhaustion and fear. She caught tender melodies coming from a very nearby source, the soothing notes a welcoming balm to her battered psyche.

Moments bled into minutes, then a slow calm began to fill the room. Hiccupped breaths echoed in the darkening room. Cal relaxed in the shelter of the sexy specimen of pure masculinity currently wrapped around her like a warm blanket. Inhaling deeply, grateful for the pain-free gesture, she pulled the wild clean scent into her blood and her skin grew hot and cool. She wanted to stay like this, locked in his arms and feeling safe. But now, she was ready for answers. Not to mention, by asking her questions, she would be rewarded with the sound of his voice, its rumbling tone brushing against her flesh like a mink glove.

"Why me? I just don't understand why me. He knew who I was. I mean, whoever it was who grabbed me, he knew my name. Why? How? I mean, how did he know my name?" She felt panic rise in her mumbled voice and she struggled to regain her calm. "I'm nobody, just a dumb grad student working on a dry MA in Ancient Civilizations and Medieval Lit. What kind of threat could I possibly be?"

"For reasons beyond me, agapi, somehow they knew you were my spiritmate and intended to—"

"Whoa, wait a minute." Cal pulled back, his sensual voice had lulled her into a sense of security until a certain phrase caught her attention. "Spirit...what? Did you say mate?" She looked up into his piercing eyes, at his deeply tanned skin, and his mouth that promised nothing but endless pleasures. Her heart quickened its pace the longer she gazed up into the face out of antiquity. She had a sudden image of him standing upon a field of battle, sword raised high above his head, his partially naked body encased in leather and armor, bathed in blood and mud.

Here was her own personal mythic hero. *And he was Greek to boot. Girl, you couldn't have asked for anyone better!*

The devilish hint of a smile touched the corner of Galen's mouth. "Does the thought upset you?"

"I...uh...well, no, I mean, but..." She gaped like a beached goldfish, her jaw moved but no intelligible sounds came out. Her mouth and her brain argued, the words caught in a violent tug-of-war. Her mouth begged to taste those yummy lips and her brain wanted answers. She felt a flood of heat rise from the collar of her shirt (or would that be his shirt?) coloring her cheeks. Even the tips of her ears warmed up as he gradually leaned in.

She sat frozen, her eyes entranced by the full lips getting closer and closer. Her heart raced, speeding the blood from head to toe, warmed her already flushed cheeks, and tingled intoxicatingly everywhere else. The distance between their lips disappeared until her breath danced across his lips.

"Just...one...sip..." His whispered words brushed against her lips before he closed the final gap. At the first gentle push against her lips, her body jolted, eyelids fluttering down over her rolled back eyes. Deepening the kiss, he dragged his tongue along her full lips, asking quietly for entrance. The pressure against her mouth became more demanding, his tongue tracing the seam of her lips. She opened up to him with a needy groan, relaxing further into the soft bed, her arms snaking up around his neck and shoulders, pulling him closer to her.

She poured her throaty sigh into his mouth and was rewarded with a wickedly possessive growl. His tongue swept and savored every corner of her mouth, his kisses sweeter than rich chocolate and she was lost in the incredible sensation of his mouth on hers. He tasted wild, dangerous and decadent. Her fingers caressed the butter-soft leather around his shoulders before wending through his thick black waves. They were just as soft as she imagined them to be. His tongue delved deep into her mouth, entwining with hers in a passionate dance. Never had she experienced such passion, such heat. His movements shifted slightly, and the bed sank beside her, dipping in support his massive frame.

An instant later, her body rolled against a very solid and very masculine shape, a set of arms wrapping around her shoulders, dragging her across his muscled chest and pinning her in a gentle cage against his hard body. Strong fingers tunneled through her hair, tilting her head to give him greater access to her mouth, while his other hand strayed lower, finally coming to rest on the hollow of her lower back.

Her heart began to hammer a panicked tattoo as she realized her hands met with bare flesh. *What the hell am I doing? Too much, too fast.*

No sooner did the thought race through her brain then he ended the kiss. Her eyes refused to open as he settled her against his side, one arm draping over her shoulder as loosely as his rock-solid body would allow.

Her lungs heaved, sucking in deep gulps of air as she rested in the hollowed curve in the bed. She heard the thundering beat against her ear and her lips curved upward. Wow, this total specimen of yumminess was just as spun as she was. And it was only a kiss. Not that she had much experience, but something told her it had been more than a simple kiss.

"I…um. Wow. I, uh, don't even know where to start." Her voice sounded breathy to her ears. Clearing her throat, hoping to add more power to her soft voice, she tried again.

"Was it truly that unenjoyable for you?" the voice against her skin did not match his words, his deep voice gravelly and winded.

She groaned, covering her embarrassed blush with her hands. "Yeah, wait, no, it was… I mean, but that's not what I meant. I just…" She stopped talking, allowing a moment for her tongue to untangle and for thoughts to unwind. If she moved away from him, maybe she could form an intelligible sentence. But her body seemed unwilling to make the all-important first move. "That was very nice, really. Ok, so it was a lot more than nice."

The bed shook as Galen tried to contain his mirth. "Well, I am pleased I measure up. Perhaps I should try again? See if it can be much more than nice?" He tightened his arm with a flinch, keeping at bay his growing desire to make good on his casual words. He expected to meet with hesitant resistance, but he did not intend to practically terrify her off the bed.

With a frantic scramble, she half crawled, half fell to the far side of the massive King size bed. "No, really. That's all right. I, uh—"

Ashamed of his misconstrued tease, he dropped his gaze, but not before he caught the innocent panic firing in her bright green eyes.

"I am sorry. I did not mean to insinuate I would take anything not freely offered. I have offended you and—"

She sat back on her heels, her knees just shy of sliding off the mattress and landing on the floor. "No," the word tumbled out in a rush as she reached out, scooting a little closer to him. "No, please. Don't apologize. You didn't do anything wrong. Hell, to be honest, you didn't do anything I didn't want. It's just that, well... All I know is your name, and that I'm supposed to be your...your mate? I don't even know what that means, much less why those people were following me in the first place, or why they kidnapped me and then that guy in the office..." Her hands flew to cover her mouth, eyes wide as the events prior to his appearance played out in her mind's eye.

"Yes, about him...I saw the aftermath, but what started the short-lived row?"

She tried to look contrite but instead, a mischievous smile tugged at one corner of her kiss-swollen lips. The devilishly seductive grin had his cock knocking so hard against his zipper he swore she could hear it.

"Umm... Well, he pissed me off." She made a feeble attempt at a pout, her shoulders drooping to add to the illusion of admonishment. He rested back on his elbow, smirking at the ease of her reaction.

"Remind me never to piss you off, then."

He studied her from her safe distance. She had just suffered tortures for the gods only knew how long and she managed to keep her wits about her in a dangerous situation. She handled herself with confidence and did not balk in the face of violence. Yet her panicked response to his kiss gave him pause. She gave a nervous laugh before she plopped into a less-than-graceful seated position, running her fingers through her hair.

"Yeah, well...I, uh, guess I sorta lost my temper and I, um, slammed his head into the table." He blinked deliberating, waiting before she added, "After I stuck a 4,000 year old Dynastic Sumerian dagger through his hand, which I guess is how I popped my rib out of whack. The table thing, not the dagger thing, I mean."

He threw back his head, his rich laughter bouncing off the white walls. She was feisty. He liked that. He had opted to spend much of the last century alone, most of the women he came across being more interested in style rather than substance. But here, now, he had found a true Renaissance beauty. Intelligent, resourceful and not to mention arousingly sensual in ways even she did not realize. She was more than capable of handling herself, with graceful reserve or fierce action. The gods had truly given him a worthy mate. Now, to assure her he was worthy of her. That would be a task he would gladly pursue for the rest of his life.

But his heart skipped a beat as a sobering reality hit home. She'd had to defend herself against an opponent, most likely much larger than she, judging by the size of the suit hanging from the table, and he had been helpless to aid her. If she had remained here with him, safe in his arms, this situation would have never occurred. A situation in which she returned to him injured, not to mention, almost in the arms of another man.

"You should have stayed here, Cal. You could have been seriously hurt." His voice was soft, yet undeniable. Sidling closer, his hand crossed the short white distance between them, cradling her cheek in his palm. Her soft skin beneath his rough fingertips sent a delicious fire through his body. Her eyelids fluttered down, giving him a moment to gather his thoughts, and her a chance to respond to his statement.

"Yeah, well…One of those jerks talked about my roommate and—" Her eyes flew open in a panic. "Maggs—" She tried to move away, but a gentle touch on her cheek calmed her frantic actions.

"Shh, agapi. As long as you stay by my side, you are safe." Galen spoke gently, filling his words with compassion and honesty. Her eyes were filled with such fear, his heart felt as if it were going to crack. His first urge was to gather her into his arms, kissing away all traces of fear and not to stop until both of them were entangled in each other's arms, drenched in sweat.

However, the small part of his brain still functioning beyond animal instinct belayed his current plan in lieu of a more, socially acceptable response. "And you still need time to heal before going another round, don't you agree?" Smiling as innocently as he could muster, he looked into the beautiful emerald green eyes before him, drawn in to their bottomless depths, happily willing to drown in them.

Her chin quivered and the edges of his smile faltered. "She could be…"

In the space of a heartbeat, she was in his arms, his fingers wending through her short black hair, holding her close to his chest. "If I were able to tell you your friend is unharmed and safe, would that do?"

"How? Yeah, I mean, yes, it would but—"

"Close your eyes, *órmorfià*, and picture your friend in your mind." He stroked her back, drawing light, lazy circles with his fingers, his voice lulling her into a more relaxed and open state of mind. "Her hair…" His lips drifted over her soft, straight tresses. "Her face…" His fingertips grazed her jaw line. "Her eyes…" To punctuate his words, he trailed kisses across her closed lids. "Picture every detail and focus your thoughts on only her, Calliope." He pressed his forehead against hers and his eyes drifted shut as he whispered, "Now breathe with me."

He drew in a slow, deep breath and guided her lungs to follow his lead. As he exhaled, he slipped into her thoughts. Silently, he trailed behind her as she walked through her mind, dodging around the all-too-vivid pictures of the two of them, naked and writhing. Her thoughts even included a soundtrack, moans, cries, and sighs of pleasure echoing through the dark He raised an eyebrow at the seductive visions of their coupling. She wished for it as well as he did, that was a good sign indeed. He watched as the images of their passionate joining faded to be replaced by the face of a young woman, long blonde hair hanging in thick ropy bands, blue eyes framed in thick round lenses and clothes that smacked of the sixties, which he had avoided by losing himself in any booming metropolis he could find.

Narrowing his focus on the New Age disciple before him, he traced her, following the heart link shared by her and Cal. Friendships, he had learned, created clear pathways easily followed if one knew where to look. And this friendship was strong and true, lighting the trail brighter than the noonday sun. Soon he found her pacing around a small room, a young man clad all in black watching her from a bed against the wall. She was worried for her friend who had disappeared and could not be consoled by his words. Calling upon his Marshal skills, he directed her companion to gather her into his arms and within their embrace, he flooded both of them with the assurance of their missing friend's good health and well-being. He wished he could guide the male's voice, but his talent did not lie with the skills of the Conduits. So he did what he could. He stayed for another heartbeat, relieved as both people relaxed a fraction, telling each other of their newfound belief in her safety.

As he returned, he caught the sounds of a telltale hitch as Cal fought to hold back the threat on impending tears. Brushing his lips against her sleek hair, he hugged her close, using his body to reassure her. "There is no need for your tears, agapi. She is unharmed, worried about you, as is her lover. But they are in no danger."

Her shoulders collapsed, laughing in shaky bursts. "Oh, thanks the gods." She pulled back, her bright green eyes misty and damp, the smile reaching from her soul to every part of her. "Thank you. I don't know how you know, but thank you."

Galen thought he would pass out, from the blinding brightness of her smile. There was an innocence about her that touched his heart, a breath of fresh air that called to him. As long as she continued to look at him as she did now, he would do anything. He was happily ensnared and forever he would delightfully remain so.

Heat spiked through his body, curling his lips into a seductive grin. "There is nothing for which you ever need to thank me. I will always do everything in my power to see that you are happy."

"Oh." The single syllable drained all coherent thought from his brain. Her tongue flicked out, wetting her parched lips and her innocent action ignited the powder keg of desire inside him. Her lips still slightly parted, his lips descended, devouring hers.

His mouth slanted over hers, his tongue eager to chase hers back into the sweet recesses of her mouth. He pressed her hungrily against his body, fitting the soft curves of her full breasts against his chest. One hand kept her firmly in place as he slowly levered them both down toward the beckoning monstrous bed. He labored to keep his deeper instincts at bay, the ones screaming for him to shred their clothes and plunge himself deep into the hot and sweet confines of her body.

Cal's groan was swallowed by the hot, passionate mouth latched onto her and by the cushioning softness of the snowy expanse of linen. Her body sang as his heavy frame pinned her sweetly to the bed. Well, until she felt the massive length pressed against her inner thigh. *Holy shit!* Her brain and her inexperienced body went into self-preservation mode. Her eyes flew open as she placed her hands against the solid wall of excited male above her. Fear nearly overtook her as she pushed on his chest, but her light touch had him flying halfway across the room, landing silently like a cat with his back against the wall.

"I did not intend to frighten you." His voice was shaky and winded, the normal deep and controlled timbre ragged. "I am—"

She waved off another apology from the panting giant across the room from her. Her other hand, however, was busy attempting to shove her heart back into her chest, the damned thing still bouncing around after the make-out session and his hasty retreat. "P-p-please...don't..." Pausing to inhale as fully as her body would allow, her efforts gaining her only enough to giggle lightly. "Don't apologize again." Sighing, she shifted against the cooling sheets, her body tossed and turned by every emotion she had sought to bury. "I'm the one who should be apologizing. I mean, all I've been doing is sending you mixed signals and you've been..."

Kissable? A-friggin'-mazingly hot? A perfect gentlemen when you could have been ripping my clothes off?

"I assure you, I have not been the perfect gentlemen you think me to be." Racking a hand through his disarrayed hair, he offered her a simple smile, exhaling slowly as he leaned back against the sturdy stucco. "Perhaps it would be best if I were to remain here to answer any questions you still may have."

Cal laughed lightly, shaking her head, her straight bobbed hair swishing as she crawled into a seated position. "I'm not going to bite." Tucking her legs beneath her, she turned her attention to the shadowy temptation currently taking up residence on the other side of the bedroom. *On second thought...*

He smirked, arching a black brow over his sparkling eyes as his arms folded across his powerful chest. *"You do know I can hear your thoughts, right?"*

She covered her mouth as her nervous giggling seeped between her fingers. "That is so unfair. How come you can peek into my brain? Or can you read everyone's mind?"

The Greek Adonis across the room gave a subtle shrug. "I can read the minds of most…"

"Humans?" The word came out as a rushed whisper, her eyes went wide.

His deep laughter filled the space, warm and delicious. "No. I was going to use the word 'mortals.' I am human, my beautiful muse, perhaps with a bit longer of a lifeline than most."

"Well, how much longer?"

A crooked grin matched his arched brow. "I thought a lady never asks?"

Cal laughed, answering with an easy smile. "Nah, the line is that a gentleman never asks and a lady never tells. Not too sure if it goes the other way around, though. But, I'm glad to hear you're human. Hoped I hadn't fallen for a space alien or something."

He called her his muse. As a child, she'd learned about the origins of her name. Calliope, the ancient Greek muse of epic poetry, was said to have inspired Homer to write the Iliad and the Odyssey. But Cal had yet to inspire anyone, much less any boy. Well, until puberty hit and she was blessed by the Boob Fairy. Too bad the Brain Fairy had made a major stop years before, all but cementing her reputation as a "geek."

Then again, not that she really cared. She did only have eyes for those a little bit older than her. *Yeah, like a couple hundred years old and long since dead.*

Galen stood glued to the wall a second time in the span of as many minutes. He fought to bring his body back under his brain's control, waiting blood to return northerly as he dragged air into his shrunken lungs. In deference to her current train of thought, one earlier idea flared brighter than all the rest: inexperienced. Rewinding the clock, he replayed the healing of her injured body. As he had found no evidence of any forceful violation, he did not search any further.

Was she truly unknown to any man? Yet, in her own words, she had fallen for him. His heart soared, his body wanting nothing more than to take those scant few steps separating them and to continue with their earlier, interrupted activity. She still needed time and now he had a few questions of his own.

"I know you have more questions, but perhaps I can sidetrack you with some food first. How long has it been since you ate?"

Food. At the mere mention of the word, her stomach growled so loud, he had to squash the urge to look under the bed for some small animal. "God, honestly? I can't even remember. I…I don't have any memories of-of eating while, um, while…" Her brow furrowed as she struggled to complete the sentence, but her mouth seemed unwilling to comply, frowning and gaping.

That did it.

He stepped away from the wall, kneeling before her, cupping her face in his hands. "You never need to go back to that place ever again, Cal. You are safe, and by all the gods in the heavens, I will do all I can to keep things that way. I know it's going to take time for you to truly recover. I am able to heal your physical injuries. I can even take away the memories of your ordeal, if you would but ask me to." He paused, holding her gaze. "Yet, I somehow sense you would not wish me to do that. However…" He rose to his feet, carrying her along with him. "I believe the first order of business should be food."

Keeping a careful and gentle hold on her elbows, he stood on guard as she tested her still-shaky legs. She was taller than he had expected, yet his chin rested easily on top of her head, her eyes staring straight into his chest. Her gaze traveled upward, locking onto his, her sparkling emerald eyes drawing him like a moth to the flame.

Another rumble from her empty belly cooled the moment.

He smiled down at the beauty in his arms. She had gone too long without many comforts. Leaning over, he placed a chaste kiss atop her forehead, dragging her scent into his lungs. Beneath the aroma of a new spring day, he sensed a lingering sadness, something stemming back long before her horrific nightmare of recent days. He would discover the source of her sorrow and make this right as well.

Color crept onto her cheeks. "Yeah, food, then shower, then bed, then phone call, then…" He lifted his hand, a finger touching her lips and stopping her laundry list of tasks.

"I'll get food. You can freshen up. Does that sound good?"

"Yeah, that sounds wonderful." Aware of the current bedraggled state of her attire, her eyes dipped away from his, dropping down to the starched-stiff denims encasing her legs.

He pulled her in for one last embrace before leading her toward the bathroom, chuckling at her bout of self-consciousness. "All you require is in here. Take all the time you need. Dinner will be ready when you are." He watched as she gaped at the marble, glass, and chrome escape from the world complete with sunken tub and six-head shower. He did like some luxuries. His thoughts strayed as his eyes followed her around the room, his body holding up the door frame as visions of her emerging from the steamy glass box had him digging into his pocket, eager for some release. "And as for your clothes…" "Burn them." Cal's words slipped out without thought. Turning quickly, she blushed at her harsh command. "Crap. I mean, not your shirt. It's just—"

His laughter cut off her ramblings. "I understand, agapi. You've no need to defend your words. Towels are in the cabinet, and I'll leave some fresh clothes for you as well. I will be downstairs should you need me, but for now, I will leave you to your tasks." He moved toward the door, his chivalrous heart warring with his demanding body. A frightened wave hit him hard enough to shake his balance. Lifting his eyes, he caught her panic, oozing unbeknownst from her soul. "Calliope?"

Cal stood in the opulent beauty of a bathroom straight off the showroom floor and her mind pulled up the words of Nickelback's song, "Rockstar." Looking around, she realized you could definitely play nine innings in here, not mention other, more intimate games. And the tub. She thought she might actually need to leave a trail of breadcrumbs to find her way back to the door. Her eyes took in each sparkle as her mind processed his words. One word caught her ear and made her heart race.

Leave.

She was suddenly terrified of the thought of him not being near. Her head snapped up, hoping he hadn't picked up on her fears. The sound of her name on his lips confirmed her suspicions. His voice had been pleasant, his deep timbre lulling and comforting. That one word, however, carried a different tone. He had changed from tour guide to protector in the blink of an eye. One heartbeat and he was ready to battle any foe to keep her safe.

She smiled as warmly as she could muster, trying to stave off the cold threatening to seep into her blood. "Yeah, I gotcha. Towels.

Cabinet. Clothes. Downstairs. It's all good." She spun away from him, avoiding the questions she knew were in his eyes, just as she knew they were in her heart. She had left him earlier to handle her own things, even though that little excursion did not quite go as planned. So why was the thought of him leaving her so scary now?

"Calliope? Do you wish me to stay?"

Cal leveled her gaze, catching his reflection in the gleaming mirror above the porcelain standing sink, his eyes full of concern and compassion. "Wow. That's quite a weighted question there." He held his post, hand hovering above the doorknob, his eyes staring past her shoulder.

Her voice, breathy and veiled, carried through the room. If she turned to face him, she would be lost. She would ask him to stay, cry, and rush into his arms like he was the only solace keeping her from the encroaching darkness threatening to swallow her heart. Like some little bit of fluff in one of those cheesy romantic comedies Maggs always dragged her off to see.

But she was made of stronger stuff. Sighing and giving him a smile that didn't reach her eyes, she said the words her heart screamed against in protest. "Nah, I'm good."

The silence grew and she wondered if her inability to deliver a convincing lie would be her undoing now. She wished he was closer, his dark eyes completely unreadable at this distance. After the longest seconds ticked by, he offered her a pensive smile. Dipping his head reverently, he nodded to her and let himself out.

CHAPTER EIGHT

Cal grabbed the sink as soon as the door lock clicked into place, shoving one hand into her mouth to stop from calling him back. She squeezed her eyes, shutting off the impending tears. *Take a breath. Count to ten.*

She fought to regain her composure until her knuckles matched the porcelain holding her upright. Seconds droned on as she reined in her racing emotions. Why did she feel so connected to him? Well, yeah, he had swooped in and saved her life. Healed her wounds. Twice, in fact. Not to mention, he kissed her as if she were air he needed to survive. In his arms, she felt treasured and beautiful, two things she had long since walled herself from experiencing.

She was dying. Why the hell did Mr. Perfect have to show up now? A bitter laugh escaped around her fist. Opening her eyes to her reflection, she spied the ever-present dark circles, the sallow tones replacing the fading blush brought on by his presence. She huffed out the rest of the air growing stagnant in her lungs, shaking her head and clearing away the cobwebs.

"Get a grip, Cal. Stop jumping at shadows and tilting at windmills." Yanking off the black T-shirt that had been serving as a dress for the past day, she smiled briefly until her hands reached the waistband of her blood crusted jeans. Her arms trembled, her body frozen mid-tug as she was violently thrown back into that room. She gasped for air, valiantly trying to force her heart to slow its thunderous beats against her rib cage as phantom chains held her arms above her head.

The shaking grew, tipping the Richter scale along her spine and threatening to bring down the tenuous house of cards keeping her emotions intact as the memories turned tactile. The foul breath, the stench of sulfur, and a dirty ashtray burned in her nostrils. Hands pawed at her while fists smashed into her body. Panic rose like bile in her throat, choking off her air supply.

A gentle voice seeped through her fear-locked mind. *"Agapi, do you need me?"*

She closed her eyes, shaking her head swiftly, but not before a single tear trickled down her cheek. Ripping at the offending zipper, she clawed at the fabric, scratching her legs in her haste to get them off. She practically dove into the shower, her fingers fumbling with the dials until the six jets sprayed her and she cried out at the icy blast.

The water continued to pound her from all directions, the temperature one step above freezing as she huddled in the corner, her breath coming in short fast gasps. Her mind spun as voices out of her waking nightmares taunted and tormented. She wrapped her arms around her head, trying to hold back the continued onslaught of memories. Her eyes opened and shut like torrent-blown shutters, the dark as terrifying as the light, for both backgrounds served as blank canvases for the endless roll of visions.

Once again, as the threads of her life were coming unraveled, the ground disappeared beneath her, and the arctic cascade warmed to a more tropical clime. Maybe it was the warmth seeping out of the arms cradling her that drove away the chill. Her arms tightened, tucking her head further into her chest in an effort to again hide from the faces.

Galen *moved* as soon as he sensed her terror. He found her cowering in the shower, the frigid water raining on her skin. Not wasting a precious second, he stepped under the flow, adjusting the temperature with no more than a thought while he gathered her into his arms. She looked so fragile, his precious spiritmate hovering on the edge of shattering. She was quaking so much, he feared she would fly apart.

"Shhh. I'm here now." He gently lifted her up, settling her onto his lap and whispering soft words against her skin. His hands stroked her arms, bringing much needed warmth back into her trembling body. He increased the water temperature a few more degrees to speed up the reheating process.

"Can't…can't…can't" The single word became both a prayer and curse as it fell repeated from her lips. He pulled her close, wending his fingers through her damp hair as her hands clenched his shirt so tight he thought it would shred on its own. "C-c-can't get the damned p-p-pictures out…" Her shoulders tensed as she fought to draw a full breath. "…out of my h-h-head. Won't st-st-stop. Won't…won't…won't stop." Clinging tightly to the arms around her, she gave in again to her despair, tears falling in rivers down her face, mingling with the warm spray. "D-d-dammit all! Make it stop!" Her voice was a sorrowful cry to any who would listen, and the sobs began anew.

His lips pressed kiss after reassuring kiss against her head, humming soft lullabies and tunes from memories long since passed. He rested his cheek along her damp hair as he rocked her with tender care, silently willing her all of his strength as the demons of her ordeal tore at her damaged soul. Her narrow shoulders bounced as the ragged tears streamed down her face.

Galen growled at his uncharacteristic sense of helplessness, his hand moving in soothing circles on her pale back. "My beautiful muse, if you only say the word, I will gladly remove all traces of those memories for you. I will do whatever is needed to see you smile."

"I just want to be able to s-s-s-stop frickin' crying! I never cry."

"What about swearing?"

She barked a harsh laugh at his attempt at lightness. "Yeah, well, that I do all the time. That's easy. All this…this emotional shit. This, I don't do too well." With each word, her voice gained in strength, her tears still falling with each breath, but the tide seemed to be receding.

"Then perhaps you should swear when you feel the emotions return."

This time, her laugh sounded more natural, the tears shifting from downpour to a trickle. "If I did that, you'd think I had Tourette's or something. Probably have me committed or put on some serious meds." Their harmless banter had her relaxing by subtle degrees, her fingers loosening their death grip on his shirt.

His shirt?

Cal inched away from the comfort of his embrace to take in the scene. Naked, tucked in the corner of his humongous shower and he was here, sitting on the floor with her. Fully clothed. She pulled her eyes up to stare into his face, his jet eyes dancing yet tinged with a hint of sorrow.

"I would never put you far from my reach, in any state." His honest words sent heat blossoming on her cheeks, the foreign sensation becoming more familiar the longer she was within touching-distance of him. She ducked her head as the blush spread to cover her entire body, a coy smile hiding her naked embarrassment.

She gradually returned to herself, his fingers trailing along her jaw line as her chin lifted to stare into his piercing, fathomless eyes.

"Do you feel a little better?"

With a staggered sniffle, she tested her lungs and found them in decent working order. She nodded with a slow exhale, smiling weakly. "Yeah. I guess I wasn't as good as I thought I was. Sorry to pull you away—"

"You have nothing for which to apologize."

"But your clothes. I mean, they're all wet and—"

His smile was warm and open, reaching up to touch his mesmerizing dark eyes as he shook his head. "A small price to pay, I assure you. The real question is are you OK to stand?"

Her body was a knotted mess, and she ached to stretch her limbs. As her shoulders flexed and rolled, the state of her own undress stilled her movements. She had never been embarrassed by her body, feeling blessed to have been gifted with decent breasts, a narrow waist and long limbs. However, she had never stood naked before anyone. Ever.

"Uh, yeah, but…um…" Her eyes darted to each corner and nook, the blush deepening as she struggled to find the right words. She desperately wished for hands the size of pie plates.

His brow furrowed in confused disbelief. "Has no one else seen you so…exposed?"

Gnawing on her lower lip, she looked up hesitantly. "Not since I was a baby. Even then, I avoided that spotlight as often as possible."

The frown deepened as he pondered her words. "Why? Not that I am suggesting you take up streaking or to join a nudist colony." He paused, flashing her a wicked grin before going on. "You are more beautiful than a dream. Why would you hide from the world?"

Cal didn't know if her skin was pink from the water's heat, from the heat of his stare, or from her own blush. Shrugging, her eyes glued to the interesting grout pattern on the tile floor, she fumbled for some rational explanation. Instead, she opted for avoidance. "Can we please talk about this later? Like when I'm not naked?"

Fidgeting nervously, she lifted her pleading gaze to his. A sympathetic sigh won out over the wicked smile, and he nodded, carefully untangling his long limbs as he rose to his feet, the gentleman prevailing over the scoundrel. "I would feel better knowing you are safe. Would you mind if I stayed?" As she faded from pink to pale, he amended hastily. "Outside, of course. I...I need to be near should..."

"Should I freak out again. Yeah, yeah. I get it." Cal breathed, finishing his sentence, her legs starting to ache from their cramped confinement. "OK. I mean, it is your house, after all. You can do whatever you want and I wouldn't be able to stop you."

The air grew frosty as a dangerous emotion played across his handsome face, followed by an air of sadness. She had done it again. In her usual, blundering way, she had opened her mouth and something hurtful had fallen out. Why did she keep doing this to him? Years of honing her emotional security protections, sharpening the knife-edge of her wit to stave off feelings of intimacy or closeness beyond superficial friendship, had built unbreakable walls around her heart. She dropped her head, her shoulders slumping as the weight of her words dragged her down.

Galen was once again back in that room with her, wishing he could kill those who harmed her yet again. They had broken her faith in the kindness of others and that would take patience to rebuild. He fought to temper his rage. She did not need his anger, she needed his tenderness, and he continued to think only of himself.

His body trembled, his muscles locked in conflict as his internal battle began in earnest, logic versus libido, knight versus knave. "If you wish me to leave, you need only to say the word." He struggled to keep his desires out of his voice, hoping she only heard his concern for her.

Time crawled forward. He swore he heard the sands from Chronos' hourglass sifting from top to bottom as he waited for her decision to be voiced.

"I...I..." she stammered, "I'm sorry. I don't mean to keep pissing you off. And I really would like it, if you'd kinda stay nearby." She looked up hesitantly at him. "I mean, if you wouldn't mind."

His heart took up beating again, his lungs expelling the breath he held. "I would not mind at all. In truth, I would be honored. It would be my greatest pleasure." Grinning wolfishly, he continued. "For now."

Her jaw unhinged as a gorgeous blush raced along her skin. His eyes drank in the sight of her pinked flesh, resting a moment longer on her promising lips. A wink and a smile broke the spell, releasing her from his enchantment and as a reward, her laughter bubbled through the chamber.

"I will be just outside the door. Now, if you don't mind, I think I'll change into something a little less wet." The edges of his mouth lifted, helping to keep his tone gentle and lighthearted. Due to her tattered state, he knew he must tread softly, allowing her to set the pace. He nodded once, touching her damp hair before exiting.

Erring on the side of caution, afraid of the return of her anxiety, Cal jumped to her feet, eager to finally get clean. As she grasped the shampoo bottle from the stainless shelving tower, she spied her pruny fingers. How long had they sat under the cascading waters? And it was still beautifully temperate. Three minutes into her showers in her apartment and the chills would start. If she managed more than five minutes, icicles would start to form on her nose and other protruding body parts, not to mention the glass etching quality her nipples would take on.

Lathering rapidly and rinsing just as quick, she kept her mind focused on the act of showering. Her eyes caught the rust colored water as it swirled against the white and chrome flooring. She shook her head violently, her hand reaching for another bottle, coming away with shaving cream.

"Oh c'mon, Cal. Look at what you're doing." Chuckling, she checked again, retrieving a bar of soap, its scent wild, like him. She held the thick bar under her nose, inhaling the fragrance as her eyes drifted close for a moment. Her mind slipped her tight hold and rushed toward a devilishly erotic fantasy. In her reverie, each drop of water was replaced by his lips, his hands trailed down her body following each rivulet and his tongue...

Dear Gods, she's going to be the death of me.

Galen stood outside the door as he had promised, his forehead pressed against the thin wooden barrier. A thin sheen of sweat formed above his lip, his mind riding the same wavelength as hers, following her indulgences and wishing for more. He ground his hand against his crotch, his erect shaft biting into the zipper teeth of his drying leathers. He knew some of his Guardians, upon finding their mates, suffered for days, even weeks, while they wooed their match. For the final coupling necessary to begin, the Claiming Ritual must be her choice. Once the ritual had begun, each Warrior had only five days to complete the process, or risk becoming one of the foes they fought so passionately.

He had only been near her for a matter of hours and already, he felt dizzy from blood loss. But with the added layer of her virginity, he knew he had to move even slower than he could have imagined. His heart sang at the knowledge that no man had touched her. No other suitor had caressed her cheek, or laved her breasts, or sunk himself into her hot, womanly folds.

His fingers attacked the door frame, the wood groaning beneath his vice-like grip. It took every ounce of his willpower to not pound his head against the door, afraid she would open it up and find him coiled and ready to pounce. Water dripped down from his hair as well as his soggy clothes, puddling under his feet. Growling in frustration, he peeled out of his clothes, toweling off his body as well as the floor before pulling on a pair of black silk lounge pants. As he searched his closet for something more fitting to her slim physique, his eye caught a glimpse of the rather obvious pup tent south of his beltline.

Swearing in as many languages as he could think of, he traded the loose, more comfortable wear for another pair of confining restraints, opting for denim this time, hoping they might be a bit more forgiving than his leathers. He was inches away from discarding the thin pants in hand, until an image played into his mind. With a devilish grin, he found its mate and laid the midnight silk ensemble on the bed.

His body tightened even more at the mere thought of the fabric that had just touched him would soon cover her curves. Her pale skin would glow against the black sheen of the satiny wardrobe.

"I found something I hope will fit you," he called out over the still running water, hoping his voice carried enough. Eager to see his dream realized, he had almost forgotten his original task. Food.

He muttered, wishing his skill was as a Conduit and not a Marshal. His mind strayed as he thought of Zacarias, one of the rare Guardian Conduits who would use his ability to have any food delivered. He laughed as he recalled after one hunt when Lobster Newburg and Seared Sea Bass from Farallon had arrived to his door two minutes after they did.

Well, he couldn't mentally order food, but he did own a phone. A couple minutes later, and a Bayou special from Bruno's was on the way. Ending the call, he heard a soft click from the door behind him. His eyes snapped up to the window, catching the reflected silhouette that stole his breath. As much as he wanted—no, *needed* to watch her, he slowly closed his eyes, giving her the space she required.

After stomping on the brakes of her overactive imagination, Cal finished her shower. She took a moment to dry her hair before wrapping a thick white bath sheet around her body like a toga. Wiping down the fogged up mirror, she took a good long stare at herself. Her skin was an overall pink, but bore no real marks from her days of torture, only a little lingering yellowing along her jaw and slight dark circles under her eyes. He really had healed her. Could he possibly help her with her other little problem? She would have to think more about that question, but first she needed to leave the bathroom. Securing the towel firmly in place, she took a deep breath and stepped out into the room.

His back was toward her, but she saw his body flinch the moment she emerged from the escaping steam. He wore only a pair of low-slung blue jeans, his feet and torso bare. She felt the weight of his stare and she shifted her gaze, finding a pair of jet eyes staring at her through the large window's reflection. She didn't remember the glass being smoky when she watched the City by the Bay earlier. Their eyes locked, a faint smile touching his lush lips. A heartbeat passed and his lids shuttered down, leaving her in relative privacy.

She spied the outfit laid out for her, a slip of a shadow against the snowy backdrop of the bedding. Silk pajamas? Yes, she was actually going to be wearing a pair of men's black silk pajamas. Slipping her arms into the soft shirt, she smiled as the hem hit her mid-thigh yet again. A couple folds of the cuffs and her hands were once again visible. She eyed the pants suspiciously. If the shirt was long…

Galen imagined her actions as he listened with the ears of a fox to each movement. In his dark, he saw her slide the lucky shirt over her full breasts, her deft fingers nimbly sliding button through their slots, cocooning her body in the slick fabric. The sound of giggles drew his curiosity, an eyebrow leading a lid to creep up and hazard a peek.

"Is something amiss?"

She chuckled as he turned toward her. Fully opening his eyes, he took in the scene and joined her in a shared laugh. She swam in his shirt, but the pants were a whole other issue. The legs extended far beyond her toes, dragging a good foot along the floor. "I think I might go with just the shirt, if that's OK with you."

"I would be fine with neither, *órmorfià*." The look in his eyes burned away any doubts she might have had about his intentions. She laughed shyly, ducking her head to hide her growing blush.

"Yeah, I can tell."

The electric tension was sliced by a chime, followed by a knock. Galen raised an eyebrow, his lips lifting into a crooked smirk. "Saved by the bell?" He bowed slightly before heading out to answer the door.

Cal felt the air rush back into the room, filling the space left by her gorgeous protector. Damn, but he sure knew how to make her feel like something special. His heated glances and fiery smiles, the Old World way he spoke and how could she forget about the way he kissed. Looking down at the miles of silk on the floor, she sighed and stepped out of the bottoms. If only she had met him earlier.

Dropping down on the bed, her mind raced. *Oh, come on. Who am I kidding? I should have never met him at all. This is such a huge mistake.*

"Agapi? Do you have need of me?" His scent permeated the room, clinging to her skin and flowing through her blood.

"Again with the loaded questions," she murmured into the empty room. Unable to sit by and allow the rest of the night to pass her by, she headed out of the bedroom, following the luscious aromas of his dark fragrance and something equally as yummy.

Pizza.

CHAPTER NINE

Stefan de Coldreto paced around the rented Tenderloin room, pinching the bridge of his Roman nose in an attempt to halt the burgeoning headache. Leaning his Hugo Boss-coated body over the dingy couch, he sighed as he faced the three remaining agents he had recruited over two weeks ago.

"So please, by all means, stop me if I need to be corrected. Two days ago, the bait finally caught our target, but since your 'professionals' did not heed my warnings, not only did the fish get away, but we lost our bait. You now have to find three more men." A dismissive gesture froze any attempted rebuke.

"And one more no longer has the use of his left hand and needs to breathe through a tube for the next few months?" His eyes flickered from face to face, though no one dared to meet his stare. "Does that sound about right?"

Silence sucked the air out of the narrow space.

Feet shuffled against the cracked linoleum as the quiet deepened.

"Shoulda left me to it, man," someone said.

Stefan's lavender eyes snapped in the direction of the only one brave enough to dare utter a sound. Emmet Fischer, a massive wall of blackness, leaned against the far wall, his heavily tattooed arms coiled across the wife beater stretched over his barrel chest. Testosterone oozed off him, creating a thick fog of alpha maleness that had the rest of the players shrinking back to keep all their body parts intact. His bald pate gleamed under the garish fluorescents, his eyes concealed behind wraparound shades.

Stefan grinned at the young man's arrogance. *Oh, he will make a worthy addition. If he survives the final test.* Grinning at his boastful companion, he crossed the room to stand nose to nose with him, the hint of a sardonic grin playing across the edges of his lips. "Yes, but if I had done that, then we would have lost both with absolutely nothing to show."

A slight shrug told him the words sunk in, but no other response was forthcoming.

"So," he turned his attentions to the rest of the team. "We need to recruit replacements." Rubbing his fingers, brushing off some unseen dust from his cuff, he stepped toward the door. "And, if you would be so kind as to make sure that these listen more carefully to my directions. I know who we are dealing with, so please, trust in my knowledge."

With one foot in the hallway, he glanced over his shoulder. "Oh, I already have one in mind. You'll find he has a connection to the lure, which should prove quiet helpful. His name is Paul McCormick. Happy hunting, gentlemen." A quick nod and the door closed, leaving his companions to begin the job of locating three more saps for him.

Cannon fodder. He laughed, knowing he would gladly throw most of this accursed city to the fires of Hades to see the mighty Guardians fall. Smiling slyly, he fed himself daily on the thought he might actually live to see that day.

Soon, meus vetus hostilis. Soon.

Whistling, he headed down the hallway and out into the cold autumn night.

CHAPTER TEN

The last traces of pizza lay scattered in the cardboard square, one narrow sliver of a slice the only remaining survivor. Cal sat back smiling, stretching her legs out and groaned, rubbing her full stomach.

"Oh my God. That was the most amazing thing I think I have ever eaten. Then again, since it was the first thing I've eaten in a while, I think I could've eaten deep fried shoe leather."

Galen watched her with hooded eyes from across the kitchen island as she took a sip from a beer bottle. From the moment she stepped down the stairs, he watched her, catching every move out of the corner of his eye. He catalogued the way she walked, entranced by the subtle sway in her hips as she headed across the cherry wood floor. He studied the way she sat, her left leg tucked underneath her beautifully curved ass. She covered her mouth when she took a bite and never once spoke with her mouth full. Her eyes sparkled like stars when she laughed, and he would do anything to hear more of her laugh. It bubbled up like champagne, flooding his senses with lightness and passion.

Everything about her intrigued him. She was perfect for him, strong, sure and beautiful. From her lean legs peeking from the hem of his silk pajama top to her bobbed black hair, her entire being practically begged for him to touch. He forced his hands to remain engaged in the act of eating, tried to keep his mouth from imaging it was her soft flesh, and not pizza, between his lips. His jeans continued to shrink the longer the meal went on.

"But I believe that would not have been as enjoyable for either of us, so I am glad you liked the pizza." He laughed and added, "At least I know what to order you the next time."

"Ah, that's so sweet."

Grinning like the cat with the proverbial canary, Galen retrieved his beer bottle, taking a long draught, hoping the cool liquid would quench his thirst for her. But he knew nothing would ever satisfy him, not if she were close enough to taste. Needing to change his current train of thought, he decided to return to one unanswered question that had been plaguing him.

"Calliope, I have something to ask you. If you choose not to answer, I will understand."

She leaned in, resting the Red Tale Ale bottle on the counter for a heartbeat. "Wow. You used my full name. This must really be important."

Her apprehensive smile did not fool him; he had sensed her trepidation before the bottle touched down. He reached across the Formica barrier, covering her hand with his. "I do not mean to frighten you. If you would rather not..."

Cal's smile stunned him into silence. "You have been amazing to me, Galen. I think you're entitled to a couple of answers." She looked up, her dazzling green eyes pinning him with a serious stare. "But I might have a few questions of my own."

"Quid pro quo?" he asked, quirking an eyebrow.

She nodded. "Definitely. Like, what does that word mean?"

His brow furrowed at her odd query. "What word?"

Lifting the brown bottle to her mouth, she mumbled around the lip of the bottle as if afraid she was going to botch the pronunciation. "Um, that, uh, a-ag…"

He chuckled lightly as she tripped over the familiar phrase. "You mean 'agapi'?"

Sighing with a smile, she nodded. "Yeah, that's the word."

"It is simply a term of endearment in my native language," he answered with a smile. "I hope you don't mind."

Her silent answer appeared as a tempting blush, pinking her cheeks, as an innocent grin melted across her face.

His eyes drank her in, his heart filling with a loving pride. The corners of his lips curled up as her eyes sparkled with emerald fire. Those evil men tried to break her, tried to take her away from him.

Never again would anyone bring her harm. The thought clanged around his head, the edge of his smile faltering.

Her eyebrows pulled together as he let his anger slip out of his grip. "Gee, I'd hate to be on the receiving end of that glare."

His rage disappeared in the blink of an eye, his gaze softening as he captured her hand. "Agapi mou, you need never fear that. For those who have felt my anger never do so again." Bringing her hand to his lips, he brushed a tender kiss along the rapid pulse at her wrist. "But my question, I hope, will not cause you alarm." He sat patiently, giving her time to change her mind.

She exhaled in a huff, her short locks swaying from side to side. "Nah, I should be good, I hope." She lifted her gaze, her bright green eyes wary but willing. "OK. Let's hear it."

Galen threaded his fingers through hers and phrased his query as delicately as he could. "While I was healing you, I sensed something was very wrong." He paused, gauging her response. When he met silence, he pressed on. "And twice, you tried to awaken too early into your healing rest. Is there something that stops you from sleeping?"

A sad smile graced her full lips, her eyes slipping away from his face. "Yeah, about that…" Gnawing her bottom lip, she paused and studied the floor, as if searching for the best way to explain her situation. "Well, straight answer? I'm dying."

He blinked at the words hanging suspended between them. "I'm sorry, but did you just say…?"

A sigh tangled with the weak laugh as they slipped from her lips. She crossed to the sleek silver Viking refrigerator to escape the weight of the unspoken words behind his stare, her shoulders dropping as she turned, resting her back against the cool steel. "I, ah, can't, um…don't sleep. And I'm not talking about the occasional insomnia. I mean I *don't* sleep. I'm not able to sleep for longer than one hour a day, in short naps and my body is going to shut down one day for good. So, um…yeah, that's about it…" She told her story to the floor, unable to meet his eyes as her hand crept up the back of her neck, rubbing nervously at the ever-present tension. A shadow fell at her feet, dousing her toes in darkness as the heat from her close companion filled the space separating them.

Undeniably gentle fingers touched her chin, urging her eyes away from the deep brown wood. As much as she wanted to resist, she felt powerless against her own growing desires. She wanted him to hold her, tell her she was not going to die and everything was going to be all right. *Yeah, and Santa Claus is gonna join the Great Pumpkin and hand out presents with the Easter Bunny.* She steeled herself and raised her eyes to meet his.

"Look, I've known this was gonna happen. But it's OK. I mean, I've kinda come to terms with the whole—"

Bottles jangled behind her as she leaned hard against the cool metal, using its solid bulk to remain vertical. Her palms rested flat on the firm muscles of his chest, wishing she knew more about appropriate behavior when pinned by a half-naked god against the refrigerator. Beneath her hands, his heat beat out an enticingly compelling rhythm, her body yearning to join in the dance. He had healed her broken and battered body once before, could he possibly help her with a more permanent problem?

Galen forced himself to stand rigid as she struggled with herself, her inner conflict and his need to comfort her pounded against the walls of his self-control. When she at last leveled her gaze at him, her troubled eyes called to him, her pleas reaching into his soul.

Her brave façade fired the protector in him and his lips devoured hers, stopping any further protests. His palm glided along the slim column of her throat, tickling the racing pulse beneath. Climbing his hands upward, he dug his long fingers into her hair, cupping her head and pulling her closer, deepening the kiss. His tongue wrapped seductively around hers, allowing her to choose the tempo and the intensity. Her innocent passions stole his breath as well as his reason, his urge to fully claim her roaring through his veins.

Shuddering at her tentative touch, his blood raced toward his already aching groin as he kissed her as though she was the very air needed to survive. A long forgotten voice of his mentor screamed in the far corner of his mind, Diolocys' gray eyes clear and unyielding. *"Time bears the sweets of fruits."* With restraint he did not believe he possessed, he slowly broke the seal of their kiss, giving himself one final sip before resting his head against her damp brow. He sucked down oxygen into his starving lungs and opened his eyes to gaze down at her flushed cheeks and passion-darkened emerald depths.

"Calliope. I have only just found you. I have no intention of letting you slip into the Here After so soon."

Tears rimmed her eyes and her chin quivered in the fight to keep them from falling. He gently stroked the pad of his thumb under her eyes, wiping away a gathering drop before it descended.

"It would be nice if that were possible. Hell, I'd be happy to have a full night's sleep. Too bad I live in the really real world, not this very nice fantasy I know is gonna come crashing down any minute now."

Cal tried feebly to sound light, but her voice was too breathy, still reeling from his kiss. Her head lolled back and her eyelids drifted down, needing to find solace in the comforting dark. In here, she could get her heart to slow to its normal pace and she could hide from those gorgeous ebony depths mere inches from her. The heat from his bare chest warmed her soul and made her believe in fairy tales.

Even for a moment.

Rough fingers brushed her chin, dragging her once again out of her dark hiding place. She raised her lids to meet his gaze, gulping down a strengthening stream of air before locking on to his fathomless black eyes. The honest purity reflected in his eyes shook her stubborn resolve, the wall protecting her heart wavering.

"What would it take to convince you that this is, indeed, the real world? Maybe not the side you have seen before, but real nonetheless." With a wicked grin that curled her toes, he dragged the back of his knuckles along her jaw. "Or do other men normally kiss you senseless in this fantasy realm? Please do not tell me I have yet another suitor with whom I must compete in your dreams as well."

"Another suitor?" The words wriggled through the heated blood thundering in her ears. A frown touched her brow until she remembered how he found her on the street. He eyes flew open in panic. "Oh, hell no! Paul is, I mean…oh, puh-lease, you have got to be kidding me! He's…ewwww!"

Warm laughter flowed over her skin, deep and rumbling as Galen tossed his head back. She grimaced as her very over-active imagination took a hiatus into the bizarre, recalling an earlier incident during her second year when Paul actually tried to kiss her. She had stayed late after Professor Laurant's Crimean Warfare lectures and was meeting friends for coffee. Her hands brushed away the lingering memory of his clammy hands on her skin, which only added to his mirth. The more she squirmed, the harder he laughed.

Blushing for more reasons than she cared to count, she shoved at the muscular wall before her. "Yeah, ha ha. Very funny." She tried to pout, but one corner of her mouth had other plans, tilting up crookedly as she eyed him.

"Well, I had to be sure," he managed to sneak the words out between chuckles. "After all, he did seem to be standing possessively close to you and was quite upset when I arrived."

"Yeah, well…he can get pissy all he wants." Hesitating for a moment, a secret confession fell from her lips. "Truth is, he kinda gives me the creeps. Always has. I don't know why, but he's always been sniffing around me and…" She left the rest of the thought unvoiced, shrugging away her suspicions. Her attempt at nonchalance morphed into a shudder as a disquieting cold touched her heart.

The chill quickly melted as his knuckles brushed along her cheek, his fingers weaving through her hair, tucking a stray lock behind her ear. "I believe you are safe from his sniffings here."

She giggled, her smile lightening up her eyes as she basked in the warmth of his closeness. "In that case, I'm staying here." Words continued to spill from her lips as his gaze turned molten, her rubbery legs wobbled as her blood raced, a fiery river flowing beneath her skin. "I mean, that is if it's, um, all right with you. For me. To, um, stay…for a while."

Galen leaned in, his forearms resting against the shiny silver box behind her. His eyes searched her face for any fear or apprehension. Instead, he saw only open honesty and purity. Pressing his lips to her brow, he inhaled deeply, her newly bloomed floral fragrance coiling around his soul and invigorating his spirit. Yet, hiding behind the clean rain was an oily tang, very faint but still troubling. She confessed a terrifying truth, and he was damned if he was going to sit by while she faced an early demise. His Guardian powers might not cheat death, but he had a couple tricks up his sleeve.

"*Ómorfiá mou*, you can stay for as long as you wish. It will be my pleasure to ensure you wish to stay forever." He dragged his lips along her cheek, closing in to whisper in her ear. "And hopefully, it will be yours as well."

Her body trembled against his, her head rolling lazily on her slender neck as her fingers gripped his forearm. "I don't know if..."

Her uncertainties bled into his skin, the unnamed darkness seeping into the space between them. She was truly convinced she was destined to perish unknown to man. Galen backed away half a step, needing to assure her of his intentions. On both counts. "I am taking things too quickly for you. I do not mean to frighten you. You still need time to come to terms with all that has happened to you." His dark eyes captured hers.

The words tumbled in a rush from her lips. "Do you really think you can help me?"

"My beautiful muse..." He twined her short locks around his fingers, trailing them along the line of her jaw and coming to rest over her heart. The pounding beneath his palm was strong, the steady rhythm tuning to his own. "Should you but say the word, and I will do all to see you past this crisis. On my honor as a Guardian."

One delicate brow arched up at his comment. "Guardian... Ok, now I've got some questions of my own. Like, for starters, what is a guardian? And why is it when you say it, I picture it capitalized?"

He laughed at her astute and amusing wit. He stepped away from the fridge, taking her hand and leading her out of the kitchen toward the large gray sectional couch that took up the far wall of the spacious living room. "I suppose it could sound rather ominous. Perhaps we should be sitting somewhere a little more comfortable to have this talk?"

The trek took a couple steps and the soft microfiber fabric was soon beneath the backs of her bare legs. She sat facing him on the sofa, and he forced his eyes to stay on hers and to be the gentleman she still believed him to be. He lowered himself stiffly onto the couch, keeping his rioting body in check as he determined the best course of action.

To his recollection, never had a Guardian been claimed by his mate. He would need to contact others, namely Eamon, to see if any such feat had been recorded. Dragging in a deep breath, pulling her sweet fragrance into his lungs, he studied the beauty before him. Although she did not realize her power, he saw her as a pure temptress, which made her all the more exotic to him. She sat— patient and eager—her emerald eyes bright and sparkling, enticing and encouraging him. He smiled warmly then launched into his story.

Paul approached the familiar red and white brick row house two blocks east of campus. Third floor, second window from the far-east corner was Cal's room, or the room she shared with those two freaks she called friends. Shaking his head, he still couldn't fathom why such a brilliant girl would want to spend time with a flower child and damned emo wannabe.

For fuck's sake, who named their kid Ajax? More thoughts screaming about the general stupidity of hippies and their dumbass names rattled around his brain as he entered the building, ascending the stairs toward the window of his fantasies. With each step, his mood grew darker and darker, especially when he remembered how she looked all goo-goo eyed at that fucking Neanderthal.

Would he be there and answer the door? His fist clenched and twitched the closer he came to the silver 3G on the pine portal. Rapping sharply, he shifted back and forth on his loafers, peering down the empty corridor and watching for shadows beneath the door. He tugged his sleeve back and glanced at his watch. His Seiko Kinetic proudly proclaimed 11:42 p.m. He angrily yanked the tan fleece in place, brushing lint off his navy Dockers.

Another round of knocking finally had shadows shuffling in the cracks between door and floor. After a long second, the door swung inward, and he sneered as he met a thick pair of lens peeking from nappy blonde ropes.

"Hi, Maggie." Point for him, he remembered her somewhat normal name. "Can I talk to Callie? I mean, Cal?" He sneaked glances over her shoulders trying to catch a glimpse at the rest of the room. Sprawled on the ridiculously large couch was the lanky Jack Skellington stand-in, his slitted kohl-rimmed eyes curious as to the late night caller, his face illuminated by the flashing of the TV screen.

No other signs of life.

"Oh, hey Paul. Cal's not here right now," she said, clinging to the door sleepily. "Do you want to leave a message for her?"

Fucking hell. She's with him. Maybe he could use this to his advantage.

"She's not?" Feigning concern, he stepped in closer. "I saw her a few hours ago and she looked pretty bad off. Have you talked to her?"

"Oh, no!" A shaky hand flew to cover her heart over her faded flowered shirt. Her head jerked toward the reclining figure on the sofa. "I knew something was wrong with Cal. I just knew it!" Wringing her hands, she paced away from the door, crumpling dramatically onto the narrow armrest. "When did you see her? Was it here? Was she OK? No, you said she looked bad. Oh dear."

Paul bit the inside of his cheeks to keep from grinning. *What a couple of maroons.* He bided his time as the daft bespectacled roomie fretted and worried, reaching out to seek solace in the arms of her equally lame boy toy. He held and coddled, stroked and shushed. Leaning in, he picked out the words, "all right," "with a friend," and finally "not far away."

"I'm sure she'll be fine, but I was just so worried when I saw her near campus today. She was so pale and she said something about an accident." He glanced sidelong as a choked sob rang through the silent space. "But you know Callie. She's a real fighter and I'm sure that guy she was with wouldn't take advantage of her. I mean, you said he's a friend, so he's gonna make sure she's doing OK, right? So I'll be—"

"Guy?" Blonde dreads bounced as her head whipped up from the shelter of the pasty embrace. "What guy? You-you mean she was with, like a guy-guy? Not some...Oh dear."

"Yeah. I thought he was someone you knew. He wasn't?" His eyes widened as he watched the blue pools glass over, her head whipping violently from side-to-side. He pushed on. "But I didn't like the look of him, though. Too much of that dangerous bad boy feel to him." He leveled his eyes at her, seeing the hysterical panic rise. Turning his gaze, he locked eyes with the skinny Goth, expecting to see the same irrational fears. The clear and direct stare he met gave him pause, black-ringed eyes of clear blue causing his smug smile to falter.

"Shh. Don't worry, babe. I promise you Cal is just fine and she'll be back home in no time at all." Paul dropped his eyes first, unable to hold the unyielding pale blue eyes. Stepping back, he headed toward the door.

"Well, please tell her I stopped by and ask her to call me as soon as she can. I'm really worried about her. I'll talk to you later, I guess."

He ushered himself into the hall, closing the door firmly behind him. Pressing his ear to the wood, he strained to discern the muffled words beyond. Two voices, one high and distraught, the second deeper and soothing rose and fell for a few minutes. Finally, the faint sound of sobs dissipated as silence took center stage. His eyes narrowed, his early self-satisfied gloat tempered by that fucking boyfriend of hers.

Lucky for him, the dippy roomie grabbed the bait and that was enough to start. Now he only needed to sit back and watch them squirm.

CHAPTER ELEVEN

Galen was impressed by her patience as he gave her a brief glimpse into his life. She leaned in with each new wrinkle, her eyes bright with delight. He could tell she held her tongue for as long as possible until her inner historian screamed to come out and play. Soon, questions were fired at him in rapid succession, ranging from the color of the true Hoplite armor to the actual size of the Library of Alexandria. All the while, through each new inquest and inquiry, he answered openly and patiently, smiling at her hunger for knowledge.

"So, let me get this right. During the first Macedonian War, the Romans did ally with the Greeks, but not in the second?" Cal edged closer to him, her knees a breath away from his stretched-out body.

"Oh, no. Philip did try, but did not meet with much success." Galen glanced at the brightening sky beyond the smoky windows. "History lesson over for tonight, agapi. Time for you to rest and continue healing. I should have insisted on you staying abed. You are wearing yourself out." Rising to his feet as he recalled her earlier confession, he extended his hand toward her, awaiting hers to join his. He hesitated, his open hand a welcoming invitation to fold herself into the warmth of his arms. "And before you think of it, you are going to come to bed and you are going to stay there until I think you are ready to return."

Her brows furrowed in a childish pout, her stubborn nature rearing its demanding head, until a stray yawn tugged on her chin. Unfolding her legs, she rose from the couch, her eyes locked on his. "Uh, stay?" Her voice cracked, the words both breathy and heavy. "In bed? I mean, I could just take the couch." Each word grew fainter as heat blossomed on her ivory cheeks and his eyes were drawn to her lush, full lips. His mouth watered for another taste.

"Agapi, if I had my way, you would stay...in bed...with me...forever," he whispered against her mouth, his gaze locking with her darkening green eyes.

Her tongue flicked out to wet her lips and the space between their lips vanished. His mouth slanted over hers as he cradled her face. His tongue darted and swept, twisted and twirled with hers, and the fire in his blood licked higher and higher.

The floor dropped out beneath her feet, her knees wobbling as his ravenous kiss threatened to steal her senses. Her heart stuttered against her ribs, lightning spiking through her body with each thrust of his tongue. She wanted to give in so badly, desired to know, just once, how it felt to be loved thoroughly and completely. Heat pooled low in her gut, working its way down between her legs.

But would "just once" be enough? In her mind, her heart, hell, in her very soul, she knew the answer was no. Tears of frustration sprang unbidden into her eyes as her logical brain fought to rein in her raging hormones. She placed her hands flat against his broad, bare chest. The strong beat of his heart pulsed through her fingertips, promising passion beyond her imagining, and her heart ached as it were breaking. A choked cry escaped her lips as she pushed away from the desire she wanted so desperately, but knew would never be hers.

"P-please. I...I can't." Dropping her eyes, she turned away, embarrassed by her own fears. *Dammit all! It's not fair!* Afraid another bout of tears was close to spilling out, she struggled against the hands holding her firmly rooted to the spot.

"Calliope." His deep rumbling voice flowed over her skin, raising goose bumps down her arms as heat rose to her cheeks. "I would never force you to do anything you did not want. But I can sense you have spent far too long denying yourself life because you fear leaving things undone or unsaid." Reaching down to cup her chin, he tilted her face to meet his hot gaze. "Please. Let me show you what you desire." Her cheeks pinked, her lips parting as need darkened her eyes. "I hear your thoughts, agapi. I know you have imagined our bodies entwined. I have seen this. And if I did not, your body is calling to me as no other has before. As none shall ever again."

As if to prove his point, he trailed a hand down her back, stopping only to press his hips into hers, the solid bulge in his jeans nestled tightly against her core. Her eyes flared wide before closing, a breathy moan slipping between her lips. Shivers raced down her skin, fiery chills chasing away doubt and apprehension. Her fingers clamped down on his arm, holding her firm in the center of the gathering storm.

"I'm afraid..." Her voice wavered, trembling with anticipation.

He brushed his lips feather-light against the corner of her mouth, the tender touch sparking her passion. "I could never do anything to harm you, Calliope."

Words tumbled out, warm against his cheek. "That's not what I'm afraid of."

"Do you fear I will not stop?" He froze, his lips hovering above her ear.

"No. I...I'm afraid I won't want you to."

The breath Galen held escaped in a rush of warmth as his tongue laved her earlobe. Images flashed behind her fluttering lids, an erotic blend of her pale skin blanketed by his deeply tanned flesh poured into her mind. His arms snaked around her waist, pressing her trembling body against his.

"We will take things slowly, ómorfiá." *Slow? Good luck with that*, his libido practically sang. Already, he struggled with the overwhelming urge to shred the slick black wrapping and devour the creamy center. His own personal candy bar. Smiling at the delicious idea, he let his hand trail from her chin along her throat, her pulse pounding beneath the pads of his fingers as they continued their journey, stroking her collarbone and slipping beneath the crisp lapel of her shirt. "Let me show you pleasure."

His heart remembered how to beat as her head dipped in answer.

He palmed her cheek as his lips brushed against hers, the tender kiss a silent promise and a show of thanks. He languidly dragged his hand down her arm until it met her warm fingers. Lifting her hand to his lips, he pressed his mouth against the racing pulse at her wrist, licking along the dancing beat. He grinned as her green seas vanished, the bright jade shoved to the fringes by the encroaching black heat of passion.

"May I?"

Her brow furrowed at his open question.

"It would do me a great honor if you would allow me to carry you to bed."

A shy smile warmed her lips as he brought up his earlier attempt at chivalrous behavior. "Well, since you did ah—" A surprised squeak finished the simple word as he scooped her into his arms and he took the stairs two at a time.

The short trek ended as abruptly as it started, his eyes locked with hers, his face descending slowly. Their lips touched as her body met the cool comforter, cushioning their tangled limbs. Only the patience honed by centuries of tactics stopped him from falling upon her, shredding the offending fabric, and burying himself to the hilt in her hot core in one swift stroke. Words, foreign yet familiar, ran on an endless loop through the back of his mind. The claiming ritual begged to be spoken, syllables bouncing around his skull, demanding to be given voice. *I claim you, body and spirit.*

Groaning against her mouth, he plunged his tongue deep to keep the words from spilling out. He rested his heavy weight on a stiff arm as he cradled her head, giving her time to sink into the bed. With her laid out like a buffet of the soul before him, he eased back, savoring instead of conquering. Leaning on his side, he let his fingers do a little walking, blazing a trail from her shoulder down her side, finally coming to rest on her hip. He feathered light kisses along her jawline while he crawled his fingers across her thin fabric barrier, inching the bottom edge closer and closer to her waistline.

A smile curved her lips as the shirt began to creep from dress-length to mid-riff. "Hey, that tickles."

"Is that a bad thing?" His hoarse voice rumbled against her throat, setting her pulse racing higher. Her breath caught in a needful sigh as his tongue flicked out, lapping at the rhythmic beat beneath his lips. "Or is this what is tickling you?"

She gasped as her entire body jumped at his deft strokes across her skin. Her hand shot out, clamping tightly against his wrist as her shirt continued its disappearing act. He froze, his teasing movements halted as a myriad of new pleasures cascaded down her skin.

"Calliope, do you wish me to stop?"

Her head shook as her eyes remained closed, her lower lip pinned between her teeth.

"No." The word was nothing more than a sigh with sound, her arching back coaxing movement from his immobile hand. The splayed fingers returned to their earlier task, nudging the shirt back the final inch, as his hand caressed the quivering skin beneath. He pressed his lips along the edge of the silken collar, his tongue darting out, tasting her sweet skin.

She struggled to stay on the mattress, her body in jeopardy of bucking clean off the bed. Butterflies morphed into elephants deep in her belly, stampeding their way through her bloodstream and trampling all thought in her brain. So many sensations, hot and cold, tingles and shivers. Her mouth was dry, but south of her belly button… Yeah, that was where all the moisture in her body seemed to be heading. As his lips continued to tease, she released the death grip on his wrist and trailed her hand up the length of his arm.

His fingers eased toward the buttoned opening, nimbly sliding one disc after another free until the sides parted. Cool air kissed her bare skin as the fabric slipped away and an appreciative growl rumbled against her exposed flesh, raising the color to an impassioned pink. With his hands trailing along her toned midsection, a pleading sound escaped her. His mouth and his light touch were pure magic on her hot flesh, her body writhing hungrily as his palm traveled across her ribs and kneaded her heavy and waiting breast. Her nipple tightened in a flash as she dug her hands into the rippling shoulders that held her onto the mattress.

She bit her lip, fighting not to cry out as he teased her aching breast. She shivered as fire leaped through her body. Should she move, arch her back to give him more access to her still-hidden body, or scramble to cover herself and let her panic at the unknown hold her prisoner for the rest of her short life? It all just felt so…good. But could she?

He must have sensed her trepidation, as her body reveled in the torrent of sensations flooding her being. Feathering butterfly kisses up the column of her throat, he pressed his lips against her ear.

"You have nothing to fear, agapi. Let your body go."

His words unleashed the fiery desires building within her and she climaxed, its ferocity coursing through her veins and pooling between her legs. A strangled moan escaped her slack jaw, the diamond hard nub peaking in pleasure under his careful ministrations. Her hips rolled on their own accord, undulating against the strong leg pinning her to the cushioning mattress. Her arms also seemed to answer an instinctual call, one hand delving into his hair while the other clung to his solid shoulder.

His mouth slanted to cover her parted lips, swallowing her needy cries, his tongue twirling and dancing with hers. Flattening his palm against her sensitive flesh, he stroked and caressed, adding fuel to the five-alarm fire burning just beneath his fingers. The passion-heavy air filled the room as he snaked his free arm behind her shoulders to hold her close, riding the wave of her orgasm with her.

Her lips trembled against his as her fragmented body slowly returned to earth. Blood thundered in her ears and her skin was slick, the cool moisture doing nothing to chill her fire raging below the surface. Something trailed down her cheeks, something wet.

With the seal of their kiss broken, she blinked back the tears that surprisingly filled her eyes. He caressed her cheek and whispered against her lips. "Did you not enjoy it, my beautiful muse?"

Her eyes tightly clenched as she nodded repeatedly, her quivering chin causing more tears to cascade. Did she not enjoy it? She just had her first orgasm, in the arms of the most gorgeous hunk of man she'd seen outside of a fashion magazine and here she was, blubbering like a ditched date on prom night. Yet the onslaught of emotion and sensation was too overwhelming, her inexperience and fear spoiling the moment.

"You have spoiled nothing, my beauty. What man would not be honored to see his mate moved to tears of joy in the heat of the moment?" His comforting voice soothed her frayed nerves, his words a balm on her still-burning body. She drew on the strength of his corded arms around her shoulders as well as from the hard, solid, and still denim-encased body pressed against her legs. He brushed his lip against her closed lids, kissing away any lingering tears. Still unsure of her response, she pried her eyes open, greeting the sparkling ebony pools before her.

"I sensed you were holding back," he said, his hand tucking a stray strand of her disheveled hair behind her ear. "And pleasure is best experienced with an open heart." She shivered as his thumb skimmed her lower lip. "Especially for your first."

His face blurred before her, his strong features wavering behind a misty halo. Swallowing hard, she struggled to find her voice, so many emotions bubbling past the lump in her throat that was her heart. "So I didn't do anything wrong?" She held his gaze, falling deeper and deeper into the black depths inches above her.

"*Tóso ómorfo,*" he whispered, his lips brushing her brow. His steeled arms wrapped around her shoulders, pulling her into the warm shelter of his body. "You enjoyed yourself, yes? Then you did nothing wrong. Rest now, Calliope. Rest safe."

"If it were only that easy…" she murmured into his chest, curling herself closer to the pure masculine scent that flooded her senses. Rich, rolling laughter rumbled under the hand pressed against his heart. A smile tugged at her lips. She definitely could get used to this. All of it.

"Perhaps it can be, agapi." he said, kissing her damp hair. "But we will think more about later. For now, sleep."

"Will you be here when…I…wake…up?"

Galen smiled as her voice diminished, exhaustion and a slight push on his part finally sending her into a deep and restful state. He slowly stroked her arms, willing her into a safe place, hidden from the nightmares he knew lurked beneath her calm exterior. Closing his eyes, he delved into her mind, armed and ready to slay the memories awaiting her.

"Yes, my muse. Today…and tomorrow and after…until the end of days." Simple words, the meaning not lost on him, tumbled easily from his lips, ruffling her hair and warming his heart. An intoxicating inhale later, and he followed her into slumber.

CHAPTER TWELVE

Mutters and muffled words bled into the silent space yet again. Galen pressed his lips against her damp brow, pulling her closer to his body. Barely more than a few minutes had passed when the nightmares began. For each painful image popping up behind her eyes, he was there to cast it away, sending it back into the darkness. Monster after hideous monster rose up, armed with whips, pliers, and red-hot pokers. Baring his teeth at each new grotesque, he could do little more than hold her protectively, unable to truly destroy these phantasms.

Time crawled on, her body and mind fighting against its forced inactivity. He had hoped vainly if he were able to keep her asleep for a long period of time, her body would adjust to change. Yet, the longer he held her, the more he realized it would not be so simple a problem to solve. Now, he wished his old friend, Eamon were closer. Eamon had been splitting his time between San Diego and Las Vegas, occasionally hitting his territory if he had a craving for chocolate or garlic.

Another strangled sob caught his attention. His gaze snapped down to her furrowing brow over her tightly clenched eyes. Her head thrashed from side to side, her arms and legs fighting off an unseen enemy.

"Cal?"

A scream ripped from her lips, her lids flying open as her body jackknifed off the bed. She slapped at her arms, smacking and pushing away the clawing fingers of her imagination. He moved quickly, wrapping his arms around her shoulders and pinning her flailing limbs safely to her sides.

"Shh. I have you. You're safe, *mikroúla*." Galen kept his voice soft and soothing, his lips pressed close to her ear, whispering calming words in as many languages as he could muster until he ran out of words and resorted to humming half-remembered lullabies from years long past. He held her until the screams subsided into sobs, finally ending in stuttered gasps. All the while, he fought against his own demons, those voices crying out for vengeance and for retribution for what was done to his beautiful spiritmate.

The only thing keeping him on an even keel was her. She needed his strength and he needed her, in more ways than he dared to admit. So his anger and rage was pushed down, shoved into the furthest, darkest corner of his gut. Cradling his trembling beauty, he tenderly kissed away the tears until she was quiet once more. He slid his fingers through her tangled black waves, the short locks sweat damp and cool against his hands as he sheltered her close to his heart.

"Ómorfi ángelos mou, sas eínai asfalí mazí mou."

His beautiful angel. That is what she was, the proof of heaven on Earth, right here in his bed, held against his chest. Her breathing evened out, the rhythm beating beneath his palms calmed. Slender fingers resting on his bicep tightened before she turned her delicate face up to him.

"Sorry. I hope I didn't wake you." Her voice sounded small and fragile. He smiled, his rough fingers stroking her cheek as her soft pale skin returned to a rosier shade.

"Shh, you've done nothing you should be sorry for, agapi. I've been more worried about you than you should ever be about me." Unable to resist a moment longer, he leaned down, brushing his lips against her cool forehead. Her light, flowery scent sent his blood into a fever pitch and his still-confining jeans shrunk another size or two.

"Bad dream?" He knew the answer, but also knew sometimes a simple statement of the obvious could do wonders to help break the ice. He felt her nod against his chest. "Do you remember anything about it?"

The breath that rattled her chest nearly destroyed him. He stilled until her hair tickled his pecs, her head shaking in resignation. Again, he tamped down his own violent emotions, focusing his resolve. Pressing light kisses on her smooth hair, he rubbed lazy circles across her back, sending healing energy through his hands, hoping to sweep away the bad and ugly of the past few days.

"So I guess asking if you slept well would be kind of a silly question, huh?" Though she struggled to keep her voice light, he heard the veiled hint of fear scream through his mind. His arms tightened in a comforting hug.

"You were by my side, Calliope. I couldn't have been happier." His sleepy voice rumbled, ending as a painful groan as the minx at his side rolled and stretched, struggling to extricate herself from the cushiony cocoon. "But if you continue wiggling, I'm never going to let you out of this bed."

His throaty growl stilled her languid movement. Her head swung up, her breath warm and a hair away from his throat. His jaw clenched tightly, swallowing hard as he fought to contain his growing desires, his muscles vibrating to remain loose under her innocent perusal.

"Is that bad?" She held her breath, her body still while so many emotions and feelings battered at his mind. At the timid desire in her question, his eyes opened, meeting her wide emerald stare, her full lips parted and too deliciously close not to taste what she was offering.

"Not as far as I'm concerned," he purred against her skin. His mouth descended, slanting possessively, his tongue sliding into the hot wetness of her welcoming mouth. He held her gently against him, pinning her shoulder to hip to his solid frame. He didn't think he could get any harder for her, but as each glorious second ticked by, his body ratcheted up higher and higher, the pain/pleasure threshold moving dangerously closer.

His tongue swirled and danced with hers, hot and insistent, but never demanding more than she was willing to give. Breaking away to let her breathe, he licked and nibbled his way down her jaw, leading to the long column of her throat. He dragged his tongue along her jittering pulse, smiling impishly as he teased the thundering beat below his lips.

Pushing himself onto his elbow, he gazed at the lean beauty before him. He trailed his fingers along the edge of black silk still hiding the rest of her body from his eyes. Before proceeding, he drew his heated stare to her face, searching for the true answer to his unvoiced request. What he found was the picture of pure passion, her kiss-puffed lips and flushed cheeks in heated testament against the creamy stillness of her skin and the sleek black of her hair. Her eyes were half hooded by heavy lids, desire all but blocking out the fiery jade rings.

He pressed a simple kiss against her collarbone, nudging the soft lapel aside. "But yours is the final word here, my sweet." Another kiss, a breath lower than the first. "I will never take more…" another soft kiss, his voice rolling over her skin in warm waves, "…than you freely give."

He lifted his gaze in time to see the corner of her bottom lip vanish, pinned between two dazzling white teeth. Her back arched, grinding her ass deep into the thick mattress as she lifted her breasts toward his nibbling mouth.

Pleasurably slow, his mouth brushed along the soft swell of her firm mounds, savoring the lush flesh as it peeked eagerly from the slinky covering. He listened carefully to every sound she made, noting each gasp and sigh as his fingers swept her thigh, grinning at the throaty moans as his lips moved closer to her stiff peaks. Kneading his hands along the length of her strong, supple leg, he nosed aside the dark silk, drawing her plump breast into his mouth. A heavy groan escaped his lips as he swirled his tongue across the tight nipple.

Cal squeezed her eyelids shut, watching the fireworks blossom in the darkness as heat burned through her entire body, focusing on the delicious point where his lips met her skin. Desire and Want stormed into her brain and locked the slack-jawed Logic behind a firm door. A strange tensing grew deep in her belly, warm and wicked, and she knew the Athenian Adonis in her arms was the reason for it. She'd experienced a hint of this last night, a small taste. Now, she wanted more. She wanted it all. Her hands frantically sought out every curve and plane of his back and shoulders, her scrambling fingers trying to touch each exposed inch.

"Relax, my eager one." The warm voice in her ears hinted at deep, rumbling laughter. *"This time is all for you."*

"But, what about…you?" she breathed, hoping her lips were forming actual words. Maybe she only wanted to believe she said it. Truth be told, she wasn't even sure she was thinking in any language known to man.

"I assure you, agapi. You have no need to worry about me. I am more than enjoying this."

Air rushed out of her lungs and dampness pooled at the apex of her legs as he pressed his hammer-hard shaft against the hot and yielding flesh of her inner thigh, her breaths coming in short pants and gasps. She dug her fingers into his firm shoulders as his lips slid to tease the other sensitive globe. A strong hand traveled along her back, holding her firmly against his consuming mouth as the other caressed her leg, moving upward toward her hip. Unable to keep silent, a needy plea slipped from her lips, her head thrown back, ecstasy painting her flushed face.

He growled possessively against her skin, her hips rocking against him, dampness and heat flooding the sheets. His mouth suckled and pulled, each tug causing her groans to ring higher and higher. With her release so close, he slid his hand across her quivering stomach, reaching down to touch the soft curls covering her slick folds.

She cried out, his delicate and tender ministrations sparking lightning that raged through her blood. Her hips danced and rolled beneath his hand, pushing hard and urgently against him.

Answering her call, he lifted his face to her, slanting his mouth across hers as he dug his fingers further down, stroking the pebble-hard knot between his thumb and forefinger. Her body jerked and spasmed, bucking hard against him as her scream of pleasure spilled into the warmth of his kiss. His fingers continued to ply her, groaning in anticipation as she writhed and thrashed. He paused for a moment, before asking the question she had scarcely dreamed.

"May I touch you deeper?"

His tentative words struck her profoundly. She knew what he was asking and she wished she could spend forever here in this moment, in his arms, with his question answered over and over again. How could she ever let go of him if she felt him buried deep inside of her? She turned her face away from him, seeking to hide as tears gathered, sitting precariously balanced on her lashes.

Galen had been so deeply entrenched in her body he neglected her fragile psyche. When the shift happened, his world shook to its foundation. She believed she was going to die and did not want to leave him. Primal possession raced through his blood, his Marshal skills put on overdrive. Power unlike any he had experienced burned white-hot in his soul and zinged along his skin. His eyes flew open, his gaze meeting her shocked gaze.

"Your life I tie to mine, your joy and your sorrow."

The words were out of order. This was wrong, but he would worry about that later. The building energy poured from his hands, skittered along his fingers and soon her whole body flared with an unearthly silver glow. His head snapped back, yanking a guttural grunt from his lungs, the howl from her lips laced with fear and pain.

His eyes flew open at the sounds of her terrified shriek. *By the gods, what have I done?* He scrambled to gather her still-thrashing body into his arms, his hands brushing her cheeks, guilt strangling any words at the sight of the tears raining from her still closed eyes.

Tears he had directly caused.

Torn between wanting to crawl away from the damage he had done and his own selfish need to feel her skin against him, he held her close and reached out to the one person who might know what he had just done and how he could fix it.

"Eamon!"

Muddled voices buzzed around in Cal's mind, swarms of incoherent sounds all vying for understanding. She batted them away, pushing through the cotton candy wisps of consciousness clinging to her fingers. No color penetrated her cocoon, only the deep rumbling voices, and they sounded angry. Had she done something wrong? Again? Her brain fumbled for balance, grabbed out for an anchor in this sea of nothingness.

She had a physical body. She remembered one, but it was as if someone had unplugged her. She tried to laugh, images of The Matrix forming in the gray, but no picture held its shape for long enough for her to truly be amused. *Think, Calliope. Think. What do you remember last?*

She was…with him. Galen. Her dark warrior. She remembered his mouth on hers, his hands sliding down her body. A distant sensation tickled her. Her brain identified the feeling as heat. Passion. Desire. She recalled his growled request, his fingers teasing her clit and sweet seconds away from plunging deeper inside when…

What happened? And how long ago was that?

One of the voices sharpened slightly, as if the radio dial moved a little bit closer to the station. The sounds rose and fell in waves, riding a tidal pull of emotions. Maybe with a little more time, she could pull in a clear signal. Feeling silly, she imagined herself a face and a mouth so she could speak.

Um, hello? Ah come on, Cal. Now you've really gone over the edge.

The far off voice grew more audible, even encouraging if she thought about it. She knew this one. The second voice, one unfamiliar, also beckoned hopefully. Hushed words spun around, meanings lost and tumbling in her mind.

This is crazy. Ok, so here I am. Back to talking to myself again. I mean, really? Is this even normal for crazy people? The more she rambled, the louder and more defined the words became. One voice, deep and rich, was in counterpoint to the other, the tone more mischievous and light. She recognized the warm velvet timbre, but the other was new.

Haven't heard that voice before. Sounds nice.

"Be careful there, agapi. Guardians are very protective of their mates."

She wanted to smile. Even thought about it long and hard. But she still couldn't feel anything resembling a body connected to her rambling sentiments. What was happening?

"Can you open your eyes, my love?"

Cal listened to the beautiful but sad voice floating into her drab little world. *How? I...I can't feel my body.* Her voice sounded frightened and small. *I do have a body, right? I'm not like a ghost or anything, am I?*

"Can you feel this?"

A tremor ran across the length of what she knew to be her arm, a gentle touch that warmed and tingled. With a renewed sense of purpose, she clawed at the suffocating cellophane, the promise of more of his touch spurring her on. She struggled and fought, kicked and scratched for release.

"That's it, Calliope. Come back to me."

A final rip and she felt something solid against the back of her body. The solid mass collapsed around her, two steely bands wrapping around her shoulders as soft kisses brushed through her hair. She moved stiffly, her skin feeling two sizes too small and over-starched to boot. Opting for caution, she tried her eyelids first. They were small, she could manage them. Using sheer will, she hoisted the heavy weights up, cringing at the sudden sensation of light.

"Could you—" Before more was said, the room grew dim, a pale glow illuminating a halo around the shadowed figure surrounding her. Her brows flexed and furrowed as she strove to bring her eyes into focus. "Thank you again, *filos*." The naked skin beneath her fingertips thrummed as more words poured forth, flowing over her skin like sweet honey.

"I'm sorry, *ómorfiá*. I never meant to hurt you. Ever. I only wanted…" The remainder of his statement vanished in a heavy sigh. Arms tightened around her and darkness descended, but this time, she was not scared.

Galen listened as her breathing deepened, her sleep natural and easy. Sighing, he placed a chaste kiss along her brow before peeling himself away from her. Taking a breath, he rose to his feet to meet the troubled blue eyes before him. He didn't know exactly when Eamon had lost the long ponytail and chieftain braids from years past, but his copper hair would always belie his Gaelic origins. The stylishly chic gold- and bronze-toned spikes fell bedraggled, probably from the exertion from his sudden trip through the Void to offer his aid, or from yanking on it to think of a solution. More than likely, it was a combination of the two.

"She's asleep. For now." He tried to sidestep the other man, only to be stopped by a gentle but firm grip on his shoulder. Eyes downcast, he stood statue still.

"Galen, are you wantin' to be tellin' me what happened now?" The playful lilt was slurred, a sure sign of his exhaustion. "How 'bout ya start from the start?"

"I just found her. I am not about to lose her." The venom in his words surprised both of them, and Galen shook his head, his shoulders dropping slightly. He combed a shaking hand through his hair, reining in his raw emotions. "I don't mean to loose my ire on you. Were things this bad for Malakai and his mate?"

Eamon hesitated before leading Galen away from silent sleeper, needing to get some distance and privacy. "If I said no, it might be an over simplification. Kai's mate had been marked by Konstantin and that got a bit sticky for everyone involved. But I'm more worried about you. Who is she and what exactly did you do?"

Galen paused at the threshold of the bedroom, casting a longing look toward the still figure wrapped in his bed. "Come on. I think I need a drink to try and put this one together."

Chuckling, Eamon slapped him on the shoulder. "Now, far be it for me to pass up a drink." He pulled Galen from the doorway, heading down the stairs and straight for the refrigerator. Grabbing two tall black bottles from the fluorescent depths, he cracked open both bottles and jumped up to his favorite perch atop the counter. "All right, boyo. Start talkin'." He took a long draught from the Guinness bottle, handing Galen the other.

Galen grasped the cool glass, staring into the deepening shadows filling the room. He had her in his arms, her body so responsive to his every touch and he wanted more. Wanted it all. But his question sent things into such a strange spiral, even he didn't rightly know where to begin. So, he opted to bide his time, tipping back the bottle as he drained half of it for strength before launching into his explanation.

Eamon raised a hand quickly. "I already know she's your mate, so we can bypass on that little fact, if ya don't mind."

"Gee, and that was going to be my opening line," Galen said, his voice bored and flat. "But have you ever heard of a spiritmate calling to her Guardian?" He raised his eyes, watching the stunned expression of his friend's face. "Yeah, you wanna try that whole bypassing of facts thing again?"

"She did what?" He leaned forward, resting a hand on the counter to keep his balance.

"Right after I got off the phone with you...Gods, was that only two days ago?" A slow nod and he continued. "Well, I hang up and I hear this voice, screaming out in my head."

Eamon shook his head violently. "No, wait a sec. She called out to you? That's...that's..."

"That's what? Not possible? Well, she did."

"But how?" Eamon narrowed his eyes in confusion. "I knew the link between a spiritmate and her Guardian was powerful, but I've never heard of the contact being initiated by the mate. Where was she?"

Galen took a long pull from the bottle, needing more liquid courage before continuing. "She was being tortured, Eamon. I found her hanging in chains from the ceiling in some beat-to-shit cabin out in the middle of the damned forest. Come to find out she'd been there for a week. A whole fucking *week!*" Slamming down the empty bottle on the counter to punctuate his sentence, he turned his angry black eyes to his stunned companion. "*My* spiritmate had been in the hands of fucking psychopaths, beaten and tormented for *days*! She..." His voice trailed off, the visceral memories of her captivity choking his words.

The eyes across from his flared open, fear turning the normally friendly blue into stormy oceans. "Oh God, they didn't—?"

Galen let out air still trapped in his lungs in a rush. "No. She hadn't been violated. But that would have been the outcome if I had arrived a few minutes later. She's a virgin. Could you imagine what that would have done to her?"

"Fuck." Eamon breathed out the curse, lengthening the word.

Galen gruff laugh barked out. "Yeah, that's one way of putting it. And, to top it all off, she was being used as bait to try and trap me. Now, don't ask me how the fuck that bastard de Coldreto knew she was mine, but he intended for me to find her. And that worries me."

Shaking his head, Eamon tossed back the rest of beer. "Why can't any of you guys have a normal relationship?" Sliding off the counter to stand beside Galen, he clapped his shoulder, smiling sadly. "Ya got quite a problem to work out, but we gotta figure out what ya did to her."

"She believes herself to be dying, and I think there might be something to it. When I healed her, there was something simply not right. And when the mends didn't take, I knew then it was more. I was going to call you and see if you had any idea of what to do."

"Let me guess, ya got busy, right? Never mind, don't bother answerin'. So, how 'bout tellin' me exactly what you did do."

Galen paced away from the confines of the kitchen, needing space to think this through. "I had asked her permission to go further and she balked. Not for the reason you're thinking. She thinks it would be better if she had no ties, nothing to leave behind or anyone to mourn her. I just lost it. The words came out. I knew it wasn't right but there was no way to stop what was happening."

Eamon peered up from beneath the shaggy mop of hair, one curious eyebrow arching as his gaze trailed after him. "Now what words exactly would they be there, boyo?" The question was answered by a deep silence.

Grumbling curses echoed from the wood and tile room as he stalked out, following Galen into the living room. "Do ya have any idea what ya've done? The claiming ritual words are in their order for a reason. And to top it all off, ya bespelled her as well." Sighing and shaking his head, he slumped down onto the couch, massaging his temples. "You've tied her to you, all right. But not only is your life hers, hers is yours. As she weakens, so will you." Galen halted as the familiar lilt vanished, the weight of his words darkening his tone, and piercing blue eyes speared him with a serious stare. "Unless you can convince her that she is your spiritmate and finish the ritual, real damn soon, like in the next two days, you will leave this world, and she'll be stuck in your place. For the rest of eternity."

CHAPTER THIRTEEN

A forceful knocking disrupted Stefan's most recent entertainment. With an exasperated sigh, he lifted his gaze from the naked redhead currently tied to the bedframe.

"Enter."

Returning his attention to the pale and trembling skin beneath his hands, he pinched the pink nipple, grinning at the needy whimper laced with fear in response. He touched the black satin blindfold across her eyes as he stepped away from the bed to greet his newest potential agent, yanking his slacks back up around his waist but leaving the crisp button-down open.

Two shadows darkened his doorway, the first belonged to his current second in command. Emmet stood like a looming onyx statue, his meaty arms folded across the Bulls jersey covering his chest. A knit beanie covered his shaved dome, deep indigo blue jeans hung off his hips, and his eyes were flat and cold. The second looked more like a fashion arrest in the making. Blue polo shirt tucked into conservative khakis ending in sensible loafers. Gods, what he wouldn't give for more soldiers like Emmet and his kind. Men that commanded loyalty and fear by sheer size alone.

"I take it from your untimely interruption you have some good news for me. Did you find him?"

Paul fidgeted nervously, bulging blue eyes jerking in all directions while conspicuously avoiding the naked and bound female on the bed. "Not exactly."

He arched one eyebrow. "Oh? Then why are you here? I thought I was quite clear about my wishes." He crossed the room to the cherrywood bar. Ice jingled in the crystal glass as he splashed the strangely pale green liquid. Sipping delicately, he faced the jittery figure again. His gaze slid toward Emmet, stoically silent yet very much interested in the conversation.

Paul shifted like a puppet getting its strings jerked. "You were right. She hasn't been back yet and her roommate freaked when I mentioned she was with a guy. But her boyfriend seemed to know more. Don't know how, but he kept trying to tell the bitch that Callie was OK and not to worry." He lifted a shaking hand to rub at the back of his neck, his gaze bouncing from the floor to the whimpering plaything struggling against her silken restraints

Stefan snorted a bitter laugh at the stench of fear oozing off the scrawny man. *Of course I was right, you stupid twat.* He kept his opinion silent, not wanting to scare off the man when he was still of some use. "At least you've managed to unnerve the pair. She might make a mistake and lead us to them both. Now, keep a watch on the house. Bug the phones, put a cup to the keyhole, I don't care, but don't come back to me without more detailed information."

He appeared at the door before Paul could reach the handle. "I don't mean to sound ungrateful, but I am concerned about her. Every moment she is in his presence is time away from your arms. You do want to have her back, right?" His gentle voice added to the impulse seeping from his hand where it touched Paul's knobby elbow.

Paul's face split into a slow smile. "Fuck yes. That bastard better not have done anything to her yet."

Stefan released his hold and ushered his self-deluded schmuck out. Sighing as he shook his head, he marveled at how easily some of these humans could be manipulated. One sniff of a woman's crotch and they lost their damned minds.

No matter.

As long as they did his will and helped him reach his own goals, he would throw them a few bones. He turned his attentions to the still stoically silent statue in ebony.

"We don't need him."

"Ah, Emmet. Always such a flair for the obvious." Spinning on his heel, he crossed to the bed and perched next to the bound beauty.

Her body shivered in both fear and anticipation as he reached out to twist one pert nipple, earning a sharp cry for the blood-red lips. He grinned, removing his hand but not before slapping the jiggling mound, leaving a red handprint across the pale skin.

"As you stated, we do not 'need' him, but he can be useful nonetheless. He can get into places where, shall we say, people like us do not quite blend in." He drew his attention away from his whimpering prey to lock eyes with his lieutenant. "So, until we have obtained our prize, we have to deal with the slimy little shit. Have you found replacements yet?"

"Got a bunch of my boys willing to do the job." The deep voice was clear and without hesitation. Stefan studied Emmet. The large black man was a mountain of rage looking for an outlet. He had found him on the streets of Los Angeles, running with the Eighth Street Angels gang. Most Rogue Warriors avoided the gang members since their job required more finesse than firepower.

But there was a dark intelligence behind those cold eyes. He was cautious and deadly, the perfect combination. His methods of interrogation and intimidation were second to none. Best get him back where he needed him the most.

"Good," he said. "Keep an eye on that one, would you? I don't want to find out he's lost his nerve."

Emmet nodded sharply, heading out the door.

Alone once more with his confined companion, he stalked over to the nightstand, fingering the tools displayed for his entertainment. He gripped the black leather, fur trimmed cat-o'-nine-tails firmly by the wrapped wooden handle and trailed the dangling strips against her quivering stomach.

"Now," he purred menacingly into her ear. "Where were we?"

CHAPTER FOURTEEN

Galen stood in silence, resting an arm against the door frame, watching Cal sleep from the safety of the hallway. Eamon had turned in a few moments ago, taking a much-needed break from their unfinished discussion. Each new detail only revealed more questions. Yes, he understood the Claiming Ritual had to be completed within a certain time frame, seven days if his memory served him right. Yes, the words were more than simple words. Now, he'd discovered exactly how much more than simple words they truly were. By jumping the order, if she didn't accept him, allowing the ritual to be finished in the next 48 hours, not only would he lose his Guardian status, becoming one of the enemy, but she would forfeit her life in the process.

There were still too many details he needed to know, but his eyes drifted between his friend and the nearest clock. Eamon, sensing his torn attentions, graciously excused himself to the guest room on the lower floor, giving him the time to ponder this new batch of information as he studied her quietly.

He wanted to keep her safe, but he needed this to be on her terms, not his. His eyes shifted up, glancing at his watch. A few scant hours ago, his hands had caressed the softest skin in his imagination, his mouth sampling her sweet breasts and he was oh-so-close to bringing her the pleasure she had so long denied herself. Nineteen minutes ago, her eyes closed, her splintered spirit returning to the shelter of the flesh. Now, he counted the seconds that ticked by, nearing the allotted time she said her body was able to sleep on its own.

Five…four…three…two…

The blankets moved, cresting and flowing as her long limbs moved, shaking off the mantle of sleep. The desire to cross the space and pull her into his arms had him trembling. Only his guilt kept him nailed in place. He felt powerless as she crawled up into consciousness.

Cal felt the upward tug of her eyelids, her cursed biology stirring her aching limbs to sluggish movement. The bed was huge and soft. And very, very empty. Her heart stuttered, dropping somewhere near her kneecaps, remembering what it was like when she awoke in his arms. Swallowing hard, she fought against the fluffy comforter, the bitter sting of tears slipping down her cheeks.

"Did you sleep well?"

She jumped at the whispered words from the darkened doorway.

"Galen. Geez, yeah. I'm fine. But where did you sleep? I hope I didn't kick you out of your bed."

"Calliope," his voice still managed to tingle her skin. "You have only been asleep for a short time."

"Oh." She raised a hand, dashing away the tears that sneaked out. Sitting up, she folded her legs beneath her, watching as her beautiful Greek stayed far out of her reach. He called her by her full name, and didn't use the beautiful words as he had before… before whatever happened happened. *My fault. It's all my fault.* "Look, I'm sorry this isn't working like you want it to. I know I'm screwing things up for you. I'm not what you need and I…I know you don't need all my shit messing everything up and—" Her words lost form as her emotions strangled her. Panic set in and she jumped from the bed, crossing quickly toward the bathroom, hoping to find a hiding place among the warm wood and cold tiles.

She had almost reached the doorknob as his shadow silhouetted her and his warm hand covered her frantic fingers, putting the brakes on her escape attempt. With a gentle touch, he spun her to face him before she could twist the handle, pinning her between the solid wooden door and his rock-hard body.

"By all the gods, why would you ever feel that, much less give those thoughts voice?" His breath stirred her hair, his brow furrowed in confusion. "Is that truly what you believe?"

"Yes. No. Hell, I don't know!" She held his gaze for a moment before breaking the dangerous connection. "You're gonna have to forgive me, all right? The past week has kinda been a cluster fuck. I don't know which end is up any more and…" Closing her eyes, she dropped her head back, connecting with the door in an audible thud. "Then you show up and I start to believe all the shit wasn't for nothing. I think that maybe, just maybe for once in my fucked up life, I could… And now… Aw, screw it. Never mind. It doesn't matter." Shaking her head violently, she turned again for the bathroom, but Galen refused to move aside.

The tension in his arms practically vibrated the dark wood at her back. "Please. It does matter."

"What happened to me?" she asked the floor, unwilling to fall into his beckoning midnight eyes. "Back there, in your bed. I heard you, and you sounded so…angry and sad."

Swallowing hard, Galen reached out to gently tip up her head, bringing her frightened green eyes back to his and seeing the wheels of her mind turning, fighting to make sense of this new connection.

"Calliope?" Breathing her name like a prayer, he saw the door behind her eyes crack open and he pressed forward. "The fault here is mine. I did something unthinkable. If you wish to leave now, I must caution you. I…" Pausing to find the best way to state this delicately horrific situation, he sighed, unable to speak the words he had to. "I never meant to hurt you. Ever. In any way."

"Galen, I just don't know what to do here," she said, breathy and nervous.

His voice was heavy and regretful. He was doing this all wrong. A deeply frustrated growl rumbled in his chest, his own fears reading more like anger. Her glistening eyes slipped from his, finding her feet. *Think, you fool. She's going to leave if you don't handle this right.*

"I am sorry. What would ease your fears?" A slight shrug was her answer, her shoulders trembling as they dropped back into place. He cupped her cheek and drew her gaze upward, forcing down his uncertainties as she broke her staring contest with the floor. His mouth watered at the sight of the corner of her bottom lip disappearing between her teeth, a sudden rush of heat firing through his blood. Gods, he needed her. Needed her to stay with all his heart and soul. This was more than passion-induced lust. If he did not see her smile in the next two seconds, he feared his life would not be complete.

A simple answer screamed out in his mind. He dipped his head to catch her frightened gaze. "Agapi?" He whispered the single word with loving reverence, becoming a multisyllabic prayer.

She barked out a sharp laugh to hide her burgeoning tears. "That's a good start." Her chin quivered against his palm for an instant before he enfolded her in his arms, filling his lungs with her April rain scent, pulling it into his blood.

"God, I'm such a sap," Cal mumbled.

A slow smile warmed his lips as her thoughts mocked her own silly fears. Now that he knew how important that single word had become to her, he would never hold it from her. Soft strands slid against his rough fingers as he stroked her hair, holding her lovingly as doubt washed out of her.

"Please don't ever think I do not want you." He placed light kisses atop her head, inhaling deeply and sensing a new layer to her fragrance. A dark and wild undertone flickered beneath the surface, marking her as part of him. The undeniable knowledge of his link to her tightened his groin another painful notch. "Even now, I have to stop myself from shredding that hateful shirt and burying myself so deep inside you I lose myself. If I am guilty of anything, *mikroúla,* it is of wanting you too much. I am guilty of other things too, but please, never doubt my desire for you."

Cal ducked her head to rest against his strongly beating heart, drawing strength from the steady sound as she hid the fiery blush starting at her cheeks. She wrapped her arms around his waist and waited for her breathing to return to normal.

One more deep breath and she had the strength to pull away from him.

"I just don't understand it." Shaking her head, she quickly staved off his words, her fingers resting against his mouth. "So much has happened and I'm still trying to wrap my mind around it all, you know? And I still haven't seen or talked to Maggs. I'm sure she's gotta be driving Ajax crazy with her worrying."

The lips beneath her fingertips curled, and he pressed a kiss on the pads before releasing her from his embrace.

"If you would permit me, I will take you to see your friends."

She raised a quizzical brow. "Permit? Do I need to remind you I'm talking about my roommate, and I am quite capable of handling myself?" She narrowed her gaze up at the ancient warrior looming over her an instant before turning back toward the bathroom door. The room spun and her hand shot out to grasp his forearm, her vision blurring with her overly quick motions.

His deep voice swore rapidly and eloquently as her legs buckled. Wrapping his hands around her shoulders, he steadied her wobbly stance.

"Agapi, you will be the death of me. Now, will you please rest and—"

Her head shook violently, stopping his words. "No, I've rested enough. I need to see my friends." Taking a full breath, she brought her eyes to lock with his. "Please." Her gaze was unwavering, her mind firmly made up.

The exasperated growl rumbling in his chest told her she had won this round. "If you will not rest, then I must insist that I accompany you. After your little argument with gravity just now, not to mention the outcome of your earlier sojourn, I am not about to let you out of my sight." He tightened his hold on her shoulders, ensuring she remained vertical.

She wanted to be angry at his Alpha-male actions, but the truth was she kinda liked it. She never let anyone close enough to become so protective of her. The longer their staring contest continued, the more she realized she was going to have a traveling companion whether she liked it or not.

The truth? She did like it. Very much so.

Still she would not let him off the hook so easily.

His full lips curled into a sexy smirk as he folded his powerful, corded arms across his chest. "Do we have a deal?"

Standing akimbo, staring up into his eyes, she struggled to lock her jaw in fierce determination. Her eyes narrowed as a sly smirk tugged at one corner of her lips. "I'm not getting out of here without one, am I?"

"'Fraid not, my little minx. You may be strong, but need I remind you that you still need to heal from—"

"Yeah, yeah." She most certainly did not need the reminder. She was quite aware of how much she still needed to process, but it could wait until after she saw her roomie. Her shoulders drooped as an exaggerated sigh slipped from her lips. "Fine. I guess I'll let you tag along. Just to make sure I don't pass out or anything. But what am I going to tell them? I mean, seriously? Do I open the door and say 'Hey there, Maggie. Sorry I haven't been home in a week. I got tied up...then beaten. Oh, and tortured and burned, too."

Pulling her into the shelter of his arms, he held her close and she took comfort from his strength. "Soon, agapi, this will all be behind you, I promise. Perhaps you can tell them you were in an accident and were unconscious for a few days." He kissed the top of her head. "Come. Let us get going while we still have some daylight."

"I don't want to lie to them." Her voice was quiet and thoughtful. "But I'm afraid the truth might be too much, for them and for me." Cautiously, she pulled out of his arms, fixing him with a serious stare. "Are we going to travel normally this time?"

A rumbling chuckle vibrated through his chest. "If by 'normally' you mean by car, that can definitely be arranged. But wouldn't you like to get there faster?"

"No," she said too quickly. "Thanks, but I think I'll stick to the old-fashioned modes for a while."

He smiled broadly. "As you wish. By car, it is." Stepping back, he held her at arm's length, surveying her current attire. "Perhaps we should find something more suitable for a public appearance first."

Light laughter bubbled up from her as she looked down at her outfit. "Oh. Yeah. That might be a good idea. You wouldn't happen to have any sweats, do you?"

A few minutes and a rather roomy pair of black sweatpants later, they were in the elevator, rapidly descending toward the parking garage. Cal bounced nervously from foot to foot, his socks swallowing her feet. It would be nice to get some shoes back on her feet. She didn't really mind wearing his clothes, overly gigantic size notwithstanding. But shoes? Yeah, there was a whole other story. Looking down, she glanced at his massive motorcycle boots. Those monsters had to be a size 12 or so. Her mind spun as an old, silly childish rhyme circled in her thoughts, a hot flush creeping from neckline to hairline in a steady climb.

Galen sensed the temperature rise in the close confines as she stared at his size 14 River Roads. The longer she gazed down, the harder he grew, his body eager to prove the truth of the words zinging through her brain. A wicked grin split his lips, lighting his eyes with delicious intent.

"We could do a little literary research if you would rather, my beautiful muse." He stepped in closer, his breath hot against her skin.

"Geez! Would you stop that? Can't a person fantasize in peace around you?" She wriggled out of his reach, her back knocking against the wall of the falling chamber. He knew his laughter only added more fuel to the growing blaze now threatening to singe the paint off the panels. He watched as she tugged at the sleeves of her ill-fitting garments, trying to hide the blush threatening to cover her entire body. "Is it possible for someone to pass out from excessive blushing?"

His knuckles brushed against her flushed cheek. "If you're feeling faint, perhaps we should return at another time?" Her rapid headshake was the answer he was expecting, but he'd felt the need to ask the question anyhow. Sighing, he smiled sadly at her determination. "I had a feeling that was going to be your answer."

The high-pitched ding signaled the basement seconds before the doors slid open. They walked in silence passed the rows of vehicles, stopping at the shiny gunmetal gray Jaguar XJ3. Keys jangled in his hand, followed by the disarmed beep at their approach. As he opened her door, she glanced around the remaining cars in the lot. He grinned as he easily picked up on her inquisitive thought, wondering which of these were his.

Leaning down as she settled into the cream leather seat, he whispered into her ear, "All of them."

He continued to laugh as he rounded the hood and slid into the driver's seat. She swiveled her gaze around to drink in the multitude of vehicles, so many makes and models, shaking her head slowly. "Seriously? All of them?"

The engine roared to life, and the car glided out of the parking space. "Something tells me I don't need to give you directions to where we're going, do I?"

A knowing grin tugged at the corner of his lips. "If it makes you feel better, I wouldn't mind hearing you tell me a little more about yourself."

She cocked her right brow, the shapely curve arching over her sparkling emerald eyes. "But don't you already know everything about me from, oh I don't know, reading my mind?" Her arms folded under her full breasts, lifting them higher before they dropped with a visible bounce.

Growling, he forced his eyes to remain on the road as his cock jumped to full attention yet again. "I do not pry into memories. The only things I know of you are what you have thought of. And what your emotions have told me." The buildings changed from steel and glass to redbrick and whitewash the closer they traveled toward the college.

"Oh." She slumped down a notch. "Sorry. I didn't mean to... Aw hell, who am I kidding? Look, Galen. I have to let you know something before you think I'm a nice person. I'm actually a horrible person, as I've shown you numerous times already. In fact, the only reason I want to see Maggs and Ajax is because..."

"Because you do not want to have anyone worry about you. Yes, I did get that message quite clearly. And regarding your character, agapi, you are not a nice person." He paused, his gaze sliding to the passenger seat before continuing. "Nice is the word most people use when they don't want to say the truth. 'Nice' is weak and indecisive. You, my sweet muse, are beautiful, inside and out. Your heart is always set to the needs of others before yourself and your mind is sharp and resourceful. Your body and spirit... Well, let's just say if I start in on those, I'd probably get arrested for reckless driving." Trailing his fingers along her cheek, he smiled warmly. "And, for the record, you could not be horrible if you tried, my love." He took one of her hands and brought it to his lips, brushing her knuckles tenderly as they sped down the street.

Cal swallowed hard past the lump caught in her throat, her mouth dry and cottony. "Yeah, well. You've only really seen me in action for a day or so. Just wait til I get rolling. I get under everyone's skin sooner or later."

The journey was over all too quickly, the familiar landscape telling her they had reached their destination. She frowned at his growled mutterings, her ears catching the creak of the straining leather steering wheel beneath the shattering grip of his fingers. *Good job, ace. Pissed him off already. Must be record time for you this time.* Sighing, she reached for the handle as a metallic click met her ears and the door lock disappeared from view. Her head spun and froze, her eyes locking on his dark pools hovering so near her.

"Calliope, for the sake of my teetering self-control, I would ask you not use the words 'action,' 'rolling,' and 'under my skin' again in the same sentence. My plan is to make your first time special, and me ripping the clothes off your body and ravishing you in the front seat of this car is not quite what I had in mind."

Her eyes popped wide at his forward words and his gravelly voice, her cheeks heating up in record time as fire pooled between her thighs. She held his predatory gaze, her jaw slack as flames of desire flickered within the depths of his ebony eyes. Unlatching the doors and letting in the cool autumn afternoon air saved them both, the welcoming hint of the upcoming winter of the Bay area snapping her brain into full functioning mode.

She watched as he disappeared from the car, only to reappear to open her door. Her socked feet touched the cold gray concrete and her eyes stayed glued to their path as the door loomed on the edge of her vision. Automatically, she swung her hands around, reaching for her bag that had accompanied her for so many days. But today was different. Today, her hand met…her own ass. No comforting weight of books, no jangling of keys and pencils. She froze, her arms locked as her eyes verified the information she already knew in her soul.

Gone.

A large, deeply bronzed hand swallowed her shaky one, giving it a tender squeeze. "It's OK, Calliope. I'll handle this." She heard the annoying buzz of the automated doorman. Her whole body refused to budge as she stared at the place where her bag should be, yet was not. An opening appeared on her periphery, but still she stood.

He pushed the door open, pausing as he sensed her rising panic. With a gentle touch on her shoulder, he pulled her back into the present and out of the darkness surrounding her. "Do you wish to go back?"

His tender words anchored her into the here and now, giving her the drive she needed to finish her journey. She shook her head, not ready to trust her voice yet as she convinced her feet to move. She peeled herself from her frozen state, but not before her hand found his, gripping it tightly.

The crappy threadbare beige carpet led the way to the elevators, but she bypassed them, rounding the corner at the back stairwell. She needed to move, needed to think. She felt the silent companion by her side balk at the flickering red EXIT sign.

"The stairs dump us out right in front of my door. Really, it's faster than that friggin' rickety elevator."

His hand captured her fleeting arm as she continued toward the end of the entryway. "Do you not think the elevator would be best? You still are not at your full strength, agapi."

Her cocked brow, as well as the hand fisted on a determined hip was her first answer. "I think I can handle a few stairs." She turned before he could protest and pushed down on the metal bar, unlatching the creaky fire door. "You coming or what?"

CHAPTER FIFTEEN

Galen sighed heavily, shaking his head as he watched her curves disappear into the garishly lit tunnel. *Was he coming? Talk about a loaded question.* The longer he stared at her backside as it ascended the stairs, the closer he was to actually making it a reality. Her innocent phrases, coupled with the gripping confines of his jeans... He pulled his mind off its current path, derailing the momentary lapse of control as another door swung open, signaling their floor's arrival.

He followed closely, his eyes narrowing as they approached her doorway. Inhaling deeply, he scented a faint tinge of sulfur and ash. He halted her motions mid-knock, his hand resting on her shoulder with her knuckles a breath away from the wooden barrier.

"Is something wrong?" she whispered, looking up at him as his eyes studied every corner visible and otherwise. She remained completely still as he continued his survey.

"I'm sure it's nothing."

A frown creased her brow. "I doubt you'd get this freaked over nothing."

He pursed his lips, glaring at the minx whose head reached to his shoulder. "I am not freaked. I prefer to think of it as healthy caution, my dear. And whatever was here is long since gone. Let's not stay in the open any longer than necessary."

Shaking her head, she turned and rapped at the door. "Fine. Trust your instincts, and keep me out of the loop," she muttered as she waited for someone to let them in.

Bending down, he placed his mouth so close to her ear, his stubbled cheek brushed the curved tip of the delicate shell. "Where you are concerned, *glykiá mou*, I would rather be over protective than thought lacking."

Her knees buckled a second before the door was flung inward and a flying paisley freight train burst out of the doorway.

"CALCALCALCALCAL!OMIGODOMIGODOMIGOD!"

Galen wobbled as the two girls collided, using his chest as a backstop. Shaking his head, he quickly ushered them out of the hallway and into the safety of the room. Even in here, he caught the faint hint of electricity and brimstone, telltale signs of a Rogue visitor. His eyes scanned the vibrantly eclectic furnishings. A large avocado green horseshoe couch devoured most of the living room, leaving a narrow trail to the back bedrooms. It didn't take a genius to figure out which was Cal's room as the other was hidden behind a curtain of hanging beads with the word "Marguarette" painted in swirling letters above the entryway.

"OK. OK. Maggie? Maggs, I can't breathe," Cal squeaked out in easy laughter as her favorite hippie crushed her in a tight embrace. Ajax ambled his lanky body off the couch and joined in the Kodak moment. "Gleah. Come on, you two. Seriously, can't breathe here."

She gave her roomie a final squeeze before she led her to the Big Green, their behemoth sofa that came with the apartment. Both of them figured it was because the previous owner couldn't be bothered to get the damned thing out. Cal looked at her friend for the first time in what seemed like months. Her blue eyes were rimmed in red, her normally bright complexion dull and ashen.

"Oh, damn, Maggs. I—"

"Where the hell have you been? You scared the heart out of me! You head out for class a week ago and then you just fell off the planet!" Tears streamed down from beneath the coke bottle glasses as the tirade continued. "I called Professor Archibald and called your cell and finally called every hospital and morgue in the area code. Hell, even Paul came over to see if you were here."

Cal groaned at the sound of that name, dropping in a heap onto the arm of the avocado monstrosity. "Aw, crap. Was it yesterday?" Galen stepped closer, resting a hand against her shoulder as she met Maggie's concerned expression. She nodded, her bouncing ropy bands jumpstarting another defeated groan from Cal. "Maggs, I am so sorry you had to deal with that trouser snake."

She dropped her face onto her hands, her head shaking as she tried to think of how this moment could get any worse. Only the undeniable presence at her back gave her the strength to face this. The face of her savior lit up the dark behind her closed eyes and she dragged herself away from the study of her palms, a curious frown pulling her slender brows together. Ajax, his pale gray eyes artfully lined, gazed over her shoulder, a slight smile on his lips before his head dipped down to the Adonis at her back. Puzzled, she started to look over her shoulder until the continued words of her terrified friend bled into her head.

"...I don't know why you're upset, Cal. He cared enough to check here after he ran into you by the college. Why didn't you call and tell me you were OK?"

"I was on my way here, but—"

"And who is this?" She stabbed a finger in Galen's direction before going on. "Paul said you were with a guy and he didn't like the look of him and—"

"All right, Maggs." Cal's soft but firm voice cut through her friend's words with surgical precision. "You want to know where I've been? Fine." Closing her eyes, hating the words about to spill from her lips, but she had to tell them something. "I...When I left class last week, I—"

"Shhh, agapi. You still needed to rest." The deep rumble washing over her soothed her jangled nerves as did his touch on her shoulder. He took over the story when her voice failed her. "Your friend was in a terrible accident and has been recuperating for several days in my care. She is still quite weak and has much recovery still needing to happen."

"An accident? What kind and just who are you? Are you a doctor? What kind of care? The kind that doesn't let people use a phone?" The words shot from Maggie in a rapid-fire attack, her normal tone of open acceptance and understanding shadowed with an edge of mistrust. Cal dropped her jaw a fraction at this uncharacteristic shift in her peace-loving roomie's voice.

Galen turned his dark eyes toward the narrowed stare of her flustered roommate. Her spirit was pure, but the taint of the Rogue influence danced along the fringes, nothing too damaging. At least not yet. His skills were more tuned toward the physical, but with his spiritmate's life in the balance, he spoke again, his voice adding the push of Insistence as he continued. "My name is Galen Alexiou and I mean you no harm. Calliope was on her way to find you, to let you know where she was when she ran into this Paul person. I am sorry, but she was still too weak and I brought her back to continue to rest. She should be fine with a few more days of rest."

The magnified blue eyes dilated and contracted, a frown edging across her forehead. He kept his voice soft, yet the flicker of power crept through his words, charging the air around them. Needing a stronger connection with his target, he stepped around Cal, splaying his hand before him, the fine blond hairs along Maggie's pale Scandinavian skin standing on end. Whoever this Paul person truly was, he had ventured into very dangerous territory. Fueled by his anger, Galen pushed harder, needing to clear away any lingering stench.

Panic radiated from his beautiful angel, and she reached out, gripping tight onto his wrist as Maggie shook her head. He dropped his gaze, telltale bright flecks of silver reflected back to him in her shining emerald eyes.

"Do not fear, agapi. I am not hurting her. She has felt the touch of one of my enemies and I am working to rid her of that stain."

Cal struggled not to interfere, her face paling as she thought of Maggs, her tree-hugging pacifist in the hands of the men who had brutally beaten her, and her heart skipped a beat. "Maggs, I'm OK. Honest." Her voice was tight, holding rein against the fall of tears. "Galen's been a great help. He's a real life saver."

Out of the corner of her eye, she spied Ajax stepping up, his black-polished fingernails curling under as his knuckles brushed the blond dreads off his lover's shoulder. "See, baby? I told you she was fine. I knew she'd be back, safe and sound." The boys seemed to be on the same wavelength, she thought, noticing another secretive nod between the two of them. "And Paul's not someone I'd really trust. He seemed kinda overly interested to me."

Maggie's gaze pinballed back and forth, bouncing between the three faces focused on her. "Did he? I mean, he just wanted to make sure Cal was all right. Didn't he?"

"Maggs, I never told Paul where I lived because the guy always creeped me out. Come on, he doesn't even use my real name! He thinks I look more like a 'Callie.' Puh-lease. How could he have known..." Cal's words faded as she watched her friend's expression change from confusion to embarrassment. "Please tell me you did not tell him where we lived." Sheepishly, her roomie gave a cringing frown before nodding her head.

"Aw, Maggs. Why?" Cal ran her fingers through her hair, frustration wrinkling her brow.

"It wasn't like I did it on purpose I just ran into him a few weeks ago as I was coming out of the library and I had my hands full of books for Professor Synder's project on the cellular decay during forced photosynthesis in hydroponic greenhouses and you know how much he hates anyone to use the Internet as the only research tool and well, he, um, maybe helped me carry them back home oh Cal, I'm sorry I didn't know you didn't like him *that* much and I wouldn't have even said anything at all if I'd known you had someone in your life already oh and hi I'm Maggs I'm Cal's roommate and this is Ajax he's, well, he's my boyfriend OK, so maybe that sounds kinda juvenile, but lover is, well, maybe too much information you look foreign, don't you think so, sweetie, and that accent is so yummy I mean you can't be from around here no one talks that way who's from the States and I mean...Omigod. I'm rambling, aren't I?"

Cal looked over her shoulder, catching the stunned expression on Galen's face. He blinked slowly, his brain probably attempting to pick apart the longest single-breath sentence on record. He shifted his gaze and leaned close to her ear, but spoke in a deliberate stage whisper, his words loud enough for the other two in the room to hear. "Was that supposed to make any sense at all?"

She covered her mouth as an easy giggle sneaked between her fingers. "I've found if you record it and play it back in slo-mo, you can catch enough of the words to figure out what she's trying to say." She laughed as the words continued to tumble from her roomie's lips.

Ajax shook his head, his black and red streaked hair curtained his eyes, but even the hanging bangs could not hide his mirth. "Baby, you really need to learn to put a speed limit on your mouth."

Maggie's cupid's bow pout on her lips showed no real remorse, nor did the sparkling blue eyes magnified by the thick lenses. "But I just have so many questions and sometimes if I stop talking, I forget completely what I was going to say." Her voice finally trailed off and she shifted her gaze from Cal to the stunned olive skinned god behind her. "But you're going to take good care of her, right?"

Her innocent question and big, blinking eyes brought a reassuring smile to his face. He found himself warming to both of the two people Cal considered friends. He watched the interactions between the unlikely pair. The goth and the hippie shared a strong bond, visible to his mind's eyes. They would be happy for many years yet to come. Yet there was still the lingering trail of the Void here. He sensed when they first approached the hall in front of her door. This Paul person had brought it with him. He'd stake his reputation on it. The little worm who tried to put his hands on his mate was willingly manipulated by de Coldreto.

He needed to get her back to his home. The wards imbedded in the windows would keep out any prying eyes, but here... Resting his hands on her shoulders, he spoke without hesitation. "I will, I promise you. Now I think it would be best if I got her back to where she can complete her healing."

Cal frowned and spun around to face him, the protest poised on the tip of her delicate tongue dying as he pinned her with a direct stare. Something was up and he didn't want to frighten her friends. *Please, agapi. I must ask you to trust me on this.* Sighing in silent defeat, she nodded and rose to her feet, heading into her bedroom at the end of the hall.

"Is she OK? Really OK?" Maggie's hushed whisper from the couch drew his attentions away from her swaying hips. "I mean, I'm sure you know about her not sleeping and I just worry something bad might happen to her and..."

"Yes, Marguarette. I am working to help her with that problem," he said, his voice strong and sure. "Which is why I would like her to remain with me. I know you are concerned about her, as am I." He gave a gentle nudge of Insistence to his statement. "I am sure you had no intention of angering Calliope when you allowed Paul to follow you home. But I hope you will not let him know of her misgivings. I'm sure you understand."

Blonde dreads bobbed as her head dipped repeatedly. "Anything. Please, she's so amazing and I don't want anything bad to happen to her."

Galen answered with a warm smile, thinking he couldn't agree with her more. "Neither do I." He caught a muffled sound centering from the room at the end of the hall. "Excuse me," he murmured a second before his long strides ate up the distance between him and the source of the heartbreaking sounds.

Entering the room, he found Cal kneeling amid a pile of random clothing items, her shoulders hunched over and shaking, her fingers splayed against the knotted beige carpet. He raced to her side, scooping her into the circle of his arms as he sat on the floor, one large hand cradling her face against his chest.

"Shh. I'm here, agapi. I'm here." She shook, her limbs tempest-tossed as he rocked her, brushing tender kisses and whispering soft words against her hair. He rubbed her back in slow, soothing circles, channeling calming energy through her body. Closing his eyes, he reached out to her mind, finding her spirit cowering in dark, the position exactly as he had found her in the cold shower.

Approaching her softly, he crouches beside her. "Calliope? Please come back to me." He holds his hand out to her, inches away from her trembling form.

"Why...why do I keep ending up in this place?"

"We all have a place where we go to hide when life becomes too much to bear."

Her chin lifts at his soft words. "Do you have a place like this?"

A smile curls his lips. "I did, but I no longer have any need for it."

"Why not?"

He waits until her eyes find his.

"Because you found me, and now I can bear anything."

Strong arms surrounded her yet again. She remembered leaving the living room and going to her bedroom. She puttered around the room, grabbing some necessities; a couple pairs of pants, socks, underwear, shoes that fit her. Her hand hovered over the space where her Pumas should have been when everything went blank. The room began to shrink as if someone were pulling tight the drawstring that kept the space open, her vision narrowing as the floor rose to meet her palms.

She sucked feebly at the disappearing air, her body frozen.

Then he was there, his deep voice filling her ears with beautiful exotic words driving the cold away from her heart. He crept into that dark place and gently drew her back to the world of the living. Her surroundings became visible once more, the clothes she planned on carrying back now scattered across the floor.

"I'm OK." Her voice was thin and distant, at odds with her intention. She gave his arm a light pat before pushing to her feet. The grumble over her head voiced his disagreement with her flippant statement, but he remained stoically silent as he aided her to her feet.

A quick scan of her room aided her in locating a spare pair of flip-flops and her old, beat-up New Balance trainers she was meaning to throw out. Rummaging through her closet, she found a free gym bag and stuffed her gathered goodies inside, her movements jerky and stilted. She stopped for a moment, flexing her fingers to dispel her nervous energy. Her gaze climbed up and found Galen watching her warily through sidelong glances, his lips a tight line ringed with concern. She dropped her head, sighing.

"If you're thinking coming here wasn't such a good idea, I'm beginning to think you were right."

He crossed over, pulling her into his arms. "You needed to make sure they were fine. It was important. But," he paused, pinning her with a serious gaze. "I suggest we get back quickly. I fear things might get sticky soon and I'd rather have you out of danger."

Cal opened her mouth, intent on giving him a piece of her mind when his lips covered her, robbing her of any remaining argument. His arms coiled around her, hands moving north and south along her back, threading through her short-cropped hair and grabbing her ass, holding her firmly in place. His tongue danced and twirled with hers, his dark, wild scent assaulted her senses and threatened to push her over the edge.

Her eyes rolled back into her skull, her bones turning to mush as every firing nerve ending sent passion-laced messages to her brain. Something primal and undeniable had been awakened by his skillful caress, some part of her now howling for complete satisfaction. These tiny nibbles, hot and delectable, only whet her growing appetite. She clung to his broad shoulders as his lips pulled away from hers.

"That. Wasn't. Fair." She shoved the words past her panting breaths. Resting her forehead against his chest, she swallowed against the rocketing pulse at her throat. A thin sheen of sweat has begun to form along her bare arms, heating her as it chilled her skin.

A wicked rumbling laugh hummed through his chest as he placed a final kiss atop her head. "Perhaps we can discuss the fairness of life in a more private setting later. Do you have everything you need?"

Cal couldn't contain her crooked grin as it tugged at the corner of her lips. "What is it with you and the loaded questions? Yeah, I think I'm good." She stepped out of his embrace and grabbed the gym bag at her feet. As she stood, the room swung slightly to port before finally coming to rest in its upright and locked position.

"Calliope Adriana Vandeen."

Her name took on an entirely different meaning as it fell from his lush lips, the growl in his voice only added to the embarrassed blush on her cheek, desire kicking up the shade up a notch or two. She spun in hasty retreat, moving toward the open doorway.

She took two steps forward before her gaze snapped back to his. "Hey, wait a minute. How did you know my middle name?"

He gave her a devilish grin, his eyebrows dancing over his laughing eyes. "I have my ways." Her jaw dropped a fraction when until he placed his hands on her shoulders and directed her gaze toward the wall across from her bed. "And it's framed, in rather large black letters next to your mirror."

Laughter followed her down the hall as she headed back into the living room. "Smart ass," she mumbled, spying her roomies cuddled in their usual place on Big Green. She sighed, thinking of the danger she had placed them in, the taint of evil Galen detected still burning guiltily in her memory. Until this puzzle was solved, she needed to stay away to keep them safe.

"All right, guys. I'm, um, gonna be, ah, staying with—"

For the second time, Cal was run over by steam train Maggie. "Oh, I'm so happy for you! You deserve someone gorgeous and yummy to make you incredibly happy."

"Maggs!" The word squeaked out as the last of her air was hugged out of her body. And for the second time, she was grateful for the muscular backdrop that saved her from landing in an unceremonious heap on her ass. But this time, the wall was laughing.

"And I do believe, on that note, we should be getting back. Marguarette. Ajax. Thank you for all you have done. I will be sure to keep her safe."

"Everything will be OK," Maggie whispered into her ear. "I just know it." Giving her one more hug, she released Cal and stepped back to the couch.

Cal felt an endearing smile warm her lips at her friend's easy words. "Thanks, Maggs. I sure hope so. I'll call you in a day or two, OK?" A strong hand on her shoulder guided her toward the front door. One last look back, a nod, and they were off.

They walked in silence down the stairs, but Galen's eyes narrowed as they headed to the front door. *Fuck.* They were waiting, two figures in the shadows. Lucky for him, they had not sensed their approach. He reached a hand to her shoulder, pulling her to a slow as they neared the glass entryway.

"Is there another way out of here? A back entrance?" He hoped his use of their connection would not startle her. Her gaze lifted to catch the determined glint in his eyes. Immediately, she scanned the hallway, following his eyes until she caught a flash of movement in the dark. She jerked her head toward the hall opposite of them, lifting two fingers and tapping her right arm.

His eyebrow arched in astonishment, and he gave her a crooked grin. *"You are full of surprises, agapi. Stay here."* Yet, as he turned away from her, she reached for his arm, whispering. "I have a better idea." With a wink, she continued on her path to the front door, whistling and singing to herself.

His statue act lasted only a second before he *moved* down the hall, opening the second door on his right, which dumped him a few yards behind the shadows. Sliding his fingers against his side, he found the short staff again. He searched for a sign of their origins, discovering the tainted aura of a twisted heart, the true mark of a Rogue. He snapped his wrist as he withdrew the wooden handle, the blade sliding into place just as Cal opened the doors.

Cal held her hand to her ear as her head bopped from side to side, her eyes half closed as she danced down the two steps to the path and sang along with her own version of "Telephone." By an untrained eye, she seemed as distracted as any, lost in the music and oblivious to her surroundings. The two in the dark thought the same as well. Galen struggled to suppress an angry snarl as her performance moved her closer to the group, his crouched steps bringing him directly behind the pair.

The trap was set so perfectly and Cal did not hesitate when a hand grabbed for her arm. She gripped his wrist, wrapping her fingers tight as she pivoted easily on the ball of her foot and her leg snapped up, her knee connecting with his gut. He huffed out any air in his lungs, doubling over and she drove her elbow down between his shoulder blades. As the body crumbled to her feet, she watched as the other man froze mid-stride, his mouth held in a perfect O a breath before vanishing in a puff of black smoke, a long thin slice of gleaming silver in the neighborhood of where his heart used to be. A hand wrapped around her ankle, reminding her of the villain pooled in a heap, throwing her off-balance. She windmilled her arms before her unfettered leg spun around in a graceful arc ending at the man's face, sending him flying onto his back as blood poured from his shattered nose.

One dispatched and Galen blinked slowly as the second became airborne for a moment. Taking two quick steps, he slashed across the man's chest, driving the tip of his blade into his heart, flicking his wrist up and another cloud of shadow covered the ground. His gaze lifted, darting into the dark and the light areas as well. No more agents were near, but he dare not risk staying out in the open any longer.

"Lady Gaga?" An eyebrow arched up as he quickly wiped the dark smear off his blade and snapped it safe into it hiding place. He held out his hand, entwining his fingers with hers as she reached down to retrieve the bag she'd dropped during the short skirmish.

Cal gave a light laugh, lifting a shoulder in feeble apology. "It was the only thing I could think of at the time. Personally, I thought it was friggin' genius." Her toothy smile was broad and self-satisfied. Galen rolled his eyes at her mirth, pulling her closer to him as they continued down the path to the car.

She did know how to handle herself, Galen mused. That much was evident in not only her strategic distraction, but also in the speed of her reactions. The Fates had truly blessed him with a worthy mate. He ushered her inside the car, grateful for well-timed the appearance of a group of laughing students. The key turned and the engine purred to life.

He took her lead, giving her time with her own thoughts and the silence remained as the car pulled away from the curb. Darkness had descended during their short visit and the city lights shone ghostlike through the famous pea soup nightly fog. They drove through the silver shimmers, light and shadow dancing before the bright halogens.

He split his focus from the inky road in front to the quietly pensive beauty at his side. He could feel the turmoil of her thoughts, so many emotions and several of them bordering on dangerous. He brushed his hand along her arm as she stared into the dark beyond the steel cage.

"I can't help but think this is all somehow my fault, but for the life of me I can't figure out why." Her voice was faint and breathy, her words laced with a deep sorrow. "I never did anything out of the ordinary my whole life. I never stood out in a crowd. I never even went out on many dates." He could hear the tears in voice and saw the damp trails reflected in the passing streetlights. He gunned the engine, pushing the car faster toward their final destination.

"Why? I mean, can someone please tell me why I got chosen for the shit storm of life? All I ever wanted was to have a nice, normal boring-ass life. School, for, like, the rest of my life. I just wanted to spend my life locked in a library, or on a dig, or in a classroom." Her panicked rant spiraled as he whipped through the streets, his otherworldly skills keeping lights on their return trek. The garage mouth gaped open and he slid the car easily into an open space.

Slamming the car into park, he swept her trembling body into his arms and *moved*, returning them into his bedroom. With her once again close to him, he trusted his voice to speak. "Agapi mou, the fault here is not yours. Never once do I want you to believe you have done anything wrong. Please."

Tears of impotent rage and frustration continued to course down her face, her shoulders wracked by sobs she could no longer contain. Her back bowed as she pushed feebly against his chest. "It's all my fault. There has to be something with me. I mean, I never knew you, or about you, or any of that until…until…" Her legs buckled and she collapsed into his embrace.

Galen swore silently as she fought against the demons of Chaos. This was what his enemy did. And now, they had their hooks deep into his spiritmate. Leading her carefully down to the floor, he closed his eyes, cradling her face in his hands and pressed his forehead gently against hers.

As he entered her mind, he was jolted off his feet by howling winds and icy torrents. *What the…?* Gale force winds buffeted him as he searched for her spirit in the midst of the storm.

CALLIOPE!

CHAPTER SIXTEEN

Cal wandered through the maze of unfamiliar faces in the dark. Bouncing off invisible walls and careening though the barrage of groping hands, she clawed her way out of the fray, her head swiveling to find something tangible. She grasped and clenched her fingers feebly at the thick air, finding no solid purchase.

Wait. I've been here before. She continued to search, her eyes narrowing to find some clue. She took a deep breath, exhaling in a slow huff. In the foggy trails, she spied a doorknob.

Ha! I do know this place. Grinning, she gripped the knob, but stilled before turning it. *No, this is too easy.* Taking another deep breath, she centered herself, listening intently to the white noise surrounding her. *I'm not alone here, and not in the good way either.*

Evil laughter rolled oily off the walls, bleeding down and pooling at her feet. She stepped back to avoid the gunk as it oozed between the door and the frame. A cold light seeped around the entryway, burning from edge to center, leaving a gaping maw in its place.

"I see your Mate has trained you well. Too bad it will not be enough to save either of you."

Was he serious? "Dude, we gotta work on your material. Hell, all you need is a little black moustache to twirl and go 'Muahahahaha' while you're at it."

In retrospect, maybe taunting the Big Ugly in her mind wasn't the smartest of actions, but she was getting tired of the roller coaster of emotions and wanted off. Now.

A figure clad in a rather expensive-looking business suit coalesced before her, hair slicked back, but it looked blondish in color. Eyes an unreal shade of blue pinned her with a stare seething with hatred, and a vicious slash of a mouth broke a face too angular for her to think of as handsome.

"Your false bravado will do you no good here, Calliope. This is my world and you-"

"No, assmunch. This is MY mind, not your anything. So, if you don't like it, then you can just get the fuck out. Right. Now."

Cal watched as the stunned face before her unraveled into the mist surrounding her. A Cheshire Cat grin lingered in the haze a moment longer, then it too vanished.

This was not over, not by a long shot. But at least she felt she had won this round. For now.

In the fading wisps, a new face came into focus. This one, rushing toward her, was much more to her liking. Smiling broadly, her eyes drifted close as familiar strong arms surrounded her, pulling her from the blackness and back into the warm cherry wood floor beneath her.

Galen fought against the hell-born winds of Chaos that tore through her mind, calling and searching for her spirit. Bitter rain needled his skin, nearly blinding him to his quarry. Following the faint trail of their connection, he finally discovered her.

Standing nose to nose with Stefan.

The only way the bastard could have found her is if he had orchestrated the whole kidnapping in the first place. His heart sank as he realized the depth of his opponent's scheme. All the minor skirmishes from the weeks leading up to her abduction, the bodies of females closely matching his newly found spiritmate washing up along the shores of remote beaches or found in grisly disarray in the seedier parts of the city should have sent the claxons firing in his brain.

Please, by all the Gods, let me not be too late.

Wanting nothing more than to pour all his energy into a dead run, he settled instead for a snail's pace as he moved sluggishly toward the two figures, his lips still sending up prayer after prayer. As he neared the pair, he watched as one shape simply flicked out like a candle. As his nemesis faded away, his legs picked up speed, finally racing to the object of his heart's desire. His eyes widened as he realized his mate was still standing. Calling to her again, he wrapped his arms about her, pulling them out of her dream state and back into the world of the physical.

"I'm sorry, my love. I'm so sorry. Please forgive me, please." The words tumbled from his lips as he pressed frantic kisses on her slowly warming lips. The pale skin beneath his palms began to lose its ashen cast and her dark lashes fluttered, the heavy lids revealing cloudy seas of green.

"Why do I need to forgive you? Did you do something wrong?" she asked, and his body tensed fractionally beneath her hands. He dragged in a deep breath, her innocence, undaunted by the encroaching void, giving him the strength he needed to continue. "Galen?"

Looking down into her eyes, Galen felt like such an ass. He had somehow drawn her into his world and stole the most important choice from her, her choice to remain. And now, the bastard de Coldreto was only going to grow bolder in his quest to claim her first.

His arrogance and his ego forced him into a corner. Unless… No, there was no way he could keep this a secret from her. He wanted her trust, her respect, and most importantly, her love. And deception was not going to earn any of those.

He rose to his feet, still cradling her within his arms. "I am sorry for what just happened. That person you saw…His name is Stefan de Coldreto. He commands legions of the chaos agents we call the Rogue Warriors. And I believe it was on his orders you were originally taken. But I still have no idea how he knew who you were when even I didn't know of your existence. I had hoped, prayed perhaps someday I would find my spiritmate, find you."

Setting her on her feet, he stared into her eyes, now clear but still troubled. "There has never been an instance of a Mate finding her Guardian, much less under these circumstances. Forgive me, but there are so many questions I'm sure you have, and I'm afraid even I don't have the answers."

He rested his hands on her shoulders, feeling the warmth from her skin. "But I do have one question for you." He paused as he redirected his train of thought, gathering some mental courage. "As I was healing you, you asked me if it would be possible for me to help you. Were you serious?"

A slight frown wrinkled her brow, her mind backtracking through their previous conversations. "Um, when did…oh. You mean about me dying and stuff. If it were possible, then, um, yeah. I mean yes, I guess." Her eyes widened and the color faded from her cheeks. "I'm not...I mean. Am I like you? You didn't—"

"Gods, no." Laughing lightly, Galen sat hard on the bed, carrying her into the shelter of his arms, his face inches away from nuzzling those perfect breasts. "I cannot make you like me. But would it truly terrify you?" He forced his eyes to stay on her face and not buried in the warm flesh at mouth level. "To live forever?"

"Life is meant to have an end." Her voice/was airy, though her words were not. "Had I been able to see what you have, I might take you up on the offer. But in this, this über modern, technological world? I can't think of anything I'd really want to see on the horizon."

"Truly?" He raised a quizzical brow. "You wouldn't want to see space colonized? First contact with an alien race? Perhaps solving the human genome?" With each new idea, his hands trailed down her arms, entwining his fingers with her long graceful ones.

A timid smile warmed her lips as a tempting blush painted her cheeks. "And how about a cure for the common cold and flying cars while we're at it?" Her eyes danced as she chuckled lightly. "Nah, all the really cool things have already happened."

"Are you sure about that?" His gaze wandered across her laughing face, drawn to her lush lips as her thoughts did some wandering of their own. She was a lover of ancient history, names such as Xerses, Julius Caesar, and Aristotle rattling in her curious mind. And she hadn't even asked him about the recent historical events he had witnessed.

"Well, yeah. I mean, come on. You've met Plato, Socrates, Beethoven, Alexander the Great. Who do we have now? Bill Gates, Donald Trump and Björk? No way. You've already seen all the good stuff." Sighing sadly, she looked at his eyes, guileless and innocent.

Galen's grin grew hotter at her naïve comment. He had seen a lot of good stuff, but there was one event he prayed was still on the horizon. "I have experienced much, this is true. But there is one event I would give anything to see."

"Really? Like what? I mean, you saw the face of the world change and lived through the most incredible time periods and places in the history. What is it?" Her open and sincere eyes coiled the blood pooling in his lap, firing it into action and his cock snapped to attention. His gaze stayed glued to hers as he brought her hand to his lips, placing a heated kiss against the inside of her wrist.

"I would give my dying breath to see you deep in the throes of pleasure." His voice was a whisper, a promise of passion as it tripped from his tongue and bled through the flimsy shirt covering her quivering flesh. He led her hands to rest on his shoulders, needing to feel her touch him. "To hear your sweet voice, lost in ecstasy…"

Unable to hold his control any longer, he leaned in, pressing his lips against the fabric-shrouded valley between her lush breasts. Twisting one of the button in his teeth, he snaked his arms around her waist, cradling her back from shoulder to ass, holding her firmly for a moment before sliding his hands down her sides. His fingers tangled around the elastic and drawstring band, tugging the offending heavy covering down her sleek legs and leaving it to pool at her feet.

"Maybe even screaming my name, perhaps." An easy tug of his teeth and the thin thread gave way without a fight. "A man can dream, can't he?" The words flowed around the small plastic disc before he reached up and discarded it. He trailed his hands down her legs, lifting each foot and finally tossing the baggy sweats far from sight. He drank in the sight of her smooth lean limbs before his gaze climbed again to lock with her desire-heated eyes.

"Calliope, before I lose what little control over my baser instincts, I must be honest with you. About what has happened to you."

"You mean aside from getting kidnapped, tortured and now hunted in my dreams by strange men?" Her ever-sharp wit did little to hide her apprehension and her desire, her voice a husky blend of innocent flirtation.

Please stay with me. The words screamed through his mind, his heart. She was intoxicating to him, her quick mind, and her thirst for knowledge. Throw in a healthy dose of passion and a body to die for. Yeah, he was lost. Happily so, but lost nonetheless.

"Yes, agapi. Besides those things." His hands trembled, the desire to savor her soft skin a fabric scrap away nearly overrunning his sense of duty. "When a Guardian finds his spiritmate, words known as the Claiming Ritual will form in his mind. It is how a warrior bonds with his other half." He breathed, searching for a reason to stop in her eyes. Finding none, he continued. "These words, once begun, have to be completed in a finite amount of time. Seven days, to be exact."

Cal swallowed hard. "So this, uh, Claiming Ritual, does it, um, entail…" Her voice faded as his eyes bore deep into her, peering straight to her beautiful soul, a slow smile curving his lips.

"Oh yes," he growled, his words whispering against her heated skin. "It does indeed 'entail.' Sometimes, I've heard tell of it 'entailing' for hours." He grinned as her cheeks pinked. "Days, in some cases."

"Oh, wow," her escaping breath formed sounds that almost made sense. She leaned heavily on his shoulders, arms rigid to stop from falling into his lap.

Galen inhaled as her deep fragrance filled the narrow space between them. Heat radiated from the skin a scant inch from his lips. He wet his lips in hopeful anticipation. "You could say that. Once buried deep inside his mate, the words ring out, binding the two souls together and joining them for the rest of their days. The Guardian then has the choice to remain in the service of the cause, or find one to take his place and lead a mortal life." He finally gave into temptation and gently pressed his lips against the creamy flesh before him.

She dug her fingers into his shoulders, his denims shrinking as he imagined those long, strong digits tightening around his shaft. "What would you choose?" He lifted his gaze to see her eyes roll back as her head lolled, desire drunk, on her shoulders.

"I suppose the answer would depend on my spiritmate." He stayed riveted to her face, waiting until her lids slowly peeled back and found his. "For, you see, if she wished for me to leave the struggle, I would do so. I would do anything to see she were happy."

"But what if she were more of a fighter? Hypothetically, I mean." Passion all but hid the green in her eyes, her skin flush and responsive. "What then?"

"Ah, then I would be the luckiest of all the Guardians ever born. Only the most blessed of all warriors find a mate who is their equal in battle. Her fire and strength adds to his, as his combines with hers." His arms flexed and tensed, bringing her closer in the circle of his body. "Oh Gods, Calliope. I want nothing more than to pull you down onto this bed and lose myself in you, but I have to be honest with you. The ritual words are set forth in a specific order. And by starting in the middle…" He paused, sighing heavily and rubbed his hands along her back, looking for the strength to continue.

"Wait. You mean those words you said when we were, um, were… They were part of it?" Her eyes widened, her eyebrows dancing across her forehead. "But, why? I…I don't understand. I mean, why would you start the—"

"How could I not? You are my match, in every way I could have ever dreamed. Your mind, your beauty, your fiery spirit. If you would accept me, there is nothing I wouldn't give to you. I only hope I haven't ruined my chances." His head tilted, her rapidly beating heart pounding against his ear and his eyes slipped closed, focusing on the whirling thoughts in her mind. He waited patiently as her mind worked through his words, sending up a silently prayer to all the gods in every pantheon he knew. *Please, stay with me.*

Cal wrapped her arms around his shoulders, relying on him to remain on her feet. She pulled his words apart, let them rattle around in her brain as she picked out their meanings. The bottom line, he started those binding words, the ones that meant he wanted to be with her, and only her, for the rest of his life. And, from what she could tell, he'd botched it up somehow.

"So," she started, her voice thin and reedy, "how do you think you've ruined your chances? Is it because of the whole 'things-weren't-said-in-order?'"

She felt his lips turn upward against her skin, his breath tickling her heavy breasts. A tender kiss was pressed along her flesh and her breath escaped in a deep groan.

"That," he purred, turning his face up to hers, as he dragged his tongue along the cleft between her breasts. "And because you may not want me as much as I want you."

Cal gasped as the blood drained from her face, racing through her body before settling between her legs. Her mouth opened and closed, but no coherent sounds came out. How could she possibly not want him? He was the most amazing man she had ever seen, a hero worthy of song and stories. He looked like he just stepped off the Calvin Klein billboard by Union Station. Add to the fact when he looked at her, she felt like a priceless work of art or some other treasured object. Plus, he made it abundantly clear he found her sexy.

She continued to gape, her thoughts spinning and vying for release. Her gaze captured his and her jaw stopped moving, her own reflection cast back at her from the depths of his ebony eyes. He wanted her. Those words rang out in her head, the truth of them seeping into her whole being.

And the words gave her strength.

She dragged her fingers along his neck, threading through his hair. Holding his face in her hands, she lowered her lips and pressed a hesitant kiss on his upturned lips.

He deepened her tentative kiss, his tongue savoring each corner of her mouth, his arms coiling around her waist. "I know you're scared, agapi. I wish I didn't scare you so much."

"Y-you don't scare me."

He smiled impishly at her stammered words, one eyebrow arching up. "You sure about that?"

Her smile was shy, but honest. "Well, not like you mean. I know you'd never hurt me. It's not that. I'm more afraid of…" Her eyes drifted shut as her thoughts trickled to a stop.

His strong hands cradled her face, his palms rough against her heated skin. "Of?" He trailed his fingers along her jaw, his silence hopefully giving her the encouragement to continue.

Cal tried to sort her thoughts into logical patterns, but one image kept jumping to the forefront of her mind. One with the two of them, naked and entwined around each other. Her heart flip-flopped at the chance to make it more than a fantasy, but her inexperience worried her and her eyelid refused to lift. "Of…hell, of doing things wrong."

A confused frown puckered his brow. "Cal? Agapi, look at me." After long seconds ticked by, her eyelids fluttered open. He held her gaze, his dark eyes of molten night locked with hers. "It is I who has already done things wrong. I have forced you into a corner from which your decisions may not be your own. I wanted only to ease your mind, to give you a chance at something real, something more than you had thought possible for yourself. Instead, my brash foolishness may well have doomed you to a life you do not desire. How could you do anything more wrong than that?"

"I don't think you did anything wrong. But…" She squirmed nervously under the intensity of his stare. "What if…" Exhaling in a huff, she poured her deepest fear out in a rapid string of syllables.

"What if I don't make you happy? I mean, you don't know. I could be horrible in bed, or maybe I snore or leave the cap off the toothpaste? You might have gotten the proverbial short end of the stick forever and—"

Her protestations ended as his warm laughter curled up her body, soothing and promising. She fought to keep the corners of her mouth pulled down. "I'm serious, Galen. What if I'm not the person you think I am?" Even in the cocoon of mirth, she felt her eyes brim with panicked tears.

"My sweet muse." With an easy sweep of his arms, he carried her down to the bed, resting his massive form alongside her lean body. The soft cool sheets did nothing to staunch the heat radiating from her skin. "Have you forgotten I can see into your mind? I know the person you are. As long as you are by my side when each day ends, I don't care about anything else. I can recap toothpaste and I am certain you don't snore. And as for the rest of your question…" His gaze grew hungry, fixating on her lips before climbing back to lock with her eyes. "With what I have already seen, pleasure looks very good on you and I would love to see you draped in it."

"Oh." The word was merely a breath as a pink rush painted her cheeks and the corner of her bottom lip slipped between her teeth.

Galen sensed her conflicting emotions, her scent growing heavy and dark with anticipation and desire even as her naivety fueled her apprehension. Propped up on his elbow, he gently trailed his fingers along her arms, watching as goose bumps flowed in the wake of his touch. He wanted her to trust him so badly it truly caused him pain. Every breath he took drove his need to a fever pitch, but the idea of not drawing in her heady fragrance was no option. He lightly brushed his lips against her shoulder, flicking his tongue to taste her soft skin.

"You set the pace, Calliope. I will give you all the time in world if you wish me to." Nibbling his way to the graceful column of her throat, he tasted the salty skin covering her dancing pulse. "We will go only as far as you desire. Say the word and I will stop. I have waited a hundred lifetimes to find you. If you ask, I would gladly wait a thousand more."

She sunk deeper into the pillowy mattress as her eyes floated toward the back of her head. Her head lolled back as her spine bent, her lush breasts straining against the slippery fabric barrier.

"I probably would not be of any good to you if I waited that long, though." With a wicked grin, he nipped his way toward her ear. "For I do hope you wish your mate to please you in every way imaginable." He swirled his tongue along the delicate shell, growling at her breathy moan. "Because I plan on doing so, for a very long time."

He dragged his hand down her side and splayed his palm against her quivering midsection, the heat rising up through the black silk still covering her. His fingers made short work of the three remaining buttons, slipping free the final closure before peeling back the thin barrier and marveling at the creamy flesh before him. There was no hint of the yellowing bruising from her ordeal, only soft and perfectly toned skin met his eyes.

"*Theoí. Tóso ómorfo.*" Every inch of her was laid out for his eyes. Her full breasts and sleek muscular torso leading toward her narrow hips and the small patch of deep chocolate curls at the juncture of two lean strong legs. His pants remained on his body by the sheer willpower of the threads alone, although he swore he could hear the fabric groaning and fraying under the pressure of his straining cock.

The shy blush that warmed her cheeks fired his desires to a fever pitch as his mouth descended, burning away any of her lingering fears.

Growling, he covered her lips with his, thrusting his tongue into the soft recesses of her mouth. He caressed the curve of her hip with his free hand, following the path along her side, grazing her ribs before palming her perk breast. His fingers kneaded the yielding flesh, gaining hungry groans that he eagerly swallowed. He tore his mouth from hers as he licked and nibbled his way down her throat, nipping at her collarbone as he scooted further down. His lips seared a tempting trail down to her lush mounds. When his tongue flicked her peaked nipple, she cried out in a gasp, her fingernails digging into his shoulders.

"Yes, agapi. Let it go. Let it all go."

Cal writhed in anticipation, her skin was on fire and two sizes too small at the same time. Her back arched and bowed, hoping to entice his hands to caress more than her arm. His words had her head spinning in delicious circles. As long as he kept talking, he could be reading the friggin' phonebook for all she cared. That accent of his rumbled through her bones, weakened her knees, and dampened her panties in record time. She gripped his corded shoulders tightly as her legs slid slowly against each other.

A myriad of erotic and unknown sensations coursed through Cal's body, each one bringing her to greater heights than the one before. It was too much, yet not enough at the same time. Her breathing picked up its pace, racing to stay in time with her heart as it thumped out a jackhammer's rhythm. A coiling sensation centered deep in her gut pulsed and grew with each caress. His touch tantalized her as it traveled down her body, his strong deft fingers walking across her undulating hips before tunneling through the curls between her legs.

Heat, undeniable and all-consuming, rocketed through her veins and a strangled cry broke from her lips as the dam of desperate desire shattered, her slow building orgasm rippling through her as his fingers gently stroked the edges of her hot core. The part of her brain she had slammed into a closet so many years ago had broken down the door and now screamed for attention. It was this neglected part that controlled her arms as they pushed against his shoulders, guiding him further down her body.

His mouth added one final suckling pull against her sensitive nipple before leaving a trail of butterfly kisses along the flat path of her stomach. One hand stayed behind, rolling the hardened tip between his thumb and forefinger. He whirled his tongue in slow circles further and further down, her hips dancing in intuitively erotic gyrations. As his teeth grazed against her hipbones, she felt the deep rumble that vibrated through his chest and poured into her very soul as his mouth inched nearer her thatch of soft curls.

Her skin tingled with electricity as his skilled hands stroked and caressed her. The decadent weight of his body slightly atop hers was the only thing keeping her anchored to the bed, her body bucking uncontrollably, lost in the flood of feeling. His warm breath tickled places on her no other human had ever seen, much less touched. Words rattled around in her brain, but her tongue and lips had other plans. She wanted to tell him how good it felt, how he made her feel complete as no other had before, yet her body seemed bent on a different course, one craving nothing but touch and sensations. Her jaw swung on its hinge, her throat convulsing around inaudible sounds.

"We have no need for words, agapi. I can hear your thoughts and desires. You only need to let your imagination speak for you and I will do whatever you wish."

Dark, erotic images danced behind her eyes at his simple statement while her head dug back into the mattress. She clung to the solid olive flesh as her legs trembled in anticipation. Tender kisses tickled the inside of her thighs, his hands caressing the length of her body before gripping her hips.

"Calliope? Look at me."

His gentle urgings set her to lift her head and rest her weight on her elbows as her gaze traveled down her body to meet his wildly possessive gaze. She fought to keep her eyes riveted to his, her breath coming in short, anticipatory gulps as he slowly lowered his head and his mouth devoured her hot core.

For Cal, the world disappeared in a flash as her body shattered in a wash of sensation and lightning sped through her veins. He lifted her higher and held her captive to meet his urgent demands as jolts of fire centering at their joined lips threatened to consume her. Growling hungrily, his tongue licked and delved deep into her, savoring the sweet honey as it flowed from her.

Her eyes drifted shut, unable to remain focused on the devilish god feasting on the bounty between her legs. With each drag of his tongue, she thought she would ignite into flames if it weren't for the sweat pouring off her body. Her breaths were more ragged and shallow, her throat sore for the cries ripping from her soul the longer he laved her core. And she wanted more. Her arms flailed at her sides and her long fingers clawed first at the sheets before grasping at the broad shoulders between her thighs, hoping to find purchase in the rising storm of pleasure.

Sweat dripped between her breasts as the pleasure built once more, reaching toward another mind-shattering peak. Her mouth seemed incapable of rendering coherent words, so groans and sighs were her only way to communicate. Her muscles spasmed and clenched, her body lost in the waves of passion as the rough pad of his thumb stroked the pebble hard knot seated below her soft curls.

The building fire scorched her soul as he slipped one finger into her tight channel. Her eyes flew open as a deeper cry flew from her lips, her nails clutching the strong muscles that held her tethered to the earth.

His lips broke away from their intimate lovings, desire and hunger reflected in his rumbling voice. "Mine."

Her hips bucked and rocked, driving his touch further and deeper. "Oh, God yes. Please. Don't. Stop." Her words, laced with need, spilled from her, her hands clinging to his shoulders as her body trembled.

First one, then a second digit was sucked between her folds. Kisses fluttered along her skin and traveled their way up her writhing body, his mouth devoured her breast, her keening cries rising higher and higher. Her head tossed from side to side as his long fingers twisted and scissored deep inside her. When she thought she'd reached her limit, he dragged his lips back down and buried his face between her thighs.

She felt her heart pounding in her chest. It was bouncing on the trampoline of her lungs as they pumped the much-needed blood and air through her tingling limbs. Rational thought had disappeared the moment she felt his gentle invasion. Her body, acting on raw primitive instinct, dipped and arched, urging his fingers further inside her. She threaded her hands through his thick hair, gripping his head tightly. Biting her lip, she found nothing could contain her throaty and needful sounds as his masterful touch brought her again to a screaming, all-consuming orgasm.

She clung to him as she rode wave after powerful wave, time losing meaning until the world beyond her immediate sensations began to reappear. With her still-functioning brain cells, she fought to bring her heart rate back down to a somewhat non-marathon pace. Every nerve ending tingled, especially the ones centered between her legs and wherever his skin touched hers. Her lungs burned and quivered as she gulping down air, eager for its cooling sustenance.

Galen watched her closely, holding her as she rode out the rippling ecstasy, her fingers clawing and grasping as the wave overtook her a second time. He memorized the beautiful play of emotions dancing across her face as he continued to lap at the heady cream that flowed from her dripping core. His heart pounded in perfect synch with hers, only proving the strength of the bond he had forged. Carefully, he withdrew his fingers, her strong inner muscles reluctantly allowing him escape. She was so tight and he knew he would be painful for her to endure, his enormous shaft throbbing in earnest against his jeans. When he finally claimed her, her knew the grip alone would be enough to disarm him.

"God. That. Was…" The words tripped out on her exhalation, more breath than actual sound. Her chest heaved as breath after deep breath was dragged in. He wiped clean his chin with the palm of his hand before crawling up the length of her body. She still jumped at his light touch, her taut midriff dancing under his fingers.

Leaning in close, he pressed a kiss along the warm shell of her ear. "Only the beginning, my beautiful muse. Just a taste of what is to come." His whispered voice brought a heady moan in response, his straining erection weeping in frustrated anticipation. He gathered her limp limbs into an organized pile and draped her across his chest, swirling lazily patterns with his fingertips across her slick back.

"But after you rest from this first round, my love." His breath blew hot and cold against her damp hair. With one slow exhale, he stared up at the darkness above, a grin still playing upon his lips as sleep claimed her. He lingered awake until he was certain she was asleep.

"I pray you forgive me for this, agapi. But know my reasons are sound." Closing his eyes, he touched her temple, worming into her mind. A path into the Void had been opened and it was now his job to ensure it was forever sealed and guarded. Yet, as though he were in the room with him, he heard Eamon's voice echo in his ears, warning him off tampering any further.

Gnashing his teeth in his impotent frustration, he pulled back to himself, but not before setting a metaphysical bell on that door. Now, if de Coldreto tried to sneak in, he'd know it before too much damage was done. He reached out, brushing the short-cropped hair off her cheek as he drew the soft blanket around them. Assured he had done as much as he could for the moment, he exhaled one controlled breath and joined her in sleep.

CHAPTER SEVENTEEN

Crushing his cigarette against the heel of his boot, the mountainous shadow kicked off the wall. For the past two days, Emmett had been trailing the skinny fucker around the sprawling campus. His boss, Stefan, seemed to believe this little twat was somehow useful. Scoffing, he knew he'd make good mulch somewhere. That was the best he'd give the guy. Watching as the lime green tropical print moved easily through the throng of young academics, he kept an easy distance, since the students parted before him like the proverbial Red fucking Sea. He shook his head, his eyes dispassionate behind his glimmering wraparound shades. Cattle would always be cattle, and the predators, like him, would always cause them to run away like little fucking rabbits.

And back to the stuffy classrooms he went. With a disgusted growl, he waited as the flood of eager underclassmen flowed past him as he stood at the threshold. His presence caused one young lady to become so flummoxed she nearly spilled the entire contents of her bag in a struggle to clutch the pack closer.

The urge to growl and bare his teeth, proving himself to be the animal they all suspected him to be was almost undeniable.

Almost.

Instead, he simply stepped over her as she continued to mutter civil apologies. "Yeah, whatever," he grumbled as he left her scrambling to regain her composure. Jerking his head in all directions, he again caught sight of the fluorescent fabric as it slipped into a closing classroom door.

This is bullshit. This fucker ain't gonna be of any use at all. Ready to leave, he caught a glimpse of the hippie girlfriend of their quarry as she bounced into the room. Hmm. Maybe this wasn't as pointless as he first thought. Lingering back in the shadows as his mentor had taught him, he melted into the dark and listened.

The bubble-headed blonde with the somewhat hot body spoke in agitated tones, gesturing wildly, her finger jabbing into the other guy's chest numerous times. Boy, she was sure worked up over something. Narrowing his gaze at the pair, he stared harder at their mouths, willing the words to come into his ears.

"…and he was a perfect gentleman! You made me think some monster had snatched her out of the skies!"

Holy fuck! This shit works!

"How can you be sure he isn't? She could be brainwashed by him. Come on, Maggie. We know nothing, I mean, *nothing* about this guy. I've just been so worried and then when I saw her on the street, looking two steps away from death's door." A gasp made Emmet laugh. *Damn, fucker's laying this shit on thick. Color me impressed.* "You saw the guy. He's a giant. God only knows what he could have done to her by now."

"Oh dear. She looked fine when she stopped by to get some clothes. Oh, did I do the wrong thing?"

"I sure hope not. Did she say where she was staying? A phone number, some way to get a hold of her? Anything?"

The blonde ropes swung right and left as she wrung her hands, obviously sick with worry. "No. Well, not really. I mean, I think she might still have her phone with her. But then she would have called me or at least answered all the messages I gave her when she was gone before. I mean I texted, I called, I e-mailed…"

Emmett rolled his eyes. *Jesus Fucking Christ on a cracker. Could that bitch talk any more about nothing?* He folded his beefy arms across his chest as she continued to drone on. Tuning back in, he hoped the motormouth had reached some kind of point.

"…but he seemed like such a nice guy and he didn't let her really out of his sight. Are you sure he's a danger to her?"

"Well, I just don't think either of us should let her disappear without a way to find her. Or at least to be able to check on how she's doing. I know you're her friend and are only concerned about her, right?"

Emmett gave a begrudging nod. Fucker was slick and she was eating it up.

"Please, Maggs, let me know if she contacts you. Please. She is my colleague and more than that, I…I care for her deeply. If anything happened to her, I don't think I could bear it." He touched her hand, squeezing her fingers reassuringly. "Here, here's my number again. Just in case. Thanks so much."

A moment passed and the dreadlocked hippie nodded like a bobble head and flounced down the hall. Emmett stood silent as she walked beyond his vantage point, the clinging stench of patchouli following in her wake. Well, he didn't learn anything, other than the weasel actually might be of some use. He watched for a little longer, waiting to see if anything exciting happened.

The students continued to file into the room as his object of observation took out his cell, his fingers flying over the screen before a cruel smile formed on his lips. The phone disappeared, but the creepy-ass grin remained.

Twenty minutes later, after the start of a boring lecture about something he couldn't begin to give two shits about, he kicked out of the alcove and headed out of the building. His phone vibrated, the text read, "coz r u in 4 2nite?" A wicked grin slides across his face. After this little tidbit of good news, he could afford to take some time fucking around. He'd earned a few drinks and a good solid fuck. His feet led him away from the bricked-in eggheads and all that liberal shit.

"Fuck yeah, I'm in," he mumbled as he sent his response. "hellz ya c u @ shortyz." Taking out another smoke, he continued down the tiled hall. He had barely made it out the main doors when the blonde raced past him again, heading back toward the classroom. *What the fuck, girl?*

The scent of incense and fear laced the air, making his stomach growl and his mouth water. *Fuck, this shit got interesting.* He took a step back into the shadows and resumed his listening duties as she barged into the classroom. Once again, he tuned into station K-BMBO and waited for something important.

"*They took Ajax!*" Her voice squeaked shrilling as the door whooshed closed behind her. He frowned. Ajax? You mean like the cheap-ass shit his grandma used to use to clean the sinks? He dared a closer look and moved down the hall.

And he wasn't the only one. Her panicked cry caught the attention of anyone still wandering the hall, not to mention every dog in a three-mile radius. The door opened again, this time, she was being comforted by the beanpole. Hmm. Ducking into the nearest dark corner, he amped up his hearing again, needing to catch this convo.

Hysterical sobs.

"Calm down, Maggs. Who took Ajax?"

More hysterical sobs.

"Maggie." The voice had the same power like his boss was teaching him to do. Nice. Good to know that shit worked too. "I need you to calm down and tell me what happened."

The sobs stopped, but now neither of them were saying anything. Fuck. Were they making out or what?

"Oh my God. Have you called the police yet?"

Shit. They must be reading a text message.

"It's not safe for you to stay by yourself. Come on, you'll stay with me tonight. I insist."

More blubbering broke the air and it was gaining in volume, getting closer and closer to him. He let the pair pass by before stepping out behind them, his footfalls silent as he crept in their wake.

"It's OK, Maggs. I'll take you someplace safe." The twig actually turned his head around, looking through the halls for a sign of someone to stop him or question his motives. He stepped into the light as the guy gave him a sharp nod, evil glinting off the blue in the guy's eyes.

Emmet nodded coolly as he tailed them around the corner of the building. Had to give the guy props. He didn't think the little shit would be of any use, but it seemed the fucker was more devious than he gave him credit for. Sending the bitch a message saying her boyfriend had been nabbed. Damn. That was some cold-ass shit there.

Grumbling, he lagged behind as they went up one street and down another. Block after block kept passing under his feet, moving him further from Tenderloin he called home. He followed as the pair closed in on the boss's Victorian place on Stater Street, its whitewashed walls and picket fence hiding the dank evil that dwelt within. A dark chuckle slipped between his lips as they disappeared into the house. Yeah. Shit was getting real now.

The lighter half-forgotten in his palm flared to life as the first scream rang out in the night. His teeth clamped down on the end of his cigarette, puffing the rich smoke as he laughed and headed back to meet up with the rest of his crew, figuring he could get one quick fuck in before he got called in to help with the bitch.

Two bitches in one night. This evil ass shit rocked.

CHAPTER EIGHTEEN

Galen awoke with a start, his hand snapping out as his fingers wrapped tightly around the throat of the figure looming over his bed. Half a heartbeat passed as he took in his surroundings. He exhaled heavily, releasing his hold on who he now recognized as Eamon.

"*Theós mou.* You trying to give me a heart attack?" Slipping his arm free from the sleeping beauty next to him, he extricated himself from the tangled sheets. One final brush of his lips across her forehead and he motioned Eamon out of the bedroom. As he started down the stairs, he grumbled under his breath. "So what the hell is so important you had to wake me from a lovely dream, I might add?" The smells of coffee spiraled up as they descended.

Eamon smiled the moment he watched the nose crinkle in appreciation. "Figured I'd at least ply ya with coffee to make up for it."

As they approached the aromatic liquid, Galen found his thoughts growing more and more troubled. An early morning visit from Eamon could only mean one thing and it wasn't he was getting a raise. He quietly accepted the steaming mug before him.

"How are ya holdin' up?" Eamon's question seemed innocent enough, but Galen knew better. Nothing Eamon ever did was casual or without importance.

"That all depends. How long had you been in the room?" The aromatic mist wafted up, clearing away the lingering fog in his head. Granted, the memories of his evening with Cal locked in his arms were in the foreground of his mind. If Eamon had been able to get the jump on him, things were in more dire straits than he wanted to consider. When the silence lengthened, a grumbling string of profanities in his native tongue filled the air. "It's started, hasn't it? Fuck. I can't force her to take me. If this is to be my end, then—"

"Don't give me that honorable warrior shit, Greek." Menacing power dripped from the harsh words, Eamon's blue eyes turning to pools of dangerous ice. "This is a war and I cannot afford to lose a soldier because he's got cold feet. Ever wonder how they knew she was your spiritmate?"

The wooden island pressed into the small of Galen's back as he collapsed against it. "I have been asking myself the same damned question. I mean, no one's ever tried to figure out about the women we are drawn toward. Do they all have similar heritages or genetics? By all the gods, man. I couldn't have dreamed of a more perfect match. And you say Kai's female is his anchor as well." Sighing, he set down the cup for fear of wearing the scalding brew, his hands tangling in his sleep-tousled hair. He started with two strides, but soon he was pacing laps around the spacious kitchen, his thoughts ahead of his feet by a few miles.

Eamon shook his head and folded his arms across his bare chest. "Boyo, y'aren't listenin' to the question I asked. Not askin' 'bout all them. Of course, the strong ones're the ones more suited to handle the likes of us. Have ya been tryin' to figure how Stefan *knew* she was your mate? There are, what, a few billion females on the planet, and he just plucked yours out of the phonebook?"

"I know. I know!" His voice hissed as he closed the distance between them. "They had her for a week. A full fucking seven days. He knew her name, where she could be found. How the *fuck* could he know that when I didn't even know about her?" Fighting the desire to howl at the rage in his heart, his voice sunk into a growl, frustration punctuating each syllable.

Eamon leveled his bright blue eyes at him. "He knew because— Damn, can't believe I have to say this. All right, boyo. Stefan knew because he was one of us." He paused as Galen let his jaw drop. Leaning back against the countertop, Eamon rested his hands flat on the cool surface. "Yeah, time to come clean. Stefan was a Guardian. Remember the lessons 'bout free will and choosin' sides? Yeah, well. He started with us. He's an Oracle." Shifting his eyes to meet the expected stare of disbelief, he raised his hands as he shook his head.

"The real deal, boyo, not the TV bullshit 'I see the future.' Figured he'd be a good asset, right? Well, too bad for us his heart was too full of darkness and the Rogues made quick work of his desire to rule. He switched sides 'round about the time of the ascension of the Borgias." He took a fortifying gulp of his coffee. "So, he only needed to wait until the visions told him the spiritmate of any of us and then he'd…kill 'em."

Galen's eyes narrowed. "Wait. So he's done this before? He's peeked behind the curtain, grabbed a name and…and fucking slaughtered some innocent soul to keep his side on top? Fuck me." How many others had he killed? How many of his fellow Guardians had he condemned to death, or even worse? The rage he felt was becoming a tangible force, dimming the lights in the hallway. "He has to die."

Eamon barked out a mirthless laugh. "Ya think now, do ya? Not that ya don't have my vote on the whole idea, but don't ya think it's been tried?"

"Not by me." His answer was laced with venom and vengeance. This man had tried to deny him his future and almost extinguished the life of his beautiful mate. He no longer deserved the right to draw breath. "Not by me."

Folding his arms across his chest, Eamon met his friend's fierce stare with an equally unmoving gaze. "No. Too risky. You're staying out of this one."

Galen's anger drove him right into Eamon's calm face. "So you expect me to stand idly by while he continues to search for her, or wait until he moves on to the next target?"

"I expect you to pull your head outta your ass and *think*. He found her once, right? Tell me this, what's to stop him from finding her again? Who's to say he doesn't already have a bloody army of informants combing the damned city for her. And for you, as well. You. Have. To. Think." Eamon struggled to keep his voice calm. "You think you're the only one who wants to see Stefan's blood flowing like rivers for all the lives he'd destroyed? But to do that, we have to find him first."

"We?" Galen narrowed his eyes for what he knew to be more fun and fucked up news.

"I've contacted Kai. He should be here by morning, probably with his mate as well." Eamon snapped his hand up, stopping any further discussion on the matter as Galen threw both of his up in mute rage. "This needs more hands than yours alone. This ends now."

Galen opened his mouth to argue he could protect his own mate, but the unyielding blue eyes offered no room for discussion. He picked out a strange, errant thought from Eamon. *Damn the consequences this time.* Gritting his teeth together and tamping down his headstrong nature, he snarled out his demand. "I *will* take the final blow. That honor is mine."

And so began the silent battle of wills. Years of commanding troops had given Galen the advantage of knowing how to stand and menace without much effort. His arms draped low across his chest, the tension in his shoulders climbing higher as he prepared for a fight. Power dripped down his skin, calling the hairs along his arms to stand at attention as his force leaked across the gap between him and Eamon.

The seconds ticked by and the pictures on the walls began to rattle. A minute down and the windows groaned. The air sizzled between them, the true force of each Guardian Warrior's strength growing until it became a palpable entity, threatening to consume anything stupid enough to still be in the same room. Galen even swore he could smell smoke as the temperature climbed up notch by notch. Sweat beaded on his forehead, more proof that his powers were indeed beginning to diminish and a glance to his opponent showed the same recognition. One strong push from Eamon and he would be on his knees.

"Do you two plan on the continuing this Mexican stand-off all night or just until your shorts catch fire?"

The sleepy mumbles from behind him took all the wind out of his sails, his shoulders drooping a fraction of an inch as he glanced toward the doorway at his back. "I am sorry to have woken you, agapi."

Still rubbing the sleep out of her eyes, Cal shuffled her way to the only thing in her tunnel-visioned mind. Coffee. But before her hand reached the key to her morning salvation, the pot vanished. Drawing her brows together, she stared in mute frustration at the empty space until a steaming mug crossed the plane of her bleary eyes. A sleep-drunk smile warmed her face as she gratefully accepted the gift from the java gods.

"Well, since it's technically mornin', I guess we did continue it all night."

The lilting voice caught her befuddled attention. Looking up, she blinked at the disarming smile above her. Spiky cooper-hued hair shaded a pair of the bluest eyes she had ever seen. Her jaw fell open as her brain fought to create intelligible word sounds.

As she gawked, the GQ model's laughter blended in cacophonous harmony with the deeply possessive growls coming from behind her.

"Eamon?" The single word hissed through clenched teeth as Galen snaked an arm around her waist, stepping forward to cover the distance, ending only when her ass was nestled against his groin. With a perplexed frown, she glanced over her shoulder, ping-ponging her gaze between the two alpha males trying to assert dominance over the situation until peals of laughter from the lilting stranger filled the room.

"Sorry, boyo. She just looks so cute wearin' your shirt like a dress there. Couldn't pass it up." The easy tone in his voice did little to hide the steel in his piercing blue eyes. She had interrupted something, but the discussion was far from over, judging by the look in both of their eyes.

"That may be, but I still can't have you bewitching her with your practiced charms." He inclined his head toward their guest. "Calliope, this is Eamon. Eamon was just leaving."

Cal rolled her eyes as the primitive display carried on. Cocking her hip, she rested against the counter top to better watch both their faces. "Geez. What is it with you? Look, I'm not some prize in a Cracker Jack box. I'm a grad student working on a very dry Master's thesis in shit the rest of the academic world forgot. And I'm suddenly a hot commodity? Nah, I don't buy it." She shook her head before taking a sip from the mug in her hands. "Now, someone had better tell me what I need to do to get these creeps off my back and out of my head or you're *all* going to find out just how non-helpless I really am."

She gave them her best glare, but standing toe to toe with two behemoths of pure ancient male warrior, she came up a bit short. Still, she did have an older brother and enough martial arts training to hold her own if she got cornered. She stood silent as the two men regarded her coolly. With a perturbed huff, she stomped out of the kitchen, long strides taking her quickly away from the testosterone poisoning.

Galen growled, starting after her before Eamon put a hand on his arm. His eyes locked with Eamon's narrowed gaze as he shook his head. "She's got a point there, boyo. She needs to know."

"Know what? That I might not be able to protect her as I should. She's already faced those fuckers and…I will not put her in any more danger."

"I can hear you guys. You know that, right?" Her voice rang down the hallway from the living room where she stood, staring out into the filtered daylight cityscape and out to the bay. Opting to keep her back to them, she held the warm mug under her nose, dragging in the head-clearing aroma. Why did men get it into their heads all females were weak and in need of protection? She managed to survive all this time without one, and just one little kidnapping and torture session, plus God only knew what was going on with her dreams, and *now* she fell into the damsel in distress category?

A set of hands on her shoulders drew her out of her grumblings. "And we can hear you as well, agapi." Her chin met her chest, cringing as strong hands turned her away from the silent lights beyond the glass. She wished she had the strength to break away from his gentle hold, but her traitorous body was too ensnared by him to offer any real resistance. Her gaze crawled past the carved chest, making the journey to the destination she sought. A tired smile curled the edge of his full lips, warming the dark depths of his eyes. "And you *do* need protection. I know you not weak, but even the strong are smart enough to know when assistance is needed."

As if on cue, a sharp rap on the front door broke the mood, drawing her attention to the sound. Her eyebrow arched up as she met his exasperated growl. "You expecting company?"

"As a matter of fact, *he* is." The carefree lilting voice rang out from the kitchen as Eamon headed for the entryway. "He's gonna be takin' a bit of the advice he just gave ya now." The door swung open and another giant stood at the entryway.

What the hell? Did this group have some kind of height requirement? The lethal power of this newcomer told her he was indeed a force to be reckoned with. He stood shoulder to shoulder with Eamon, long dark hair held back in a loose ponytail away from a face of pure masculine beauty with a body wrapped loosely in black linen. But the skin was paler than Galen and the eyes seemed almost unreal in their pale green hue. Cal blinked a couple times to make sure she wasn't hallucinating this latest runaway male model as he shook hands with Eamon, flashing a dazzling smile of perfectly white teeth.

The growl behind her drew her gaze. Galen narrowed his eyes as his arm wound tightly around her shoulder, pulling her back against his chest.

"Vadim," his head giving the slightest nod toward the other man.

"Alexiou." The response was equally as sharp.

For a second time, she rolled her eyes at the ridiculous territorial pissing contest only inches away from leaking out onto the beautiful hardwood flooring. "Oh, for chrissake." Wriggling her arm free, he reached out and forced herself to cross the distance, wearing Galen as a very irritated coat. "Hi, I'm Cal, resident troublemaker and the source of your visit, I'm sure. It's nice to meet you." Her smile was genuine, earning her a bout of laughter from her approaching target.

"Damn, and I thought my mate was direct." Dazzling was a weak descriptor of the smile directed toward her as a huge hand engulfed hers. Without hesitating, he raised her hand to his lips, brushing his lips softly against her knuckles.

"I am Malakai Vadim and I am pleased to meet you as well." The man sure knew how to turn on the charm, but she did catch the word "mate" in his previous statement, couched within a faint accent that belied an Eastern European origin.

This time, her back vibrated with the rumbling growl from the warrior pressed close enough to be her second skin. The space around her chilled a degree or two as the two men locked eyes.

Eamon threw his head back, roaring in laughter and drew all eyes as he leaned back against the wall. "So glad to see some things never change with the two of ya." He peered over Malakai's shoulder. "Siobhan, darlin'. How did ya manage to fit both you and his ego in the car to get here, anyway?"

"It was a tight squeeze, I'll tell you that much," the answer emanated from behind the well-dressed warrior. Cal watched as a tiny girl emerged, jabbing her elbow into the other man's rib cage. She was lithe and moved with such grace Cal felt a little like one of

Cinderella's gawking stepsisters in comparison. Thick, dark curls were pinned hastily off the nape of her neck, and the crooked smile on her face caused the light to dance in her hazel eyes. The young girl held out her hand, chuckling as her warrior placed a hand on her shoulder. "Don't worry, you'll get used to their over-bearing natures. And please, call me Voni."

After giving her hand a good squeeze, *it's nice to see a girl who knows how to shake hands,* Cal watched as an arm appeared over her shoulder to do the same. Quirking a brow, she turned to Galen with questioning eyes. "You haven't met?"

Galen shook his head as he stepped around his confused beauty to raise Voni's hand to his forehead, pressing it to the back of her hand. "Well met, Siobhan." Returning his attention to Cal, he smiled warmly. "I knew of Kai's spiritmate, but had not yet met her." When he lifted his gaze, he locked eyes with the piercing pale green of a fellow warrior. Swallowing back on the domineering pride threatening to choke him, he whispered the words caught in his throat.

"Malakai, I thank you for your offer of aid." Galen brought his fist to cover his heart as he bowed his head. A hand on his shoulder prompted his eyes to lift. Warmth and understanding replaced the earlier envisioned disdain.

"To save those who save us, brother, no offer will ever be ignored." Both warriors stood toe-to-toe, years of battle-honed skills boiled down and concentrated, taking the form of two men now fighting for one female, one who held the key to a brother's soul. Galen nodded slowly, with great reverence before stepping back to once again stand at Cal's back.

"Well, now," a lilting voice broke the tension with a chuckle. "As much of a touchin' moment this is, we do have a bit of problem to be handlin', in case ya'd forgotten."

Galen nodded swiftly. "De Coldreto is using his skills as an Oracle to find potential Guardian spiritmates and killing them, ensuring the demise of the gods only know how many of our brother Warriors. And he's using human pawns to further his plans."

"You sure about this? I know these fuckers are devious, but…shit." Kai breathed the last word as he shook his head, his arm tightening around his own mate, drawing her a little closer to him. "That bastard needs to be put into the ground. Like, now."

As the men muttered about plans and tactics, Cal looked over at the other girl in the room. She stared the petite female as Voni listened intently, her intelligent eyes absorbing each mumbled word. Sighing, she turned her attention to the rest of the room, hoping to find something that made some sense. Some way for her to help. All around her, she saw ancient weapons, reminders of centuries of battle-tested strategies. A few of the weapons had seen much better days, attesting to strong foes and hard won fights. Yet, the longer she stared, the more one word spun in her mind.

"Waterloo."

She whispered the word, her gaze roaming as her feet joined in the path, slipping out from Galen's embrace and seeking out each piece of battered armor and every saw-edged blade. "That's it. It's pride."

Galen froze mid-word, his jaw hanging agape as Cal hurried back to the group, his brows pulling together in a confused frown. "What?"

"Pride goeth before the fall," she muttered to herself as he headed back to the group, bouncing excitedly from foot to foot as she stood before the hulking men. "You said this…this de Caprio guy is using his Superman vision to find the girls, right?" Her hands fluttered as her ideas spilled from her head. "So he knows he's right, right? Knows it without a doubt, right?"

"De Caprio? That guy from Titanic?" Kai asked, one eyebrow arched over his impossible green eyes. The hint of a smirk creased the corners of Eamon's mouth.

Galen shrugged a shoulder carelessly, the growl in his voice tempered by the mirth of his words. "If only we'd been so lucky for this fucker to go down with the ship. No such luck, huh?" With a warm smile, he turned his attentions back to her. "A little off, agapi, but I think I'm following your logic. Yes, he does believe himself to be infallible. You believe his pride will be his undoing?"

Cal's short black hair bobbed as she grinned, nodding her head emphatically. "Call it a gut instinct. That asshat who tried to jump me in the collections room had the same misogynistic, alpha male crap attitude. They *know* the world will do just what they want it to. That is how we'll beat them." The longer she talked, the more sense it made to her. She was just bait, the Warrior before her, and others like him, were the true targets. Her gaze locked with Galen's, his eyebrows tugged together, cutting a deep furrow across his forehead. She reached her hand out, resting her fingers lightly against his arm. "Galen, you yourself told me you were able to defeat Darius the Lesser because he was overconfident, right? He thought he had all the cards?"

Her gaze shifted, taking in the expressions of all the parties in the room. Eamon's amazing blue eyes sparkled with a curious light. The two newcomers stood in silence, their thoughts a mystery to her, but every subtle gesture between them spoke to her heart with only one word.

Love.

The tender, yet protective way his arm curled around her tiny frame, keeping her close even in this semi-friendly environment. Galen was offering the same measure of belonging, but still she balked. Her dreams had never included another person, ever. And now?

Raised voices pulled her out of her reverie and she shook her head, dragging her focus back to the room. The masculine interplay ebbed and flowed as the men gestured boisterously, further animating the deepening discussion. Her gaze gravitated to Galen, his thick bare arms folded across his chest, jaw set in defiance. Eamon's blue eyes were locked with his, fiercely trying to calm the anger she could feel building.

Voni tapped her lightly on the shoulder, a knowing half smile on her lips as she motioned her away from the men and into the kitchen. "Trust me on this one, they'll be at this for a while. So, how about a little coffee or whatever else we can find in here?" As Cal followed her, she watched as the petite girl gracefully reached up, grabbing two cups from the cabinet, her weight precariously balanced on the very tip of one sneaker. Moving quickly, she jumped to catch what she thought was going to be the falling mugs. Instead, the other female simply lowered down with such ease it was breathtaking.

"So, how long have you known Galen?" Voni turned to meet her surprised and wide-eyed stare. She laughed as she filled the mugs. "It's not that much of an amazing feat. Be short for as long as I have and you learn how to reach the top shelf pretty quickly."

Cal shook her head to reactivate her mouth. "If I had even tried that, not only would I have broken both the mugs, I probably would've done a number on myself and the rest of the kitchen too. Are you a dancer or something?" She gazed in fascination as Voni jumped nimbly to sit on the counter, still sipping her coffee.

"Or something? Wow. Haven't heard that in a while. And yeah, I do dance. Trained in ballet for waaay too many years but just recently switched my focus to a more contemporary bend." Her legs swung as she flashed an easy smile. "But, you and Galen? Tell me. How did you meet?"

Cal fidgeted with her mug, her finger tracing spirals along the white porcelain. "That. Um, yeah, well." She found her eyes even more restless than her hands, her gaze darting around the pristine kitchen. "We, uh, just…"

Voni offered her a knowing smile and leaned forward, resting her elbows on her knees. "Kai saved me from, well, from my darkest hour. I was trying to kill myself."

Shock popped Cal's eyes met wide at her heartfelt admission. Voni smiled, nodding her head. "Yup. Standing on the bridge and everything. He's been the best thing that ever happened to me."

"I was…being tortured," the words came out in a hushed whisper, so faint Voni leaned closer to hear. "I…I didn't know why I'd been grabbed at the time. They kept on talking about, well, about things I now understand. But at the time, I tried to tell them they made a mistake, but then…" She paused, a heavy sigh filling the gap. "Then Galen swooped in and rescued me."

Voni sighed sympathetically and offered a comforting smile. "Kinda funny how they still need to play hero, isn't it?"

Cal found herself liking the other girl. A lot. Even though she originally thought her to be so much younger than her, now she wasn't so sure. Now she felt like the child. "Yeah. Definitely is gonna take some getting used to."

Feeling the tension ease a fraction, Voni smiled as she sipped at the coffee. "That it does. And I've only been around these guys for a few months. I guess after so many years of swinging swords, thumping their chests, and getting their brains beat in has reverted them permanently to Cro–Magnon standards."

Cal coughed to stop herself from drowning in her coffee, laughing as she wiped off the escaping caffeinated goodness dripping onto the T-shirt serving as her current wardrobe. Voni joined her, her deep throaty laughs blending with the lighter tones before she continued with her gentle inquiry. "Yeah, I've never been much into the whole politically correct crap. But back to you. Do you have any idea who 'they' were, or are?"

As Cal leaned back to rest her elbows on the counter, she shook her head slowly, the smile faint, yet still present. "You know, I've been trying to figure that out. Not to mention how they even knew how to find me. I mean, it's not like I announce what my daily schedule is. I guess I could have been followed, but why? Yeah, I get the whole chosen one kinda stuff now, but beforehand? It was as if someone had told them…what…my…" Her words slowed as a stray thought crept into the back of her mind. With a groan, she dropped her head into her hand. "Maggs, not again."

"Maggs?" Voni paused, her gaze darting over toward the male gathering on the other side of the room before she took a sip.

Cal nodded slowly, sighing with an exasperated chuckle. "Yeah, she's my roommate. She's a bit of a… Well, she can be a little flaky at times. I love her to pieces, don't get me wrong. But, sometimes, she always sees the best in *everyone*." She shook her head slowly as she looked around for a phone to use.

The men had been discussing in hushed whispers the best strategies to draw the Rogues out into the open when Kai chimed in with a strange non sequitur. "Who's Maggs?"

Galen frowned, his mouth agape as the question hit him mid-word. "She's Cal's roommate. Why?"

Kai shrugged in response. "Voni wanted me to ask."

"When we stopped at her apartment, I did sense a lingering trace of the Void, both inside the home and within her friend as well. She's a bit naïve. But Cal seemed quite upset when she mentioned being visited by a strange man who seemed to think he had a claim to her. The man was off, and had I more sense about me at the time, I would have realized this, but I was…"

"Preoccupied." The single word was voiced simultaneously by all three men, even though each gave it an individual intonation. Eamon's friendly admonishment melded with Kai's sympathetic understanding, Galen adding a tinge of possessive hunger to the mix.

With a resigned nod, Galen did a quick review of the events on the street corner.

"The man definitely had more than his toe in the pool of the darkness. Could have been a recruit they were still working on."

A gasp from the other side of the room grabbed their attention, all heads snapping over to where Cal staggered back, the phone slipping from her trembling fingers. Galen sprinted the short distance, catching her as she collapsed to the ground, his other hand grabbing the phone before it hit. As he held the phone to his ear, mournful, tormented wails echoed behind dark laughter.

"Who is this? What sick fuck kind of game are you playing?" he growled, his anger slipping through the connection with ease. The laughter was cut short on the other end as what he assumed was another speaker took the phone.

"Ah, Galen. How nice of you to finally answer my call. Didn't you get my other message?"

He shook, his hand nearly crushing the innocent electronic device. "De Coldreto." Soon he was flanked by the other Warriors, each of their expressions intense and captive. "If you call torturing females a message, then you need to learn how to use a fucking computer. E-mail is much neater and easier on your henchmen budget. Exactly how many fucktards have you lost so far?" One look toward Eamon and he gave a sharp nod, yanking out his phone, hastily pushing buttons as he moved away from the current conversation.

"You think you are so amusing, Greek. I—"

"Oh, I know I am fucking hilarious. You should hear me on open mic night." He glanced over to Eamon, watching as his friend spoke frantically to a voice on the other end. As they caught eyes, Eamon spun his hand around in fast tight circles. With a nod, Galen went back to his taunting. "I can really bring down the house with stories about what a bunch of pussies the Romans were. And I've got a great one about Nero."

"You seek to bait me? Well, soon you will see that I do hold all the cards this time." A weak cry whimpered through the phone, turning to a howl of pain before the line went dead. He shot a look toward Eamon, who sighed heavily and shook his head.

Galen glared at Voni as he held his trembling mate. "What happened?"

Voni shook her head as Kai moved to stand at her back. "I don't know. We were just talking and she needed a phone to call her friend and then…" She shrugged sadly. "I'm sorry."

"Maggs. They've got Maggs. They…they…." Cal stared at nothing, her eyes wide and unfocused as she clung onto Galen's arm. "It…it was Paul who answered her phone. He…" Her breath quickened, her eyes slamming shut to try to stem the tears filling her eyes. *"Goddamn you, you fucking sonofabitch!"*

Galen rubbed soothing circles on her back, growling. "Don't think about it, agapi."

"How can't I? Fucking hell, I *heard* her screaming in the background. I can't leave her there. I can't. I can't…" Her eyes flew open, leveling her furious green eyes at the crowd of testosterone. "She's not strong, Galen, not like me. She doesn't believe people in this goddamned world are bad. I know what that'll do to her. And Ajax. Fuck!" She shoved her way out of his arms and scrambled toward the door. "I have to find Ajax. He's gotta know."

"Calliope. Stop." Galen's voice was soft yet firm, brokering no argument as his hands gripped her shoulders, stopping her frantic movements. "We will find him. You need to stay-"

"No!" Her eyes were wild with self-loathing and despair. "They are not going to kill her!" She grabbed onto his wrists, tears streaming unchecked in angry rivers down her flushed cheeks while she fought to break his hold on her. "You saw her, Galen. You know these people and what they're capable of. Tell me I'm wrong. Tell. Me!"

Unable to say the words she needed to hear, Galen pulled her struggling body tight into the shelter of his arms, pinning her to his chest. He pressed his lips against the top of her head as she sobbed uncontrollably. "I'm sorry, agapi. I am so sorry." His heart stuttered and cracked as she sagged in his embrace.

Eamon leveled his eyes to Kai, watching as the warrior held his mate close by, offering her comfort. "This has to stop." His thoughts spun as he mentally cursed his only living family member. *"Cabal, you fucking bastard."* The ring of dark chilling laughter was his answer. Swallowing the urge to call him onto this plane, he turned his attentions back to the room as it stood, both of his strong Guardians comforting their troubled spiritmates.

"Malakai. You have been brought here to fight this menace. As you have yet to hand over the mantel to your successor, you cannot lead where this path must go and your mate will be of more use in our fight. Do you give your wordbond, consenting to her the right to choose?" Gone was the playful lilt, and in its place was the unyielding authoritative tone of one who was used to being obeyed. The shift caught Kai off guard, his eyebrows pulling together in confusion. Eamon didn't give him a chance to second-guess his question. His hand clamped onto Kai's shoulder, his piercing blue eyes reached into the pale green eyes and bored straight into his heart.

"Do you consent?"

Kai coiled his arm tighter around Voni's narrow shoulders, sheltering her in his embrace as his jaw worked in silence. He glared back at Eamon, a deep, possessive grumble serving as an answer.

Eamon spoke again, his words measured and powerful. "Do. You. Consent?" His hand slid from his shoulder to grip the back of Kai's neck, leaning forward as he pressed his forehead against the furrowed brow of his friend, his arm bunching to the point of pain. This time, the words crept out in a desperate and harsh whisper. "You know I would not ask if there were another course." He would force the answer he needed out of him if he must, even at the risk of their friendship.

His friend stood his ground, every muscle in his body locked. Eamon sensed the strong urge for Kai to pull Voni behind his back, the protective drive worthy of a true Guardian Warrior. Eamon hated the Scylla and Charybdis choice, but they were running out of time.

Not wasting another second, Eamon swiveled his head down, his stormy blue eyes capturing the confused honey brown of his friend's fledgling spiritmate. Although only recently coming into her powers as a Conduit, she showed great potential and a sharp mind. "Siobhan, there is need of your Conduit skills. Will you join in this foray?"

She blinked several times, her gaze ping-ponging between him and Kai. He knew she had never seen this side of him, but there was too much in the balance to play nice. Eamon kept his gaze neutral as he watched the wheels turning behind her hazel eyes. She shifted her gaze to the other pair in the room. Then she straightened her shoulders, lifting her chin in more of a show of courage rather than to gain any height advantage in this crowd.

"I will." Her voice was clear and without hesitation.

"No. I won't allow it. You don't have to do this. I can... *we* can take this fucker down without putting our mates in the line of fire. I'm not about to put her in danger again." Kai felt the words tripping out of his mouth faster than his heart could form them, his head shaking frantically. His eyes narrowed into dangerous slits, the venom a tangible force as it crept across the tiny space separating him and his mate from the rest of the group.

Voni spun around to face him. Reaching her hand up, her fingers brushed his cheek, shattering his primal display as she tenderly pulled his focus to meet hers. He wanted to drown in her warm hazel depths and protect her from the monsters and demons in his own head. She stroked his stubbled chin, her smile taking a good chunk of the wind out of his sails.

"This is my choice, Kai. I can do some real good. I can help." With a gentle nudge, she pointed his gaze toward the mirror image of the embraced lovers on the opposite side of the room. *"Kai, you know what he's going through. If someone could have stepped in and helped, wouldn't you have wanted that? I can help her. Please. I know I can."*

He remained still, his gaze fixed on Galen and his newly discovered mate. He heaved a heavy and resigned sigh the instant before his lips descended, burning his claim onto her soul as his kiss took on a hungered quality. Cupping the back of her head, holding her in place as he molded his body around hers, he felt the tickle of long lashes across his cheek as her eyes drifted shut. As he poured his love and his apprehension into her, she answered him with compassion and a strength forged by her unending devotion.

An aching groan slipped from his lips as he ended the kiss. Unwilling to completely break the spell, he slowly raised his eyes, intent on the petite beauty in his arms as he spoke to the room, his words aimed toward Eamon.

"Any harm comes to her and I swear by all the gods of old, I will hunt you down and no one, not even the best forensic expert will be able to identify the remains." His gaze remained fixed on her, his fingers slipping through the thick sable waves that tumbled around her shoulders. Swallowing hard, he mouthed two words to her, his strong brow deeply furrowed.

Be careful.

Voni smiled, but he detected a tiny flicker of concern in her eyes. She rose up onto her toes, pressing a soft kiss onto his lips, whispering against his mouth and into his heart. "With you waiting for me, I can do no less." She paused, holding his gaze. "*Te iubesc*."

Kai swallowed back the next bout of Neanderthal behavior that rumbled in his chest as the simple, loving phrase in his native tongue slipped from her lips. "You keep talking like that and we're gonna give everyone a show they'll not soon forget." Only through sheer willpower was he able to release his hold around her shoulders, giving Eamon a curt nod before stepping back.

"I mean it, brother. One hair out of place and I'll make you useless to females for the rest of your days."

The stern look on Eamon's face was only slightly tempered by a pale hint of a smile. "I will guard her, *braither*. Keep an open eye." He clasped Kai's shoulder, giving him a comforting squeeze before he moved quickly away, taking Voni's hand and leading her toward the other pair of lovers. Without giving anyone a chance to change their minds, he placed his free hand on Galen's arm.

"We must go now while the trail is still hot." He turned his gaze to Cal, her red-rimmed eyes breaking his heart even as they strengthened his resolve. "We will return as soon as we can. I'm sorry you've had to be thrust into this so fast, but there is no time."

Eamon stood by, giving Galen time for a quick farewell. Feeling like an asshole wedding crasher who just interrupted the ceremony, he placed his hand on Galen's shoulder and pulled him away from his intended. He couldn't meet Cal's eyes, the unshielded grief too much to face.

"I'll get her back, agapi. I promise you."

Cal blinked, stunned and bereft as the trio simply vanished. One second, strong arms surrounded her, loving words hanging on her lips, a breath away from tumbling free and the next she stumbled, her knees buckling without his presence to keep her afloat. Before she crumpled to the ground, a pair of hands gripped her arms and gave her a chance to regain her legs.

"Come on. Let's get you to a seat." As he spoke, Kai lead her deeper into the living room, lowering her onto the overstuffed couch. She stared into nothing as he knelt beside her, his forearm propped against the cushy armrest. "Can I get you something to settle your nerves? Water? Coffee? Bourbon?"

"Got any Hemlock on you?" Cal wiped at the tears that refused to stop. *My fault. It's all my fault.* She had put Maggs in danger, and now Galen had disappeared, literally, with two someones she had only met. She still struggled to get her mind to accept she just saw three real live human beings go poof.

A deep chuckle crept into the empty space, making her acutely aware of how much she had come to rely on Galen's presence. It had only been a couple of days since her ordeal and his sweeping rescue, yet she felt cold and alone without him within arm's reach. She stifled the growing sob before it could surface. *Come on, Cal. You survived having the shit kicked out of you and now you start losing it?*

Yeah, she answered. Because now she had something to lose.

"I seem to have left my poison in my other pants," he said. She rewarded him with a weak smile, so he pushed on. "Perhaps you can tell me a little more about what's going on here. I feel a bit in the dark."

She drew in a stuttered breath, gulping back her tears and using the back of her hand to dash away the few escapees that managed to sneak to the surface. "You're not the only one, and it's my life I'm talking about. I went from a nothing grad student on a fast track to an early grave to the center of some bigger-than-life battle between good and evil. And now it's spilled out to the other person who's ever really given a shit about me." With the words hanging in the space between them, her resolve locked, calming her frantic mind.

"I have to find Ajax. I have to…know." With a strength she didn't believe, she rose to her feet, pointing her nose toward the front door. She managed two steps before being jerked to a stop, the iron grip on her shoulder unyielding. The backward yank became her ally as she bobbed her head down, ducking under his arm and grabbing the wrist, her movements seamless as she sought to bring her opponent to his knees.

Stunned, Kai scrambled to regain control of the situation that had quickly disintegrated from a female meltdown to a WWE championship bout. She might have had him too, were he any other man. But as his spiritmate was out of his protective sphere, his intense focus was not so easily duped. He spun in counterpoint with her aggressive move, their dance smooth and well-executed as he twisted his arm and turned her into the shelter of his body. Sure to keep his face out of reach from her head, he wrapped his arms tightly around her, using his size to still her movements.

"Whoa. Hang on there, killer." Kai fought to keep the softer parts of his anatomy out of her attacks, shuffling his feet to avoid the jabbing heels.

"*Let me go!*" Panic laced her words and her frenzied struggles continued. She kicked and bucked, using all her body as a weapon.

"Shhh. Calliope. I am not going to hurt you. Please, calm yourself." Kai pushed with his voice, pressing close to the side of her head. "I cannot let you go out alone. Galen would hand me my mate's favorite body part if anything were to happen to you. Shhh." His arms remained tightly wound around her, sensing the vibrating tension humming through her, recognizing the heavy scent of survival mode. "We can check in with your friend later, once the others have returned, OK?"

He dared a peek into her mind and found a chaotic whirlwind. Images flashed past like Polaroids caught in a blender and none of them seemed pleasant. Pain dripped in thick sheets as her thoughts spun, reaching for fragments and her words repeated on a fear-laced loop.

"Let me go let me go please please please."

He didn't dare let her go, but her body didn't recognize his arms, and no amount of talking could make the strong binds around her familiar or comforting.

Crap, Kai thought. She was about to have a full-blown panic attack and if she called out to Galen in her distress, she could put not only his life, but the life of his spiritmate in deadly jeopardy. Calling his skills as a healer, he stepped inside her jumbled thoughts as he slowly eased the tension from his arms. He whispered softly in her ear and echoed the words in her head.

"I know you're scared for your friends, Calliope. But you need to calm yourself. Your mate needs you to stay calm and stay safe for him." His voice echoed his heartbeat and his breathing, deep and even. "Nice, slow breaths. That's it. You can do this."

Her eyes grew heavy as she pulled in air in slow, deep gulps to the spasming sacs beneath her rib cage. Inhale. Exhale. Inhale.

Exhale. The process repeated as a controlled action, the necessary oxygen feeding her brain until the edges of the world regained their contrast. Thoughts fell into neater piles in her now functioning mind, bouncing against the walls of her head, with each new idea centering on the fact her only friends were in danger. Yet now, the hero who swooped in to save the day for her, more than once, had entered the mix again, wading in to save someone precious to her.

She had to help. She could not just sit by and let everyone else do the work and take the risks. That was not who she was.

"Malakai? I need your help."

She looked over her shoulder, finding a deep furrow across his forehead as a smirk curled one corner of his mouth. "Why does that scare me?"

Steady once more, she stepped away, meeting no resistance from the formerly viselike embrace. "I have to check on Ajax. If he's hurt... Hell, if he even knows Maggs is...is..." The words "is currently being raped repeatedly and probably wishes she was dead" screamed out in her head, but to actually hear them uttered aloud would destroy her. Maybe it was nice torture. Just pleasant stuff, like tormenting her with cheap dime store Halloween spiders on strings over her head or making her watch a Jerry Springer marathon.

Yeah, and little happy unicorns fart rainbows. Vicious fear began to rear its ugly head and she drew in a ragged breath, forcing it back, swallowing it down once again. Her eyes blinked rapidly, clearing the tears teetering on the edge of her control.

"I—" A strong pair of hands slipped down her arms, cupping her elbows as he groaned in defeat.

"Galen is going to have my nuts hanging from his rearview mirror if anything happens to you, you know this, right?" His voice, though even and deep, held a tinge of capitulation. Pulling his eyebrows together in a dangerous scowl, he mumbled words she could tell he prayed he wouldn't regret.

"You stay by my side and don't move, got it?"

Cal was tempted to hug the big guy, but she wasn't too sure how well that would fly. In the end, she gave one sharp nod, gathering herself for the upcoming funfest. Oh, whee. This day couldn't get any more fucked up, could it? Her eyes flashed to the ceiling, praying the Fates would not take her previous thought as a challenge.

CHAPTER NINETEEN

The In-Between slipped around the trio in a vicious blur. Galen was armed before the floor formed beneath their feet, his wickedly curved Falcata razor sharp and gleaming like a beacon as Eamon drew forth his bladed staff. Voni stood in the shadow of both warriors, her hands open and relaxed at her sides. Silence cocooned their entrance, and Galen hoped their luck would hold out.

"Siobhan, I need you to step into Galen's mind. He has a link with the one we seek."

Galen felt an eyebrow tug upward as he turned his eyes to Eamon. The flat look he received in answer offered no hint of discussion. "Dammit, man. We don't have time for you to start getting nervous about what goes on between your ears about your girl. Just let her in and we'll be—"

A high-pitched yowling screeched from the surrounding abyss, marching an army of goose bumps up Galen's arms.

"Fuck."

The trio voiced the same single syllable in perfect synch.

"Time to go." The playful lilt in Eamon's boyish voice was scarily absent, replaced by the direct, no-nonsense "kick this shit into gear" mode Galen had only heard on very rare, and usually potentially violent, cases. He reached out, lacing his fingers into Voni's trembling hand. Locking onto her pale amber hazel eyes, he gave her a soft, confident smile and a gentle, strengthening squeeze.

"Watch our backs, man." Galen closed his eyes, pulling the image of the be-dreaded blonde hair, thick glasses, and pale blue eyes. Footfalls echoed against the stone walls as soon as they took form, and he forced his eyes to remain shut, sharpening the lens of his mind's eye.

"Don't listen to them, Siobhan. Don't pay them any mind. Close your eyes. You can do this." Raised voices and the clash of steel clanged in the darkness at his back. *"Eamon? Why the hell are we still here?"*

Something was very wrong. With their combined strength, Marshal, Conduit and Channeler, they should have blasted out the other end of this shit hole seconds after their feet landed. *Shit. Shit. Shit. SHIT!*

"Lockdown." Eamon tossed the word over his shoulder as his staff landed a solid blow against the temple of the nearest Rogue.

Shit. There was only one way for the Void to be locked down. Someone knew they were coming. Two voices muttered two different words, but the conclusion was the same.

De Coldreto.

A growl rolled deep in Galen's chest as he spun, dropping to his knees, blade in hand before the first Rogue closed in. The silver in his hand flashed and the crimson spray followed the graceful arcing blade as he regained his feet. As he followed the staggered gait of his combatant, he drove his knee up, and earning a satisfied oomph, he let the man crumple at his feet. His gaze darted around the space, hoping to catch a glimpse of an escape route. Instead, he found Eamon, his bladed staff whirring in the slice and dice, the odds remaining equal as the body parts piled up like split logs.

"This isn't happening. This can't be happening." The words tumbled from Voni's lips as she squeezed her eyes shut. She was searching to find the way out, and judging from the panicked litany, Galen guessed she was running into more walls than windows. Time was ticking like nails on a taxi's dash, the sands slipping through their fingers the longer they were stuck in enemy territory.

Galen rammed his elbow back to satisfying sound of the shattering crunch of a nose followed by the warm splash of blood on his sleeve. He tossed his words back over his shoulder, dragging Voni out of her confusion. "Just focus, Siobhan. Find the path and open the door. You can do this. Just keep your mind calm." A stray right cross rocked his head back, spinning him about to face a curled lip scowl. With a flick of his wrist, the speckles of red dotted the ground around his feet.

"Step on up, fucker. See if your luck is any better than your buddy's." Beckoning his new opponent closer with his hand, he kept his eyes on his new prey as they circled each other, testing and daring until someone blinked first. His mind flashed forward, anticipating every move before his foe took step one. The scenario unfolded exactly as it did in his mind, every step, each assault and feint. Thrust right, dodge left, leg sweep spiraling into a roundhouse kick. Normally, the fevered strike would have crippled any normal opponent.

Guess I'm lucky I'm not normal. No sooner did the bare arm wind up for the initial attack, Galen cocked his arm back and pistoned forward, his clenched fist shattering the nose with a single blow. The blank look on the stunned face only earned a single shoulder shrug from Galen. "Sorry, pal. Maybe next time, I'll let you win." He placed his palm flat against the bastard's forehead and shoved, then stepped over the groaning body.

His gaze sought out the next opponent as a phantom pain struck his ribs. Gasping, he wrapped his arm around his midsection when another imaginary fist found the same spot and his legs buckled. He dropped his sword, the metal clattering on the unearthly ground of the Void as his stiff arm stopped him from eating the same surface. He sucked in air, forcing his eyes open to find the source of this latest beating, but could find no adversary.

Too bad the scenario didn't remain that way for long. Two Rogues saw him falter and descended fast, their eyes lighting up with the hope of seeing his blood. His leg shot out, catching the leading asshole a hair below the kneecap. Tucking his shoulder, he rolled away, but not quick enough to escape the slashing blade. He gritted his teeth, the cut shallow but continued to grow in length until his ribs were out of range.

"Mother…" Galen muttered in an angry hiss, his fist connecting with the Adam's apple of the stumbling bastard. He shook his head as he sucked in a shallow breath, his hand wrapped around his throbbing side. The blood added another layer to the fatigue tugging on his mind. Fingers dug into his shoulder and he swiveled his eyes up.

Eamon glowered over him, anger written all over his face. "Just couldn't wait to get the whole ball rollin', could ya? Had to jump the gun and go right to the good part. And don't even try sayin' it ain't what's goin' on here, *adelphos*. Bet me on it." Between the two of them, Galen regained his feet, but the lingering pain coupled with a growing weakness pointed to the truth and depth of his error. His spiritmate was in danger and had been injured, and because their connection had not been sealed, he would continue to feel the drain on his powers until the ritual was complete.

Or until they were both dead.

"Found it!"

Her eyes still closed, the satisfied smile grew on Voni's lips. The crack was small, a tiny thread she'd missed the first five times she scanned the wall. She studied the images from Galen's memories until a faint spark rekindled the connection. Racing to the wall and sliding under the flailing arms of the fighting men, she placed her hands against the pulsating glow. She remembered Kai telling her that her powers would take on different forms in the In-Between, but she had to stay focused on her final goal.

"Hurry up, boys! I'm not sure how long I can hold onto it."

Two sets of eyes jerked up and locked, both men nodding as a combined wave blasted the remaining Rogues off their feet and they walked casually across the room toward her.

Voni motioned them on, frantically urging haste until she remembered the laundry list of house rules in this wicked place. *Dammit, this is so unfair.*

She forced herself not to fidget as they strolled toward her in silence, blades vanishing and returning to their innocent guises. Blood smeared both of their faces, but neither appeared too worse for wear. She extended her hand toward Eamon and Galen. With their physical connection reestablished, they stepped back through the Void.

The opening fizzled into the darkness as Stefan and four other Rogues appeared. Deep lilac eyes narrowed into dangerous slits as he took in the minor damage. His brethren groaned, staggering back to their feet and gripping severed body parts.

One nice thing about creatures generated from pure chaos? Regeneration was the norm. After all, even a small piece of chaos was enough to start a revolution. A final glance and he shook his head, scoffing under his breath.

"Looks like we will be needing a new place to call home. Pity. I did like the neighborhood." He shifted his eyes to the gathering Warriors and signed impatiently. As he tapped his foot, waiting for the last Rogue to reattach his arm, he raised a hand, tracing a new portal in the air.

"Come. The new recruits must be prepared."

CHAPTER TWENTY

Ducking the swinging fist, Cal delivered a strong kidney punch to the baggy shirted intruder closest to her.

The repeated growl over to her left did echo her own frustrations. "OK, OK. So maybe this wasn't my best idea today. But it beats watching reruns of *Law and Order*, right?"

Her ribs were still aching from the two driving kicks from the now unconscious thug. The short drive to her apartment had been uneventful, unless she included the litany of reasons this was a bad idea that had poured from the driver.

The door off the hinges should have been her first clue, but her fear for her only friends overrode any sense of self-preservation. She glimpsed the slumped and bloodied body of Ajax a heartbeat before the knee jabbed into her gut. From then on, things became a little fuzzy for her. She remembered being pulled behind the massive wall of Kai's back as he flew into a rage.

He was right. It had been a trap and she walked both of them through the front doors.

Might as well have gift wrapped my ass and worn a damned bow.

Fists and limbs flew in all directions, arms leveled bone-shattering punches, and the blood sprayed the walls. Cal narrowed her focus, the voice of her sensei ringing in her ears. One target at a time. Right. Easier said than done since there were five nasty-looking and uninvited, thugs in her living room.

"Cal! Get down!"

She could feel the rug burns on her cheeks as she ate carpet fast. *Shit, please don't make too much of a mess. I need this security deposit back.* To be on the safe side, she covered her head and shut her eyes. A jolt creeped up the back of her legs and made her hair stand on end, the eerie charge crackling in the air, then nothing. Blinking, she slowly sat up.

Three body shaped piles of clothing littered Big Green, looking like the aftermath of spontaneously passionate evening while two other sloppy bundles decorated the floor at their feet. But she knew these hastily tossed discards wouldn't be finding their previous owners, at least not in this lifetime.

"You guys are seriously beginning to freak me out. It's cool. Don't get me wrong. I mean, breathing is one of my favorite hobbies. But…dayam."

Kai lifted the back of his hand, swiping it across his mouth and smearing the blood away. "Well, let's hope this bought the others the time they need to find your friend." He stepped over the carnage and knelt by the battered body crouched in the corner. Cal swallowed hard at the sight of Ajax, the stench of burnt hair and other things she'd rather not think about thickened the air. Soft prayers fell from her lips as she watched Kai check for signs of life. She wrapped her arms about herself, her fingers clinging tight in an attempt to drive away the chill creeping into her bones.

"Please, let him be alive. Please, God."

The massive shoulders blocking her view dropped a fraction and her teeth bit into the knuckle of her raised hand.

"He's been through one fuck of a beatdown, but he'll live." Kai ran a shaky hand through his hair as he rocked back, sitting on the floor. "I'd fix him up myself, but that blast took a big chunk out of me. He needs a hospital."

Cal's strangled cry of relief slipped from her lips as she threw her arms around Kai's neck, almost taking both of them to the ground. "Thank you. Thank you so much." Scrambling, she managed to find her phone as the sirens grew near. She had never been so happy for nosey neighbors in all her life. Still, her fingers flew over the keypad and the 911 operator answered the phone as the police rounded the shattered doorway.

"Please. My friend needs an ambulance! I walked in on—" She gestured wildly as she scanned her apartment, her tongue halting as the words dried up in her mind. Shit. How the hell was she going to explain any of this?

"Freeze! Get on the ground! Now! Now!" Guns swung into every corner of the room as more officers poured into the small confined space. Her phone slipped from her fumbling fingers, hands trembling as she reached toward the ceiling.

Kai raised his hands, his back to the door but she did catch mumbled curses before his voice shifted. *"We are not your target, officers. We found an assault in process and were injured as the culprits ran out the door only moments ahead of your arrival."* His head turns slowly, his eyes almost glowing with power as he continued. *"Our friend is badly injured and needs immediate medical attention."*

Cal blinked as the officers lowered the guns, one officer grabbing his radio and calling for the ambulance. A couple seconds passed before she realized her hands were still slightly raised.

"Ambulance is on the way. Are you two all right? Can you identify your attackers?"

Cal gaped like a beached fish while one of the officers took out a small notepad and waited patiently for her to fill in the blanks. "Huh? Oh, um. Yeah. Well, they were, um…"

"We only saw the backs of the three of them as they rushed past us, Officer Hardy." Kai's soothing voice turned the questioning gaze his direction, giving her the space she needed. She nodded thankfully before dropping down beside Ajax, lacing her fingers with care into his broken and bloodied hands. Tears fell unrestrained as his swollen eyes fluttered open. His cracked lips fought to form words. She placed her fingertips lightly onto his mouth, her head shaking in hopes of silencing him.

"Shhhh. D-don't try to talk, Ajax. You'll be fine. Oh God. I'm sorry. I'm so sorry. This is all my fault." She had a hard time trying to force her voice to work as the air was trapped in her tightening chest, not to mention squeezing past her locked throat. Her butt found the floor as grief and self-blame pressed upon her, the guilty sting of tears blurring her vision.

"M-m-m-Maggs?"

Voices bled in from her back, the words making no sense. Finally, a set of firm hands gripped her shoulders, guiding her to one side as the gurney wheeled up. She maintained her grip on Ajax's hand mutely, carefully avoiding the EMTs as they stabilized him.

What could she say?

"We will do what we can to find her." Once again, the accented voice behind her provided the words when her tongue refused to budge. *"You need to sleep now. Rest. You need to heal."* A weak smile blossomed on his swollen lips as Ajax let his eyes droop shut. One word slipped out in a whisper as the paramedics hurried him out.

"Thank…"

Kai placed a hand on Cal's trembling shoulder, keeping her on her feet as the officers finished their questions, his responses vague yet oddly satisfying to the gathered men. She was aware of people moving around her, but she was lost in fog, tied to the tiniest shred of sanity by the fingers on her arm. The gurney vanished, along with the last cop, leaving her unmercifully alone with her screaming conscience.

Ajax. Maggie. She never meant to hurt them. They were innocent bystanders. Now, they were collateral damage. Or worse, pawns in a chess game that liked to change the rules at the drop of a hat.

"My fault," her voice rasped out. "This is all my fault."

Her world tilted and spun until a black fabric wall crowded her vision. "No. Listen to me, Calliope. These fuckers will use any tool they can find to destroy the world. That is what they do. Hey? Hey!" A jolt shook her gaze away from the sea of ebony, lifting up to meet a fierce pair of pale green eyes. "You're Galen's spiritmate and he needs you to be strong for him. You cannot blame yourself for this, kid. Don't let them win."

"Win? What the hell is this? Some fucked up pissing contest?" Cal yanked her arms out of his grip and gestured to the scattered clothes knocked around the monstrous sofa. "These assholes broke into *my* place, beat one of my only friends half to death and…" She paced the room, hoping movement would derail her current train of horrific thought.

Galen would find Maggs. He just had to.

Kai could only watch as she circled the room like a caged animal. He knew how she felt. And it sucked. Leaning back, he rested his shoulder against the wall, letting her walk off some steam. "So, what do you want to do? We can stay here or head back to Galen's place? See if they're back yet." He read her hesitation, continuing as he stepped in her path. "I gave my phone number to the paramedics and they'll contact me as soon as your friend is admitted and able to receive visitors. The doctors will find most of the damage is not life-threatening."

Cal shook her head, the last phrase sinking into her despair. "What? H-how? I...I saw him. He..." A relieved sigh slipped from her lips as the words took on true meaning. She blinked, dipping her chin in silent thanks. "Look, I'm...Fuck. I don't know what I am anymore."

Kai set his hand on her back, a soft smile across his face. "You're angry, tired, scared, probably pissed off and maybe a little hungry to boot. The last one is only a guess since personally, I feel like I can eat the asshole out of a dead horse. OK, maybe a thick steak might be tastier, but you get what I mean."

"Ugh. The idea of food has my stomach doing back flips." She shuffled toward the door and cast her gaze over her shoulder, the impact of the violence hanging heavy. "Tell me they're going to be all right. Lie to me, at this point." She turned to face Kai, his face an unreadable mask. "Because, I'm really getting sick of this shit."

Kai's weak chuckle flowed around her as he steered her out the doorway, maneuvering between the crisscrossed yellow tape. "Welcome to the family, kid. But if I know Eamon, he'll bring them back. He'll bring them all back."

CHAPTER TWENTY-ONE

A familiar darkness surrounded Galen as he stepped out of the Void, the night air cool and welcoming after the confining stench of the nothingness. "Thank the Gods. That place smells like Frat Row on a Sunday morning."

"Speakin' from a little experience there, boyo?" Eamon narrowed his eyes, peering into the shadows for a sign of their current location. "Got any idea of where exactly we might be now, do ya?"

After helping Voni regain her land legs, Galen took a quick glance around. "Yeah, I do. Looks like Alamo Square. Had a place out here before the Millennium was finished." Another look and he nodded, pointing to the Stater Street sign on the corner. "Yup, Postcard Row. Perfect place for de Coldreto to hide. Clean, tidy, posh and away from the more seedier element." His eyes settled on a green and white-trimmed number with a beautiful bay front window, the thick drapes keeping out any light, but something more sinister dripped off the picturesque tiled roof, oozing out onto the sidewalk a step away from them.

Voni and Eamon followed his line of sight, Voni rubbing her hands against her arms to hide the creeping chill along her bare skin.

"Burning the night here, brother. Let's go."

Galen led the way to the front door, his gaze seeing past the wood and stained glass barrier. Not hesitating, he drew back his leg, grunting as his foot slammed into the fragile door, the sound splintering the night as the blow splintered the wood. Two long strides later, the dark inside replaced the darkness outside.

Eamon rolled his eyes as he cast his face skyward. "Ya know, boyo. Doors have these things called knobs and if they get twisted, they open. Quietly, too." He continued to grumble under his breath as he led Voni inside the strangely silent house. "Oh-kay. That shoulda woken the whole house." He gripped the staff hiding under his coat as he scanned for signs of an incoming attack.

Galen shared his friend's sentiments. The racket of the breaking door should have called forth every asshole in the place right down onto their heads. But instead, the air was deathly still. A couple dogs barked down the street and a television droned in a nearby house. Yet, in here? Silence.

Not good. Somehow, de Coldreto must have been tipped off and the Rogues scrambled to make a quick getaway. Galen ground his teeth, nostrils flaring in unchecked rage and impotent frustration.

A faint whisper echoed off the Victorian paneled and papered walls, a soft whimper of pain that tore at his heart. Hitting the stairs at a dead run, his legs gobbled up the short flight before he skidded to a halt in an open doorway. He swallowed hard, finding sheets scattered on a ruined bed, a bloody and bruised leg peeking out from the stained ivory fabric.

"Oh, God. No." The hushed feminine voice at his back mirrored his thoughts. Galen froze at the entry, his feet locked to the hardwood beneath him. He edged forward, but Eamon shoved past him to check for signs of life. As the rumpled covers fell aside, he had to curb his deadly urge to slam his fist into the paneled wall nearest to him. Blond dreadlocks hung in rusty red clumps, those bright blue eyes hidden by purple rings and swollen lids. The fact she wore no visible scrap of clothing made his stomach spin and pitch.

"Man up, Galen." Galen nodded to the voice in his head before he turned to the ashen cheeks of a fellow Warriors' spiritmate. "Stay here. You don't need to see this."

Eamon spoke from beside the bed. "No. We need her help. She can help ease her mind while we stabilize her wounds." Two sets of eyes stared his direction. "Mind, Body, and Spirit. If we are going to put this Humpty Dumpty back together, it's going to take all our efforts, got it?"

Galen took a deep breath before his eyes glanced down to the tiny female at his back. She was so unlike his spiritmate in appearance, but both had the same indomitable presence, that sense they could, and would, tackle any obstacle head on. He placed a hand on her shoulder, giving a comforting squeeze, waiting until she pulled her eyes away from the grisly scene on the other side of the threshold. She was a Conduit, a fledgling one, but a Conduit nonetheless. Once her eyes found his, he held her gaze until the immediate shadows vanished. A firm nod to her and together, they stepped into the room.

Eamon knelt alongside the bed, his hand brushing the exposed leg. The pale skin was bruised and battered, the dark pool of dried blood at the semi-covered apex of her legs a testament to the past twenty-four hours. *Damn you, Cabal. You need to get your dog back on his fucking leash.* A gurgled cry pulled him back into the present and he sidled up onto the bed, shoving the covers aside. "Hurry. There isn't a moment to lose. She's alive. Barely, but she lives."

Voni tiptoed closer to bed, grief pouring off her as she worked up the courage to close the final distance.

"She might not want to, judging by what they've done to her. Good God, what is wrong with people?" Eamon had no words, no way to answer the question his best friend's spiritmate raised. *What indeed?* Rather than dwell on the imponderables, he turned his attentions to the problem at hand. She had been raped. Repeatedly. Her skin was mottled with handprint shaped bruises and grip indentations on her legs and arms. Bite marks stood out as centerpieces, ugly purple hickeys blossoming around the vicious red divots.

He tipped his chin, guiding her to sit along the edge of the bed. With great care, she lifted the young girl's head, cradling her into her lap. Knowing the poor girl was in the best hands possible, Eamon inclined his head toward Galen and the three of them took up their stations; Conduit at her head, Channeler at her heart, and Marshal at her feet.

As one, their fingers touched her exposed skin, Voni's hands resting on her forehead, Galen on her feet and Eamon pressed his splayed hand across her heart. The shock rocketed through all of them as the true depth of her pain and torment flooded the room.

Images overlaid the still room, ghostly figures wandering through time as the recent events spilled into their time stream. Galen sneered as the spectral scene played on.

"The scrawny, polo shirt wearing shit-stain talking to Stefan is Paul." Galen spat out the answer. "He must be the one who brought Maggs here in the first place."

The little fuck had a lot more than a toe in the waters of evil.

Too bad.

Now he would pay with his life for it. More faces weaved in and out of the room, all of them leering as they waited for their turn.

Galen forced his anger down as his eyes turned to the broken and battered body of the once vivacious young female. He remembered her open and exuberant hug attacks as Cal returned from her own darkness. Grabbing onto that memory, he lowered his eyes, blocking out all the agony lingering in the room. He opened his mind, allowing the happy and whole version of Cal's daffy roommate to fill the room.

A sob from Malakai's trembling spiritmate cut the silence, slashing straight to his heart. Unwilling to break contact with Maggie, he reached out with his mind to Voni, wrapping his spirit around hers in a supportive mental hug. "She needs your strength right now. Cry for her once she's safe and whole."

Voni reigned in her tears. In all the times she and Kai had worked on her Conduit skills, the situations had been controlled and quite harmless. She was completely unprepared for the frantic and soul-wrenching misery that bombarded her mind at the first touch. She gulped down air in gasps, slamming her eyes shut as she struggled with the painful memories, crying for everything from easement to death. Her immediate urge to pull away was almost crippling.

If not for the comforting and steadying warmth pouring into her head, she would be in the farthest corner of the tiny space, rocking to hide from the hell she had only seen. The whispered words boomed in her heart, and her mind focused on the poor young girl who needed her. She began to sift through the tortured screams, ducking from the angry blows as they rained down on her from all directions. Kai's voice brushed against her mind, lessons and focusing techniques rolling back in a calming wash.

The mind is as strong, if not stronger, than the body. Great moments of physical strength come in moments of mental clarity. But the mind can be as fragile as newborn babe, and it has to be defended. Think back on how you protected yourself and this will help to help others.

She hid. She forged a hiding spot, safely tucked into a corner of her mind to use as an anchorage when the rising tides became unbearable. No sooner had the thought crossed her mind, she found her feet rooted. A door appeared in the midst of the vast emptiness, the old whitewashed wooden piece looking straight out of The Twilight Zone. Tentatively, she reached for the handle, giving a twist as it swung open.

Inside, she found a gentle young woman sitting on a small Oriental rug, her nose deep in a thick book. Ropey blonde dreadlocks adorned with the occasional shell or bead wiggled as her eyes moved across the lines.

"Um, excuse me, but are you Maggie?"

Bright blue eyes shielded by coke-bottle lenses peered over the giant tome. "Why, yes. Yes, I am." A smile hovered on the fringes of her lips as she cocked her head inquisitively. "How did you know? Are you a friend of Cal's? Is she here? And where is here? How did you find here, I mean?"

Voni smiled, shrugging a shoulder. In spite of the remembered horrors she'd waded through to get to this moment, the girl before her seemed untouched by it all. "I took what was behind Door Number One." When she earned a light laugh in response, she extended her hand. "Would you like to go home?"

The blonde eyebrows before her pulled together in curious confusion, and she shook her head sadly. "Oh, no. It's much safer in here, with my books and…huh. I can't seem to remember why, why I needed to stay in here. But I know that it's safe in here. I just…just had to…to leave." Her blue eyes misted over as the atrocities crept closer to her. "The…the bad is out there. And it hurts."

Yowling figures shrieked and clawed their way through the viscous dark, glowing pinpoints from red eyes promising more pain and torment. Voni narrowed her eyes and turned to glare out the still open door, uttering the word Kai had taught her. *"Pleacă!" Be gone!*

The harsh word flung the door shut, locking the leering faces away from their peaceful sanctuary. She stepped closer, dropping to her knees beside Maggie. "I know. What was done to you was horrible and unfair. I am so sorry, but I can help take away the memories of all of this. My friends are taking away the physical pain, and I can remove these memories if you want. The main thing you need to hold on to is knowing there are people who care about you and they're waiting on the other side of all of this. They miss you and want you back with them."

Maggie bounced up to her feet, the book vanishing as she quickly rose. "Cal? Ajax? Are…are they all right?" She pinballed her gaze in an eager search for her friends.

With the other woman on her feet, Voni chuckled as she stood. "Well, I know Cal was fine when I last saw her. I don't know who Ajax is, but I'm sure they're both fine. All I need is-oof!"

The force of Magg's exuberant hug froze any other words. She remembered Cal saying her roommate believed in the good of everyone. This one simple act proved that point. *I could have been one of the bad guys.* Somehow, even with all the horrific things done to her in the past twenty-four hours, this kind soul still believed in the goodness of strangers. She returned the gentle embrace, taking comfort in the unexpected gesture from a very grateful person.

Patting her back, Voni pulled away, smiling up at the magnified and enlarged blue eyes. "Take my hand and we can go." She held out her hand, waiting as Maggs hesitated a moment.

"It was Paul. He…he did it. He…he…"

Voni gave a sad nod as she reached for Maggie, touching her fingers against her temple. "I know. He will pay for what he did to you. But you don't need to worry about that." The betrayal of one she thought was kind had cut the young woman deeply, the jagged wound across her psyche festered during her ordeal. As she pulled into the Conduit powers still new to her, she took care, pouring trust and friendship into the breach. Under her tender gaze, she watched as the fissure began to close, the dark memories and anguished pain sealed deep in the healing scar.

"We cannot control the hateful and selfish actions of those bent on seeking their own goals. All we can do is rely on the strength of our true friends, those who put our names on their lips before their own. You have that, Maggie. Your friends are waiting for you. Please."

Once again, Voni extended her hand. She smiled, remembering a similar situation in her own past. Yet, this time, she was the one doing the rescuing. Maggie nodded, her dreads bouncing as she took the small hand, squeezing it tight.

Voni gasped in a deep breath, her eyes popping open as a weak cough sounded from the head cradled in her lap.

"Welcome back there, sweet. Been wonderin' when ya'd be joinin' us out here."

It took her a moment to untangle the words from Eamon, her eyes squinting and flaring wide, her focus out of whack. She ended up giving her head a firm shake to settle her swimming brain. Following the sound of the lilting voice, she found Eamon sitting on the floor, the standard smirk wilted around the edges. But there was something else in the enigmatic smile. It was pride.

Her mouth opened to peg him with some colorful retort, but a bottle of water appeared under her nose. "Drink this. You need it. Are you all right?" The richly accented voice of Galen rumbled over her, his powerful voice sounding drained and weary. She merely nodded, accepting the offer and took a long drink. Her immediate need met, she bent down to help Maggie only to find her charge no longer resting in her lap.

Eamon reached out and gave her foot a shake. A strange, calm and numb sensation flowed from where his hand met her body.

"You've done good, kiddo. Now get some rest."

The world became soft and fuzzy as her eyes slipped closed.

With Voni deep in her Conduit trance, Galen and Eamon worked to mend the physical damage to Maggie. Galen stopped counting the number of growls that escaped from his clenched teeth. She had been violated in every manner imaginable. After they had set her dislocated hips and jaw, they focused on deadening the overloaded pain receptors and nerve endings.

Galen wiped the sweat beading on his brow, the lingering weakness from the fight passing through the In-Between coupled with the screwy bond with his spiritmate making his gestures clumsy. And he needed to be precise here. Rape was a difficult wound to heal, since the places injured couldn't be sealed. It took care and patience, the latter of which he was running short on at the moment. What he wanted more than anything was to have that slimy,

Hawaiian-shirt-wearing asshat's throat between his fingers while he squeezed until his eyeballs bugged out.

"Stay with me, Galen." Eamon's calm voice cut through his mental rage, bringing him back to the task at hand. He filed away the graphic image for later reflection.

"Not going anywhere."

The silence lengthened, the synchronized sounds of three pairs of lungs breathing in perfect timing centered him.

When the last injury had been tended, he stood on rubbery legs, fetching water and wash clothes. Galen heard the shredding of fabric behind him as he returned with a plastic tub of water from the bathroom, towels under his arms.

"Fuck."

They breathed the word out in a strange two-part harmony as they took in the stench. With great gentility, they cleaned the filth off her skin, wiping away the blood and other fluids without moving her from Voni's lap. Galen lifted his angered eyes to meet with the soul-saddened peacock blue across from him.

"I know, *adelfós*. I know."

Galen cast a glance back down. They had to get her off the dirty sheet. Who was he kidding? They had to get her out of this fucking Hell. But right now, all he could do was wait, forcing his breath to keep the structured cadence, the steady inhale and exhale in synchronous harmony pulsed against the ratty walls.

At the sound of Voni's gasp, the trinity split. Fatigue crashed down heavily, knocking both Eamon and Galen off their feet. It took Eamon a couple attempts to climb back to a somewhat more respectable position than flat on his ass, that being draped sloppily across the bed. Galen scrambled to stand, moving to the small fridge tucked behind the bathroom door and rummaged until he came up with a couple bottles of water.

He placed one directly in Voni's field of vision, watching as her sweat-sheened face and unfocused eyes struggled to make sense of reality. He had heard she was training to hone her Conduit skills, but as far as he knew, this was her first real test. What a fucked up maiden voyage this was. As her fingers gripped the bottle, he swept Maggs up into his shaky arms, nodding to Eamon. The stained sheet vanished with a tug, his companion using the nearest drapery as a makeshift blanket.

"Let's get the fuck outta Dodge."

The words passed Galen's lips as he caught a glimpse of Voni collapsing into an exhausted heap. His tired eyes raised, the sleeping bundle in his arms getting heavier as the seconds ticked by.

"You're on your own with that one, man. And I vote we take a cab or something. I don't feel like walking up the fucking hill to get to my place."

Eamon's weak laugh barely crossed the rumpled bed. Galen forced in and out of his lungs as Eamon bent down to scoop up their now unconscious third, cradling her protectively against his chest. "Aw, c'mon now, boyo. A big, strong strappin' lad like yourself should be able to manage a little incline."

Galen would have flipped him off if he'd had a free hand. Instead, he simply glared blandly at his chuckling friend. A quick scan of the room brought some measure of comfort. Satisfied that they were unobserved, he stepped closer to Eamon, careful to keep Maggie from slipping in his awkward hold. He furrowed his brow as Eamon fished his Guardian staff from his jacket. With a flick of his wrist, the short stick elongated into an impressive eight foot staff, the ornate carvings glowing faintly, charging up for the impending journey.

Since both of their arms were occupied, Eamon stood with his back against Galen. "I'd say hang on. So instead, how 'bout ya click your heels three times and say 'There's no place like home.'"

"Oh, you think you're…" Galen managed just the start of an appropriately rude comment before the four of them slipped into a crack in time and space, vanishing into the silence of the night.

CHAPTER TWENTY-TWO

Stefan sneered as his gaze took in the less than modest interior of the flophouse in the Tenderloin. He had hoped never to return to his particular locale. *I guess no one passed that little nugget on to that fucking Greek.*

Sirens faded in and out in the distance as the rest of the night soundscape was punctuated by car horns, the thump of a passing car's overly loud stereo system and his personal favorite, the screech of arguing females. He dug his thumb into his temple, hoping to diffuse the headache a moment away from making this first appearance this night. And since his superior was on his way for an initiation, things could only go up from here.

Too bad the accommodations were not the ones he had hoped to present.

Yet as the temperature dropped like an anvil, his thoughts turned to his own rite, perhaps this crappy place was the best choice. No one would notice the stench. Or the bloodstains that would soon paint the room from floor to ceiling.

He slanted his eyes toward the awaiting recruits. Seven had stepped up, five anxious and eager for the honor, one calmly prepared for his fate, and the last trembled in abject terror. An evil smirk curled one corner of Stefan's mouth, knowing what awaited the last in line.

Paul.

Granted, he thought, it was his actions that drew out the girl of hiding, weakening the link between her and Galen. But with the amount of cringing and mewling he did during the "questioning" of the vapid roommate, Stefan knew he was not Rogue material. He only wanted to wet his wick in the virginal slit of his adversary's plaything.

He scoffed, thinking of how much longer that was going to last. Galen might be strong warrior, but he was still a man. The thought alone of the pain the bastard must be feeling made the cruel grin on his face deepen. An oily chuckle sneaked out as a figure clad in all white stepped out of a crack in time, the yowling backdrop of the abysmal In-Between receding behind him. Linen and silks flowed around him, clothing the lean and statuesque figure with an ethereal air.

He knew better. He knew the angelic form before them was nothing more than Death wrapped in an ivory box. He inclined his head toward the man as his true features become more apparent. Long white-blonde hair surrounded a face straight off of any number of high fashion billboards wallpapering the sides of nearby buildings. But it was the eyes that made the gathered hopefuls drop their gaze, the blood drain from their faces, each kneeling in turn as the unearthly red eyes scanned the room.

All but one.

Only Emmet stood his ground, his iced ebony eyes leveled at the crimson depths. Stefan watched curiously as the staring contest moved to its inevitable end, one sleek eyebrow arching up as the big and bad gangbanger lowered his gaze from the slender, yet powerful master of pure evil.

"Oh, Stefan. I do like this one."

Stefan dipped his head lower, hiding the self-satisfied grin splitting his face. "I thank you, my lord. I hoped you would be pleased."

Cabal moved between the groveling recruits. Stefan lifted his eyes, hoping to gain approval on the others as well.

However, once Cabal stopped before the quaking form clad in yet another hideously vibrant flower print shirt, Stefan knew his luck was about shift dramatically.

As the Master of the Rogue Warriors stood over the trembling rabbit, he watched as goose bumps rose on bare arms around the room, the hairs on the back of his neck standing up as it grew more and more frigid. *Here we go.*

Cabal flared his nostrils, the previously heady aroma of fear now soured by the unmistakable stench of someone losing their bowels. As well as their nerve. The focal point was most definitely the quivering glob in the Day-Glo shirt. Sweat added another unnecessary layer to the vile perfume. Whispered words fell in a frantic jumble from the thin lips. Curious, he leaned closer, cocking his head to help decipher the exact plea.

"It wasn't supposed to be like this. Please, I don't wanna die. I didn't mean any of it."

He bent lower, his lush mouth hovering above the ashen cheek. "Oh, come now. Were not those the same words uttered by the little beauty you so recently aided in defiling?" His gaze drifted up, locking with each of the panicked gazes of the recruits. With deliberate slowness, he lifted his hand, resting it on the hunched shoulders, and the sobs began in earnest.

"I didn't...I didn't..."

Cabal *tsked* him, the clicking of his tongue sounding like a death knell as his fingers tightened, squeezing in an almost lovingly gentle and supportive gesture.

"You didn't what? You didn't think anything bad was going to befall her? Is that what you expect your soul to believe? Truly?"

He scanned the room, the only true Rogue watching the interplay in sidelong glances, his gaze more intent on the more stalwart hopefuls. His lieutenant was well aware that he had no patience for weakness of any kind. And this pussy who blubbered on his knees was about to learn firsthand what he thought of frailty.

He continued to squeeze, the pitiful whines emitting from the pathetic creature at his feet was making him ill. First, this waste of skin shat himself in terror. Now, the little worm actually hoped to appeal to him for mercy.

"I am afraid compassion is a commodity I do not possess. Too bad." He shifted his gaze as he rose, once more finding the eyes of potential new Rogue Warriors. "I speak now to the worthy gathered before me." His voice boomed, driving his words straight into the heart of each man as the flesh beneath his fingertips trembled. "In order to become better than what you are, you must destroy what you were. Only through Chaos can you rise above."

The sickening snap of bone interrupted his speech, followed by a weaken cry. "Ah ah ah. All in due time. You must be patient and wait your turn." He hissed the last three words out, baring his clenched teeth in forced grin. Adding an additional squeeze, he returned his cool eyes back to the collected group. "Do you believe yourself worthy to rise above and become more?"

"Yes." The word rang out, unison and strong.

A pale blonde eyebrow arched up as he noticed a lack of reply from the blubbering body curled on the ground. "Paul?" He cupped a hand behind his ear, cocking his head in an exaggerated effort to listen to the stuttered and incomprehensible words. "Is there something you needed to add? No? Are you certain?" Before another sound escaped, he straightened, yanking his hand back, careful as he wiped off any lingering taint of the weakness oozing from the whimpering blob.

"I—"

Cabal's eyes never wavered from the group as the man at his feet started to twitch. Seconds ticked away as the tremors gained in ferocity, the body thrashing and jumping like a drop of water on a hot grill.

"Weakness will not be tolerated, nor will excuses. To become more than you are, you must accept the weight of all your actions, for true Chaos reigns when form and function are altered."

An evil smirk tilted the feminine, full lips as Cabal drew all the wide eyes down toward the spasming form. Paul's fingers clawed at his throat as red froth dribbled from the corners of his gaping mouth. His terrified blue eyes popped wide, turning in a pathetic plead, searching for a voice to speak on his behalf, one of those gathered to vouch for his worth.

Paul struggled to scream as pain unlike any he could ever imagine coursed through this body and gnawed at his bones. Neither heat nor ice, it was liquid fire that froze and shattered every muscle in his body and tunneled through his bones, turning the very marrow against him. His skin was frail paper, absorbing what it could but the frigid flames scratched and tore at the weakening barrier. The part of his body once called "arm" extended, the gelatinous glob plopping with a sickening splatter onto the grimy linoleum.

No. This isn't supposed to end like this. I'm supposed to win.

"You truly thought yourself worthy of the mantle of Rogue Warrior?" the angelic face above him whispered in painful truth. "And of the spiritmate of a Guardian to boot? My dear, she never knew of your existence, nor did she care of your desires or sacrifices. For you never made one. Every action was selfish and motivated by greed."

The voice shifted and boomed out as he continued to flop like a fish on metaphysical line. "Greed merely confuses, only Chaos controls destruction and rebirth."

Paul blinked once, his final word lost in a strange pop as his skin burst, splashing the remaining contents of his insides at the feet of Cabal. Even the primordial ooze knew better than to sully the flowing white fabric.

Cabal clapped his hands twice, the sound ringing and bouncing off the confining walls. The remaining men froze, statues locked in apprehension, only their flickering eyes and heaving chests proved them to be alive. As Cabal peeled his hands apart, lightning crackled and sparked between his palms, the charcoal gray tendrils illuminating the room in an eerie glow. The cold fire of the In-Between poured into the room, emerging through the floor, scenting the air with the telltale blending of sulfur and charred flesh as it floated in like thick fog. As one, the gathered men began to quake, bony fingers clawing out of the haze, crawling up their legs, pulling the Void with them.

Cabal's eyes shifted from smooth ruby to dangerous crimson, the fathomless pools aglow, illuminating his sinister and beautifully cruel smile as he threw his arms outstretched. The howls from the recruits hit the ceiling an instant before dark streaks charged through the living fog. The mist rushed to fill the gaping mouths, sliding down throats, and began to take control. Once, they had stood tall and rigid, Cabal thought as he chuckled darkly. Now, they clattered to the floor, hands scratching at their necks and coughing in an attempt to disgorge the encroaching darkness.

"To become more, you must shed what you once were. Who you once were."

Although Cabal's voice did not rise above a whisper, the initiates roared, pressing their hands to their ears as inky wisps climbed out of every orifice, small glittering shreds of what was left of their souls melting into the oily dark. Some of the young men crawled to their knees as the steady flow of their humanity was yanked out amid the shrieks and cries of agony. Others writhed on the floor, vomiting up buckets of blood intermingled with their dwindling milk of human kindness.

Stefan had watched with pride as the recruits stood in rapt attention during the pre-show entertainment. Not one wavered, not one blanched. His prize pupil, Emmet, even gave the shadow of a grin at Paul's demise.

Now however, as they trembled to gain their legs like recently birthed colts, they were not so self-assured. Then again, he remembered how he'd fared in his own initiation, and the bilious recollection became visceral, forcing him to swallow hard as the memory trickled down the back of his throat. His hand reached for the handkerchief tucked in a pristine square in the lapel pocket of his Hugo Boss slate blue three-button jacket, filtering the tainted air through the fine weave linen. Perhaps they were mistaken in avoiding the back alleys in their search for new agents. These gang bangers might turn out to be a true asset.

"Stefan de Coldreto?"

Snapping out of his moment of self-praise, he bowed low. "Yes, my Master?"

Cabal stepped over the slick stain that was once a man and placed a hand on the bent head. "You have chosen wisely, Stefano. Now get them out there and find that fucking Greek. Bring me his head." He leaned closer, brushing his lips almost tenderly against his ear, adding in a hushed whisper. "If you fail in this, I will devour your soul."

TWENTY-THREE

Cal made her fifteenth lap around the living room. Kai knew the exact number. On each completed circuit, he carved a notch with his thumbnail into the uneaten apple that rested in his palm. Fifteen divots. His stomach grumbled in protest at his waste of precious food as well as prolonging the necessity of eating. Yet, each time he lifted the fruit to his lips, an exasperated huff from his companion stalled his desire to chew.

"Girl, I'm getting tired just watching you." His feet propped onto the table as he balanced the low-back captain's chair on its back two legs. "And don't even think about picking up that phone. A phone call could put your mate, as well as mine, in serious danger. They are handling things on their end, so you might as well sit down."

Cal paused, looking over at him. "How can you sit there so calmly? How can you be so sure?"

He arched an eyebrow. "Do you think I'd be sitting here if things were truly that fucked up? You know about the connection. If my mate were near death, the pull on my soul would demand that I find her." The blank expression on her face drew his eyebrow down as the furrow grew on his forehead. "I know that damned 'by-the-rules' Greek of your wouldn't have left out that little detail."

Cal shook her head as she made another pit stop at the mantle. "All I know is that until about two weeks ago, I was only a lame grad student, and now, I'm in the middle of something I still don't fully comprehend and I'm fated, or destined, or whatever you want to call it, to be with someone I've never seen or met before three days ago."

He understood her confusion and apprehension. But there was something missing. "But you have accepted him, right?"

Her cheeks flushed quickly and she gave a sheepish shrug. "Sorta? We're, um, not, um…aw hell. We haven't quite sealed the deal just yet. We're taking it slow, all right?"

Kai blinked once, leaning forward until the chair sat squarely on the floor once again. "What? I thought Eamon said that you two had been… Shit, kid. Why didn't you say something? Shit." Now it was his turn to begin doing laps. "But you know what he is, what we are? How far into the Claiming ritual are you?"

Cal huffed and plopped down on the couch in agitated resignation. "What does it matter?"

"It matters tremendously. You mean you let me take you into combat and you didn't tell me things were not finished?" He changed direction, striding angrily toward her. "Don't you know what you've done? A Guardian Warrior can gain strength from his fully Claimed spiritmate. Conversely, he can be weakened by any injury to her should their rite be incomplete. Simply put, you get hurt, he feels it. He is in jeopardy until the ritual is completed."

He didn't want to be cross with her, since his own control was hanging by a thread as well, and she didn't need to see that. With the strength of his connection with his spiritmate, he saw much of what the others found after his impromptu rescue attempt finally released them from the In-Between. But once she slipped into the Triumvirate, the strongest of all the healing spells known to the Guardians, aligning Channeler, Marshal and Conduit to repair the brutal damage done by the Rogues and their allies, he closed their link, allowing her to focus solely on her task.

His thoughts raced, knowing this was unlike anything she had ever faced in their training sessions. Not only did she have to negotiate through the Void, but she also needed to repair the shattered mind of an innocent. He did not doubt his resilient mate, but he did worry for the other young woman. He forced himself to be patient and to send nothing but love and encouragement into the ether for their friends.

And the wait was killing him.

Her jaw gaped open as her head swiveled from side to side, disbelief and confusion twisting her expression. "Wait, what? You...you don't mean I...I put all of them, even your wife..." Cal noticed something flicker behind the stern face towering above her, a spark lingering for an instant before vanishing. She bit her lip, closing her eyes as her fist came up to her mouth. Her head dropped, a new wave of guilt building as the air flowed out of her.

"I am so sorry."

He reached out, patting her shoulder and she dragged her eyes back up to see the same concerns reflected back at her. "You have no reason to apologize, kid. I know there's a lot to take in and it can be overwhelming. But worrying about them is not the energy they need from us right now, OK?" He gave her shoulder another brotherly squeeze when a bright flash lit the room.

As a crackling buzz charged the room, two figures, each laden with another in their arms, stepped into the room in mid-conversation.

"...you're just mad since I thought of it first, boyo. Admit it." The laughing tone of Eamon's brogue did little to mask the fatigue in his movements.

Kai vaulted over the couch, quick to steal his spiritmate's still body from Eamon before his knees buckled and hit the floor. Answering with her own burst of speed, Cal leaped from her seat, rushing to Galen's side, helping him both find the ground with some dignity and to relieve him of the burden he was carrying

"Oh, dear God, no. Please, no."

Without the weight in his arms, Galen pitched forward off-balance. Had Kai not remained close, he would have successfully taken down his lady and her roommate as gravity reinforced its law.

"Whoa. Slow the roll there, brother," Kai mumbled as he guided him down. Galen nodded his heavy head in thanks as he followed the earth's pull, landing in a semi-dignified heap next to the cocooned snoozer. The next pull, even stronger than gravity, was the need to see relief in the eyes of his beautiful mate. He remained still as her face stayed glued to the rise and fall of the sleeping bundle at his side.

So engrossed in the serene scene, he failed to prepare himself for her exuberant tackle, the impact of her grateful embrace causing him to reel backward, landing half on the Persian rug and the rest on the hard wood floor.

"Thank you, thank you, thank you." The words tumbled from her lips as the tears fell from her eyes. She knotted her fingers in tight fists, curling around his damp T-shirt. A cross between a cough and chuckle slipped from his lips, and the choked sound caused Cal to snap her head up. He mustered a weak smile until she looked at the crimson splatters on his once-white shirt. "You're hurt? Oh, God. I'm sorry, I'm so sorry. I…" A feeble sob locked her voice from continuing as her arms folded in close between them.

Galen panted, a drowsy smile on his face as he forced his eyes to remain semi-open. He brushed a light kiss onto the top of her head as a voice drifted up from the ground not too far from him, the words halted and heavy. "Think I might…just sleep here. The floor seems…quite comfortable."

He scoffed, coughing a couple times before trusting his voice enough. "Speak for yourself, Celt. I know what's been on these floors. I'll take my bed, thank you very much." His arms wrapped around the shuddering shoulders, dragging his fingers in tiny circles along her back. "Shhh. Please, don't cry, agapi. Just let me hold you."

The scene took on a surreal quality for a moment before Galen lifted his head. His eyes narrowed as he searched for Kai and his woman, and found none. He listened a moment longer, giving a nod as he faintly heard a door close from somewhere down the hall. He, as well as every Guardian, always made sure their accommodations came equipped with several guest rooms. Never knew when company would drop in unexpectedly with a body or two. Eamon sprawled on his back, dragging in deep gulps of breath with his eyes closed.

When he moved his focus from his brethren and to the huddled form pressed tight against his chest, he was drawn to the soft sounds of her stifled sobs. He sat up gingerly, keeping a hold on Cal as he heaved a heavy sigh. Her panicked and disarrayed thoughts rained down against his throbbing mind, with one self-recriminating voice screaming louder than all the rest.

My fault. All of it, it's all my fault.

Galen gripped her arms, coaxing her gaze up to meet his. "Calliope, I need you to listen to me. None of this, any of it, is your fault. *You* did not set any of this into motion. This…this is what they do. This is the 'gift' of the Rogue Warriors. They breed and foment chaos and destruction and they are very good at playing the mindfuck."

"How can this not be my fault?" her eyes cooled even as her voice rose, her arm flinging out and pointing toward the drapery-wrapped cocoon surrounding her roommate. "She had nothing to do with this. *Nothing.* Neither did Ajax, and we found him beaten half to death and the assholes were well on their way to finishing the job if we didn't get there when we did. You're hurt." She paused in her tirade long enough to gesture toward Eamon, a tired smile on his sleeping face as he lay sprawled on the floor. "He's not looking too hot, and I don't know where Kai and his girl disappeared after the three of you beamed back here."

"Ya owe me twenty bucks, boyo."

Galen groaned, screwing up his face as he pushed up onto his feet and pulled Cal to hers. "Bite me, Celt."

A weak chuckle reminded him they were not alone in the room. "No thanks, Greek. Too hairy in all the wrong places for me. But it ya'd be so kind, I think I'm gonna take one of your spare rooms and collapse until the next catastrophe strikes." Eamon pushed off the floor, giving an agonized laugh that melted into a groan. He knelt down, gathering up the drapery cocoon before regaining his feet. "You kids play nice and don't wake me unless death is the only other option."

Galen tilted his chin toward Eamon as he shuffled down the hall, disappearing into one of the several open guest rooms. With only the two of them still in the living room, he let his eyes drift down, meeting the turbulent emerald depths pleading up at him, the swirling range of emotions chasing each other across her face. Digging deep into his power reserve, he forced himself to stand on his own feet, his hands resting lightly on her narrow shoulders as he fell into her stormy green eyes. "As for Kai and Voni, I'm sure they're fine. But it's you that I'm worried about, agapi. What were you thinking? You could've been hurt."

He slid his hands along her arms and over her shoulders, moving higher until he cradled her face in his blood-speckled hands. He lowered his lips, giving her mouth a light brush, stealing her sigh as it sneaked between her lips.

"Ah, Calliope." Her name became more of a prayer as he breathed out. He pressed his forehead against hers, his drooping lids blurring his vision. "Why did you not stay put as I asked?"

Cal wanted to be mad at him, but his voice was so weary, she didn't have it in her heart. "Galen. I know this is gonna come as a surprise, but I'm not used to being the damsel in distress. Normally, I'm fully capable of saving my own ass." She wasn't sure who started moving up the stairs, but soon her feet were stepping up and up, their path leading to the massive iron four-poster bed.

The door to his room was still open and her eyes darted over to the hastily arranged sheets. She vaguely remembered climbing out of the welcomed fluffy confines what seemed like weeks ago. Her skin flushed as her mind replayed the events of her last moments on the sea of soft whiteness. The heat dripped down her tired limbs, stopping briefly to set her breasts on fire before pooling to rest at the juncture of her thighs, filling each step with an aching need.

A dark chuckle rumbled against her side and shivered down her spine, adding to her growing arousal. "*Glykiá mou*, I have yet to see you in the role of a helpless damsel. Now, as for that ass of yours, I would prefer to do the saving, and savoring, of this on my own." He slid his hands down her back and punctuated the sentiment with a light squeeze that made her jump, her muscles clenching under his fingers as an uncharacteristic squeak slipped between her lips.

Cal caught herself before any further humiliation, rolling her eyes as she hastily guided him down to the bed. Ok, if she was honest, she practically jumped out of skin, half-tossing him onto the bed in her attempt to escape her own burning desire.

"Galen, I'm serious." She paced around the spacious room, her eyes straying to the inviting bed. She had to get her head clear before she allowed her body to take control. Kai's words tumbled around in her mind. She had put him in danger by rushing in to find Ajax. Their connection was too tenuous and he had felt every strike and punch during the short fight.

She could have gotten him seriously injured, or worse.

Swallowing hard past the lump in her throat, she turned away from the beckoning whiteness, away from his questioning gaze. "I…fuck. I don't know what to say to you, Galen. I can't seem to do anything right. You've done…so much more than I can ever…shit."

Galen sat further up in the bed, her turmoil tearing at his heart, shredding his soul. "Agapi, come to me." He extended his hand to her, his voice free from any additional push, but his words carried the concern. When she remained frozen across the room, locked in her fears, he rose, covering the scant distance between them. Without another thought, he wrapped his arms around her, stepping in close at her back.

The feel of her trembling shoulders against his chest forced a deep and possessive sigh from his clenched teeth. His enemy was still plying his evil tricks on his spiritmate. His mate was in agony, those friends she treasured used as nothing more than pawns in a sick game and she felt responsible for all of it. Stroking his cheek against her smooth midnight hair, he breathed in her scent and whispered words against the sleekness just below his lips.

"Calliope. What I have done, I will always do for you. You are my spiritmate and I can do no less than all I am to see that you are happy. I know your heart is aching for your friends and what has befallen them, but do not think for a moment that anything you have done was wrong. You are not a fault here. What has happened is horrible and evil and it is what my enemies do. I am truly sorry you have been pulled into a war you do not truly understand."

Pausing, he trailed his hands lightly along her arms until he felt her sobs settle. Soft kisses brushed against her hair as he angled his head, his lips finding the sweet curve of her ear. He pulled her tight against him, gripping her shoulder with one hand as the other pressed her hips back against him. As he nibbled his way from her lobe to the thundering pulse at her neck, he let another groan hiss from his lips. Her mind was a whirling, chaotic frenzy of panic and heartache, her emotions turbulent and confused. He stroked his hand along her tense arm, cradling her close as he rested his cheek against the top of her head. Silence filled the room as her breathing evened out and he spoke from his heart.

"But, I am afraid that I can never apologize for finding you, my sweet love. You have brought a peace into my life I never thought I would find." At his whispered words on her heating skin, he felt her rigid body relax into the cage of his arms. He tightened his arms as she instinctually ground her hips back against him.

He turned her in his embrace, exhaling in a sharp hiss as her strong and lithe body fit perfectly against his, her soft curves tucking in harmoniously into his body. With his fingers resting beneath her chin, he gently guided her eyes up to his. He had to see them, needed to know she was as affected at this moment as he was. When her face tilted up to meet his, he exhaled while holding back the primitive howl. With their eyes still locked, he reached down, finding the hem of her shirt. He paused, ever the gentleman until her chin dipped in silent approval. An easy tug upward and the cloth flew across the room, landing in a discarded heap somewhere behind him.

"I promise that I will cherish you with my last breath, my love." His gaze drifted over her face, a smile of wonderment curving his mouth as he committed this moment into memory. "I could have never asked for a more perfect match to spend forever."

A timid heart beat hard against his chest, trails of recent tears painting silvery streaks of sorrow. Yet, the green eyes that rose to meet his spoke only of curious passion and of unfamiliar need. The emerald seas flickered and vanished, desire darkening her eyes as her hand reached up to touch his cheek. The slight brush of her soft fingertips along his unshaven jaw ignited his blood even as her face lifted toward his, her lithe body sliding against him as rose to her tiptoes.

Her kiss was tender, the touch full of innocence. Galen forced his body to allow her to set this pace. He coiled his arms around her back, pinning her lightly, his solid cock against her hip, weeping and eager. A breathy moan was swallowed as he deepened the kiss, his tongue sweeping into her mouth, tasting every corner. He tempted her tongue to join in the dance, twisting and entwining as he cupped her head with his palm.

The drive to control and claim was burning through his mind and body and only through a willpower he did not know he possessed was he able to leave the reins of this moment in her delicate hands. Slanting her head, he continued to ply her mouth with his tender assault, pulling the breath from her lungs into his, sharing the very air they both needed. As her fingers gave a tug on his hair, he slipped his lips from her, nipping and licking his way along her jaw line and down further to lave the pulse dancing under his tongue.

Cal gasped, her control shattered as her lungs sucked in burning gulps of air. She needed more, she wanted more. She wanted it all. Why couldn't she want to take what he offered? If she truly was meant to be with him for all her life, was it wrong to allow herself this sensation? Her body melted, the heat of his passion too much for her physical form to deny.

She felt. For the first time, she truly felt.

The floor disappeared under her feet even as his body stayed pressed against her. Her mind flashed back to another moment, another time when she was weightless, cradled in the strength of his arms. He was her hero, her savior who swooped in to save the day. Even as she denied her role as helpless damsel, she knew she would never deny the fact he was the armor-clad knight.

Soft waves of white linen cushioned her back as his rock solid body pressed her further into the bed. His lips had not stopped the barrage during their short excursion across the room, his teeth grazing her collarbone, sending heated chills along her skin as a now familiar dampness pooled at the apex of her legs.

"But what...what is forever?" Her voice stuttered as she clung to the thick biceps bulging by her head. His shaggy head lifted and animalistic dark eyes met hers. Her heart pounded in her chest, but not out of fear. It was desire, unfamiliar and yet exhilarating. And she could see the affect it had on him. The feral hunger on his face, the air heavy with his dark, wild scent that she dragged deeper into her soul with each and every breath. All of it was arousing but terrifying, creating a mysterious dichotomy that held her captive into this one defining moment. He pushed onto his elbow, sliding his fingers through her hair as it spilled across the white pillow beneath her head.

"With you in my arms, agapi," he whispered, feather-light kisses dancing across her face. Her eyes rolled back, her body arching, hungry for more. As he rocked his hips against hers, she groaned in heavy need. "Forever can be as long as this moment and it would be enough for me."

With deliberate and maddening care, he slid one narrow strap off her shoulder as his fingers nimbly unclasped the lacy scrap hiding her sensitive breasts, the pliant fleshy mound hot and the tiny nub of her nipple diamond-hard, cutting into his palm.

"By the gods, agapi. You are so beautiful." The words seemed trite and did not do her justice. He needed her to see how he saw her. Using their connection, he filled her mind with the images of her perfect, unblemished body, her long lean legs, the narrow waist, and the bountiful breasts that lay beneath his hands. He added to the picture, painting the delicious contrast of her porcelain skin wrapped around the dark olive of his body, her legs hitched around his waist as his muscular body plunged and drove deep into hers. Sounds and scents joined as additional layers, the needful moans filling the air as the heavy perfume of their love clung to each molecule.

She threw her head back as he brought her to orgasm with nothing more than the visuals he poured into her mind and the light touch of his hands on her breast. She screamed in sweet agony as her body writhed, her fingers clinging to his arms in search of an anchor for this unexpected storm. Deep in the throes of sensation, she grabbed onto his head, yanking him down to meet her eager mouth, her kiss demanding.

Once his mouth was fused to hers, she reached for his shirt, tearing at the offending fabric in an effort to feel more than his hands on her. His tongue plundered her mouth as she scrambled to remove the rest of his clothes. A dark chuckle bubbled between their mouths, his lips curving into a wicked smile.

"Slow down, *my eager one.*"

She shook her head, her breath flowing in and out in a quickening pace. Finally, his shirt disappeared and her fingers fumbled for the zipper on his jeans. Her eyes were staring intently at his fly, her single-minded determination broken when his dark hand covered her trembling fingers.

"Cal?"

Unresponsive and intent on the task at hand, she batted away his hand as she returned to the fight with his pants.

Once again, he reached for her hands, stilling their movements as he rolled onto his back. Frowning deeply, he held her hands to his chest as he lifted her chin to capture her eyes.

"Calliope? This is not like you. Please, speak to me."

Cal struggled to break his soul-piercing gaze. "No. No talking. I don't want to talk. We've wasted too much time talking already. And I can't...I mean, I want..."

Her mouth froze, the words trapped but he saw the truth in her mind. The crease on his brow deepened as he caught her desperation. Somewhere in the back of her mind, he heard the words of his fellow Guardian flittering like tiny moths near a flame. *He is in jeopardy until the ritual is completed.* His eyes drifted shut as the weight of his actions hit his gut. He lifted his fingers, trailing his knuckles against his cheek.

"Remind me to kick the crap out of Kai for divulging trade secrets." He hoped the mirth in his mind was strong enough to override his frustrated groan. "My beautiful muse. You have no need to rush this. I will wait until you are ready."

The thrashing hair tickled his neck as her head jerked from side to side, her frantic actions anything but playful. "But I am ready. I really am. I can't keep putting you in danger just because...because..." Fear and uncertainty clung to each word, outweighing her passionate intentions.

His eyes cracked open, tightening his arms fractionally to hold his spirited mate together as she threatened to shake apart. "Ready, are you? Yes, I can tell." He sighed, pressing a chaste kiss on her forehead, a gentle smile on his lips. "You have held onto your gift for the whole of your life. I would not force you into feeling you must give up your purity before you are certain." He pressed his fingertips onto her opening lips, silencing the denial he knew waited beyond. "I do not doubt we will be one, but too much has happened today. You need to let your mind and your body rest."

Her lips pursed, kissing the tip of his square finger as it touched her mouth. Her eyes remained locked with his, glittering and beckoning. Using the same tricks against him, she pictured the two of them entangled, naked and writhing, cries of passion echoing through the dark. To add to her ploy, she swirled her tongue across the pad of his finger before pulling in into the warm heat of her mouth.

I need you to be safe. Please. Her voice bordered on sorrowful desperation and was tinged more with regret than romance. He sighed and pulled her down for a tender kiss. Needing to calm her frantic nerves, he crept into her thoughts, found her rational self cowering in a corner. Knowing both of them were in desperate need of rest, he did not hesitate and he reached out for the small figure, cradling her carefully in his arms. *"Sleep, agapi. I promise we will continue this in the morning."*

He pulled back to gaze at her, her eyes drifting shut as he released the flood of exhaustion she struggled to hide. A tired smile warmed his lips and he rested her head on his chest, placing a kiss on her head as she tumbled into sleep, tucked safely at his side.

Soon, he would finish what they had started.

TWENTY-FOUR

Malakai closed the door to the room at the further end of the house. Galen and Eamon had kept her from the battle, the blood marring her clothes was not hers.

But the mere fact she was covered in it and unconscious did not make him the best company. It made him dangerous.

He stripped off the ruined clothes, his gaze scanning her creamy skin to ensure she bore no wounds. Her petite body, deep in sleep, was revealed inch by inch until she lay before him, completely bare and completely beautiful. Once satisfied she was indeed in the same physical condition as she was at the start of her trek, he now had to check the state of her psyche. This was where any damage would be found. He knew this and he steeled himself before he took the first step inside.

His shirt ended up on the floor as he sat on the bed, gathering her into his lap. As he held her against his chest, feeling the soft tickle of her breath on his skin, he closed his eyes and delved into her mind. He prayed he had prepared her enough.

The link between them fired brightly, the light a beacon he followed through the forest of recent events and unsorted memories. Images of the trek through the In-Between, her fears and apprehension as their party met with resistance flooded past him as he continued down the path, her light pulling him further on.

"I am here now, with you, dragoste meu. You have no need to hide."

Onward, he ventured, traveling through her mind when a door appeared in his path, blocking her light from him. Frowning, he reached out to touch the strange barrier. The red paint was chipped and worn around the Victorian decorative stylings. He pressed his hand flat on the surface and a wave of grief and torment raced into his body, slamming into his heart like a fist. Pitiful and mournful cries crept around the edges of the freestanding barrier.

"Siobhan, my love. Where are you? Allow me to help you through this."

Her voice, muffled through the door, whispered, heavy with sadness. *I know what she felt, what happened to her. I saw it through her eyes.*

He slammed his shoulder into the flimsy wood to no avail. The barrier stood firm, mocking him and he narrowed his eyes in impotent rage. He was a Guardian no longer. He had yet to make the final Commitment Ritual, handing over his mantle of power to his young protégé, but the Void knew his vacillation weakened him in this world. Dark laughter echoed in the corners of his mind as he thought of his mate alone in this place without his protection.

"Voni? You saved her. She will bear no lasting scar of this. You have done well. Please, let me in."

She suffered alone, at the hands of those monsters. And one of them she knew and trusted. How can people like that live with themselves? She trusted him.

The tears she spilled gave Kai the power he needed. With a tremendous roar, he howled into the In-Between. *I AM MALAKAI GREGORI VADIM, GUARDIAN WARRIOR FOR ALL TIME AND YOU WILL RELEASE MY SPIRITMATE!*

The door vanished in a cloud of red smoke, vaporizing as power flooded back into him. As long as his Conduit mate drew breath, he would fight for honor and for her. He took one step and he was before her as she sat on the tattered and ruined bed. Kneeling down, he cupped her face into his hands and turned her gaze away from the gory memory. He struggled to hold her troubled gaze.

"Look at me, dragoste meu. I am here to bring you back home."

Her long lashes fluttered before lifting, the pinpoint black spots in the sea of amber grew and focused until a curious frown furrowed her perfect brow. "Are we home?"

That sexy, whiskey-deepened voice warmed his heart until the radiance spilled out to form a dazzling smile. "Just click your heels three times, baby and we'll be there." His lips brushed against hers, the briefest taste to tide him over until they were safe. As she snaked her arms around his shoulders, he scooped her up, one hand sliding around her back as the other looped under the crook of her knees. The slight, yet so familiar weight of his spiritmate's body falling against him shattered any remaining barrier between Kai and his Guardian powers. He was committed, now and until the breath left his mate.

The darkness around them melted, the inky blackness replaced by rich wood tones and warm burgundy and forest green hues. With his mate still held tightly in his arms, he peered out at the early morning glow through frosted windows, the rising sun chasing away the lingering shadows. She gasped, dragging in a rattled breath as he lowered her onto the soft bed.

"Well, hello there." He smiled, the teasing phrase had become his go-to words when she was gone from him. She blinked rapidly before leveling her grateful yet confused gaze at him.

"How did you find me? I thought you were, I don't know, banished or something." Before he could speak an answer, she slammed her face against his, kissing him as though he was the air she needed to live. Her tongue drew his into the warmth of her mouth, their spiraling dance firing his now frantic fingers.

He sought out every curve, her bare skin heating under his touch and the drive to ensure his spiritmate was indeed whole and unharmed almost as strong as the need to bury himself so deep inside her he lost where he ended and she begun. He ripped his lips from her mouth, trailing a hot path along the column of her throat as he fought with the zipper on his jeans.

"I'm so sorry I left you alone, baby. I won't ever again. Not as long as I live." With a growl, he slid his freed shaft into her waiting and welcoming hot folds, his back bowed as inch by inch, he delved deeper into her. At the sound of her gasp, he opened his eyes to catch the familiar glow on the ivory complexion of his chosen spiritmate. She dug her fingers into the thick muscles, biting with a pleasurable pressure against his shoulders as she rolled her hips, her hot sheath gripping and milking him as she rose to her own release.

"Gonna h-h-hold you...aah...hold you to that, mister." Her husky voice poured hotly against his cheek. Her passion darkened eyes wore only a slender ring of hazel, but a flicker of fright still lingered. "I was so scared."

The catch in her voice drew his gaze up and he slowed his pace. Balanced on his elbows, he brushed the thick, soft sable silk from her forehead, his knuckles caressing her tear-spilled cheek.

"I know, baby. I know. But don't think about that." Words fell from his lips as he nuzzled his nose into the crook of her neck, kissing and laving the pulse beating just below his lips, the heady scent of her jasmine and spice bleeding into his soul with each breath. His mouth lingered a moment more before crawling back up to cover hers, swallowing her muffled cries.

"Stay with me here and now, dragoste meu. Let all of that go, baby. Be right here. Right now."

Finally grounded, surrounded by the strong embrace of the man who time and time again had saved her sanity, Voni let slip the death grip on her emotions, pulling the air out of his lungs in an effort to feed her oxygen-starved brain. His voice warmed her from the inside out, the velvet tones stoking the fire raging beneath her skin, fanning the damp inferno where their bodies met.

He was her rock. Since the moment his fingers brushed the tops of her battered New Balances, he was the anchor in her life. Even when the strange seas roiled and crashed, he never failed her.

Her back snapped up off the mattress, the ferocity of the sudden climax catching her unprepared. A heady groan poured from her mouth, spilling between the broken seal of their kiss as her head dug into the pillow, whipping her hair into a sable cyclone.

Words had long melted from any discernable language into soothing sounds and loving whispers as he plunged with long strokes into her hot, wet sheath, his pace languid and tender. He allowed her the time she needed and desired to take her full measure of pleasure. And at her powerful release, his body could do no other than follow where she led, his seed pulsing and filling her, heating as it cooled them. Not wishing to move and spoil the moment, he shifted to his side, gathering Voni's sweat slick body and cradled her against his chest.

Kissing the fragrant waves under his lips, he inhaled deeply, the comforting blend of her spicy jasmine and the deep musk of their love making settling his heart. "Looks like we're both in this for the long haul, baby." His voice rumbled, the rough words resigned to the path he had placed them on.

The tips of her fingers drummed against his chest as she snuggled into his tense embrace. He felt her lips curved as her eyelashes tickled his skin. "That's OK. I mean, what else would I expect you do to? Become an accountant?" At the sound of his deep chuckling, she lifted her head to find his eyes, her hazel eyes warm, love and relief mingling in their honey depths. "Kai, when I met you, you were the hero I had always dreamed of, but never really believed was real. I can't ask you to become something else just because of me."

Kai didn't think he could ever love her any more, yet her honest words never failed to bring him to his knees. His relaxed smile changed, the depths of his love and respect for his spiritmate altering the simple joyful expression into one speaking volumes of compassion and adoration.

"Siobhan Brigit Whelan, I love you. I thank the gods every day for bringing you into my life." The longer his eyes held her, the deeper the blush on her cheek grew. His lips landed soft upon her forehead before tightening his arms about her shoulders. "Ah, my shy one. And I should mention I love the fact that, even in light of what we just did, I can still make you blush."

She swatted his arm lightly even as she scoffed and shook her head.

"Yeah, yeah. Laugh it up, mister. You have to sleep sometime."

Laughter shifted to a hungry growl of primal need and his hand cupped her ass, holding her against his grinding and growing erection. "If that is a threat, dragoste meu, we need to work on your technique."

No more need for playful words, or any words at all, she raised herself onto her arms, slinging her leg around his waist. Her eyes locked with his as her straight arms braced against his chest, the knowing smile on Kai's face giving her all the encouragement she needed. His arms slid up her sweat slick sides as the long slow session continued until well after dawn, both of them finally falling into an exhausted, spent tangle of limbs.

TWENTY-FIVE

Fists thumped against Galen's temple, lights flashing behind his swollen lids. The voices bleeding through the cottony cocoon currently encasing his head spoke in harsh, intelligible tones. The disconnect grew as the scent of old blood and stale tobacco assailed his senses. Familiar yet foreign.

He was here, but this was not his memory.

Calliope.

This was her recollection. Her nightmare.

His lip curled in disgust as clingy hands pawed at his/her body, each lecherous grope and responding flinch driving another jolt of pain rocketing through his/her outstretched arms.

"Such a shame your boy didn't care enough about you to save you."

Impotent rage choked him as dread filled the pit of his/her empty gut. Alone, she had suffered, tortured and tormented without ever knowing the true reason. Without knowing he was waiting for her, just beyond the night and the dark.

"Wake up, agapi. You do not need to stay in this moment. Wake up with me, safe and in my arms."

Chunky fingers on one hand fumbled with elastic band holding up the stained cheap track suit, drool dribbling down in lascivious anticipation as the other hand bit into his/her scalp, yanking out a healthy handful of hair. Fear ratcheted up, thickening the putrid air with desperation.

"Wake up, Calliope. Cal? Cal!"

The thrashing and cries pulled Galen out of their shared dreaming, his arms tightening reflexively around her shoulders as he cradled her head against his own pounding heart.

"Shhh. *Écho écheis. Eísai asfalís.*" Mumbled words full of love and comfort slipped from his lips even as sleep pulled heavy on his eyelids. Damn, he knew the battle and the healing was going to take a toll, but this was different. An unusual force sucked his body back against the mattress, threatening to yank him deeper into the nightmarish territory.

Cal awoke with a start, Galen's slurred speech snapping her eyes open. Entangled in his embrace, she squirmed until she was able to raise herself onto her arms and look upon his face. His dark olive skin was slick with a sheen of sweat, a deep frown furrowing his strong brow as his eyes fluttered under shuttered lids. Frantic, she scrambled to her knees, crawling in search of some shirt to cover her nakedness. Once she had punched her arms into whoever's shirt she nabbed, she returned to the bed, swinging her leg over his waist as she pressed her hands against his shoulders, shaking them wildly.

"Galen? *Galen*! Oh shit. Oh shit. Oh shit!"

When his feverish mutterings did not stop, she called for aid over her shoulder, hoping someone else was awake or could hear her through the thick walls. Her bottom lip quivered as it disappeared between her teeth.

"Please, Galen. Wake up. Don't do this to me. I'm sorry. Fuck. This is all my fault."

"Don't be wearin' that guilt all on your own, darlin'. He's as much to be blamed as you."

She swiveled her gaze toward the soft lilting voice just behind her. "How? It seems since I showed up, his life has just been one fucked-up mess." Spite filled her mouth and tainted the words she spat out. "Or maybe unfucked would be better. Dammit all. I'm a goddammed albatross. Everything I touch turns to shit. My roommates—"

Eamon stepped close and his strong fingers gripped her shoulder, stemming the flow of grief driven self-hate as an unexpected sense of calm melted through her knotted muscles.

"Your roommates are both going to be fine." A tremor of steel ran the length of his words, a tender squeeze centering her attention as he continued to speak. "Maggie will never remember much of the past day. Not ever. So it's important you not bring it up, right? Too much to try and explain. Her boyfriend? Kai got a call from the doctors and he's being released in a bit. Now, hold on," His words, coupled with his raised hand, put the brakes on her voice, her mouth agape. "Kai and Voni are on their way to the hospital to pick him up. They're bringing him here, since your place is still a crime scene and without a front door."

Cal blinked back the stunned tears as her mind spun, forcing meaning into the words. "But…but all of this is… How do you guys do this? I mean, I just feel like I've made a complete clusterfuck out of it all. Now, he's gone all catatonic and you can't tell me this has nothing to do with me."

Eamon sighed, dropping his hand from her shoulder, his influence lingering as a sense of peace and tranquility in her troubled mind. "Calliope? Life gets messy. It's just the way of it sometimes. Terrible and unfortunate events have played out in your world these past few days and though none of it's been your fault, you have been at the center of a good bit of it. Not too easy to separate the two at times, but that's the truth of it. And as for Sleeping Beauty there…"

A groggy groan from beneath her jerked her gaze down to the thick black lashes fluttering slowly up, revealing the ebony depths that kick started her heart rate and sent lightning through her veins. Full lips curved into a sleepy smile as he lazily lifted a hand toward her. Panic spurred her into action, grabbing onto his outstretched arm and resting her cheek against his palm. She blinked rapidly in a weak attempt to hold the frustrated tears at bay, her shaking fingers lacing between his.

"Aw, Eamon. I didn't know you cared." The joking words croaked soft as Galen rolled through his shoulders, angling up into more of a seated repose. "You're just pissed I've got a gorgeous female straddling my lap, brother."

Each subtle move and wiggle of his hips shot a wave of heat right into her core, the muscles jumping and quivering in hopeful anticipation. Lowering her eyes as the embarrassed blush painted her cheeks, Cal leaned onto him, taking physical comfort in his consciousness. She only wished the fire beneath her skin would burn the icy despair that encased her spirit.

Galen felt the pull of the earth heavier than he thought possible, even as the delicious addition of his chosen spiritmate's lithe limbs wrapped about his waist. This must the side effects of his botched binding. His mind spun as he vaguely remembered Eamon's warning about the now truncated time line, as well as the dire consequences. Already, he felt his body weakening, his Guardian powers draining out, transferring from him into the beauty seated conveniently atop his hardening erection.

"Right, boyo. Ya just keep on thinkin' that." Eamon's snickering tones faded toward the door, but Galen's attentions were more attuned to a much fairer companion. *"Time's runnin' out, Galen. Don't waste it."*

"Promise me you'll watch over her, adelfos."

Floorboards paused in their soft creakings, footfalls freezing at the silent request.

"I have a better idea. Don't die."

The door clicked shut in the growing sunlight while he held her troubled gaze. He wished he could smile and tell her everything was going to be all right, but his throat tightened, stalling the possible lie from falling from his lips. Instead, his fingers slid along her cheek, winding through her sleep-tousled hair. A steady pressure downward, plus a sensual roll of his hips, gained a breathy moan from Cal, encouraging her to respond to his unvoiced coaxing.

With the first brush of her lips against his, the fatigue multiplied, threatening to drag him back into the fitful dreams of their shared mental link. Trailing his tongue across the seam of her lips, he drank in the essence of his spiritmate, drawing strength from the simplest kiss. She dug her fingers into his knotted shoulders, cinching her thighs around his. With a strangled sob, she broke the kiss, pressing her forehead against his.

"You can't tell me this isn't my fault, Galen. You're slipping away from me."

Galen's lips curled into a drowsy smile, a leaded arm trembling as he stroked her damp cheek. His eyebrows pulled together and his lids slid open.

"Agapi, my powers always take a serious hit after heavy duty usage. I still need to recharge. I assure you, I have no plans of leaving you." Forcing his eyes to focus, he studied the sorrowful green gems above him, his thumb rubbing along her bottom lip as he risked a playful smile. "Some of us do need more than a blink of sleep a night, my muse."

A laugh squeaked out of Cal as her shoulders dropped with a sigh. Her eyes searched for the clock and found only half an hour had passed.

"Oh crap. I'm so sorry. Damn, I just thought that…well, since…fuck."

As his eyes drifted shut, unable to resist the lure of unconsciousness, he managed one final grin. *"Soon enough, agapi. I do keep my promises. Even if it is the last thing I do."*

Although his words were designed to comfort her, the harsh ring of finality cooled the fires fanned by his touch. Her back bowed as her forehead pressed against his brow. "That doesn't make me feel any better, bucko."

With a sigh, she sat back on her heels, resting her hands on her hips as she watched his chest rise and fall, sleep claiming him without mercy. The harsh lines on his chiseled face softened, but never veered away from the pure power and masculine strength of the honest-to-God warrior resting between her legs.

A warrior.

She was in love with a man who had stood toe-to-toe on ancient battlefields, encased in hammered steel and weathered leather. Her heart skipped a beat as her mind wove pictures of the arms resting on her legs swinging a broad battle-axe at the descending hoards of whoever was dumb enough to attack the Greek general.

Her imagination continued to weave new scenes. In each new tableau, he was standing proud and tall, the Mediterranean sun glinting off the horsetail helm, the exposed olive skin of his chest and arms splattered with the remains of his enemies. Skimming her fingers along his shoulder, her gaze stayed glued to his face as she studied the thick black lashes and the perfect crescent shadows they cast on his cheeks.

He had stepped in and saved her life twice, and now, he saved her roommate. She could do no less for him. A strange calming resolve steeled her spine, straightening her back and firing her courage. Leaning over, she placed a soft kiss on his full lips, the gentle pressure causing tingles to play chase across her skin as she climbed out of the bed. She forced herself not to look back at the sleeping god buried in the waves of white as she opened the door and stepped into the hall.

Her bare feet padded down the stairs where she found Eamon inside the kitchen, pensively studying the white mug in front of him as he held up the silver refrigerator.

"All right, so what do we do?"

Eamon lifted his dancing blue eyes up from his coffee contemplations, a coppery eyebrow arching at her open-ended question. "Come again?"

She grabbed another mug and poured herself a steaming helping of go juice, wrapping her fingers around the heating china. "I can't just sit here, twiddling my thumbs while everyone else takes the risks that are centered around my life. I'm not weak and I'm not helpless. And I owe these fuckers for the past two weeks of nexus level shit that's darkened my door."

Despite the venom and fatigue in her words, Eamon heard the underlying strength of her convictions. She did have a point, on all counts. She knew more of what was at stake here than he gave her credit. He took a slow sip, pondering the next steps, his eyes never leaving hers.

He knew she was strong, he sensed that from their first meeting. No one other than the true spiritmate of a Guardian Warrior could have withstood the terrors of the In-Between and return with any semblance of sanity. He stood vigil as she clawed her way from the Black to stand by the side of her man.

The question now, would she be strong enough to sacrifice it all?

The drumming of short fingernails against the white porcelain cup cradled between her palms broke into his mental wanderings. Blinking back into the present, he held her fierce gaze, pinning her with an unwavering stare of his own. The years spent in staring contests with his bastard of a brother had given him skills that were the envy of most cats.

It wasn't long before her eyes faltered, her elbows hitting the counter as if the cooling coffee mug grew heavier.

"Look, you might all be a bunch of badasses, but I deserve some payback, after all the crap I've dealt with the past couple days. Something. Closure, revenge, I don't know what the fuck to call it, but I am going to get it. With or without any help, guidance or direction."

Eamon nodded in slow deliberation. "Are ya now? And just what would ya be doin' there? Got any idea of where to start handin' out this divine retribution of yours?"

Her head dropped at his frustratingly clear voice of reason, her grumblings bearing a strong likeness to the Guardian Warrior currently passed out upstairs. One word fell from her lips as she stared at nothing in particular.

"Paul. I'll start with that asswipe. He's the one who handed over all of us in the first place. All I have to do is head to campus and get his home address. He has to pay."

"Campus? You think that's a good idea? What if he's there, waiting to spring another trap? He already took out your home; the next place for him to wait for you would be at school."

"Dammit." Cal leaned forward, her chin hovering over her coffee. "And it would be too much to ask for the bad guys to go back to their earlier hiding place where you found Maggs, right?"

Eamon chuckled at her wishful thinking. "Darlin', the only place the villain goes back to the scene of the crime is in the movies. But I think you're gettin' the right idea there. We do need to find where they're hidin' out, but this is an old city, with lots of alleys and hidey holes."

Her head bobbed up and down. "Hell, I can think of a dozen out-of-the-way places and that's before even leaving the campus. Talk about the proverbial needle in a haystack."

Eamon continued to sip his cooling coffee as the silence lengthened.

"Yeah. Fuck, they always make it look so easy on TV." With a scowl, she spun, planting her back against the uncluttered counter. "He's still out there, isn't he?"

Eamon quirked an eyebrow in her direction. "Him? Your friend, de Coldreto or his men? Either way, the answer is definitely yes. I'm sure after our visit, they've called in reinforcements."

Cal blinked as he let his words sink in. "Wait. Reinforcements? You mean there's probably more of these lowlifes out there now?"

His sad smile wasn't giving her the warm fuzzies, but time was not on their side, and diplomacy needed to take a backseat to discretion. "Just as the good guys try to keep their numbers high, so do the bad guys, darlin'. This one here, de Coldreto? Him and your boy have been at each other's throats for goin' on a millennia now.

Think the two of them first met during Caesar's day. And yes, I do mean the first one." One last sip from his cold mug and he headed back to the pot. "So, now do you understand that all is not completely your fault?"

Her eyebrows pulled together in a frustrated frown, but she nodded in agreement. "Yeah, I guess so. But that doesn't explain it away. Please, I need to do something, if only for Maggs and Ajax. What about Voni? Can't she just, I don't know, do that whole psychic thing of hers and find them?"

Eamon opened his mouth, his counter argument poised on the tip of his tongue as voices drifted in from just outside the front door. He lifted a finger, pressing an imaginary "Hold" button on their current conversation, the movement timed in perfect synchronicity with the front door swinging opening. Kai's deep baritone called out, announcing the obvious.

"Honey, we're home."

Cal jerked her gaze toward the source of the sound and she spied the familiar lanky, yet plainly clad, figure following the towering GQ model. Bespectacled, he leaned on the petite girl who lifted her leg in the most graceful display of ass-kicking she had ever witnessed.

"God, you are such an ass sometimes." Her playful and laughing tone brought light into Cal's heart, kicking her own ass into gear and she flew out of the kitchen, nearly knocking over the barstool nearest the corner.

"*Ajax!*"

Kai intercepted her full body check before she reached her target, wrapping his arm around her waist and pulling her to a halt. "Whoa. Slow down there, kid. He's still pretty sore. Some nasty bruises and a couple of cracked ribs, but nothing too serious." Certain her energy was semi-contained, he let go with a warm smile.

Cal swiveled her gaze from the pale gray eyes to the soft blue, squinting at her roommate's boyfriend until a small frown appeared between her brows.

"Ajax? I never knew you had such pretty blue eyes?"

A gentle laugh emerged from her friend, his straight black hair shaking slightly. "It's amazing what good eyeliner will do for eye color. Not to mention, I wear contacts."

"Oh," she paused, seeing her roommate's boyfriend as if for the first time. Without the guyliner and the black attire, he was cute, wholesome in a Midwest kind of way. His smile was easy and without guile. Plus, it was hard to think of him as Goth when he was wearing a pair of green scrub bottoms and a white T-shirt emblazoned in green letters, "Nurses need love, too."

"Yeah. One of the ward's nurses took pity on him and donated his spares."

Cal knew the voice belonged to Kai's girlfriend, but the deep, whiskey smooth tone seemed out of synch with her petite frame. She stepped back, allowing Ajax to stand on his own while she returned to Kai's side.

The strained moment dragged into the realm of uncomfortable before Cal again found her voice, tight and tense as the words spilled out.

"I'm so sorry, Ajax. If I hadn't come back home, none of—" Ajax closed the short distance and wrapped his arms around her shoulders, offering her solace and forgiveness.

"Cal? I'm no idiot, and I might not know everything that's going on here, but I do know you're just as much of a victim of all of this as I was. Your friends filled me a little with what they could, and I do get it. But, Cal? You might think you're strong, but even you can't carry all this on your shoulders."

Sobs wracked her as Eamon's words once again sounded in her ears. Her head bobbed up and down as he tried to rein in her rampaging emotions. *Dammit all, this sucks.* She had never broken down in front of anyone for as long as she could remember.

However, in the past two weeks, she'd become a poster child for Kleenex.

She released her crushing hug on Ajax, realizing there was someone else in the house who needed to see him more than her. Dashing the back of her hand against her eyes as the downpour dried out, she stepped back, sniffing and shaking her head.

"Gah. I really hate all this emotional shit." She looked up, expecting condemning stares. Instead, she found nothing but understanding smiles and a couple chuckles, proving to her these were all good people. She reached down, clasping Ajax by the hand. "Come on. I'll take you to Maggs."

TWENTY-SIX

The lights were dimmed in the spare room where that sweet Irish guy had settled her for the night. Even with this being a spare room, it was still more spacious than her apartment.

Maggs squinted, reaching to the nightstand, hoping to find her glasses.

Nothing.

Dang it all.

Where was she?

Scooting up, she pressed her back against the headboard, the blurry furniture unfamiliar. She knew this wasn't Ajax's place. He lived in the boys' dorm, sharing a closet with three others. It wasn't his parent's place either, or her parent's. She didn't know much about Cal's family, but she knew they didn't live nearby.

As the awareness of her unknown surroundings continued to sink in, she was surprised by her lack of concern. She might not know where she was, but she knew she was safe. She ran a hand through the knotted mess on her head, agitating her dreads and jangling the calming beads and clamps along the long ropes.

She might be safe, but she was also very naked. One hand tucked the thick brocaded hunter green and burgundy quilt under her armpits, the hazy pattern lost on her eyes, but not to her other senses, the elaborate stitching creating textured swirls and arcs.

A timid knock caught her attention and she swivel her head in the general direction.

"Yes?" She squeaked out, giving a cough to clear her sleep weakened voice.

Light spilled in from a growing slit in the darkness she assumed was a wall, a door the moving part. She narrowed her eyes, hoping to catch a glimpse of the bearer of the approaching footsteps. As the figure grew closer, the fuzzy edges sharpened.

"Is someone one…Ajax? Is that you?!"

Soon, she was wrapped up in the arms she knew. "Hey you." She heard the smile in his soft voice even though her eyes didn't want to focus. A kiss landed on her furrowed brow. "Don't squint, babe. Your eyes will stay that way."

Cal stayed by the door, unwilling to interrupt their happy reunion. Her mind spun as she worked on what lie she would tell her roomie this time. First, she fibbed about why she'd gone missing for a week. Now, in order to keep her sanity, she would have to come up with some doozy of a story for where she was, why she was here and what happened to the past day.

Fuck. Me. Running.

Luckily, her rather profane outburst was only witnessed by the voices in her head. Along with her spinning wheels, Eamon's warning now joined the dance. *"Maggie will never remember much of the past day. Not ever."*

Is a lie still a bad thing if it saves someone's sanity, if not their life?

"Cal? What are you doing over there?"

It took her a minute to process the words, then another to get her body to respond.

"I didn't want to interrupt." Her hands found the back of the waistband of her baggy sweats before sliding down her ass. Dammit, why couldn't she find pockets when she needed them?

"Cal, when have you ever interrupted anything? Besides, you might be the only person who has some answers for me. Like where is this place and how did I get here?"

She took the opportunity in the shuffling trip across the floor to formulate the best lie to feed her best friends. "Well, this is Galen's place. Um, they guy that's been, well, uh…taking care of me while, uh…" She was so bad at lying and this was going to go horribly wrong if she wasn't careful with her next few words.

Sadly, she discovered the room to be not as wide as she prayed it was, the bed bumping against her knee sooner than she was ready. She opted to keep a small distance and perched on the corner of the normal-sized bed.

Maggs jolted up, her cornflower blue eyes bright and shiny, no trace of grief or sadness visible. "You mean the sexy hunk that brought you over to pick up your stuff lives here? Wow. He must be loaded. Is he an investment banker? I mean I hear they make tons of money and it would make sense since this room is just huge and I don't see him here. Did you guys sleep here? Oh, what am I saying? Of course you didn't. He must have his own room, right? Am I rambling again?"

Ajax laughed, his arms relaxed around her shoulders. "Babe, you just keep on rambling. It's been a long night for me."

"Night?"

Cal leaned back as Maggs nearly took out an eye with her flying locks. A barked laugh from Ajax, coupled with a late flinch on his part, encouraged her to join in, the joy at seeing her roommates safe and whole easing her self-recriminating fear.

"What do you mean night? And how come I don't remember getting here, much less naked?"

Ajax fumbled, catching the bulk of his lover's blonde ropes before her next deadly head shake. "Don't you remember? Those burglars broke in while we were watching movies. You were just getting out of the shower when the door broke open." He held her eyes with a wink. "You panicked and passed out, baby."

That's what must've happened to Ajax, Cal surmised. Poor guy. She imagined the scene, him sitting in the middle of Big Green, wondering when Maggs would be coming home when the door breaks open and all hell breaks loose. Reaching out, she rested her hand on his knee to offer some measure of comfort. When his eyes met hers, her mouth formed the words she felt compelled to say.

Thank you.

His smile over the top of the pivoting head nearly cued an encore of the waterworks, but Cal knew it would only trigger an interrogation from Maggs she couldn't handle. She needed all her faculties on point if she was going to be getting any payback soon.

"I did? Well, that does sound like something I'd do. Omigod! Are you OK? Did you get hurt?" Maggie blinked saucer wide eyes, her hands inspecting whichever body part they could find.

"A little banged up, but I'm fine now. Honest. We might need to stay her for a couple nights. Our place is still missing a front door." Ajax leaned over, placing a kiss on her forehead. "I hope Cal's friend doesn't mind if we crash out here until the repairs get done. What do you say, Cal?"

Something jostled her shoulder, dragging her back to the conversation happening around her.

"I'm sorry, what?"

Maggs scoffed, rolling her eyes. "I don't think I've ever seen you so dreamy before. You really have fallen for him, haven't you?"

She swallowed down the unexplainable tears, the feat nearly choking her at her friend's well-meaning words. Coughing out a sharp laugh, she gave her a weak nod and an equally anemic smile. "Yeah. Yeah, I think I have."

Maggs leaned over, keeping the sheet tucked under her armpits as she hugged her close, whispering into her ear. "Then go to him. He's a good guy, Cal. I mean, he's letting us, a couple of complete strangers, stay in his house. Please, don't let him get away." As she released her, Cal looked at her friend in a different light. If she survived this plan, she promised herself she'd change things. Maggs and Ajax had put their lives into her hands, not intentionally, but by their love and caring, they both wormed their way into her heart.

"You two are amazing. I know I've never said it enough, but I...I am so glad you've always been there for me. Both of you." Magg's confused expression drew out a laugh that only added to her bewilderment. "I know, I'm not making any sense, but you're right. I do need to make sure not to let him get away."

Bolstered by the unbreakable bond of true friendship, she hugged her roommates before heading out to finish her conversation with Eamon.

"I'll check in with you guys later on, OK?" With a wave, she backed out of the room, closing the door behind her.

All right, time to deal with this, once and for all.

She turned and pointed her nose toward the kitchen, still puzzling out a solution to the bigger problem. Now, after a few necessary moments spent with her friends, she had a better plan of attack in mind. At the table, Eamon and Kai sat across from each other, Voni easily within arm's reach of her over protective male. The murmured conversation stalled as she entered the room.

"Yes, I am going out to find these fucks. You guys either can either tag along or not. I don't really care which, but you can't stop me." She punctuated the last statement with a firm and final arm fold across her chest. Her inner voice prayed the gesture came off as powerful, and not petulant.

By the arched eyebrow from Voni and the slow blinks from the boys, she had the sinking feeling she didn't quite master the tough look just yet. An exasperated sigh huffed out as her shoulders dropped.

"OK, OK. So I really do need your help. I need to make sure to keep Galen out of this as much as you can. I know how to get this guy. He's an egomaniac. I'm a girl with big tits *and* a brain. He'll never see it coming. Trust me."

Kai made a steadying grab for the table as he sprayed his coffee onto the floor. Sputtering and gasping between coughs and laughs, he wiped his mouth with back of his hand. "Damn. You don't mince words, do you?" Eamon thumped him on the back even as he shook with amusement.

Voni remained collected, her hazel eyes sparkling with mirth as the boys fought to regain their composure. "She's right. Most of you guys figure the bigger the boobs are, the lower the I.Q. must be. Present company excluded, I'm sure." She raised her hands in mock surrender, but the telltale smirk on her face said more than her obsequious words.

After brushing off the lingering go juice on his chin, Kai leveled a playfully evil glance at his mate as he addressed Cal's statement. "Be that as it may, and I'm not going to even start this battle with either of you in defense of my gender, but just where did you want to start looking?"

Oh yeah. There was that little matter still looming over her head. Her gut kept pointing toward the campus, toward Paul, but Eamon was right. She would do Galen no good if she got herself nabbed before she saved him. Thinking again about the suggestion of having Voni find them, she opened her mouth, but a stern gaze and an almost imperceptible head shake from Eamon stopped her words. As she followed his guiding eyes, she noted the traces of faint dark circles under her eyes that had cropped up since the last time she saw her. Even her voice sounded more strained, her laughter heavy and exhausted.

No way could she ask any more, not after what they had already done for her.

Her mind spun, idea after idea rolling forward only to be pulled under by the voice of reason. All her solutions were ripped straight from last week's episode of NCIS. Her gaze landed on the handsome faces of both the men sitting lost in their own musings. Mark Harmon didn't hold a candle to either of them.

Until a week ago, all the men she knew with half a brain were the older, scholarly types in tweed suit jackets and horn-rimmed glasses. The standard male student in her classes was more interested in becoming the next Jack Kerouac or George Lucas. Yet here she stood, a couple hundred years of battle tactics and know-how wrapped up in a pair of six-foot twelve, bench-press-a-Buick badasses.

Three, if she counted the one who now rested upstairs, behind the second door on the right, laying amid a tangle of white sheets and a thick down comforter. Only through her sheer stubborn will did she remain here away from him. Her heart stuttered as an invisible tether gently tugged her back to the stairs. If she shifted her eyes, she could see the bottom step. The magnetic draw sang to her blood as the discussion continued, filtering in as a staticky buzz.

The complete awareness of the distance between her and him dragged her spirit down, her heart homing in on his restful breathing.

Homing in.

She gaped in wide-eyed joy, the idea hopefully not too far-fetched.

"GPS." She skidded to the table, falling into the first available chair. "We use the GPS chip in Paul's phone to find where they are." Out of habit, she patted down all the possible pocket locations on her body, searching for a non-existent cell phone. Looking around, her eyes joined in the frantic search, even as her brain tapped an impatient foot, waiting for her to remember her phone had long since been lost.

"Eamon? Can you run a phone trace?" At Kai's question, Cal turned to Eamon, unable to hide the puppy dog plead in her eyes. Kai covered his mouth, coughing to mask the escaping chuckle. "Oh, she's good." Rocking forward to bring all four legs back down to the floor, he reached out his hand, patting Cal's shoulder. "If he can do it for you, he will."

Eamon flashed a Cheshire Cat grin, lacing his fingers together and with a twist, his arms snapped out, each knuckle popping in a flourish.

"Are ya doubtin' me there now, boyo?" His hand disappeared into his pocket, returning with a gleaming silver iPhone. "I'm sure ya got a number for me to be callin', right?"

"Ummmm. Shit. It's on my phone. Wait. I need a computer." Cal searched her surroundings, hoping to see the signs of the needed tech to no avail. "I know he sent it to me. It's on the bottom of all of his damned emails. All I have to do is access my messages. Dammit. How does someone live in this day and age without a computer?"

Eamon laughed before handing over his phone to her. "It's upstairs in his study, but there's another one in the library. And he usually keeps his laptop in the game room."

She slid her fingers around the slim case, her head lifting as an inquisitive expression drew her eyebrows higher up on her forehead. "Game room? Library? I haven't seen a library."

Two heads nodded in unison as Kai answered her. "Yeah. It's on the floor beneath us, across from the armory."

"Armory?" Her voice squeaked, fumbling the phone in her surprise. "Just how big is this place? Does he own this whole building?" Refocusing on the task at hand, her fingers flying over the familiar keys as she delved into her university Web site, seeking out her personal mail folder. As she skimmed past the unopened and impatient electronic letters, her mind flashed back to a snippet of a conversation after a certain elevator ride. *He had said all the cars in the garage were his, but...*

Her eyes began to lose focus as page after page of unanswered messages scrolled down, a never-ending stream of requests from a life she half forgot that she still lived. Strong fingers clasped her shoulder, pulling her troubled thoughts away from the tiny screen. Eamon smiled reassuringly, infusing her fractured mind with a needed clarity.

"How's 'bout ya worry 'bout askin' him that later, yeah?"

His nod waited for a responding one from her, and after a deep calming breath, she followed suit. With a renewed sense of peace, she easily pinpointed Paul's e-mail address amid the crowd. Thumbing opening the message, she handed the phone back to Eamon.

"Thank you. All of you." Her gaze moved to the three others gathered in the still unfamiliar room. For too long, she existed on the fringes of life, never daring to connect with anyone for fear of leaving someone to grieve over her. She did not want to cause anyone any pain or sadness, so better to keep everyone at a safe distance. She thought her actions to be so altruistic and compassionate.

But now, she realized she was the one who came up short in that deal. She was the one on the losing end. She missed out on laughter and on friendships. The pain and sadness were her own as she wrapped herself up in a blanket of fear, blinding her in the guise of consideration.

Here, surrounded by people she had only known for an amount of hours she could count on one hand, she learned the true meaning of life. These virtual strangers willingly put their lives on the line to save two people they did not know. People she tried not to even call friends.

The openly accepting eyes gazing back at her filled her with shame and sadness.

"I've been such an idiot. All this time, I kept thinking it would just be better not to get attached to things, or people. And now? Now I…"

Her voice caught in her throat, wedging around the lump that was her heart. A gentle squeeze from the hand still on her shoulder, a hint of tranquility seeping through her limbs.

Eamon stood as a sentinel, watching as the chosen spiritmate of one of his greatest generals puzzled and reasoned her way to the first viable solution suggested that did not involve someone traveling through the Void. From the moment Kai and Voni returned from picking up the final member of their happy troupe from the hospital, the three of them had been trying to formulate a plan as well.

He knew his friends well. He knew Galen would not sit by and allow for the heinous attack on his mate and those she held dear to go unanswered. Also, he knew Kai's caring and kindhearted spiritmate would not be able to say no if she was asked to venture into the Black once again. Finally, he knew without a doubt he would lose a testicle if he dared to mention the possibility of a return trip.

The drain on Voni still clung to her lethargic movements and her drowsy smile. If there was another, more mundane, way to find his enemy short of knocking on every door in the entire 415 area code, they would find it. And thanks to the wonders of this overly connected electronic world, the path was soon to light up brighter than the Vegas strip.

Only the impending implosion of Calliope dampened the rising spirits in the room.

"Now, you have a reason to be attached. Don't spend your time worrying about what you can't go back and change." Eamon's playful lilt diminished as he spoke, his words soft and powerful. "Just think about how much richer your life is going to be."

"And crazier," Voni added, an innocently impish grin on her face, lifting her hand as she began ticking off fingers. "And messier, and louder and let's not leave out—"

The final point remained a mystery as Kai hushed his mate in the most creative manner Cal imagined, covering her mouth with his, the kiss flirtatious and effective. Powerless to stop the giggles that bubbled up as she watched the loving pair in a good-hearted wrestling match, Voni unconvincing in her attempt to escape Kai's embrace, Cal hoped her plan met with the success she so desperately needed. As she continued to spy on the laughing lovers, she wanted to know that with Galen. Her heart quickened its pace as her mind swapped out the entangled pair before her, the fashion forward blazer and v-neck tee replaced by a sweeping black leather trench and nothing underneath.

"Now don't be scarin' her off like that, Siobhan. I'm tryin' to give sage words of wisdom here." The charming brogue had returned to Eamon's voice, his eyes focused on the flashing images on the small screen in his hand.

Cal shook her head, the grin firmly planted on her face. "Oh, I'm made of sterner stuff that than. But I do want to have some girl talk time once this is done. Ah, who the hell am I kidding? I think I'm gonna need serious therapy after this is done."

"Well, then, boys and girls," Eamon announced, spinning the device in his hand, the visible grid glowing and one specific point clearly flagged. "We now have a destination. Do we have a plan?"

They're not gonna like this at all.

Shushing the nagging voice in her head, Cal pinned both of the men with determined eyes. "Yeah, I have to go in alone."

She raised her hand in the hopes of cutting off the growls of denial, the sounds of a chair scraping against the tiles disobeying her command. "No, I've thought this out. I have to draw him out. He thinks he's smarter and he's won. If I go alone—"

"No." Eamon's head shook so furiously she feared it might fly off his shoulders. Soon, Kai stood shoulder to shoulder with him, a menacing wall of protective masculine energy. "Galen would have my head on a pike if I let anything happen to you."

Kai chimed in, his complete agreement with Eamon coming as no surprise to Cal. "Kid, you go in alone and he'll paint the walls with your entrails. These bastards don't play by the rules of polite warfare."

"Cal?" The only other female voice in the room spoke up softly. "I've been in your shoes before. Please make sure to really think this through."

Kai eyes softened fractionally as his mate mentioned her own hellish experience with their foes before turning again to hard gems of icy gray. "You might think you're ready and that you're strong, but you would be dead wrong. If we let you go, it would be like a lamb to the slaughter."

"Exactly."

Eamon arched an eyebrow as his fellow Guardian blinked slowly. "Come again?"

Cal heaved in a deep breath before launching into her plan. "The way I see it, we will only get one shot at this guy. He will be expecting all of you, but not me. Maybe if I go in first, get him to drop his guard, then you guys can come in and mop up. I may be stubborn, but I'm not stupid. Tell me I'm wrong. Tell me going in guns blazing is the best plan."

She swiveled her eyes between a pair of stormy pale green and an equally unhappy set of frigid bright blue. Kai drew his eyebrows together in an angry frown as Eamon folded his arms across his barrel chest. Well aware her idea would meet with some resistance, she kept her face impassive, waiting for the inevitable grumbles of agreement.

"Fuck."

If the situation was not so dire, she might have laughed at the simultaneously growled word. Instead, her chin dropped sharply, grateful for their begrudging faith.

"Yeah, my thoughts too. But here's the kicker." Another slow inhale, the air hissing out in a long stream. "I need you guys to stay here with Galen."

Kai barked out an incredulous laugh as Eamon tossed his hands in the air and paced away from the gathered cluster. "Stay? Why, so he can disembowel us without having to go far?"

"No. So you can help save my ass. You know where I'm gonna be and no way are you going to be able to keep Galen away. But if you can hold him for just a little while?"

Both of the guys stared at her like she had grown a second head. "Please?"

Eamon groaned, rolling his eyes, Kai burying his face in his palms.

A deep chuckle drew Cal's attention from the cringing warriors to the pixie sitting at the kitchen table, her crooked grin full of feminine pride. "You used the magic word, Calliope. Even as tough as these guys are, they're a couple of softies for one little please from a damsel in distress." Giving her a conspiratorial wink, her half smile blossomed to full flower. "I know, neither one of us really fall into that category, but sometimes being a girl can be helpful."

"Voni," The muffled word seeped through the slits of Kai's fingered mask. "You're not helping."

"Didn't say I was helping, hon. But I am still right."

Kai lifted his eyes, glaring weak daggers at his mate from her safe seat at the table. Cal watched entranced as Kai and Voni gazed deep into each other's eyes, as if in silent conversation. A warm smile touched Voni's face and melted the sadness from her eyes, while Kai beamed, the grin filled with love and pride.

Remembering her own mental chats with Galen, she realized that was exactly what was happening and wondered if all the Guardians could read minds.

"Yes, we can." The answer came as a shock even as the smirk lingered on Eamon's face. *"But sometimes, we can just guess what people are thinkin' by how they act."*

"Didn't your mother teach you it's rude to listen at keyholes?" Cal added a sidelong glare at Eamon, certain her childish pout, complete with petulant arm crossing, did not improve her score on the scale of badassness, but nonetheless, she felt it needed to be said. Her face blanched as a stray thought tugged on the heels of her indignation.

"Wait. Can the other guys listen into my thought, too?"

The unison nod dropped her heart somewhere around her knees.

"Great. Now, what?"

Eamon moved to her side, a grim smile on his face as he rested a hand on her shoulder. "Now, we teach you how to build a wall in your mind. Gonna have to keep your focus on this one and once Galen discovers you're missing, you're gonna have to find a way to hold him at arm's length. Any opening and we're all dead meat." He held her gaze, letting the gravity of his words sink in. "Sure you're ready for this?"

Her answer came swiftly, confident and without hesitation.

"I can't live without him, Eamon. I'll do whatever I have to spend whatever time I have left with him."

"Then let's get to this. Daylight's a-wastin' and the longer we delay, the more likely we're gonna get caught by your man upstairs."

His words cut out any remaining heel dragging on her part, giving him a sharp nod. "You'd better make this the Readers Digest version. I'm getting a bad feeling about this."

She hoped her gut was just leading her astray, since she hadn't really eaten for the past day. She made a mental note to grab a bite before things got rolling. She looked up for some reassurance, but the equally dreadful look in the blue eyes above her only added to her fears.

"Wish I could say the feeling wasn't mutual, but lyin' isn't something I do." He gave her a comforting pat on her shoulder before leading her to an open chair at the cozy breakfast nook. "Try to relax, darlin'. Let me and Kai do all the heavy liftin' this time." She blinked and Kai's face appeared before her, his large hands resting on her knees as he crouched down in front of her. A second set of hands settled on her shoulders and an eerie hush blanketed the space around her.

"Do I need to…whoa." She exhaled the last word, her eyes flaring wide before her lids slipped down. A shock of energy jolted through her body, snapping her spine stiff and the powerful tendrils raced like lightning on a course leading to her frantic mind. Brick by imaginary brick, a barrier appeared, walling her thoughts behind a veil of silence. The sensation was not painful, but neither was it pleasant. Her heart beat faster, the reassuring warmth of Galen's presence disappearing behind the thickening curtain. Strange that she should so deeply miss something she had only recently accepted.

And miss it, she did. Down to her soul.

"Just relax, Cal. He hasn't gone anywhere." The deeply accented baritone just beyond her closed eyes gave her little comfort, the foreign timbre similar to the one she craved to hear with all her heart. Close, but not the same. *He's fine. Well, until he finds out what I've done. God, please let this work.*

"All right. Done." Eamon pulled his hands away and moved to stand next to Kai as he regained his feet. "You can let some things come in. Think of the wall as more of trampoline. You can bounce some thoughts off it, and they'll be able to read surface thoughts, but you have to keep things simple. Even once your boy arrives. No matter how much you want to, you cannot answer him."

Peeling her eyes open, her gaze drifted up, meeting the apprehensive stares from all. After scanning the room, she found her eyes drawn toward the stairs. Her mental wandering moved down the hall and into the deep cherry wood room and French white linens waiting beyond. She refocused and gave a reassuring nod.

"I'm ready."

TWENTY-SEVEN

Cal squared her shoulders, following the magnetic pull in her gut toward the dilapidated Tenderloin hotel. Her steps remained sturdy and straight forward, her eyes focused on the flakey red and black door as she ignored the graphic catcalls riding her receding footfalls like an oily wake. She stumbled, her foot nearly missing the curb at an especially lewd proposition from the spindly dark specter standing guard at the door. As her gaze narrowed unimpressed, her mind took a pondering path, wondering how she would have reacted to the veiled threat of physical violence in his offer prior to this moment in time.

Watching the smirk slide off the thug's stunned face, she knew that had this been two weeks ago, she would never have walked willingly into this part of town. Not unless she was armed to the teeth or with a rabid Rottweiler. Maybe both.

Today was different.

Today, she was different.

The man who had put his life before hers more times than she dared to count was dying before her eyes. And unless she stopped the evil asshole behind these walls, they would never be free.

As she ascended the final step, daggers in her cold and angry green eyes, her voice rang clear and determined.

"I'm here to see Stefan."

Dark eyes flashed into view over the silver wraparounds, a sickening sweet waft of what she knew to be panic oozed out of his skin even as he fought to hold the upper hand. He lifted his hand to slide down the lens, the attempt to flex his anemic and exposed bicep humorous to say the least. "How 'bout you see how much of my dick you can—"

She snapped out her arm in a blur, straightened and stiff fingers finding their target at the base of his throat, sinking into the soft flesh. "So not happening, asshat," she replied, her tone bored. "Now, is someone gonna open this door or do I have to do everything myself?"

The baggy-clothed gangbanger next to the door stepped over his coughing and choking brother, his Bulls jersey shimmying as his shoulders bounced in laughter. "Dayam, girl. Y'all got some anger issues there or what?"

Cal nodded as she followed inside, mumbling as she passed the threshold, leaving the writhing heap alone in his suffering. "You have no idea."

Arguments and bass thumped through the thin walls. Somewhere above her, she heard the shattering of glass and the answering wet slap of flesh on flesh, groans of either pain, pleasure or a blending of the two, drifting in and out. Her sneakers crunched on debris that blanketed the cracked and pitted linoleum hallway. The stench of grief and forgotten dreams mingled in, filtering through stale smoke and the flickering florescent glow. Babies cried as a phone rang behind a door, a distant siren silencing the din for a held breath until fading into the night and the tenement exhaled, sagging on its foundation and the noise began again.

Under other circumstances, Cal would have been saddened by the whole scene, empathizing with those dealt a tough hand. Yet, with each step pulling her closer to the pulsing vile center of the building, she only felt a simmering rage. This de Coldreto guy had her nabbed from in front of a classroom, tortured her and her roommates, and until he was out of the picture, Galen was going to let himself die to keep her safe.

So not happening.

She had only just begun to think of a real life, a life that involved another person, and she was not about to let it slip away without one hell of a serious fight.

Her reluctant guide stopped before the only silent door. A sharp rap and the wood swung open. The Bryant wannabe pivoted and eyed her, the toothpick dancing between the flashing pearly whites as he tipped his head toward the opening.

"You got balls, girl. Gotta give you props there."

Cal coughed out a short laugh, giving the complimenteur a slight nod of her head. "Yeah, too bad you chose the wrong team." She waited as one black eyebrow shot up. "I think the Knicks are gonna take it this year." Mocking laughter filled the space at her back as she entered the room.

Something bad had taken place in this tiny room and not too long ago. The stench of rotten meat and vomit permeated the entire space, peppered in was the scent of spent electricity and a familiar hint she couldn't quite put her finger on. As her hand rose instinctually to catch her own gag reflex, her gaze scanned each darkened corner and dingy wall.

Another waft and she knew what that scent was.

Aqua Velva. Faint and perverted, but still there it was.

Amid a drying brownish smear on the floor was a crumpled pile of fabrics that was once a bright red and white Hawaiian shirt as well as a pair of khakis.

She swallowed hard against the bile that rose in the back of her throat, almost losing the battle. Blinking quickly to keep the image in focus, she tried to convince herself that Paul didn't deserve whatever had transpired here.

Too bad neither her heart nor her head believed the humane sentiment.

"You will have to excuse the mess, my dear. I was not expecting to entertain any visitors here."

The voice pierced the silence like a needle as the speaker slunk in from the open corridor to her left. That same voice had tormented her waking dreams and belonged to the elusive fourth man in that tiny cabin. Her heart thundered, forcing the arctic blood to resume its path through her body. A large part of her mind ran in retreat, searching for the farthest corner in solace, there to cringe and cower. Standing as a statue, she blinked as he made his way into the room, his long legs taking polite bites out of the distance between them. A white button down Oxford had been slipped on, the sleeves rolled up as the front remained unbuttoned and untucked, revealing a well-toned physique that disappeared into a pair of neatly pressed black slacks.

"How kind. You do remember me. And here I was afraid that you might have forgotten about our...previous meeting. After all, you were, shall we say, otherwise engaged?"

He circled her, his bare feet making not a sound, a shark leisurely taking in the distress of its prey. She stared at his face, the hidden or half-remembered images flooding into her mind on fast forward. Those strange pale purple eyes set into a harsh and scarily handsome face, hair too perfectly slick and an unnerving Italian accent. *You will make for a fine catch, my little minnow. You'll see.*

It was him. He was the one who grabbed her at school. The darkness dragged her down in such a blur, she almost missed this gem of a memory. It never was a random attack or a chance occurrence. He knew exactly where she would be because Paul told her. The bastard must have promised Paul something.

"Oh, I did." Lavender eyes slid to the messy pile of melted clothes. "Too bad he did not truly understand just what the price was going to be."

She dropped her hand from her mouth. Dammit, she kept forgetting these guys could read minds. Anger mixed with fatigue, brewing a dangerous concoction and once again, she found her voice.

"Listen, assmunch. I couldn't care less what happened to that fucker. I am pissed at what you did to my friends. And why me anyway? That part I still don't really get."

An oily chuckle slithered across the floor as he crossed to the battered Lazyboy and lowered onto the patchwork leather regally, a tattered throne for a passed-over prince. "My dear, why ever would you think this has anything to do with you? You were simply a pawn of convenience. It could have been another female, any other female and the outcome would have been the same." He gazed at her over his steepled fingers, a mischievous grin marking his face as he nodded toward the couch at his left.

He was lying and she knew it. She interlaced her arms across her chest, helping her keep her rage in check. "Bullshit. You think you can get me to do your dirty work, but you're wrong. I'm not playing your fucking little game. I won't bring Galen to you." She prayed her overt confidence was enough to convince the dangerous man before her. Their whole plan hinged on his ego, and she had to play it cool.

Stefan studied the self-assured girl standing defiantly before him. At their first meeting, she appeared to be nothing special. His insight told him she was to be claimed by one of the Guardians, and since that overgrown Boy Scout of a Greek was the only one local, he was certain this would spell the end of his interference. His plan was flawless. Grab the girl, Galen would sniff out the bait, then he would be rid of him once and for all.

That was over a week ago, and still both of them remained, a festering thorn in his side. He narrowed his eyes, sliding up and down her lean body. Black leggings and a nondescript olive green sweatshirt did little to hide her lush curves. But there was something else there. A new strength now radiated from her spirit. And it was familiar to him.

He arched an eyebrow as his lip curled into a sly grin. "Well, well, well. It seems like you don't have to bring me him after all. You, my dear, are all I need." The confused look on her face was precious, almost convincing too, until a commotion from just outside the door spread his wicked smile, plastering it across his entire face. "Live bait still works the best."

Loud voices in the hall pulled her pretty green eyes away from him. Her jaw dropped in shock as the wood vaporized, vanishing in a muffled flash. The red gore painting the corridor explained who now stepped through the opening. Body parts littered the hallway as a very pissed-off Greek strode into the room.

Power tempered by seething rage flowed in waves from Galen's blood-speckled face. "You even think about touching her, de Coldreto, and your hand will fall to the floor next to your head." A flick of his wrist snapped the lingering crimson drops off the gleaming sharpened steel. His black eyes burned as his gaze moved from his foe to his female. Eamon and Kai would be guarding the door, ensuring they were not going to be interrupted.

A thin sheen of sweat dampened his brow as he forced himself to stay focused and upright. He knew he could only tap into his fading powers a little longer before his body would betray his weakness. Inside his head, a voice prayed it would last long enough to finish this bastard once and for all. The look of shock on his mate's face threatened to shatter his resolve.

"Galen? No. This is my battle to fight. This is payback for—"

"Your battle?" Galen's steel voice cut her to the quick, his sharp wrath cutting off any further words from his headstrong mate. "No, agapi. You have no place in this fight. It's me he wants, and now I will oblige." The air crackled around them, electricity sizzling in the tight confines. With two strides, he stood nose to nose with the smirking Roman when a flash of movement on the edge of his vision caught his eye.

A black fist narrowly missed his nose as it barreled past. He jumped back as a mountain in a sleeveless T-shirt continued swinging. Surprisingly on the defense, he dodged and ducked, countering with a bone-crushing blow to the attacker's gut, his feet back pedaling to move the fight out into the larger living room. His punch did little to slow his opponent, the fresh infusion of Rogue energy still settling into the blood.

He swore inside his head as he drew the big man in close and he used the butt of his sword in a powerful up thrust, snapping the bald dome back. The attack took a sharp turn as the head rocked forward, the impact on the bridge of Galen's nose causing fireworks to bloom behind his eyes. Gritting his teeth, he blinked away the sporadic light bursts as he lowered his shoulder and drove the big man backward. Their feet tangled at the force of the impact, stopping only once the wall slammed them to a sudden halt, pictures and a broken clock bouncing off to shatter on the peeling tiled floor.

Cal watched as the two titans pummeled each other, the air filling with groans and grunts with each passing second. Her breaths came in short gasps. Even after all the classes and years of martial arts training she had, she had never really seen a true knockdown, drag out fight. It didn't look like it did in the movies. It was much more brutal, more visceral, and the sounds were making the hairs on the back of her neck stand at attention.

In the back of her head, she sensed the brush of his Galen's voice, soothing and calming, but the words stopped just shy of the massive wall in her mind.

"No more."

The words fell in a murmur from her lips as she squared her shoulders. Her eyes lifted, dragging away from the two struggling fighters to pin the true cause of this fight. "If I give myself to you, will you let him go?"

Had this been other than a life or death situation, Cal would have been laughing. The scene just froze, as if the hand of God pushed the giant "Pause" button in the sky. Even the fists ceased to fly as her words drifted through the room.

Stefan quirked his head, an eerie light twinkling in the purple depths that stared at her. "You think to buy his life with your own? Well, now. This is an unexpected turn of events." The glowing gaze shifted to the statues caught in mid-strike. "What say you, Alexiou? Do I accept the gracious offer?"

Galen couldn't believe his ears. Sure the blood pounding in his head must have garbled the message, he gaped in mute shock, his arm locked back, half-cocked and inches away from finishing off his opponent. The distraction was enough to turn the tide and fast. Not as damaged as he thought, a beefy arm slung around his neck, torqueing his arm uncomfortably against his back as floor met his face. Stunned to his core, he felt his spirit sink into the pitted linoleum pressed at his cheek.

"Cal? No, don't do this. You can't know what you are saying." His heart screamed in protest, his mind searching for hers, but his thoughts slammed hard against the shut door in her head, cutting him off from her thoughts. Refusing to allow her to trade herself for him, he continued to struggle and fight, even with the familiar agony of his shoulder dislocating met each new wiggle.

"Calliope? Do not give in. Please"

His weak voice betrayed his flagging resolve, yet he couldn't drag his eyes away from the hell unfolding before him. Stefan smirked. "I believe it is too late for you, Greek. She came here, of her own free will, to seek *me* out. Now she makes her choice. I won." The evil glint in those lavender eyes doubled as the devastating truth shattered the last vestiges of hope in his soul. He watched in defeated agony as Stefan extended a hand to the prize in question, smiling as he licked his lips in anticipation of his impending conquest. "Come to me and I swear he will leave unharmed."

Cal steeled her spine, her feet shuffling closer to the outstretched arm, her eyes sliding to Galen as he ceased to struggle against the imprisoning hold. The black eyes refusing to look at her were flat and empty, devoid of any heat or any life. Unable to endure another second, she glanced away, finding the hilt of his discarded blade.

Once the distance disappeared between her and the source of all the shit that had happened in her life for the past two weeks, she stopped, lifting her eyes with a strange calm. "I was right."

Stefan frowned imperceptibly, a slight crease forming across his forehead. "Right how?"

"Waterloo."

Cal slammed the palmed knife into de Coldreto's chest, the thick blade cracking the ribs as its tip sought out his heart. His saucer-wide eyes gave her all the answer she needed. "Wow, you honestly thought I'd go with you? You really are full of yourself."

Stefan staggered back, his face a wild mask of pure shock as he stared at the hilt protruding from his chest. She wished she had a camera to capture the look on his face. Evil twisted the frozen features into a scowl of rage as he yanked out the blade.

"Y-you...BITCH!" It clattered against the floor before he viciously backhanded her. The world tilted in a flash of pain and darkness swallowed her.

Galen sprung to life as he saw Cal flip back off her feet. With a lethal roar, he kicked off the floor, his strength returning in a violent rush. His head jerked back, a telltale splash of something warm and sticky identified his shot as on target. Free from the headlock, he drove his elbow back, ribs shattering and he clamored to his regain his feet.

"*De Coldreto!*" His voice shook the walls with the power of his rage. Still in a low crouch, Galen tackled him, his arms wrapping around his waist as he tossed him with a growl onto the floor. Curling his fingers around the crisp white shirt with a growing red stain, his lips curving into a sneer as he yanked hard, slamming his forehead between the seething lavender eyes. He unclenched his hands only long enough to release the fabric from between his fingers, but his fists formed a heartbeat later, a rapid fire combination of bone-crunching body blows with no sign of letting up.

Buoyed by a renewed influx of power, fueled by one truth, he aimed his attacks on the gaping hole just shy of piercing the bastard's heart. His female had only missed the mark by a cat's whisker. Pride filled his heart at her bravery, but quick on its heels was anger directed toward the punching bag under him.

Stefan shook his head, baring his blood-stained teeth in a snarl.

"No way you win this one, Greek. This ends now." Lavender eyes blazed as Stefan splayed his fingers wide, the tell-tale glow of Rogue-charged energy lancing between his palms. One more second and this fight would be over.

Galen had faced death numerous times in his long life, several close brushes as a mortal, but many more as one of the chosen Guardians. Time slowed to a pinpoint clarity of possibilities. He blinked in slow deliberation, his mind unraveling the actions just beyond the thin shades of skin. Fingers unfurled, the exposed palms beginning to glow with an unearthly light. A few feet away, a pair of wide emerald green eyes swiveled his direction, unfocused and disoriented after the vicious blow.

She did not give up on him. She bought him the time he needed.

The outcome was clear in his mind as he snapped his eyes down. He wrapped his fingers around de Coldreto's wrists and turned them back onto the man's chest, the movement nothing more than a blur made real with the power of a true Marshal of the Guardian Warriors. Galen roared in response, and he glared confidently into the stunned purple eyes as the power bolt fed back onto itself.

"There you are right, asshole. This ends now."

He shielded his eyes an instant before the room exploded in a silent burst of blinding white and the smell of burning copper filled the air. Galen cautiously peeled his eyes open, the colors slowly returning to his vision. His hand reached down, meeting nothing but a slippery residue where de Coldreto once lay. Heaving a deep sigh, he sat back on his heels and dragged the back of his other hand across his forehead, wiping away the blood and other evidence of the battle.

"Calliope?" Tired, his voice distant to his own ears, he called for her, weak in his desperation. *Please. Let her be safe.*

The bells ringing in her head did nothing to drown out the only sound her soul craved. Pain and the lingering dancing lights fogged her vision, but still she scrambled toward the source as best as she could. "Galen? Galen! Oh God. I'm so sorry. I'm sorry. Please don't be mad at me." The more she moved, the more she realized the earlier smack was not the only reason for her blurry sight, tears cascading down her face by the time she reached him.

He scooped her into his powerful arms, cradling her close as he rained kisses against her hair. "Shhh, my beautiful muse. Do not cry, please." His fingers gently stroked along her back, as her tears continued to dampen his shirt.

Above her muffled sobs, she picked out heavy footfalls that stopped in the vicinity of the shattered doorway. But she didn't want to move from this moment, didn't want to look up, and once again, see the heart broken betrayal in the eyes of the man who was willing to die for her. The guilt-laden waterworks ebbed into a sniffling stream, her tenuous emotional control safely reasserted for the moment.

"De Coldreto?" Kai's thick accent slurred belied his exhaustion.

Galen raised his eyes from the tender burden in his arms to see the two brothers as they waited in rapt expectation. His gaze swung between Eamon's bright turquoise and Kai's eerie ice green, words of gratitude unspoken but heard nonetheless. He dropped his chin a fraction of an inch before finding his voice again.

"Gone."

Cal jumped, her head pivoting around the room. "What about the big guy? Where'd he go? Did he…" A gentle touch on her cheek stopped the rapid-fire spill of panicked words and he waited until her sparkling green eyes settled on him.

"We'll find him, agapi. If he shows his face again, he will be found."

"So, the plan worked as you hoped it would there, kiddo?" Eamon's playful lilt had a slight slur. But that was not the only reason Galen drew his eyebrows together, his gaze narrowing toward the smirking mop of copper and bronze spikes in the doorway.

"What plan?"

"Ummm," the drawn out stammering syllable brushed against his chest, pulling his confused gaze downward. "Yeah. Remember when I said don't be mad at me?"

He tipped her chin up even as her eyes studied the bloodstains on his shirt. "This was your idea, Calliope?" He tried to keep his tone even and non-threatening. Yet, as soon as he saw that lower lip of hers disappear between her teeth, he knew he failed to miss his mark.

She huffed out a panicked breath, the words tumbling out in one long stream. "Well, sort of, I mean the only way to get this guy to drop his guard enough would be to make him think he had won, so I figured if I came here and just sorta, well, um, said I was giving up then he'd screw up, and I knew you would follow me here, but I had to act like I was gonna go through with it, which I wouldn't have, but I had to make sure he believed me, and Eamon and Kai were supposed to make sure you were safe, but then that guy came in from the back room and…"

Laughter, rich and full, bled in between each word, gaining in volume and momentum the longer her story continued and it seemed to be emanating from all around. As her gaze climbed up the vibrating chest before her, the corners of her lips tugged into a tentative smile even as the tears still lingered on her lashes.

"So…you're not mad?"

Eamon chimed in, patting Kai on the shoulder as they entered the room. "Oh, sweetie. I think you're gonna need to be learnin' he's gonna forgive ya for most any wrong. But I think it's time we found another place to be talkin', right?"

Galen kept his gaze focused on the brightest green eyes that captured his heart with a quiet strength and an unyielding spirit. He nodded as he rose to his wobbling legs, his arms remaining tightly wound around her. Eamon's hand grabbed onto his shoulder, steadying him as Kai's voice filtered in through the silence.

"Come on, brother. Let's get back home."

Home.

The word had a new meaning. One of hope.

"Yes, that sounds like a good idea."

"Uh?" A timid voice chirped from the cradle of his arms. "Maybe just a cab ride this time? All this popping around is making my head spin. And not in a good way either."

Galen leaned down, placing a tender kiss on her brow. "By car, it is."

* * *

Emmet glared from the shadows at the foursome stepped into the waiting cab. Breath crept in with painful gasps, one rib bending and flexing with each inhale. He continued to throw virtual daggers as the cab pulled away, disappearing at the corner.

Fuckers were gonna pay for icing his crew.

"Vengeance at this stage will do you no good, I assure you." A cold voice dripped down his back, followed by the tight grip of long fingers against his shoulder. "There will be another time, another place. Let them have their little victory."

Emmet felt the world around him melt and shift, a new doorway opening to someplace beyond the brick at his back.

"For now, you must become who you were truly meant to be."

Wicked laughter wafted up from the nothingness. Emmet stepped into the growing darkness and was gone.

TWENTY-EIGHT

The water shut off in the shower, only the sounds of the trailing drips gurgling down the drain cut into the tense silence. Cal sat in apprehension as she waited, cocooned in a voluminous T-shirt, her legs hanging off the edge of the bed.

Eamon and Kai had helped Galen heal from his physical wounds. Now it was up to her to heal his soul, hers as well. She couldn't bear it if she brought him any real harm. Throughout the entire cab ride back, he refused to let her go, his arms holding her more tightly than any safety belt. Plus, if she were honest with herself, he wasn't the only one clinging on for dear life.

She tried to kill a man tonight. Granted, the man was a monster, a creature of unforgiveable evil who had brutalized her and her friends, but she had never thought she was capable to taking a life. He gaze slipped down to her shaking hands, her fingers twisting together in nervous knots. She pulled in a shuddered breath, working to steel her roiling nerves.

A warm shadow fell across her hands, followed by a gentle touch on the top of her head.

"I can hear your thoughts, agapi." Her eyes drifted close, seeking comfort and needed strength from the fingers sliding through her still damp hair. The crisp aroma of wild darkness tickled her nose and sent tingles down to her toes. Waves of infused heat still oozing from his shower-warmed skin brushed against her face, daring her to open her eyes.

A thick white towel hung low, hugging his narrow hips and cutting a sharp contrast with the chiseled olive abs a breath away from her lips. A tempting dusting of dark hair disappeared beneath the rolled terrycloth barrier, the desire to reach out and touch him moving from a curious inclination to a soul-shattering imperative in record time. Her blood picked up speed, fueled by his nearness. Roses bloomed on her pale cheeks the longer she gazed at the heady, and purely male specimen before her.

His life was literally in her hands and she knew in that moment, she loved him. She had since he exploded into that hellish pit, and each time he swooped in to save her only further cemented her conviction.

She was in love and now, she intended on showing him.

Galen called all his Guardian skills to bear, biding his time and allowing her to set the pace. Although his own time was limited, and slipping fast, tonight was about her. She would be the one to save him, or to send him to his final reward.

He prayed for Option A.

He skimmed his knuckles along her flushed cheek, coming to rest under her chin as he guided her eyes to meet his. Her bright green eyes were clouded by doubt and shadowed by shame. He shook his head as he knelt down before her, cupping her face in his rough hands.

"There is nothing you did for which you need to be ashamed. You were strong and brave. A little too brave," he amended, his lips curving into an impish grin to set her mind at ease. His eyes drank in every inch of her face, tracing the fullness of her bottom lip with the pad of his thumb. "Calliope. My muse. Beautiful, intelligent and daring. I thank the gods for allowing me to share these moments with you."

Her tongue slipped out, wetting her lips and licking the pad of his thumb before she leaned close, her lips brushing his. At the lightest touch, he leaned in the final distance, chasing her receding tongue back inside the warm wet of her mouth. Groaning in heady need, he slid his hands from her face to cup the back of her head, entangling his fingers in her midnight black silk.

From his current vantage point on his knees between her legs, the heat from her barely covered core washed over his clenched muscles.

A deep growl rumbled in his chest, vibrating the thin veil separating her perfect breasts from his tightening body. He walked his fingers down her back, dragging the knit fabric up as he angled her head, allowing him better access to all confines of her mouth.

As much as he knew he would need to take things slow, a certain part of his anatomy was tired of waiting and judging from her amorous response, she was inclined to agree. Blood ceased to reach his brain from the moment he stepped out of the bathroom, finding her lost in her dark thoughts, her pale bare legs dangling off the edge of the bed. His towel was thankfully thick enough to shroud his growing erection, but settled between her thighs, even the strong terry cloth barrier offered little resistance.

He let his mouth slip from hers, breaking the seal and giving her a chance to suck in needed air. Nibbling along her jaw, her ragged breathing and fingertips digging into his shoulder spurred his racing libido. He eased her back gently, the hard plains of his chest pressing into her soft mounds shrouded by another cursed tee until mattress met her back. After a couple crawled scoots, a smattering of giggles and a growl from him, he sunk his weight down, pinning her neatly onto the pillowy mattress.

She dragged in a stuttered breath and the sound a need-filled groan slipping from her parted lips fired his need even more. Her questing hands grazed against his back, the scrape of her fingertips tracing the jumbled and jagged path of scars, some more recent than others. Before she could ask the questions bouncing around in her head, the unmistakable hiss of shredding fabric filled the air.

"*Theós mou*, you are so beautiful."

He slanted his mouth over hers, devouring her hungry cries while his palm followed the shapely contours of his narrow ribs to tease the diamond hard nipple that cut into his chest. Her legs scissored, rubbing along the thick towel still wrapped around his waist. The scratchy friction drove her passion spiraling to greater heights, the heady April rain scent that wafted through the air proving it. But he wanted to feel so much more.

With one arm cradling her back and his lips teasing the jumping pulse at her neck, keeping her firmly pressed against his body, he snaked his other arm around his back, releasing the last scrap of cloth separating them. He tossed the towel carelessly on the floor, seating his hips between hers, careful to keep his overly anxious and hammer-hard cock away from her tight and weeping core. A scared catch in her breathing worried him. As ready as she claimed to be, there was no way for him not to hurt her.

Rolling onto his side, he took her hand, guiding her fingers toward his thick shaft, his gaze pulling her passion-darkened emerald eyes to follow the trailing line of her fingertips. Her hesitant touch had his muscles jumping, the feathering tickles of curiosity inching his desire up another notch. A line of fire burned down the length of his body, her eyes blazing a path of want until he wrapped her slender fingers around his fully engorged cock.

As her eyes flared wide, drinking in the sight of his immense manhood, she sucked in air with a gasp, the sigh caught between passion and panic. He dipped his hips, feeling her smooth palm slipping down across the sensitive head as he thrust with careful strokes into her loose grip. Growls of exquisite pleasure rumbled in his throat, his back bowed to press his lips against her head bent in innocent study. He encouraged her to continue on her exploration of his body, needing to feel her hands on his skin. Burying his nose in the straight strands of midnight silk, inhaling the heady fragrance and pulling it into his soul, he tantalized her, filling her mind with vibrant and sensory glimpses of his physical reactions to her touch.

She gasped in erotic delight, her hot breath escaping in a ragged sign and her grip tightened around his cock. He growled hungrily as her unhurried strokes drove him to the brink of his control. With her shaking hands moving more confidently, Galen trailed his fingertips lightly up her skin. A warm smile spread as he watched the tiny hairs on her arm stand on end until his knuckles rested under her chin, lifting her swirling dark pools laced with only a narrow band of jade. A blush warmed her ivory cheeks, but his eyes were intent on her slightly parted lips. His hand covered her fingers once again, dragging her hand away from his shaft as he threaded his fingers between hers. He carried her arm up his body, finally resting her soft palm on his shoulder, his hips nestling in the heavenly juncture of her thighs.

He settled the bulbous head to rest on the bed of her soft curls, the thick and pronounced vein teasing against her hot slit with deliberate slowness while he nuzzled her, his light stubble adding to the sweet friction. "I will do everything I can to make this pleasurable for you, agapi. We will go as slow as you need."

His mouth slid down, his teeth grazing against her collarbone as they sought the object of their true questing. He feathered light kisses on the ample mound, a smile curling his lips as her fingers clawed deep into his shoulders and her hips bucked beneath him. He swept his tongue in long swirling drags, encircling her round firm breast, savoring every inch before he pulled the silken nipple into his mouth. His groan of deep satisfaction timed in perfect harmony with her keening cry, her body arching and writhing.

He slid his mouth from one flushed orb to the other, his hand moving down to the damp and moist slit, one finger sliding into her tight, hot channel. Her flowing juices sweetened the air and his cock wept in need as he added another digit. Continuing the grueling snail's pace of strokes against her tingling button nub, he wondered at his own control. His cock was on a hair trigger and the last thing he wanted to do was to shoot his load the second he entered her.

He groaned in eager anticipation at the squeezing grip on his inserted fingers. With a long, lingering lick, he trailed her tongue from her breast up the sweat-beaded column of her throat. Once he reached her lips, he slanted his mouth over hers, his tongue sweeping and thrusting in intoxicating, pulsing rhythm with his hand. A groan poured into his mouth as her back arched off the bed. He worked his fingers deeply and slowly into her, earning him a keening cry and a hand drenching.

As his hardening cock crept toward the pain/pleasure threshold, he broke off the kiss, nibbling his way to her ear. His voice blew hot against the sensitive shell as his passion fueled words teased and promised.

"Agapi, just say the word and I am yours. My life is in your hands and I await your command."

Her thighs trembled in the aftermath of yet another earth shattering orgasm, the cascade of wanton desire making coherent speech impossible. She clawed at his slick olive skin, clutching for a handhold as her body prepared for the next cresting wave. His words bled through her euphoric haze, their true meaning bouncing around the walls of her mind.

Unable to speak with her mouth, and while her body screamed for what he suggested, she opted for a blending of the two. Her hands threaded through his thick hair, cupping his face and with trembling arms, she lifted his head up to look deep into the swirling black pools.

"*Galen, I want you so much. I...I love you.*"

The three little words.

His smile burned hotter than the sun, her cheeks warming in the loving heat. In that tender moment, he bent his head, kissing her lips as he guided the head of his throbbing cock to her pleasure-damp entrance. With a needy growl, the heat of her welcoming channel beckoning him further, he stroked with agonizing control just along the slick opening.

"*My beautiful muse. I pray that I am worthy of this great gift you have given me.*"

Her body bucked and shuddered, completely out of her own control. Her mind had long since given up on trying to be logical about this. Yes, she knew she was inexperienced at this and she knew he was huge. But her urge to impale herself on his thick rod overwhelmed her, and as the broad head nudged her nether lips open, she bit back a breathy moan, her nails digging deep into the taut muscles of his back. Her eyes widened as her cheeks paled then flushed in a blink.

Heat gloved his shaft, the tight grip pulling him steadily onward. Tenderly teasing her mouth to relax, he swept his tongue inside, dancing and dueling with hers as he swallowed her groans. "*I will do all I can to make your first time pleasurable. But there will be some pain and for that, I am sorry.*" His hips dipped, inching his throbbing cock deeper, stretching her tight sheath to accommodate him. Her heavy, keening cries intermingled with the erotic rolling of her body, the combination threatening to shatter his tenuous control.

A light sheen of sweat painted her skin, adding to the sweet friction between his body and hers. She arched her back as he slid deeper and deeper, the gripping resistance chasing the fire licking through his veins. For each loving stroke, her body quivered and tightened, preparing for the coming stab of pain. She inhaled sharply, her fingers digging sharply into his shoulder in anticipation. He raised his head, breaking the seal of their lips.

"Stay with me. Here. Do not leave my eyes." He willed her to open her eyes, needing to see into her heart at this delicate moment. Her thick black crescents fluttered up, stealing away any doubts or rational thoughts from his brain. The green fires had receded, leaving behind only a glowing ring of bright emerald surrounding the passion-darkened pools. Reflecting up at him was nothing less than the purest trust and love.

"I claim you, body and spirit. I claim you, heart and soul."

The first words fell as a prayer from his lips, his hand cupping her warm cheek, trailing his thumb along her kiss swollen bottom lip. With a loving smile on his face, he threaded his other hand with hers, entangling their fingers as he surged past the thin barrier in one smooth stroke.

Cal gasped at the briefest bite of pain, her fingers tightening around his before his tongue laved her earlobe, his hot breath igniting a fire beneath her skin and dampening her feminine sheath as it gloved his velvet wrapped shaft. Her lips quivered, needy cries falling wordless from her mouth and her nipples hardened to diamond peaks, her breasts heavy as his firm body pressed against hers. She breathed a saddened moan as he slid out from her hot tunnel, only to have the sound rise in pitch as he inched further inside.

She arched her body back, creating a sweet friction between his hard cock filling her with each new stroke and the press of the cut plains of his body against her sensitive chest. Every breath that brushed her skin, each feather light touch only drove the flames higher and higher, and all these new sensation made her body weep and beg for more. Her brain struggled to comprehend the sounds whispering hotly in her ear.

Words.

She wanted more. Needed more.

"Your life I tie to mine, your joy and your sorrow. I give you all that I am, and all that I will be."

His voice rasped out, and her nerve endings fired fast, the blanket of erotic sensations spiraling her body to newer and higher peaks than the one in the breath before. Her hot silken channel gripped his shaft, guiding him deeper into her, the slow invasion of his body into hers a delicious and wanton feeling. Air dragged into her lungs only to return to the room in either a soundless groan or a pleading cry for more. His forehead dipped, touching hers with a reassuring kiss as the sweat dripped down her neck and pooled between her sensitive breasts.

"I take only what you offer freely."

She threaded her fingers through the dark hair tickling her skin, peeling open her heavy lids to see his possessive gaze fixed on her aching nipples. Emboldened by his lusty look, she pulled his head down toward the object of his obsession, pushing her head back against the soft pillow.

His tongue flicked out before tugging the tightened peak into the confines of his hot mouth. The wanton whimpers ruffling his hair encouraged him, pulling more of her plump flesh into his mouth. His teeth grazed the diamond nub before soothing the sting with a swirl of his tongue. She clenched his hair as her legs slid higher up his body, her knee nudging his hip to delve deeper.

No longer could she form coherent thoughts or words as pleasure took over completely. And she did give herself over completely to the sensations flooding her body, her blood a river of fire coursing to all her tingling parts north and south of the inferno raging where his body speared her hot core. She slid her hands down to caress the bunching muscles of his back, savoring the dip and plunge of his hips as he drove her over that delicious precipice again. Another wave crashed over her and she threw her head back, her screams falling from her trembling lips as shudders wracked her body.

Galen bit his lip as her orgasm threatened to unman him, the tight milking grip of her quivering sheath pulling the final sweet inch inside her. With his hips fully seated into the apex of her thighs, he paused, relishing the moment as he released the captured nipple, trailing light kisses up the column of her throat until he found her parted lips. Slanting his mouth over hers, he drank in her groans, drunk on her ecstasy and he slowly picked up the pace.

"By all the gods, agapi, you are more than I ever believed I deserved. And I was right. You look so beautiful draped in pleasure."

"Only because of you, Galen. You saved me. Oh, God. This is...I..."

His hips rocked and pistoned in an ever-increasing pace, each of her cascading, gripping orgasms pulling him closer to his own release. Straining to make this last for her, wanting this first time for her to be without any regrets, he forced his clenched jaw to form the final words that would forever change both their lives.

"I will be with you today…" he whispered, burying his nose in the hollow of her throat. "…And tomorrow…" He walked his hands down her sides, kneading the soft pliant flesh of her perfect ass as he drove himself deeper and deeper into her moist pocket.

"…And after," his voice a needy groan as her heavy moans echoed and harmonized with his possessive grunts. Faster, he slammed into her responsive body, her fingers biting into his shoulders as she held tightly, the storm of sensation raging unchecked and out of control.

"Galen…" Her lips formed the word and her lungs gave it sound, his name becoming a prayer, a pleading cry of love.

"Until the end of days."

His head snapped back as his powerful release roared through him, the force tearing a primal scream from his lips. Blood thundered in his ears and colors exploded behind his closed lids. His body froze, hips caught in the deepest thrust, her spasming sheath milking his shaft as he flooded her hot core.

A white hot flash of golden light flared out, enveloping both of them. Energy, the mark of the Guardians, marched along his skin, recharging his spirit as it seeped through his pores. Shudders ran down the length of his spine, bowing his back as he rested his damp forehead against hers. In the distance, he vaguely heard the tinkling of glass raining somewhere near them. He pulled his eyelids up, watching the flushed beauty beneath him shiver in the loving aftershocks, her cheeks beginning to pale.

Cal fought to drag in breath, but her body only sank further down into the damp, comforting softness at her back. Her heart labored with each beat, the blood only moments ago that flew through her veins ran sluggish, going from magma to molasses in a steady downward spiral. Gone was the energy that had buoyed her only hours ago. She fought to keep a hold on the slick olive skin even as her leaden muscles dragged her hands down.

Father Time has shit for timing, she mused in impotent anger as her vision blurred and bleached, the face of her only lover washing out, swallowed up by an encroaching fog. She fought to gulp in air, praying that somehow the effort might extend her remaining moments even as an overwhelming sorrow fired her last thoughts. *I'm not ready yet. I don't want to leave.*

She was vaguely aware of a pair of strong arms gathering up her limp body and cradling her head to a steadily beating heart. Wetness dripped onto her face from somewhere above, one of the salty drops dampened her lips. Her hero was crying? Words bled through the cottony abyss, the strained and failing thump of her heart pull her further from his beautiful voice.

"Calliope? Agapi, *akoús.* Hear me. I'll not lose you. 'Your life I tie to mine.' Remember?"

The tender brush of his lips jolted her body, her arms jerking as life jumped back into them. Her eyes flew open as power poured into her body, flowing in from his soft kiss. Panicked, her lungs struggled to remember how to work properly, while her heart danced around in a frantic flurry of rhythms. She tried vainly to control the flailing of her limbs, needing to hold onto the only anchor her body and soul wanted, but her current lack of coordination had other plans.

"Listen to the sound of my heart, agapi. Let it lead the way."

He deepened the kiss, sweeping his tongue into every crevice and corner as warmth wove its way under her skin. One large hand palmed the back of her head as he captured her twitching limbs, pinning them safely in the cage of his body. As if by magic, he seemed to inhale her confused panic and with tender care and loving patience, he retaught her body to function.

Slowly, breath after steady breath, she regained control of her body. Her lips answered his kiss, their mouths speaking without sound as her fingers dug into his solid pecs, her hands stretching higher until she reached strong shoulders and the arms holding her in their embrace. The fatigue that had plagued her for as long as she could remember had simply vanished, replaced by a never-ending warmth, a glow that seeped through every inch of her body.

Awareness spread through her, her skin hypersensitive where their bodies met, especially at the junction of her thighs. The cool air sent shivers down her damp arms and across her bare stomach while the touch of his palm on her chest as well as the press of his hips still fused with hers started tremors of a much different kind. A sigh poured from her lips into his mouth, her heart beat mirroring his as she broke the seal of his lips, her eyelids sluggishly following her directions.

As the darkness receded and light spilled in, she saw the silhouette of a god. *Or angel at the very least*, she thought since he came with his own halo. Not trusting her hazy vision, her hand moved to cup the shadowed jaw, feeling the tantalizing scrape of his stubbled cheek against her palm. His thick and still damp hair tickled the back of her hand, its light touch dancing down the length of her arm. Her pale hand stood in stark and delicious contrast against his olive complexion, but it was the sparkling pools of ebony fire that drew her gaze higher.

Daring a timid smile, she licked her parched lips before attempting to speak.

"Hi."

The word croaked out and the smile above her doubled in amorous ardor.

His cheeks hurt, smiling so broadly, as he pressed his hand against hers and watched his beautiful lover slowly return to him. The rosy glow returned to her skin, warmth driving away the chill still clinging to his heart. He nuzzled her palm as he dragged her hand to his lips, placing a simple, loving kiss into the center of her hand.

"Hi yourself."

His need to touch her more than he already was soon had his fingers threading through her hair as he set her hand on his chest. He splayed her fingers wide, his heart nearly jumping out of his rib cage, eager to feel her gentle touch as well. "So, was it good for you, too?"

A strangled laugh caught in her throat and he pulled her closer, locking her in a loving embrace in the cage of his arms and pressing soft kisses into her hair. Her shuddering body, wracked by the sobs she struggled to fight, bounced in an unconsciously erotic lap dance, her legs wound about his waist and his shaft still buried in her warm, fleshy pocket. His fingertips traced lazy, soothing circles along her back in a feeble attempt to calm her.

Sadly, the action did nothing to calm the fire bubbling just beneath his skin. Neither did the rocking. Hell, if anything, it ratcheted up his erection even faster, the rhythmic rolling of her hips nestled in his lap driving him insane.

As the emotions poured out of her, Cal felt her body respond to the gentle touch along her spine, her back arching and bowing, her catlike movements pulling a purr from her lips and a growl rumbled in his chest.

"Well, uh, right up until that last part. You know, the whole light at the end of the tunnel…" She wished her voice sounded more sexy and less squeaky and weak, but all that screaming finally caught up to her and here in this tender moment, her words grated like sandpaper against her own ears.

His lips curved into a wicked grin, a heated glow sparkling in his deep ebony eyes. "A true *petit mort?* Wow, now that is going to be hard to top the next time."

She laughed shyly as her head dropped, her cheeks going from pale to pink in record time. As she took in her current situation, naked, planted firmly on the lap of the man who just brought her to numerous peaks and a handful of complete screaming orgasms, she shook her head, pondering the ridiculousness of her sudden case of the shies. Her body, sore in places she never knew existed, wanted nothing more than to melt completely into the strong arms cradling her.

"The next time?" Her question seemed just as silly as her surprise modesty, but her brain/mouth connection was currently out of commission. Yet, if even as the words trips from her lips, his hips swayed in answer, her eyes rolling back into her head as his deep laughter flowed down her back.

"Oh yes, agapi. I assure you, there will be many more next times." He trailed his knuckles along her jaw line, his thumb trailing to lift her chin until her shining emerald eyes locked with his. With tender care, he leaned back, pressing his shoulder to the mattress as he carried her to join him. Easing himself from her moist heat, he kept one arm around her shoulders as his fingers gripped the edge of the quilt, giving a tug to cover her cooling skin. "But first I think you have more than earned a full night's sleep. How does that sound?"

A languid grin warmed her face as her eyelids drooped further down. "Full night? You're kidding, right? And to be honest, with all the shit of the past couple days, I'd be afraid I'd sleep for a month if I ever got the chance to close my eyes." The last few words fell as mumbled gibberish, the lure of sleep too strong for her to resist any longer.

He gazed in rapt adoration at the face of his angel as her breathing evened out, the rhythm peaceful and soothing. He traced the curve of her cheekbone, his fingertips skimming the contours of her ruby lips, his touch feather light. Hints of a grin began in the corner of his mouth as his eyes drank in the sight of his spiritmate, resting peacefully in the circle of his arms.

Just as she should be. Treasured, sated and purely his.

Bending to brush his lips against hers, he inhaled, savoring the intoxicating fragrance in which he would spend the rest of his days happily lost. "Sleep as long as you need, *ómorfi moúsa mou*. I will be here when you awake and I will gladly wait a mere month if that is all that you require." He poured the whispered words, laced with love, against her mouth and her throat as he nuzzled her ear.

"Smooth talker," she slurred out, the contented smile never leaving her face as Galen pulled her tighter against his chest, the steady thump of her heart keeping perfect time with his as sleep dragged him down.

ABOUT THE AUTHOR

Tessa McFionn is a very native Californian and has called Southern California home for most of her life, growing up in San Diego and attending college in Northern California and Orange County, only to return to San Diego to work as a teacher. Insatiably curious and imaginative, she loves to learn and discover, making her wicked knowledge of trivial facts an unwelcomed guest at many Trivial Pursuit boards. She also finds her artistic soul fed through her passions for theatre, dance and music, as well as the regular trip to The Happiest Place on Earth with friends and family.

www.tessamcfionn.com

@TessaMcFionn

www.facebook.com/tessa.mcfionn

Made in the USA
Middletown, DE
30 June 2019